THE STOLEN HOURS

Also by Allen Eskens

The Life We Bury

The Guise of Another

The Heavens May Fall

The Deep Dark Descending

The Shadows We Hide

Nothing More Dangerous

THE STOLEN HOURS

ALLEN ESKENS

MULHOLLAND BOOKS

Little, Brown and Company

New York Boston London

The characters and events in this book are fictitious. Any similarity to real persons, living or dead, is coincidental and not intended by the author.

Mulholland Books / Little, Brown and Company
Hachette Book Group
1290 Avenue of the Americas, New York, NY 10104
mulhollandbooks.com

First Edition: September 2021

Mulholland Books is an imprint of Little, Brown and Company, a division of Hachette Book Group, Inc. The Mulholland Books name and logo are trademarks of Hachette Book Group, Inc.

The publisher is not responsible for websites (or their content) that are not owned by the publisher.

The Hachette Speakers Bureau provides a wide range of authors for speaking events. To find out more, go to hachettespeakersbureau.com or call (866) 376-6591.

ISBN 978-0-316-70349-9
Library of Congress Control Number: 2021938717

Printing 1, 2021

LSC-C

Printed in the United States of America

This book is dedicated to Hugo Allen Koser and Arthur Carey Koser, two brilliant, new points of light in this wonderful world. Welcome to the grand adventure, boys!

THE STOLEN HOURS

CHAPTER 1

Lila Nash counted her steps as she walked from the kitchen to the bathroom of her apartment. *Ten, nine, eight*—the numbers falling silently in her head, a remnant from those days when she paced the corridors of the hospital. *Seven, six, five*—turn into the bathroom—*four, three*—close the door—*two*—turn—face the mirror—*one*.

Her last step had been little more than a shuffle, but it allowed her to stop on one, which somehow eased the clockwork that ticked inside her chest.

Lila never told Joe about the counting; she saw no reason to. It wasn't a secret so much as a private comfort—a blanket she had learned to wrap around herself all those years ago when a head full of silence had the power to coax demons out of the shadows. Now, it had become more of a habit, an echo that refused to die away. Dr. Roberts had once assured her that the counting was a good thing, a coping mechanism to distract her from harmful thoughts.

She used a cotton round on her eyes, wiping away what little makeup she used: mascara, eyeliner, and just a touch of shadow. A once-over with soap and water, and she was ready for bed—almost.

She locked the bathroom door, the tiny click far too anemic to reach the bedroom, where Joe lay reading. In a cupboard beneath the sink, in a makeup bag where she stored a collection of old compacts and lipsticks, Lila fished out a small tube of cream. Another little secret she kept from Joe.

Lifting the sleeve of her T-shirt to expose the top of her left arm, she moved a finger across her scars, seven thin lines that ran parallel to one another, the Braille that told the story of that summer when she was eighteen—the summer of her attack. Each scar was as straight as a toothpick except for the one in the middle, the first one. She had been crying when she made that cut, her hand trembling enough to give the scar a slight dip. When she confessed to Dr. Roberts that the flaw upset her more than the cut itself, he had seemed to understand.

Lila pressed a smidgen of scar-reduction cream onto her finger and began rubbing it on her arm, counting down the strokes. *Ten, nine, eight*... The advertisement promised dramatic results, but after a week Lila had seen very little change. Then again, her scars had had years to dig in, so she saw no reason to expect them to disappear overnight.

Lila wanted to believe that she'd come a long way in the eight years since she stopped seeing Dr. Roberts, but she worried her progress was more a matter of time and distance than actual healing. The trauma to her flesh had mended easily enough, her scars the only reminder of who she had once been. But the other wounds, the ones that she could only see when she closed her eyes—they refused to heal. She had hoped to drive them inward far enough that they would never escape. But escape they sometimes did.

Four, three, two, one. She finished working the cream across her arm and put the tube back into the old makeup bag, before returning the kit to its hiding place. She had become adept at hiding things from Joe, and she felt a tinge of dishonesty for trying to get rid of her scars. How many times had she told herself—told Joe—that she was okay with them? The cutting had helped her survive, had given voice to the emotion that roiled through her veins.

Back in that terrible summer, it felt as though her anger lay trapped beneath her skin, a caged animal, its scream growing so loud in her ears that the only way to find peace was to touch a razor to her flesh. But those seven scars, souvenirs brought back from a walk through hell, were now no more meaningful than cracks in a dried lake bed. Apply a little skin cream and soon they would be gone.

When she worked the cream over her arm the first time, a week earlier, she contemplated telling Joe about it. Why not? He knew about her past, about the men, the cutting, and the two weeks she spent in the psych ward, so why not tell him about her little experiment in scar reduction? He had stayed with her through every new revelation as she eased him into the nightmare of her past, which sometimes made her question his judgment.

That poor judgment came into even sharper focus just after Thanksgiving the previous year when he started hinting about marriage. First, he slipped a comment about her dainty hands into an otherwise casual conversation, guessing that she probably wore a size-five ring. Then, as Christmas approached, he struck up a conversation about diamonds, as if she might not notice his clumsy attempt to ascertain her preferences.

He was stumbling toward a proposal, and Lila reacted like a woman standing in the path of an avalanche. She responded to his diamond inquiry by blathering for half an hour about the evils of blood diamonds. Then she made up a story about a law school friend who argued that the notion of marriage proposals, as a tradition, should go the way of hoop skirts.

That Christmas, instead of an engagement ring, Joe gave her a spa day gift certificate.

By Valentine's Day, he had completely given up, his surrender signaled one night in bed as they watched a news story about a woman who organized a flash mob to propose to her boyfriend. At the end of the piece, Joe rolled over to Lila and said that it was good that women also took the lead in such things.

As Lila often did when their discussions touched on marriage, she unconsciously reached a hand up the sleeve of her T-shirt and rubbed her biceps. That's when Joe reached his hand up to her arm as well, resting his palm on the back of her hand, his index finger gently touching one of her scars, pressing a fret on a guitar eight years out of tune. When he spoke again, it was as if to apologize.

"I just think that the girl—the woman—should have just as much right to say when the time is right as the man. And if that time ever came..." Joe didn't finish his thought, and although Lila wanted desperately to say something hopeful, no words came out. In the silence, Joe rolled back over and fixed his eyes on the TV.

Lila may as well have yelled in his face that she didn't want to marry him. But that wasn't true. She loved Joe, loved him more than she thought she would ever love a man. In those moments when she allowed herself to dream about the future, she always saw Joe at her side. She wanted to tell that it wasn't him—it was her—but those words sounded hurtful and trite, so she said nothing.

Over their six years together, Lila had done her best to convince Joe—to convince herself—that she had moved past what had happened to her that night. In truth, she had survived, but she had not healed, and deep down she knew it. Keeping that from Joe meant that he really didn't know her. How could he? He didn't know about the sharp fragments of doubt that floated loose in her blood. The woman Joe knew, the strong, fierce Lila Nash, had been constructed out of spare parts. How could she marry Joe when she still kept so much from him?

Eight years ago, Dr. Roberts told Lila, "Healing requires patience. It requires forgiveness."

Lila wanted to scream the first time he said that. He had no idea what it was like. He was a man. How could he understand? Forgive her attackers? Hell no! Kill them, maybe. Put them in prison at the very least. But never forgive them.

"Don't confuse hatred for strength," Dr. Roberts had said. "The forgiveness isn't for them. It's for you."

How many times had she fantasized about finding those who had attacked her, those faces with no features, men with no names? In her dreams, she saw them as shadows, stood against them with rage as her only weapon. Never once did those encounters end in forgiveness.

CHAPTER 2

Who gets married on a Sunday? Gavin Spencer pondered that question as he stood at the edge of the dance floor, squinting through the viewfinder of his Canon Mark IV. People with any money at all got married on Saturday, which was why wedding venues offered Sunday discounts—for people like the newly minted Mr. and Mrs. Halloway.

"Peasants," he whispered to himself.

Gavin aimed his camera at the bride and one of her bridesmaids, hopping up and down in one of those half-hug-half-dance embraces, the kind of thing seen at events where alcohol is served. The bride's dress, though not a hand-me-down, was definitely off the rack, and the bridesmaid wore a purple gown with a high slit up the side, slinky and simple, a dress that could be repurposed for a date night or New Year's Eve party. They were bedecked beyond the stretch of their meager budgets—yet they were incapable of living up to those dresses.

When they saw Gavin and his camera, they raised their beer glasses in yet another drunken toast—the bridesmaid screeching, "Hey, Picture Boy! Whoo!" He aimed the camera at the two women as they squeezed in tight, their beers held high, the inebriant sloshing down, splashing to the dance floor and speckling their knockoff Dior shoes.

This was the tenth time that the bridesmaid had demanded that a picture be taken and the tenth time she had called Gavin Picture Boy.

With any luck, he had snapped the photo in time to catch her spilling her beer. Maybe she would see it later and be embarrassed, even sorry for being vulgar, but then Gavin shook his head, disappointed that he gave voice to such a laughable notion. Women like her were never sorry, not to guys like him.

Gavin had already taken hundreds of pictures of the bride and groom. He had taken pictures of the relatives and the ceremony, all of it staged like a grand tableau. As far as Gavin was concerned, wedding photography was the art of deception, creating phony memories to set the bar of their happiness so high that every day to follow would be a disappointment. It pleased Gavin to think that his pictures might one day be thrown around as the couple fought over things like custody and alimony and child support.

The sun had disappeared hours ago, as had the older guests, cutting the pups free from the restraint that had kept the affair even remotely dignified. This was the part of the night that Gavin liked best, the time when his expert eye could capture those tiny fissures that would one day bring about the end of the marriage. Harbingers of the ruination to come.

His bet: Mrs. Halloway would cheat on her husband. Earlier, he'd taken a picture of the bride dancing with one of the male guests, a man with features ordered from a catalog. The sadness in her eyes in that brief moment exposed a shared past, and Gavin quickly snapped a close-up—the bride's face raised in apology to her former lover. Gavin imagined Mr. and Mrs. Halloway sitting on a couch, flipping through the wedding album, and coming upon that picture. The thought made him smile.

Another whoop came from the dance floor, and again the bridesmaid pointed her beer at Gavin. "Hey, Picture Boy."

Gavin held his lens on the two women, but he didn't click the shutter. Instead, he used the moment to focus on the bridesmaid, a woman with bleached teeth that seemed to glow against her fake tan.

And Gavin was pretty sure she'd taped her breasts up, because she filled her dress in a way none of the other bridesmaids had managed.

Gavin knew about such things because he had watched his own mother employ those tricks, back when he was a little boy and she was hunting a new stepfather for him. A memory came to Gavin as he watched the bridesmaid, of a summer evening when he was seven years old. A man had come to visit, and Gavin's mother, Amy, had given Gavin a talking-to, pointing her bony finger sharply at his face. "Stay in your room! Don't make a sound. It's important that you behave tonight."

Gavin had promised to be quiet, yet when he heard the mix of music and Amy's laughter coming from the living room below, he couldn't help sneaking to the steps to spy.

They were dancing, but at the same time, they weren't. The man moved his hands up and down his mother's body, squeezing and kneading her as though trying to mold her from Play-Doh, touching her in places that people weren't supposed to touch. His mother's chin rested on the man's shoulder, and she twitched and pinched her eyes shut as he moved his hand under her dress, doing something that brought her up on the tips of her toes.

Gavin was on the verge of charging down the steps to save his mother when she opened her eyes and saw him. He expected her to call to him for help. Together they could push the man out of their house. Instead, Amy twisted her face in anger, her snarled white teeth standing out in Gavin's memory. She lifted her hand from the man's back, pointed at Gavin, and then at the top of the stairs, her finger a dagger. She wasn't in trouble at all. She wanted the man to be doing what he was doing. And for his disobedience, Gavin spent part of the next morning on his knees, his hands taped behind him, his nose pressed against the back of his bedroom closet.

The throng of dancers and spectators grew uncomfortably thick around Gavin, so he lowered his camera and backed away from the dance floor, taking a seat near the bar. He spent a few minutes rearranging lenses in his bag before noticing the groom's teenage brother wobbling drunkenly into a chair at the end of the table. *He'll puke before the night's over,* Gavin thought to himself. He aimed the camera at the boy, zoomed in tight, and snapped a picture. The kid sweated from his eyes and had a dead-carp expression on his pale face. *Hell, he's not going to make it another five minutes.*

Then it came again: "Picture Boy!"

Gavin flinched as the voice, loud and close, came from behind him. He turned in his seat to see her leaning against the bar. She was no beauty queen, but she had the kind of teasing vibe that had surely made her popular on the beaches of spring break.

"Whoo!" She lifted a fresh cup into the air.

It was as if she couldn't stop herself from poking him, certain that a dog like him would have no bite—but Gavin did have a bite. It had been two years since an ill moon brought that side of him out to play. Two years of waiting, his hunger building, his appetite once again aching to be satisfied.

Gavin started to raise his camera, but then he lowered it. He shouldn't engage her. Look at them from afar was the rule. Study them, but remain invisible—forgettable. To attract attention meant to attract suspicion. But this one had been pushing it all night, tacky and impolite. Her condescension demanded a response—so he went off script.

"I have a name," he said.

"Of course you have a name." She spoke as though bothered that this extra in the movie of her life dared to address her at all. "All God's creatures have a name."

Now he was a creature. She was failing a test that she didn't even know she was taking.

"So what is it, this name of yours?"

He smiled at the benevolence he felt in that moment. He would give her a chance he hadn't given the others, a chance to save herself. If she would treat him with decency, he would let her be. All she had to do was be nice.

"My name is Gavin."

He studied her face as he said the word *is* because that word exposed his speech impediment, thick and damp like air seeping from a wet tire. A squishy lisp from a squishy man. She would hear: "My name isch Gavin."

She giggled, of course, and covered her mouth with her free hand. He could feel the heat of judgment as her eyes moved from his uncombed hair down to his doughy midriff. He found himself sucking in his gut as if he cared what she thought. But why should he care? She was just like the others, ready to dismiss him.

"Kevin?" she said.

"Gavin," he repeated.

A grin spread across her cheeks. "You look more like a Kevin to me—Kevin the Picture Boy. That's your name." Then she laughed hard, as though she had just told the funniest joke.

Gavin felt assured that the world would neither mourn nor miss this woman. He lifted his camera and snapped a picture, which made her smile. But this picture wouldn't be included in the package of photographs that he would give to the bride. This one was for him, a memorial of the exact second that Gavin chose her, a memento to keep in his secret hiding place—with the others.

A groomsman bumped into the bridesmaid, causing her to spill her drink. She turned and slapped the man's broad shoulder in mock anger. He smiled at her in a way that caused her to lick her lips. And just like that, Kevin the Picture Boy no longer existed.

Gavin lifted his camera bag and walked calmly to the head table, to where the bridesmaid had been sitting earlier in the evening. Leaning down as though inspecting his camera, he carefully palmed the place card with her name on it. When he stood back up, he looked around the room to see if anyone was watching. They weren't. He was invisible again—just the way he liked it.

He glanced at the name—*Sadie Vauk*—and slipped the card into his pocket.

CHAPTER 3

The Hennepin County Government Center hogged two blocks of downtown Minneapolis, straddling Sixth Street like a steel sentinel. The building housed those mechanisms of the justice system that marked the end of the line: the courts, probation, and the office of the Hennepin County attorney—where Lila worked.

On the twentieth floor, Lila's small, windowless office had no character, but in fairness, she had done nothing to give it any. In the six months that she'd been working there, she had hung no pictures, no plaques, no diplomas. The only item that hadn't been there when she moved in was the picture of Joe that she kept on the corner of her desk. Lila had chosen not to settle in, just in case things didn't work out.

She had been hired with the understanding that she would become an attorney in October, once her bar exam results arrived—fingers crossed. For now, her title remained law clerk, one of three culled from a herd of over five hundred applicants, third-year law students brought on board to organize files, write memorandums, and draft criminal pleadings.

The rules permitted new graduates like her to make court appearances under the supervision of a licensed attorney, but Lila's supervisor, a sharply dressed man named Oscar Hernandez, preferred that she stay in her office, elbow deep in papers. Oscar worked white-collar cases, so Lila spent her time cross-checking accounting forensics and bank transactions, breaking it all down into graphs and exhibits so that a jury could understand.

The other two newbies, both of them men, worked in offices just as small and bland as Lila's, but they had tacked their law school diplomas to their walls, one from the University of Minnesota, the other from Georgetown.

That morning, as she walked to her office—counting her steps—she passed the office of Ryan Kent, the newbie from Georgetown, and heard him grunt out an anguished wail. She stopped, backed up, and peeked in.

"Everything all right?"

He waved Lila in and motioned for her to close the door.

"She's pissed off again," he said in a sharp but hushed tone. "I can't do anything right."

Lila considered herself lucky for having been assigned to Oscar. Although he didn't let her appear in court, he never yelled. That couldn't be said of Ryan's supervisor, Andi Fitch. Lila had seen it firsthand, when Fitch had tasked Ryan with filing a pre-trial appeal and Ryan had applied the wrong rule for calculating the time. Andi had let him have it.

Even when she wasn't angry, Andi was an intimidating woman: six feet tall, Black with short blond hair styled to give it sharp points. She had dark eyes that could cut glass and lips that seemed incapable of smiling. And although she hadn't actually yelled at Ryan, her words had landed just as hard.

The confrontation took place outside of Ryan's office and lasted all of three minutes, with Andi ordering Ryan to personally drive the notice of appeal to both the defense attorney's office and the court of appeals in St. Paul. And if he failed to get the documents filed in time, he needn't bother returning.

Just watching Andi take Ryan apart that day made Lila's breath run shallow, and she was certain that had she been in Ryan's shoes, she would have wilted under Andi's disappointment. Maybe that was why Lila pitched in to help Ryan whenever she had the chance.

"What is it this time?" Lila asked.

"I gave her a complaint yesterday and she threw it back at me. Told me to try again." Then, in a mocking tone, he added, "'But do it right this time.'"

"What's wrong with it?"

"I have no idea. She gives me no direction—nothing. It's like she expects me to read her mind. All she said was 'Make it so we can convict the son of a bitch.'" Ryan closed his eyes to calm down. "I passed up the feds to work here, and she treats me like an idiot. I can see why her last law clerk quit on her."

"Last two," Lila said.

"Well, I'm about to make it three in a row. I swear, I don't need this drill sergeant bullshit."

Lila settled into a chair across the desk from Ryan. "What's the fact pattern?"

"Guy named Donald Gray got into an argument with his wife—they were parked outside of a convenience store. She tried to get out of the car, and he yanked her back in and hit her. Gave her a black eye." Ryan handed a photograph to Lila. The woman facing the camera wore a scowl and had a darkened left eye.

"Any witnesses?" Lila asked.

"None. The surveillance tapes show a struggle of some kind, but it's not clear."

"Can you see the punch?"

"No. Just movement. It's too grainy."

Ryan handed still shots from the surveillance video to Lila. She could make out the driver, a man in a red shirt, pointing his finger at the woman. In the next picture, the woman had opened the passenger door and had one foot outside. The man had ahold of her arm near the biceps. In the next picture, he had pulled her back into the car. The fourth picture showed the two people facing each other, both with their arms up as though wrestling. The final shot showed the woman lunging out of the car, a hand to her face.

Lila sat back in her chair and flipped through the photos again. This time, instead of thinking about the potential charges, she took her thoughts to the trial. What would be his defense? How would she handle the case if she were his attorney?

"What did you charge him with?"

Ryan handed the draft complaint to Lila. Count one was third-degree assault, which required substantial bodily harm. The swollen eye met that element, but some juries didn't like the idea that a black eye could be considered substantial harm. The second charge on the complaint was domestic assault—a misdemeanor—which required a punch but no damage.

"Is your victim willing to testify?" Lila asked.

Ryan shrugged. "He's hit her before—twice—both times she changed her story before trial. Said she lied to the police because she was mad at her husband. Said she hit her eye on a door frame or something. Both cases got dropped. I think that's why Fitch is being such a—"

"Stickler?" Lila finished Ryan's sentence, although that hadn't been the word he was going to use. Ryan had called her Fitch the Bitch once before in Lila's presence, but Lila's look had let him know she didn't approve.

"So, what am I missing?" Ryan asked.

"What's Gray do for a living?"

"Runs an assisted living facility."

"Ah."

"Yeah, a conviction gets him fired."

"That would explain why the wife keeps recanting."

Lila stared at the pictures again, thinking the case through as if she were the defense attorney, focusing on the State's obvious weakness—the wife. The key would be to take her out of the equation. Abusers like Gray often talked their victims into not testifying—for the sake of the marriage, or the kids, or a job. But surveillance cameras don't have that particular human frailty.

Lila stopped on the picture of the woman with one leg out of the car, the man holding her arm, and that's when it came to her. "Gray yanked her back into the car."

Ryan looked at Lila as though confused. "Yeah."

"It's false imprisonment. He didn't let her leave the car."

Ryan pondered that for a second and then said, "Okay, but that's still only a three-year felony. I already have him charged with third-degree assault. That's five years. If Fitch isn't happy with five—"

"He'd have to register as a predatory offender. False imprisonment carries a mandatory registration—assault doesn't."

Lila could almost see the thoughts forming behind Ryan's eyes as he worked to catch up.

Ryan smiled. "That would be some serious leverage."

"You have the video of him pulling her back into the car. The jury can see him do that with their own eyes, so it won't matter if the wife recants on the punch. Fitch can use the big stick of predatory offender registration to get a plea on the assault. Who knows—you might just convict the son of a bitch."

"Damn." Ryan shook his head slowly. "I should have seen it...but...why didn't she just tell me? Why does she...?" Ryan leaned back in his chair and let the thought pass. "I owe you one."

"I'm sure I'll cash it in soon enough."

A tap at Ryan's door, light but emphatic, interrupted their conversation. Before Ryan could extend an invitation, the door opened and Patrick Hittle, the third of the newbie trio, entered. "Did you hear about Beth?"

"Beth?" Lila asked.

"Beth...Malone." He drew the words out to make clear to Lila he was saying *Duh!*

Lila liked Ryan, but could do without Patrick, a man who never missed an opportunity to jab at her, comments that had no purpose other than to show off his big brain. "I can't hang out after work," he once said. "I have a MENSA meeting." Another time he corrected Lila, saying, "Cats aren't nocturnal, they're crepuscular—they're active at dawn and dusk, not all night." Once, at lunch, Lila made the mistake of ordering a cheese panini. "It's pronounced *panino,* not *panini. Panini* is plural."

"It's pronounced *pedantic,* not *Patrick,*" Lila had whispered to herself. At first she thought that Patrick was like that with everyone, but when the three of them were together, it was Lila he threw darts at. So he was a misogynist. But then she noticed that he didn't treat other women in the office that way.

That made Lila think that he singled her out because she didn't belong. She was petite with small features that shaved years off her age. She used to have long, dark hair, but had cut it short after that terrible summer. It didn't help—she still looked young.

She once asked Ryan his opinion on Patrick's dickishness. "He knows you're smarter than he is," Ryan had said. "Despite all that MENSA crap, I think he knows, deep down, that you'll be a better attorney. He's making a preemptive attack." Lila didn't see it.

Patrick closed the door to Ryan's office and spoke quietly. "Beth was in a car accident last night—jammed her leg up into her hip, broke the bone in four places. They say she won't be back for weeks, maybe months."

"Oh my God," Lila said.

Then Patrick added, "Frank Dovey's taking over Adult Prosecution till she comes back."

That last bit of news landed like the blow of a fist. *Frank Dovey—the head of Adult Prosecution?* He would become Oscar's boss—her boss. Lila sank into her seat, letting the conversation between Patrick and Ryan drift away.

Frank Dovey—her boss.

The dream of becoming a prosecutor had sustained Lila through seven years of books and study and stress. Her undergraduate degree had been hard enough, but law school came with the feel of trench warfare, the competition for class rank pitting students against each other. Lila had chased a vision of herself through it all—nice suit, polished shoes, confident posture, standing before a jury and putting evil men in prison—men like the ones who had hurt her so badly. In the end, her effort landed her a job that was perfect in every respect—except for Frank Dovey.

She wasn't sure whether it had been seconds or minutes since she'd tuned Ryan and Patrick out, but soon she heard Ryan's voice breaking through the fog. "Lila? You okay?" He sounded concerned. "You need water or something?"

Lila looked around and saw that Patrick had left. "I'm sorry," she said. "I should get back..." Lila started to stand, but Ryan put a hand on her shoulder, gently easing her back down to the chair.

"No hurry. What's going on?"

"Nothing, really."

"Lila." Ryan's voice took on the soft tone of a therapist or maybe even a friend. "It's me."

"Frank Dovey."

"Yeah, I hear he's a bit of a dick."

"It's more than that. He and I...we have a history." As soon as she said it, she could hear the hint of *affair* in the words.

"You and Dovey?"

"In court," Lila said quickly. "We have a history in court. When I was a second-year, one of my law professors hired me to help him with a murder trial. We beat Dovey, and I think it cost him a judgeship."

"The Pruitt case? You were part of the Pruitt case?"

"You heard about it?"

"Just gossip."

"What'd you hear?"

Ryan sat down and laced his fingers behind his head, looking at the ceiling as though trying to remember. "The victim's sister...she was politically connected, right?"

"Personal friend of the governor."

"Right. One of the paralegals told me that Dovey was so sure he had the judgeship that he'd joked that she should start calling him *Your Honor*."

"Oh good lord."

"Yeah, and then he lost the case. Word has it that the sister went to the governor and blackballed him. The paralegal said he smashed one of his chairs against the wall when he found out."

"I was on an elevator with him back in June," Lila said. "Everyone else got off on lower floors, so it was just him and me. Once we were alone, I faced the front like a normal person, but he turned and stared at me like…I don't know, but it was creepy."

"Stared at you?"

"Yeah. He was two feet away."

"Did he say anything?"

"Not a word. He just stared at the side of my head."

"Damn."

"I know. I'm pretty sure that Beth hired me over his objection."

"And now he's…your boss."

"Yeah, well, it was fun while it lasted." Lila had a smile on her face, but the slight quaver in her voice betrayed her.

"He's not stupid enough to fire you. Beth would have his hide. At the end of the day, he's a political animal. Self-preservation will trump revenge."

"He'll find a way to get rid of me, I just know it."

"You just have to keep your head down till Beth comes back. Avoid riding in elevators with the guy. You'll be okay."

"I hope you're right about that."

Lila tried not to seem dazed as she stood to leave, counting her steps as she walked to her office. On her desk lay a stack of files. Fraud cases. Numbers. Math. Not the kind of thing she dreamt about in law school, but the kind of thing that a newbie should be working on—at least according to Oscar Hernandez.

She fired up her computer, the hum of its fan teasing the empty room, and tried to get her head into the groove. When her screen popped on, she glanced up to see if she had any emails to answer, and there, in the upper corner of the screen, blinked a message from Frank Dovey. A tendril of dread crept its way up her spine and into her chest.

She opened it and read. *Come see me.*

CHAPTER 4

Gavin Spencer always thought of himself as a man who wore his plumage on the inside. Born with a body and face that were genetically forgettable, he had been further hobbled by a tongue that wheezed a sloppy hiss when he spoke the letter *S*. He was a backdrop, a weed. He was the beige Crayola in a box of sixty-four. But once he came to understand the power of his invisibility, it suited him well. What the rest of the world saw as indistinct, Gavin used as a disguise, turning his weakness into his strength. Gavin was happy enough to let his brilliance shine behind that mask.

Part of that shine had always been the care that Gavin took to understand his craft. Excellence didn't come by accident; it took effort. Take photography: The world was awash with happy amateurs taking crooked pictures with their cell phones. They had no appreciation for balance, or ratios, or rhythm. Just point and shoot—the resulting aesthetic no more pleasing than a finger painting smeared on paper by somebody else's child.

Similarly, Gavin believed the prisons of the world to be populated by thick-minded thugs who cared not a lick for their craft. Their paths led to incarceration not because of their calling, but because they refused to take that calling seriously. Just point and shoot. Not Gavin. He was a craftsman.

He had been up late taking photographs at the wedding the previous night, so Gavin allowed himself the luxury of sleeping in until nine in the morning. A good night's sleep heightened creativity and attention to detail. His breakfast consisted of two eggs and a piece of toast, with orange juice to wash it down. Showered and shaved, he dressed like a man going to work—khakis and a long-sleeved shirt, buttoned to the neck—because that's exactly what he was doing, even if that work was burrowing through the tunnels of the internet in search of his prey.

It had been two years since he last performed this task, and that two-year hiatus had not been by accident. Police looked for patterns, their eyes and ears perked by those deaths most recently discovered. But police were human, apt to forget details as time went by. It only made sense that a connection would be harder to make over a span of years. Gavin had chosen a two-year break at random, but over the course of eight years—and four victims—it had seemed to work. And now the time had come to add to his collection.

He began his routine by spending five minutes staring at the wall to clear his mind of prurient thoughts. He had learned that passion and emotion were venoms that needed to be sucked out and spat to the ground. Rule number one—keep your head. Be patient, look for flaws in the plan, and above all else, be prepared to abort if the risk ever outweighs the reward.

He put Sadie Vauk's place card on the desk and, right away, the face of the woman at the wedding came back to him. The bleached teeth, the bottle tan, the contempt in her eyes when she called him Picture Boy. She had invited what was to come.

Gavin started to feel anger build in his chest, so he turned the card facedown and took a deep breath to expel the agitation.

When he felt calm again, he went to his kitchen, knelt on the floor in front of his lazy Susan, and reached for the toe kick. His fingers found the loop of fishing line, the handle that opened his hiding spot. One small tug and the cupboard's kick plate came free. He retrieved a small laptop, one he used for his most secret of tasks.

As a student of the craft, he understood that computer forensics could find items buried on a hard drive, bits of data that lay entombed but intact, even after deletion. This was just the first of the many mistakes made by lesser men, troglodytes who blundered their way toward awaiting jail cells. Gavin, however, planned multiple options for every contingency. Redundancy was his mantra.

For example, he would do his internet searches for Sadie Vauk on his special laptop, never on his home computer. And when he finished his research, deleting the search would not be enough. Hiding the computer under the lazy Susan would not be enough. He would also run an evidence-erasing program. And once he executed his plan, he would render the hard drive useless and dispose of the computer. It made for extra work, and extra cost, but such were the travails of a craftsman.

Sometimes Gavin entertained himself by watching true crime shows on television, where purportedly brilliant investigators pursued what passed for master criminals. Gavin giggled at the buffoonery—the sheer slapstick comedy of it all. People left bloody footprints behind and kept the shoes. They gave no thought to tire tracks in mud or to DNA sloshed around like party confetti. He lived in a world full of amateurs and idiots.

Yet despite his careful study and redundant cover-ups, Gavin understood that he had one essential weakness—an absolute violation of all his rules.

Before launching into his search for Sadie Vauk, Gavin took a moment to visit his trophy room, a collection of protected files on a private server, one that he had installed in his mother's garage attic back when he still lived with her. It was the perfect place to store his keepsakes should the police ever come to tear his house apart.

He had taken great care to devise a system of online traps and hidden passages to keep his virtual trophy room hidden from prying eyes, precautions that mollified his unease over having a trophy room in the first place.

There were four files on the server, and each held pictures of what he had done, and to whom. He would visit his trophy room on special occasions, the images taking him back in time so vividly that he could again smell their perfumed bodies and feel the softness of their skin against his fingers.

Sometimes, he let his mind wander into the future, to a time when his bones would rest beneath a marble headstone, put there by nothing more exceptional than old age. In that daydream, he pictured some clueless bastard stumbling upon his trophy room. He hoped that the guy would have the good sense to take the computer and its files to the police. Gavin imagined their faces as they came to understand his skill. It sometimes bothered him that his artistry might go unappreciated, that his secret might follow him to the grave. His magnum opus deserved to be acknowledged—but not until after he was dead and gone.

He closed the connection to his private server, letting his pulse return to normal before typing Sadie Vauk's name into his search engine.

She had already posted thirty-six pictures from the wedding to her Facebook page, godawful shots, like someone had handed a camera to a baboon.

Gavin had taken up photography when he got his first camera on his twelfth birthday, a gift that his mother could afford only because she married that man who had handled her like Play-Doh. He was an ugly man, a shaved llama with too many teeth, but he was also a man who lived in a big house with a swimming pool. Gavin called the man Dad, not because his mother hit him when he called him Mr. Balentine, but because Richard Balentine bought nice things for Gavin—things like a camera.

That birthday was the last one that Gavin would spend with Richard Balentine. A few months later, Richard would be dead, and his beautiful house with the big swimming pool would become the property of Gavin's mother.

In the comments section below the Facebook pictures, Gavin read a message from the bride, Janelle Rice-Halloway, thanking Sadie for doing her hair. Sadie was a hairdresser? Gavin opened a second search, adding the word *salon* after Sadie's name, and found a link for Queen Bebe's Hair Salon. He clicked on it.

Queen Bebe's was in the Lyndale neighborhood, a ten-minute drive from Gavin's home in Kenwood, but a world away on the socioeconomic map. The shop squatted in the middle of an old strip mall and housed two stylists, Bebe Kavenaugh and Sadie Vauk. It stayed open until six in the evening, and had no bank or convenience store nearby, which cut down on the possibility of surveillance cameras.

A plan began to form.

Sadie's social media presence extended to Twitter, Pinterest, and Instagram, but it was a collection of videos on YouTube that Gavin found most helpful. They were promotional shots taken inside the salon, showing the layout. How stupid to put her life on the internet like that—as if she wanted someone like Gavin to come along.

Gavin searched old news articles and found one about Sadie's high school swim team taking top honors at the state championship. A more recent article announced that Queen Bebe's was now offering body piercing. It had a picture of Sadie giving a customer a nose ring. Gavin hated nose piercings, although he had once dated a girl with a nose stud.

Well, to call it a date was a stretch. He had taken her to the homecoming dance his freshman year, a mistake that ultimately led to Gavin getting shipped off to a private school in Indiana.

Her name was Eleanora Abrams, and he'd only asked her to the dance because his mother had pressured him for weeks to find a date. Eleanora had sat next to him in chemistry and talked to him on a few occasions when she didn't understand her assignments. It had been the closest he had ever come to connecting with a girl, so he decided that if he were going to ask anyone to the dance, it would be her.

He found her alone in the school library one afternoon, and, summoning all the courage he could muster, said, "Eleanora, would you go to the dance with me?" But because of his speech impediment, the word dance came out as *dansche*. Gavin's cheeks turned hot when she didn't answer right away.

Then she said, "What?"

He hadn't prepared to say it twice—he doubted he could—but he pushed forward anyway. The second attempt came out even worse because he tried to ask without repeating the word *dance.* He instead muttered, "Homecoming," pointing at her and then back to himself. Was it confusion on her face, or panic? He'd wanted to run—instead, he begged. "Please?" But what she heard was "Pleasche?"

Backed into a corner, she looked around for help. No friends nearby. No lifeline. "Um..." She bit her lip. "Uh...I guess so." He could feel her regret almost immediately.

Gavin's mother drove them to the dance in her Jag, squawking the entire time about what a cute couple they made, and how lucky they were to be young. Gavin and Eleanora sat on opposite ends of the backseat, neither saying a word.

At the dance, Eleanora joined a cluster of her friends, and the group sat so tightly together that Gavin couldn't get close. He understood what they were doing, and why, and he wanted to be invisible.

After an hour of that hell, he left the gymnasium and took a seat on the stone wall, where he and Eleanora were to meet his mother after the dance. He had a cell phone and could have called his mother, but he didn't. Instead, he spent the next three hours waiting, and thinking, and plotting how he would make Eleanora regret the way she had treated him.

"Where's Eleanora?" his mother had asked when she pulled up.

He had practiced his answer as he waited. Amy hated his speech impediment, so when he had the opportunity to formulate his sentences in advance, he avoided words with the letter *S* in them. No reason to add to the revulsion she already felt for her son.

"Eleanora will ride home with a friend."

"What do you mean? She's your date. She came with you, so she should leave with you."

Gavin got in the car. Angry and embarrassed, his next words came out sharper than he had intended. "Go, would you!"

"Don't you talk to me that way, young man! What's going on? Did she dump you?"

"I told you—"

"If that little bitch—"

At that exact moment, Eleanora walked out of the gymnasium with her friends, and Gavin's mother grabbed her Styrofoam cup of coffee and jumped out of the car. Gavin opened his mouth to stop her, but the door slammed closed before he could get a word out. He watched Amy march across the parking lot toward Eleanora and the others, tossing the coffee lid to the ground as she neared them.

Gavin couldn't hear what was said, and the exchange lasted only a few seconds before his mother threw the coffee into Eleanora's face, causing the girl to fall backward to the ground. The others stood in stunned silence as Gavin's mother walked casually back to her Jaguar. Gavin cursed his mother under his breath. He had been hatching his own plan in those hours as he waited for his mother to show up, but now, any misfortune that might befall Eleanora would be traced back to him. Why hadn't his mother stayed out of it? The woman had no more cunning than a clod of dirt.

The cops arrived a few minutes after Gavin and his mother got home. It was the second time his mother had been questioned by the police, the first time being the morning they'd found Richard's body floating in the pool.

Stupidly, Amy chose to act confused. "What assault? What are you talking about?" She was about to talk herself into a criminal charge, so Gavin stepped in, laying it on thick, using words that exposed his speech impediment. He even threw in a bit of a stutter for good measure.

"Sh-sh-sche grabbed Mom's arm. That's how sche sh-sh-shcpilled the coffee. She was yelling and sh-sh-shcwearing at Mom, sh-sh-shctepping in like she was gonna hit her. Mom defended hershcelf. I schaw the whole thing."

How could they not believe the pathetic pleading of a kid so messed up that he could barely get the words out? Besides, the coffee wasn't hot enough to burn, so maybe Eleanora had exaggerated her story. The police closed the books on Eleanora's assault and left Gavin's house with a polite nod. And for the second time in his life, Gavin got away with lying to the police.

CHAPTER 5

Lila stared at Frank Dovey's invitation on her computer screen—no, not an invitation, a command: *Come see me,* three words that sucked the marrow from her bones. She thought back to that day in the elevator, the way he stared at her like a mean dog sizing up a meal. It had been two years since the Pruitt trial. For Dovey to fire her now seemed like a fight well below his weight class.

Lila took a few calming breaths and counted down from ten. When she got to one, she stood and walked out of her office. Whatever Dovey planned to do to her, it had already been decided. All she could do was hold her emotions in check as he placed her neck beneath the blade of the guillotine.

Frank Dovey's office had windows, and shelves, and a wall behind his desk chock-full of diplomas, plaques, and pictures. His door was open, but Lila knocked anyway. Frank didn't invite her in but simply pointed to a chair. She took a seat.

His face held no expression as he stared at her. If he was trying to unnerve her, it was working. Then he said, "I assume you heard what happened to Ms. Malone?"

"I did. How's she doing?"

Dovey ignored the question. "I also assume you're aware that I am in charge of the Adult Prosecution division in her absence."

Lila figured this question to be rhetorical and didn't answer.

He continued. "I've been looking over your work here, and I don't think you are living up to our expectations."

"I don't understand."

He picked up a piece of paper—Lila's résumé—and started reading. "Editor of the law review, Dillard Award with the Jessup Moot Court, teaching assistant for the litigation practice class."

In her head, Lila added, *Second chair of a murder case where we kicked your ass.*

"You've been here six months and in all this time, you've never appeared before a judge."

"A judge? No."

"And why is that? Has Mr. Hernandez lost faith in you?"

"Mr. Hernandez prefers that I do research and prepare exhibits."

"One of the purposes of a clerkship is to see what a person's made of. Trying a case isn't like moot court or sitting in an office, drafting memos. It's pressure. People's lives and livelihoods will be at stake. Victims need to know that you can handle the case—that you won't strike out on a curveball."

"I've asked Mr. Hernandez to let me—"

"Don't interrupt."

On the wall behind Dovey, Lila noticed a picture of Frank standing next to Colin Nelson, the county attorney, her boss—Dovey's boss. In the picture the two men stood in a thick wood, bonding over camouflage and dead turkeys.

"Your offer of employment here remains contingent, not only on passing the bar exam but on showing this office that you have the mettle to handle the job, and so far I've seen no evidence of that."

"What have I—?"

Dovey jabbed his hand into the space between them, his fingers clamped in a pinch, the message clear: *No talking.* "I'm reassigning you to an attorney who will get you in front of a judge. Report to Andrea Fitch. Tell her I sent you." His lips crept up into the slightest grin. Then he cocked his head as if he couldn't understand why Lila was still in his office, and said, "That's all, Ms. Nash."

Lila stood, left Dovey's office, and counted her steps in sets of ten as she made her way to the office of Andi Fitch. Dovey had moved the first piece on his political game board, a move Lila believed she understood. Assigning Lila to Andi Fitch had nothing to do with getting her in front of a judge and everything to do with building a paper trail that would justify his firing her. The quarterly performance review Fitch had written for Ryan was microscopic in its thoroughness, detailing every minor stumble and flaw. Dovey planned to kill her with paper cuts, and she would have no choice but to take it.

Lila paused outside of Fitch's door to gather her resolve before knocking. She wanted to present herself as the epitome of confidence: no shake in her voice, no fidget in her hands. At the very least, she wanted to hide the biting anxiety that roiled in her stomach. Then she knocked.

"Enter."

Lila stepped in, closing the door behind her. "I'm Lila Nash," she said.

Fitch gave her a glance and then turned her attention back to the document she was reading. "Congratulations," she said. "Why are you standing in my office, Lila Nash?"

"Mr. Dovey didn't tell you?"

At the mention of Dovey's name, Fitch put the paper down and looked at Lila. "Tell me what?"

"I've been reassigned to you."

Fitch pursed her lips and took in a slow, deep breath. "Is that a fact?"

Lila was about to answer, but Fitch pointed at a chair and said, "Sit," which Lila did. Then Fitch punched some buttons on the phone and set the ringing line to speaker. Frank Dovey answered.

"Frank, Andi here. I have a confused girl in my office who thinks she's been assigned to me for supervision. That has to be a mistake, so could you clear things up for her?"

"No mistake, Andi. I sent her there."

Andi picked up the receiver so Lila could no longer hear Frank. "What part of 'no more clerks' did you not get?" There was a long pause, after which Fitch said, "I'm tired of babysitting, Frank. We've talked about this."

Lila wanted to say, *I'm right here,* but she held her tongue.

"Goddammit! I don't know what your game is, but—"

There was another pause before Andi said, "Go to hell, Frank," and hung up the phone.

Andi looked at Lila as though she had just noticed that Lila was still in the room. Then Andi took her seat and dialed the phone again, keeping it on speaker. Ryan answered.

"Yes, Ms. Fitch?"

"Grab your files and bring them to my office."

"Which ones?"

"All of them!" She hung up the phone and pressed a finger against each temple, rubbing slowly. Lila wanted to say something but had no idea where to start. They sat there for minutes in silence until a knock announced Ryan's arrival with his arms full of files.

"Give those to... What's your name again?"

"Lila... Nash."

"Give those to Ms. Nash and then go see Frank Dovey. You're apparently being reassigned."

Ryan looked at Lila and then back at Fitch, as though waiting for the catch. When neither said anything, he handed the stack to Lila and left.

"The Gray case is your priority. I need a complaint done today. I want a draft on my desk in two hours."

"Gray... that's the one at the convenience store—the guy that hit his wife?"

Fitch looked mildly curious. "You know the case?"

"Ryan told me about it this morning. Said he was adding a charge of false imprisonment. It might be finished already."

Fitch appraised Lila for several seconds before saying, "I see." She leaned back in her chair. "I'll take a look at it. As for the rest of those, I have notes inside each file. Focus on the cases that need to be charged out. I want you in my office first thing every morning, and I mean first thing, not after coffee, not after chitchat—eight o'clock, here, so I can give you your assignments. Are we clear?"

"Yes, Ms. Fitch."

"You're excused."

Lila stood, the stack of files reaching up to her elbows. When she got to the door, she had to lift a knee to hold the stack so that she could open it.

"Wait," Fitch said.

Lila turned in the doorway.

"I just want to be clear: If you're not cut out for this job, it's best to figure that out early. I will not abide subpar. If you want out now, I'll be happy to recommend a transfer—maybe Juvenile Prosecution or Child Protection. But if you want to be an attorney in Adult Prosecutions, you will excel or you'll be out."

Lila couldn't take her eyes off Fitch. The woman scared the hell out of her, but at the same time, Andi had a presence unlike anything Lila had ever experienced. Her words moved through the room like music, the tone menacing and dangerous but utterly captivating. Lila remained in the doorway, not sure if Andi had finished. Then Andi said, "Shut the door!"

Lila lifted a shaky knee again to support the stack as she pulled Andi's door closed behind her.

CHAPTER 6

By midmorning, Gavin had reached the end of what he could accomplish on his computer and set out into the physical world for the next phase.

He owned two vehicles: a new Lexus GS and his faithful old friend, a 1986 Ford Bronco. It was a hideous rust bucket that shook at speeds over fifty-five miles per hour. But the Bronco had no GPS to record locations of travel, so as far as the matrix of cell towers and satellites were concerned, it didn't exist.

First, he drove the Lexus between his house and Queen Bebe's Salon, in search of a path devoid of surveillance cameras, altering his course whenever he saw a stoplight camera or ATM.

Once he'd plotted his route, he drove to a distant thrift store, paying cash for a complete set of clothing: jeans, a hoodie, a T-shirt, sunglasses, shoes, and socks, all of which he would destroy within twenty-four hours. He went to a drugstore and bought latex gloves, hand wipes, and a package of ten condoms. At a nearby Walmart, he bought a burner phone, twenty yards of plastic sheathing, a computer privacy screen, and a large plastic storage bin.

By eleven thirty, with his shopping complete, Gavin switched to the Bronco for reconnaissance.

An empty parking lot across the street from Queen Bebe's provided Gavin with a perfect view of his prey. With the ass end of the Bronco facing the salon, he climbed into the way-back, pulled a telephoto lens from his camera case, and settled in.

Under the hot August sun, sweat trickled down his temples as he studied the layout of the shop, noting the absence of surveillance cameras. From his nest, he watched Sadie Vauk as she worked, talked, and more important, drank from a bottle of water she kept at her station. He would need to get her to turn her back so he could be alone with the water bottle. Maybe he could ask for something to drink or to see a style catalog. He'd only need a few seconds.

Pleased with his effort, Gavin climbed back into the cab of the Bronco, started the engine, and turned on the air conditioner, aiming the vents at his face. He pulled a pair of latex gloves and the burner phone from the glove box. He had been practicing his conversation with Sadie Vauk, being careful to construct a script that would keep his speech impediment hidden. He went through the exchange in his head one more time, enjoying the slap of cool air on his hot skin. Then he dialed.

"Queen Bebe's." It was Sadie.

"Hi, I'm calling for an appointment to get a haircut."

"Oh, cool. I can get you in sometime next—"

"I've got a problem, though. I have to fly to London in the morning and I need to get a trim before I go. Do you have an opening today?"

"I'm sorry, but I'm booked full."

"I'm in a real bind here. If there were any way... I'll pay you double if you could add me on at the end of the day. My regular guy had a funeral, and I have to look good for my trip."

Gavin could hear Sadie wrestling with her decision. She was on the fence, so Gavin pushed on. "Triple. I'll pay triple your normal rate, but I can't go any higher. I'm begging."

"Okay, but you need to be here by six."

"Perfect."

Adrenaline coursed through Gavin's body, the exhilaration making him want to scream and punch at the air. How could skydiving or bungee-jumping ever compete with the thrill of bending a woman to his will? Dancing on the edge of a verbal cliff while his speech impediment fought to break free? He'd done it. Round one, and Picture Boy had bested the princess.

"What's your name?" she asked.

Gavin smiled to himself. "My name? Kevin."

* * *

Gavin went home and finished his preparations, spreading the plastic sheathing in a basement bedroom just inside the garage, and a second sheet in the back of the Bronco. From his hiding place beneath the lazy Susan, he retrieved a small bottle of gamma-hydroxybutyric acid and carefully poured a measure of the clear liquid into a vial the size of a double-A battery. He put the vial in his pocket.

The computer privacy screen wasn't for his computer. He cut it in half, fitting a section over his front and back license plates. Privacy screens were designed to turn a screen black unless viewed head-on. Placed over his license plate, it would lessen the chance that a random surveillance camera might capture his plate number.

Then he fired up the Bronco.

As six o'clock neared, Gavin found himself back in the parking lot across the street, watching the final customers of the day leave the salon. He began to worry a bit as he waited for Bebe to leave. If she dragged out her departure, it would throw a wrench into the plan. But at six on the button, Bebe walked out, leaving Sadie alone.

Gavin waited for Bebe to leave the parking lot before driving across the street and parking where Sadie wouldn't see the Bronco. When he entered the shop, he took off his sunglasses and his hood. Would she recognize him? If she did, she might make a fuss, become suspicious. At the very least, she would be reluctant to leave him alone with her water bottle. Then what? If he aborted, she would tell Bebe about him and end the game.

This was his only chance—the moment of truth. If she recognized him, he would walk away. But when she looked at him, her eyes held no sign of recognition.

"Hi," she said. "Are you Kevin?"

"I am," he said.

CHAPTER 7

Joe arrived home after Lila, his shoulders slouched like those of a man who had spent the day carrying stones. He'd been working double duty for the past month, picking up assignments for another reporter who was out on maternity leave. He walked straight to the couch and plopped down, his head tipped back, his eyes closed, knees splayed open. Lila thought he looked like a man who could use a beer. But Lila couldn't get him one, because they kept no alcohol in the apartment.

She'd never asked Joe to give up alcohol, and he drank on those rare occasions when they ventured out to a restaurant, but as an act of unspoken solidarity, he never brought alcohol home. Lila was eight years sober now, her last drink the half bottle of vodka she'd downed just before swallowing a handful of her mother's Ambien.

It took almost dying, two weeks in a psych ward, and meeting Dr. Roberts to stop the slide she had been on. Her decision to quit found its roots the day Dr. Roberts showed her his twenty-year medallion.

"How was your day?" she asked Joe.

"Same as yesterday and probably won't be any better than tomorrow. How 'bout yours?"

Lila sat down on the couch, slung an arm around him, and tipped his head onto her shoulder. "My day was... Well, you remember back in law school, that case I did with Boady Sanden?"

"The Pruitt case."

"Do you remember the name of the prosecutor?"

"Dovey?"

"Look at the whiz kid—two for two."

"Don't worry. I'll blow it in Final Jeopardy. So, what about Dovey?"

"He's my boss now."

"What? Why?"

"Beth Malone was in a car accident last night. She'll be out for a while, and in the meantime, Dovey's taking over Adult Prosecution."

Joe raised an eyebrow. "As I recall, he was something of a dick."

"Don't sell him short—he's a complete dick, a walking, talking asshat. And his first order of business was to call me into his office."

"Did he... I mean..."

"Fire me? Frank doesn't operate so bluntly. His game's more subtle. I think I see his strategy, though. He'll drum up some reason to fire me. Either that or he'll force me out... lay stones on my chest until I can't breathe anymore."

"So... what was the first stone?"

"He reassigned me from Oscar to this woman named Andi Fitch."

"White Collar?"

"No. Sex Crimes and Homicide."

"That's good though, right? That's where you want to be."

"Yeah, but this woman." Lila rolled her eyes. "She's demanding and gruff and—"

"And she doesn't know what she's in for," Joe said. "She hardly sounds up to taking on the likes of Lila Nash. Someone should warn her."

Lila cracked a smile in spite of herself. "It's not funny. It's just the first salvo. Who knows what he'll do next."

"But he won't just fire you, right?"

"I don't think so, not without a pretext. He'll hold me under a magnifying glass for a while first. He's such a—"

"Asshat?"

"Exactly."

Joe turned toward Lila, put his arm around her, and eased her back into his chest. "Then keep being flawless," he said.

Lila relaxed into Joe. "Maybe I should get my résumé back out there. Who knows, I might enjoy insurance defense."

"What would we do with all that money, though? It'd ruin us."

"I could buy you pretty things."

"It *would* be kind of nice to have my own toothbrush."

And like he always did, Joe made her laugh. "That is disgusting."

"Anyone ever tell you you're pretty?"

"Anyone ever tell you you're full of crap?"

"Every day." Joe gave her a squeeze. "It'll be okay. You're stronger than Frank Dovey, or this Fitch person. You're like a...legal ninja Jedi. They want to crush you? They're gonna need a lot bigger rocks than what they've got."

Sometimes Joe spoke with the bravado of a child; at least it seemed so to Lila, the way he jumped to her defense with both feet. He made her sound eight feet tall, but the woman Lila saw in the mirror could never measure up. But then again, how could he understand what had been carved out of her all those years ago?

He didn't see the remnants of those anxious nights in the hospital when sleep came in broken shards. He'd never heard her counting her steps. Joe saw what she wanted him to see—what she needed him to see—that version of herself that she wished were true. As much as she wanted to believe that summer was behind her, she knew it wasn't. What happened to her would never be gone.

She swallowed her doubt and smiled at Joe. "You're right," she said. "To hell with them. They don't know who they're messing with." The lie tasted bitter on her tongue.

"That's my girl."

Anxious to change the subject, Lila said, "Tell me about your day."

"Oh, you've already won the contest. My day was nothing compared to yours—although, I may be heading out on assignment."

"Oh...? Where to?"

"A tropical paradise they call North Dakota. There's a protest over a pipeline they're building on Native lands. Things are heating up."

"When?"

"Allison hasn't decided if I'm going for sure, but if it happens, it'll be soon."

Lila turned to face Joe, the ache of his absence already creeping into her bones. She would hide that pain from him and watch him go if it came to that—one more secret to put with the rest. It was always harder when he was away.

She wrapped her arms around his neck, pulled his face to hers, and kissed him. It was what she needed more than anything else in that moment.

* * *

Early the next morning, in those dark hours when the rise of the sun remained nothing more than a promise, Lila awoke from a dream. Like most dreams, it was disjointed and random. She remembered being on her hands and knees amid a pile of files, the papers scattered around her like fallen leaves. Andi Fitch stood over her, arms folded in disgust. Lila was stacking the papers, but like the biblical fishes and loaves, they continued to multiply.

Then she noticed that Andi's shoes had become a pair of men's shoes, and Lila looked up to see Frank Dovey, a vengeful grin wrinkling the corners of his eyes. That's when Lila woke up.

Joe lay with his back to her, his light snore drifting in the air. He was such a sound sleeper that he never noticed her nightmares. And while it had woken her up, the dream hadn't been nearly as jarring as some she'd had. Her new boss held no candle to the faceless men who grabbed at her from the darkness.

Those dreams sometimes affected her for days. She would see men looking at her in that certain way as she passed them on the street. The scrape of sand underfoot in a parking garage could make her heart stop. Such was the fallout that survivors like her had to endure.

She curled an arm around Joe's chest and listened to the sound of his exhales, felt the gentle rise and fall of his back against her cheek. How she loved the way his presence brought her peace. She pressed her face to his shoulder and whispered, "I need to tell you something."

She paused to be certain that she hadn't woken him up before she continued. Then she said, "Sometimes, I'm afraid."

She tried to find more words to explain the labyrinth that lay between the woman Joe knew and the one who stared back at Lila from the mirror. How could she possibly explain it? She was too tired to form cogent thoughts. Her sentences broke apart in her head, the words becoming heavy and lost before she could speak them.

"I just wanted you to know that," she finally said.

She closed her eyes and listened to the hum of the air conditioners in the courtyard below mixing with passing cars on the street and Joe's breathing. As sleep came for her, she whispered to Joe, in a voice so soft as to be as much thought as it was breath, "I love you."

CHAPTER 8

Gavin knew that his plan held risks, unavoidable gaps that could be minimized but never eliminated. Getting the women into the Bronco in public was one of those gaps; and for Sadie Vauk, that part had gone without a hitch. The second unavoidable gap came when Gavin brought them out to the banks of the Mississippi River to say goodbye.

Gavin put a great deal of thought into how best to part ways with them. Fantasizing the perfect adieu had lulled him to sleep on so many nights. The problem, as he saw it, was that if he left them dead along the side of the road, they would be found, and the foul play of his deed would flash as if in bright neon red. The game, as Sherlock Holmes might say, would be afoot. So why invite that kind of trouble?

He considered hiding them, maybe digging a hole and burying them, but that brought with it a host of new problems, not the least of which was finding a suitable location, a place where he could spend time without being observed. He considered purchasing land out in the country, but then he would own the graves if they were ever discovered. That would not do. The best solution had to be one where no one would know what had happened to them.

That's when Gavin discovered Nicollet Island.

Unlike those deserted islands of Huckleberry Finn, Nicollet Island was as much a part of Minneapolis as any other city block. It held houses, a school, a hotel, and on its lower tip, a pavilion for weddings.

That's how Gavin first discovered it. He had photographed a wedding there as one of his earliest gigs. When he'd stepped outside to get some fresh air, he'd strolled along the walking path that followed the river, and where others might have seen the peaceful beauty of one of the world's most storied rivers, Gavin saw the answer to a problem.

A couple hundred feet downstream from the pavilion lay the front edge of a hydroelectric dam built at the start of the twentieth century. The dam reached upstream in an upside-down V, water washing over a fourteen-foot spillway. But that was just the beginning of the ride. Below the dam churned St. Anthony Falls, a fifty-foot drop in the river where according to Dakota legend, an evil god named Oanktehi lived.

For Gavin, the river seemed an answer to a prayer. The medical examiner would determine that death came from drowning, but what kind of drowning? Suicide? Accident? Foul play? If they couldn't say for certain that it was a murder, would anyone ever look for him? As an added bonus, the brutality of the falls would pummel the body, threshing away any speck of evidence that Gavin may have missed. Although he never missed a thing.

The only stumbling block was getting them into the river without being seen.

West Island Avenue followed the contour of the Mississippi but curved sharply away from the river when it arrived at the entrance to the wedding pavilion. With a sleeping Sadie Vauk in the back, Gavin drove down the avenue twice, looping past the pavilion to see if anyone might be walking the paths or loitering in the parking lot of the nearby inn. At three o'clock in the morning, everything seemed quiet.

On his third pass he stopped, looked around one last time, and then backed his Bronco onto a walking path. Only thirty feet off the avenue, Gavin found a spot at the edge of the river beyond the reach of the nearby streetlights. He knew that spot; he had been there before.

As Gavin slid her out of the back of the Bronco, she acted lethargic and drowsy, more conscious than Gavin would have liked. He thought he heard her say the word "No," her voice thick with sleep. None of the others had been able to speak. Had he used enough of the drug? If she'd ever imbibed liquid ecstasy, say at a club, she could have built up a tolerance. He had no way to account for that.

"Right over here," Gavin whispered as he walked her to the edge of the river. He set her in the grass atop the six-foot embankment and slipped over the edge, finding his balance on the slippery rocks.

Sadie was trying to open her eyes. That hadn't happened the other times. And Sadie's legs seemed less wobbly. He had to drag the others to the river's edge, but Sadie had managed to put one foot in front of the other, leaning on him to remain upright. Would she put up a fight when he pushed her face under the water?

Gavin took ahold of Sadie's left wrist and she tried to pull away, a feeble effort. When he tightened his grip, she opened her eyes enough to look at him, but then she closed them again, pinching them tight as if trying to solve the riddle of how she had come to be in this place, with this man. Gavin felt a spark of charity—knowing that she would soon be dead—and in that moment of benevolence, he answered the question that he thought she was pondering. "All you had to do was be nice, Sadie." He hadn't prepared his words, so they dripped thick with his lisp. Then he grabbed her other wrist and yanked her over the edge of the bank.

Right away he understood his miscalculation. He had expected her to be heavy and inert, a bag of rocks like the others, but Sadie stumbled into him, sending them both tumbling toward the river.

Gavin spun backward, letting go of Sadie and grabbing a branch to keep from falling. Sadie sailed past him, crashing down the steep embankment, twisting on the rocks, and plunging into the water, crying out in pain just before the river swallowed her.

Gavin tried to regain his footing but tripped in the darkness and fell back into the scrub.

When Sadie came up for air, Gavin heard splashing, but no scream.

That was good—or was it? When he finally managed to get back to his feet, he saw Sadie twelve feet out, struggling to right herself.

He wanted to leap in and finish the job, but he froze. Was she awake enough to fight? How deep was the water? Would the current pull him toward the falls? That synaptic flurry of doubt lasted a mere second or two, but it was enough to keep him on the shore until his window of opportunity had disappeared.

Sadie sloshed and flailed and fought to stay alive. He waited for a scream or maybe a yell for help, but none came as the current pulled her away from him and toward the dam. St. Anthony Falls would have her soon, and no one could survive its crushing power.

But then, Gavin saw something that confused him. At first he thought that the darkness was playing a trick, but it wasn't. The splashing, which had once been erratic and wild, had taken on rhythm, like the strokes of... a swimmer. She was swimming away from the falls!

Goddammit!

The hydroelectric dam powered a station on Hennepin Island only a hundred yards downstream from where Gavin stood. He watched Sadie flutter and fight to stay alive, her clumsy strokes pulling her toward the jagged riprap on the upstream point of the power station. Lights from the plant illuminated the river enough that Gavin could see her head bobbing in the water—loose on her shoulders, but moving in rhythm with the strokes.

No! No! No!

Gavin climbed the bank and ran to the Bronco. He stomped on the gas, causing the old truck to bounce over the curb so hard that he hit his head against the roof. He willed himself to slow down. *Keep your wits. Panic is the enemy. This is where a lesser man would screw things up. You're no lesser man.*

Once again in control, he drove calmly off the island and down the lane that followed the river, toward the gate of the power plant. A surveillance camera on the building's roof forced him to circle the block and park where the camera couldn't see him.

Sadie lay on the rocks, her body limp, like a shipwreck survivor washed upon a hostile shore.

Options: He could pull the hoodie over his head and climb the fence, drag her back into the water, and drown her. She would put up a fight. Plus, the power plant had cameras and a security staff. He would never make it back off the island before he was spotted—but would they be able to identify him?

Before Gavin could come up with a better alternative, a man appeared in the doorway of the power plant, stood for a moment as if confused, and then walked toward Sadie. As he neared her, he must have realized what lay on the rocks, because he ran the last few yards to pull her to safety.

Gavin should have been apoplectic at the sight of Sadie being rescued, but somehow he wasn't. Instead of visions of prison and recrimination, Gavin saw a challenge like no other. A strange energy washed over him.

Finally they would know about him. Sadie would tell of the man who came to her salon, the man named Kevin. And with that, the game would be on.

They would come for him like hunters in search of prey, chasing him over a terrain of his choosing, his skill matched against theirs. He had been preparing for this test his whole life, and now that it had arrived, it excited him to his core.

The time had come to test his long game, march out onto a new and vastly more complex battlefield. He had imagined this moment a thousand times, prepared for it. Now he would face off against a true adversary, a detective, someone worthy of his prowess. And if he remained calm and executed his moves with intelligence, his victory would be as sweet as heaven's own honey.

The first move in this new game would be to dismantle what little remained of his evening with Sadie Vauk. Gavin Spencer had a long night ahead of him.

CHAPTER 9

It was Detective Niki Vang's turn to get the coffee that morning, which she bought at the Park Café, a cafeteria in the bowels of the Hennepin County Government Center—this even though her partner, Matty, wrinkled his nose at anything that wasn't Starbucks or Caribou. As she waited for her order, she spotted a familiar face, smiled, and gestured for the man to join her in line.

"You coming or going?" Niki asked.

George Devlemnick rubbed his eyes, heavy with exhaustion, and cleared his throat with a light cough before he spoke, a habit she remembered from the days when she worked with him in the Sex Crimes unit. "Just finishing up a long night," he said. "Worked a prostitution sting."

"All night? Must have been a big haul."

"Nothing more than usual, although we did snag a man of the cloth. Said he was only there to spread the gospel of repentance. You know, 'Go forth and sin no more.'"

"I take it that didn't fly?"

"He brought his own condom."

Niki stepped up to the counter and placed her order. "If it was just a sting, why're you still here? That should have wrapped up hours ago."

"We had a curveball thrown at us."

The woman behind the counter brought two coffees. Niki thanked her and waited with George as he ordered.

"Actually," George said, "it was nearly a case for you guys. A security guard over at Hennepin Island fished a girl out of the river. Found her washed up on the rocks."

"Alive?"

"Barely."

A cog clicked somewhere in the back of Niki's mind. "Tell me more."

"Woman. Early twenties. Groggy as hell. We tried to get a statement, but she couldn't focus. We're having the dayshift go back to give it another try this morning."

"Drugged?"

"That's our bet. We took blood and urine."

"Sexual assault?"

"Doc said she saw evidence of recent sexual activity, but the girl was out of it, so we couldn't ask about consent."

This all sounded strangely familiar to Niki. She pointed to a table and the two of them moved to take seats. There had been other women in the river. She worked the memories out of the dust.

"Fully clothed?" she asked.

George tipped his head, curious. "Yeah."

"No ligature marks?"

"None."

Niki took a moment to think, to remember them all. The most recent one had been two years ago. It hadn't been her case, but she remembered how cavalier Lieutenant Briggs had been when he assigned it to the other detective. "I'll bet fifty bucks that she just broke up with her boyfriend," he'd said.

Curious, and disliking his assumption, Niki had done some digging and found a similar death two years before that and another two years before that. When she mentioned this to Briggs, he said, "We have enough murder cases to keep us busy; we don't need to burn time on people who jump off bridges. These are low-priority cases. Focus on the ones we know were murdered." She was a rookie in Homicide back then and didn't challenge Briggs, but his offhanded dismissal stuck with her.

Niki leaned in toward George and lowered her voice. "Just after I came to Homicide, they pulled the body of a young woman from the river down near Ford Parkway. She was fully clothed, her body a mess: postmortem bruises, broken bones. Best we could figure, she went in upstream from the falls. Two years before that, another one washed ashore in Gorge Park. We couldn't really say it was a murder versus an accident or a suicide."

"Two victims?"

"Maybe three. St. Paul pulled a woman out of the river six years ago. Same MO: fully clothed, no ligature marks, no defensive wounds. They all had signs of recent sexual activity and GHB in their systems."

"Okay, but GHB can show up naturally in a dead body."

"A few years back, they came out with a new test using brain tissue. GHB doesn't get into the brain unless it's ingested. They did that test on the girl from two years ago, so we know she definitely ingested it. Whether it was voluntarily or slipped to her, we can't say. What can you tell me about the one from last night?"

"Her name's Sadie Vauk. We think she went into the river off Nicollet Island."

"Find anything on the island?"

"Some tire tracks. They ran along one of the walking paths. Stopped near a gap in the trees. We made a cast of the tread print. No surveillance cameras in that spot, but we have requests in at some of the businesses around the area. Maybe we'll catch a glimpse of something. We know what time the security guard found her, so we have a pretty tight window."

"I think you have an attempted murder," Niki said. "If we could link this girl from last night to any of the others, we might have modus operandi for three cases."

"It's thin," George said.

Thin, Niki thought. *Low priority.* How could men so easily dismiss three dead women? "It's a start, George. That's what it is."

"You want the file?"

"I do."

CHAPTER 10

Lila sat quietly in the office of Andi Fitch as her new boss read the first criminal complaint that she had prepared. Lila had stacked the files in order of her own confidence, the top file being spot on, in Lila's opinion. Yet Fitch picked up a pen and started crossing out words. "It's not *the defendant;* it's simply *Defendant*. '*Defendant* ran into his house. Officers followed *Defendant* in hot pursuit.'" Andi slid the file back to Lila. "Otherwise... it'll do."

Andi added similar changes to the next three files, cosmetic adjustments, but nothing that caused Andi to throw the file back to her the way Ryan had described it. The fifth file, a child pornography case, would be a problem and Lila knew it. She mentally steeled herself as Fitch opened the file to find no complaint awaiting her scrutiny. This one she did toss at Lila. "I wanted this done this morning," she said. "Get it back to me by lunch."

"I don't think you should charge him," Lila said.

Fitch looked at Lila as though the younger woman had just thrown feces at her. "That's not your call. If you can't do what I ask, I'll be happy to transfer you to Child Support Collections."

Lila, her hands clasped tightly together on her lap, waited for Fitch to finish. And when she spoke, she stumbled at first. "It's not... This isn't about..." She took a breath. "If you charge him, he'll walk."

Andi leaned back in her chair and crossed one leg over the other, a move she executed with the ease of a scorpion drawing back its stinger. "Go on."

Lila cleared a lump of doubt from her throat and began. "So this guy, Woggum, gets arrested because he made a child porn video and shared it with his buddy. But we only know about Woggum because we arrested the buddy—gave him a deal so we could get the guy who made the video."

Lila paused to see if Andi might offer some acknowledgment, but the woman simply stared at her.

"But when they searched Woggum's house, they found nothing. He had wiped his hard drive, so, no possession of child pornography."

Fitch rolled her eyes. "Tell me you didn't decline to charge because of that. Good lord!"

"I'm not finished." Lila spoke in a tone she meant to sound firm, but it was lacking the intended punch. "The informant said that he was there two years ago when Woggum made the video. That implicates Woggum, but it's the word of a co-accomplice."

"We also have Woggum's voice on the video," Andi said. "We know he made the video because you can hear him, for God's sake. That's not enough for you?"

"My concern..." Lila paused before taking her next step through the minefield. "Is not who made the video, but when it was made."

Andi's expression moved from exacerbation to curiosity, a wolf losing its snarl. She tipped her head to listen, a gesture that inflated Lila's confidence.

She continued. "The video proves that it was Woggum's apartment, and detectives took a bunch of pictures when they made the arrest. In the video Woggum made, you can see that the bathroom is being remodeled—the sink is on the floor and there're pipes and stuff lying around—but in the arrest pictures, the remodel is finished."

"Okay."

"I thought... Well, maybe we could look up the building permit to get a fix on the date of the construction. That way—"

"Didn't the detectives look into that?" Andi picked up the file and began paging through the police reports.

"No."

"You did?"

Lila could see that Andi had finally synced with Lila's train of thought. *Now bring it home.* "The permit was issued three and a half years ago. I called the landlord, and he said he finished the work just over three years ago."

"Beyond the statute of limitations."

Lila held her grin in check. "For Minnesota, yes, but the feds have a five-year window. You can refer it out."

A long silence filled the space between them, and Lila had to fight to keep from squirming with excitement. Andi finally spoke. "I read your résumé. You did some defense work with Boady Sanden."

"As a second-year, I worked a case with him, yes."

"I can tell. You think like a defense attorney."

"I don't—"

Andi held up her hand to stop Lila. "That's a compliment. You worked through the case, anticipated the defenses—that's good."

"I didn't like the weak timeline, that's all." In truth, she had obsessed over that small detail for hours, but false modesty seemed to be a better response.

"Tell me the truth, Lila. Were you the one who told Ryan to charge out the false imprisonment on the Gray case?"

Lila didn't answer.

Fitch nodded. "Ryan's a smart kid, but has no mind for strategy." Andi handed the file back to Lila. "Please do a referral letter to the U.S. Attorney's Office."

Lila took the file.

"And they're bringing Mr. Gray in for his first appearance this morning. I want you to handle the hearing. You *have* done a first appearance, haven't you?"

"Mr. Hernandez preferred that I not."

"Good lord." Andi closed her eyes and mumbled something under her breath. The only word Lila made out was Oscar's name. When she opened her eyes again, she looked at Lila and said, "Well, you're doing one today."

CHAPTER 11

By nine o'clock that morning, Gavin Spencer had taken care of most of the tasks on his list, and now he sat in the waiting area of a tire shop, giving thought to what he may have overlooked.

After seeing Sadie get rescued at the power station, he drove the Bronco home and got to work. First, he placed the large storage bin—the one he purchased the day before at Walmart—on the floor of his garage and began filling it with the evidence, starting with the plastic sheathing that he had laid out in the back of the Bronco and on the floor of the bedroom. He added Sadie's water bottle and his clothing, latex gloves, and wipes. Anything that either of them had touched went into the bin.

How much time did he have? Sadie would have been groggy when they found her, most of her recent memory lost to a comatose haze. The name in her appointment book at the salon listed him as Kevin. If she didn't connect him to the wedding, the police might never find him, but part of Gavin hoped they would. Chalk it up to hubris, or maybe boredom, but now that the worst had happened, he wanted a taste of the big leagues.

If she made the connection between Kevin at the salon and Gavin the Picture Boy, detectives would be at his door soon, but when? That was the question that gnawed at Gavin's thoughts. Would they wait for toxicology reports to come back? Doubtful. They might hold out until they got a search warrant, and that would take time. Pass on the warrant, and they could be at his door as early as noon. Gavin figured that he had at least until then to finish his cleanup.

He had pulled his laptop and the bottle of GHB from beneath the lazy Susan, wiping his prints from both and tossing the bottle into the bin. As for the laptop, he'd had one last project to run on it. He'd exported the new pictures of Sadie from his camera to the computer before destroying the camera's memory chip with fire and a toilet flush.

This part of the plan—saving pictures of his crime—was absolutely foolish, and he knew it, but he had no choice. His keepsakes were like oxygen for him. He couldn't live without them. Besides, what was the point of all that planning and effort if he couldn't relive the thrill through his small mementos?

Once he had secured his trophy—the memory of Sadie locked away on the server hidden in his mother's garage attic—he went to work destroying his laptop.

Of course, simply deleting the data would not do; that was the digital equivalence of hiding behind a curtain. Gavin first used his evidence-erasing software to wipe the hard drive clean. A lesser mind, at that point, would have been satisfied, but not Gavin. He opened the laptop, removed the hard drive, and drilled holes through the memory platter. In order to get data from the platter, it needed to spin like a record album. He rendered the disc useless and unreadable.

Redundancy.

Finally, he smashed it all with a hammer and put the scraps into a plastic shopping bag, which he placed in the front seat of the Bronco.

He removed the privacy screens from his license plates and put those in the bin, too. Despite having laid plastic sheathing on the floor of his downstairs bedroom, he vacuumed the carpets and put the vacuum bag in the bin. Then he loaded the vacuum itself into the Bronco, on the near impossible chance that its beater-bar held a strand of hair or a few skin cells. He would donate the vacuum to a thrift store on his way to buy tires.

Once everything had seemed ready, he'd paused to see what he might have missed.

His home computer had never accessed the hidden server, never held any of the incriminating pictures, and had never been used for research. If they examined it, they would find tedium. A search of his phone would show that it hadn't left his house in the past twenty-four hours.

What was he missing? This was the point at which most people made mistakes. They got in a hurry. He would not hurry.

He had almost convinced himself that he had thought of everything when a mistake caught his attention. The router. A router can collect browsing histories. He had almost missed it. He went and unplugged his router. Back in the garage, he wiped it down with a baby wipe to remove his fingerprints and skin cells, then took a hammer to it, pulverizing it, before sweeping the bits into a second plastic grocery bag.

He then filled eight condoms with gasoline, tucking them around the edge of the bin—a trick he learned from a documentary on special effects in movies. They used condoms to create fiery explosions because gasoline wouldn't eat through a condom as it would a regular balloon. He slipped a book of matches and a tiny cone of incense into his pocket for a detonation device.

His final act was to back both the Bronco and his Lexus out of the garage and sweep the floor clean, tossing the dirt and broom head into the bin. The detectives would find absolutely no evidence that Sadie had ever been in Gavin's home.

* * *

Driving north on Interstate 94, Gavin pulled off on Broadway to go through a couple of twenty-four-hour fast-food restaurants, ordering a small meal from each drive-through. As he pulled out, he tossed the plastic grocery bags into their trash receptacles, leaving the remnants of the laptop at the first restaurant and the smashed router at the second.

Continuing north, he came to a stretch of land along the river where they once dredged sand. He had found that spot the first time he went through this ritual. It was a perfect place to set a small fire.

As was his habit, he drove past the sand pit twice to make sure it was deserted in those wee hours of the morning. Then he backed the Bronco down to the river's edge and slid the plastic bin out of the back, dropping it to the ground. He lit the cone of incense and tucked it inside the book of matches, placing the makeshift timer where its flame would lap against one of the gas-filled condoms.

As he was about to leave, he had another thought and tossed his floor mats and cargo mat onto the pile. Crime labs had the technology to trace the dirt from a pair of shoes to a crime scene. He had been careful, but if any dirt from Nicollet Island had made it onto the floor mat, it made no sense to leave such a thing lying around.

In the Bronco again, he drove to a vantage point about a half mile away to watch.

It didn't take long for the spark from the incense cone to touch off the book of matches, igniting the first condom full of gas. Things erupted quickly after that, and in a matter of seconds, the bin went up in a pyre visible for miles, the thick black smoke from the burning plastic and rubber lifting to the sky. There would be no trace evidence found there.

Gavin's next task was to clean up his beloved Bronco.

He drove through two different car washes because seedpods and grass can sometimes tie a vehicle to a crime scene. But a car wash could not change the tread of his tires. That's what brought him to the tire shop.

At first the guy acted like he didn't want Gavin's business.

"Your tires ain't that bad. Ya got a good twenty thousand miles left on 'em."

"They don't ride well," Gavin said, avoiding his lisp.

"But why do ya want used tires? What I got here in the shop ain't as good as what ya got on there now."

"I prefer older tread."

"But that don't make sense."

"I could go to another company—"

"No, I'll take care of ya, it's just... Fine, if ya want used tires, I'll get ya used tires."

CHAPTER 12

A nurse led Niki Vang and Matty Lopez to a room in the Hennepin County Medical Center where a young woman lay sleeping in the lone bed. Her face was hollowed out by her ordeal, her hair tangled, having gone unbrushed after being wet. Next to her, a man in his late forties slept in a green chair, his head propped up by an elbow on the armrest. When the detectives entered the room, the man sat up and wiped the exhaustion from his eyes.

"This is her father," the nurse whispered.

The man blinked as if confused.

"Mr. Vauk?" Niki said.

"Yes."

"May we speak to you?" She pointed to the corridor.

The man looked at his daughter and nodded, standing to follow the detectives out of the room.

"I'm Detective Vang, and this is Detective Lopez. We need to talk to Sadie, but we'd like a word with you first, if that's okay."

"Did you find him—the one who did that to my little girl?"

"We're just getting started, Mr. Vauk," Niki said. "We need to learn everything we can—every detail. Do you know where your daughter was yesterday or last night?"

"I already had this conversation with you people."

"We're with a different unit, and we'd like to go over it again. Make sure nothing gets overlooked."

"What unit?"

Niki handed a card to Mr. Vauk. "We're with Homicide."

"I don't understand. Sadie's alive."

To avoid getting into the weeds about the three cold cases, Niki simply said, "Someone made an attempt on your daughter's life. That's why we're here. What do you know about Sadie's whereabouts yesterday?"

"Not much. She lives on her own. She came by Sunday to drop off her dog so I could watch him. She had a wedding to go to."

"Whose wedding?" Matty asked.

"A friend of Sadie's named Janelle Halloway. Sadie was supposed to come by after work yesterday to pick up the dog, but she never showed. I called her but got no answer. I kept calling until around eleven; that's when I phoned you folks. I got a call around four-thirty this morning. Said Sadie was..." Mr. Vauk paused to let a quiver pass his lips. "She was here at the hospital."

"I know this is difficult, Mr. Vauk," Niki said. "Only a few more questions. Was Sadie dating anyone?"

"No one she told me about."

Matty asked, "Did she have any enemies?"

"No." The word came out sharp and strong, as if Mr. Vauk had been insulted.

"Anyone make her nervous lately? Call her too much?"

"Nothing like that. Everybody loves Sadie."

Niki asked, "Has she said anything since the other detective left?"

"She's been asleep."

"We're going to talk to her and ask her some questions, and we'd prefer it if you weren't in the room," Niki said.

"She's my daughter."

"Exactly," Niki said. "Sometimes we ask questions that are...Well, they're the kind of things a girl might not want to talk about in front of her father."

"I'd rather be there."

"We need to speak with her alone," Niki said. "It'll help the investigation. We want to catch this guy as much as you do, Mr. Vauk."

"That's where you're wrong, ma'am. Ain't no one on God's green earth that wants to catch that son of a bitch more 'n me. I'm her father. I was supposed to protect her."

"I understand," Niki said. "We need to do our job now, so this doesn't happen to anyone else."

"You find out who did this and I'll god damn guarantee you he never does it to anyone else. I got friends who'll make sure of that, guys from the brotherhood if you get my drift."

Matty, who stood all of five foot nine, calmly stepped forward and looked the six-foot-plus Mr. Vauk in the eye and said, "Mr. Vauk, I know you're angry, but we'll be the ones handling this case. And right now, we need to talk to her alone. Is that all right with you?"

Vauk seemed to wilt under Matty's stare. He nodded. "I'm just saying..."

"We understand," Niki said. "Why don't you go grab a coffee or something. This won't take long."

Vauk nodded and hesitantly walked away.

Inside the room, Matty stayed near the door while Niki walked to the side of the bed, put her hand on Sadie's arm, and gave it a light squeeze.

Sadie opened her eyes in confusion, as if she had no memory of where she was or how she'd gotten there. She looked almost unbearably young and scared. Her breath quickened when she saw the detectives and her eyes darted around the room searching for her father.

"Sadie, my name is Niki Vang. I'm a detective. I'd like to ask you a few questions about what happened. Would that be all right?"

Sadie calmed at the sound of Niki's gentle voice.

"I know you already talked to some other detectives, but I want to have you go through it again in case we missed anything. Let's work backwards. So do you remember the ambulance ride here?"

"A little." Sadie's voice cracked as she worked the sleep out of it. "I was so tired."

"What do you remember before the ambulance?"

"I was in water, and I swam to some rocks. A man laid me in the grass. He put his jacket around me."

"He was a security guard," Niki said. "He's the one who called the ambulance. What do you remember about being in the water?"

"Swimming. The water tasted like mud, and I couldn't move my arms right, but I was swimming. There was a current. I tried to swim against it. Where was I?"

"You were in the Mississippi River."

"I don't understand." Sadie looked at Niki as if something in the detective's face might hold an answer that eluded her. "How'd I…get in the river?"

"Let your mind relax," Niki said. "What happened before you were swimming? Were you with anyone? Do you remember anyone talking to you or holding on to you?"

"No. Nothing."

"Take your time, Sadie. Just let your thoughts come to you."

She closed her eyes. "I was in the water. I couldn't see. It was dark, and I had water in my eyes. And it was loud. I could hear…I could hear the water."

"What about before that?"

"I think I remember falling. The water was so cold."

"Describe the fall. Do you remember what was around you?"

Sadie closed her eyes, pinching them tight at first, then relaxing them. When she opened her eyes again, she seemed brokenhearted. "I just remember the water. This is so confusing. How'd I get in the river?"

Niki shared a look with Matty, not seeking permission so much as letting him know that she would answer Sadie's question.

"Sadie, when was the last time you had sexual relations?"

"What?"

"When was it?"

"My boyfriend and I broke up in April, so...not for four months."

"The doctors found evidence of sexual trauma. We're running tests to see if you had anything in your system—like a date-rape drug."

"I was raped?" Sadie's face paled with fear and anguish.

"We're not sure at this point, but...I'm sorry." Sadie's eyes filled with tears and Niki rubbed her arm to try and soothe the blow. "What's the last thing you remember before the water?"

"I was at the shop—my hair salon, Queen Bebe's—and this guy came in for a haircut."

"Was he a regular?"

"No. He wanted an appointment after hours. He offered me..." Something seemed to be shifting around in Sadie's memory. "I don't think he paid me. I don't remember."

"Do you remember him leaving?"

"No. I'm not sure that I even gave him a haircut. He wanted to look at some style catalogs. We were talking and then...I don't know."

"Do you remember his name?"

"Kevin. I wrote it down in my appointment book. Kevin. I'm sure of that. And..." Sadie stared hard at the wall. "I think I've seen him before, like we'd met, but I can't..."

"His name is Kevin, though? Do you remember what he looks like?"

"My age, I suppose. Kind of chunky in the middle, light-brown hair, and...he was wearing...I think he had on a sweatshirt...a hoodie. That's all I can remember."

"Do you remember what he drove to his appointment?"

"No."

"You said he looked familiar. Think about the places you frequent—restaurants, night clubs, gyms—is it possible you know him from a place like that?"

Sadie closed her eyes, but then opened them again and shook her head. "I'm sorry."

"That's okay." Niki patted Sadie's arm. "Sometimes a memory can get blocked if you try too hard. Just take it nice and slow."

Sadie closed her eyes again as if searching, but then opened them and said, "Nice." She said the word slowly, as if she were saying it for the first time.

Niki waited for her to continue, and when she didn't, she asked, "Are you—?"

Sadie held up her hand to stop Niki from talking, her eyes burrowing deep into an empty space on the wall in front of her. Then Sadie whispered the word again to herself. "Nice."

Sadie still had her hand raised, so Niki looked at Matty, who shrugged. Sadie's face wore a look of intense concentration verging on fear. Then she said, "He said… 'nice.'"

"Who said 'nice'?"

"The guy—Kevin. He said…" She closed her eyes again and fought to remember. "He was standing in front of me…I was sitting…in the grass…and he said, 'All you had to do was be nice.'"

Niki repeated the words. "All you had to do was be nice."

"Yeah, but…he had a lisp." Sadie slowly repeated the line, but muddled the letter S. "All you had to do wasch be nische." Sadie's eyes grew big and her breath caught. "I think…I know who Kevin is."

CHAPTER 13

Gavin sat in his basement, in the very room where he had brought Sadie the night before, and pondered the myriad paths that might bring detectives to his door. There were so many variables, any one of which could change everything, and the prospect of accounting for each contingency filled Gavin with a sense of purpose. He tapped a nervous finger on the side of his temple as he shuffled through possibilities, narrowing them down to the most likely scenario.

Sadie would remember the man who came in for a last-minute haircut. She would give a detective the name Kevin, as it appeared in her appointment book. But would Sadie connect Kevin from the salon to Kevin the Picture Boy? Gavin had seen no sign of recognition as she'd prattled on about hair products and new styles. He'd managed to hide his lisp the entire time. Still, if detectives showed up at his door, he had to assume that Sadie had made the connection to the wedding.

They would want to know where he was last night. A forensic check of his phone would reveal that it never left his house, but a neighbor may have seen him leave or return in the Bronco. No need to get caught in a lie. So he would say nothing.

Would they do a lineup? Of course they would. But the question was whether it would be an in-person lineup or a photo. Should he agree to an in-person lineup if they asked? His first inclination was to refuse. Why make it easy for them. But on further study, he changed his mind.

If he refused the in-person lineup, they would show Sadie his driver's license photo mixed with a group of similar-looking guys. She would likely have no problem picking him out of the bunch. The jury would then hear about how easily Sadie had identified Gavin.

The case against him would stand or fall on that identification; it would be the prosecutor's sharpest weapon. Gavin needed to take it away from them—turn it into his own weapon. Sadie had to fail to pick him out of that lineup, or at the very least, struggle.

Gavin went to his bathroom and looked in the mirror. He didn't have time to grow a beard or lose weight, but he could shave his head. Would she recognize him if he were bald? Would that be enough to trip her up?

In the back of a closet, he found the beard trimmer he'd purchased at a time in his life when he thought that growing a beard might make him more appealing to women. It hadn't worked. No amount of cosmetic realignment could hide a lisp.

He laid a towel on the floor of the garage, knelt over it, and began shaving. When he finished with the trimmer, he went to the bathroom and used a razor to shave his head clean. Gavin's pasty white skin gleamed, marking where his hair had been, but Gavin would eliminate that as well. He washed the stubble down the sink, swept the garage, and shoved his towel full of hair into a garbage bag to be thrown away when he stopped for gas later. Then he put the clippers back in the closet and fired up the Lexus.

He drove fifteen minutes to Bloomington and found a tanning salon. There were stores closer to home, but investigators would surely check those out once they understood that he had changed his appearance. The salesperson, a girl in her teens whose own skin was the color of a coconut shell, droned on about discounts and packages.

Being careful not to expose his speech impediment, Gavin interrupted the girl by pointing to the option in the brochure for a single spray-tan session, saying, "I want that."

The girl shrugged and led Gavin to a stand-up booth, where she explained the procedure, showing him the wipes he would need to keep his hands from looking blotchy. After she left, Gavin stripped down to nothing, stepped inside, and pressed the start button. As the nozzles coated his body with a fine spray of chemicals, he tipped his head to get a little extra color on his crown.

When he'd finished, he looked at himself in the mirror. The bald head made a huge difference, and although it would take a few hours for the chemicals to darken his skin, he could imagine the effect. What else could he do?

He touched his eyebrows with his pinky finger. He could darken those with eyeliner, and maybe draw them a little closer together to make his nose look thinner. And he could put rings under his eyes, provided that he straddled the line between thick enough to make a difference and light enough that no one would be able to tell that it was makeup.

He decided to buy a few items on the drive home and test them out in the mirror. He would have time to spare as he waited for the police to arrive.

CHAPTER 14

At ten o'clock that same morning, Lila Nash sat in the back of a small courtroom, the Donald Gray file on her lap. Andi Fitch sat behind a stack of files at the counsel table, alongside another prosecutor.

Hearings were set to begin at eleven, and as was the practice, attorneys used the time before to negotiate deals. Defense attorneys approached the two prosecutors in a steady stream, their conversations starting with smiles but usually devolving into scowls. Sometimes their arms would wave around in animation, or a finger might jab the air, but Andi remained impassive, her features carved in stone.

On the elevator ride down to court, Andi had given Lila a short, terse lecture on plea negotiations. "Know your strengths and weaknesses before you make an offer, and once the offer's on the table, hold firm. You don't want to get the reputation of being someone who'll cave at the last minute. Only sweeten the deal if your case goes south somehow. If the evidence doesn't change, the offer shouldn't either."

"Oscar said to start high and meet in the middle."

"Oscar hasn't had a trial all year. Defense attorneys know he'll give away the store if they wait. Give them a reasonable offer out of the gate, and if they don't like it, go to trial. In time they'll learn to take you seriously, and your cases will settle faster. We have too much volume to pussyfoot around."

The elevator dinged to announce their arrival. Andi led the way to the courtroom.

"If you don't mind my asking," Lila said. "How many trials do you have a year?"

"I don't keep track—maybe ten or so." Then Fitch stopped and turned to Lila. "And for God's sake, don't be one of those fools who keeps track of wins and losses. When someone tells me they have a ninety-eight percent conviction rate, what I hear them say is that they're scared to take a close case to trial. You can't be afraid to lose. This isn't about you or your percentages; it's about victims. It's about getting bad people off the streets."

When I grow up, I want to be like her, Lila thought.

In the courtroom, Lila took a seat in the gallery behind where Andi sat at counsel table and reviewed Donald Gray's bail study for about the tenth time, a mix of excitement and trepidation tickling her chest. She would be asking for ten grand in bail, but it would be the conditions she wanted on top that would light the fireworks—at least, that's what Andi had predicted.

Out of the corner of her eye, Lila saw a man in his late forties approach Andi. He was wearing a blue suit that didn't quite fit him. He chuckled his greeting, the pleasantries bouncing off Andi's porcelain façade. She raised a hand to stop the man from talking and pointed to the back door of the courtroom. As they passed Lila, Andi gave a nod for Lila to join them—and like an eager puppy, Lila followed.

The three of them entered a small conference room in the hallway outside, Andi speaking first. "Ed, this is Lila Nash. Lila, Ed Chappelle." The man barely looked at Lila as he shook her hand. "Ed represents Mr. Gray."

Chappelle placed a briefcase on the table and clicked it open. Then, speaking exclusively to Andi, he said, "I thought you should know that Mr. Gray's wife called me yesterday. Wanted to talk. I didn't speak with her myself, of course. I put her in touch with my investigator." Ed opened a folder and withdrew some papers. "She gave a statement that you need to read."

Andi took the pages. "Let me guess. She's recanting."

"Like I said, I didn't talk to her, so this isn't me coaching her or anything. All I did was set her up with the investigator. Bottom line is she lied to the police. Don never hit her."

"What's she saying this time." Andi turned a page as she read aloud. "She had the black eye...before they drove to the convenience store. Got it playing with her dog?" Andi looked at Ed, her face remaining deadpan. "She's blaming her dog?"

Ed put his hands in his pockets in a gesture of blind confidence. "She's a real piece of work, Andi. Their marriage isn't the best, and so every time she gets a bump or bruise, she finds a way to make a police report out of it. She's building a case so she can take him to the cleaners if they ever divorce. The man's a wreck—lives in constant fear."

Andi lowered the transcript and faced Ed. "The man beats his wife and *he's* the one in fear?"

"He didn't beat his wife. You have it right there." Ed pointed at the transcript. "I can play the tape if you want. Bring her in and you can ask her yourself. Hell, put her under oath."

Ed painted the edges of his words with indignation as he continued. "You don't have a victim, so you don't have a case. If she takes the stand she'll say Don never hit her, and if she doesn't take the stand, it'll violate my client's right to confront his accuser. Either way, you've got nothing."

"Have you read the complaint yet?" Andi put the transcript on the table. "We served it on your client this morning—along with the bail study."

"Not yet. I wanted to talk to you first." Ed shifted his tone, turning almost apologetic. "Andi, you and I both know you're not gonna put the alleged victim on the stand if she's recanting. Without an accusing witness, you have squat. Why are you talking about bail studies? Your dog ain't gonna hunt and you know it."

"I have a surveillance tape."

"A little pushing in the car, that's all. So what? They were arguing. Arguing's not against the law. She's gonna take the stand and swear he didn't hit her. Whatever tape you have won't beat that."

"Third-degree assault, and I'll dismiss the rest."

"I bet you will." Chappelle almost laughed as he spoke. "Come on, Andi. My client just spent two nights in lockup because his wife's gearing up for a divorce. Don't make this thing drag out. We both know where it's going."

Ed put the file back into his briefcase and closed it, clicking the tiny hasps into their locks. He started for the door, but then, in a move that looked rehearsed, paused and said, "Listen, Andi, I'll grant you that Don and his wife had an argument. Like I said, their marriage is on the rocks. If you offered a disorderly conduct, I'd be willing to talk to him about it. I might even recommend it. At least you'd get something out of this."

Andi didn't even blink. "Your client has the complaint and bail study. We can talk after you meet with him."

Ed shrugged and left the conference room.

Andi gave the transcript to Lila to read. "He's going to be pissed when he finds out we've charged Donnie-boy with false imprisonment. In a few minutes, he'll come storming in here, beating his chest. He's what we call a gorilla."

"Gorilla?" Lila said.

"Attorneys like Ed will come at you like a gorilla charging out of the bushes. He'll yell and throw sticks, jump up and down, but the more he beats his chest, the more I know he's scared. That's the biggest tell of them all. You don't make a big show of it if you have a superior case."

"He seemed pretty calm just now."

"He was on his best behavior because he thinks he has the upper hand with that recantation crap, so he's keeping things understated. That whole *I'll do my best to sell the disorderly conduct* crap was an act. He had that in his pocket before we walked in here. Most cases are won or lost before we ever set foot in court. Like a train on rails, it's just a matter of riding the case to its inevitable destination."

"And you know the destination for Mr. Gray?"

"I think so." Andi paused a moment as though collecting a thought. "Here's the thing, Lila. As prosecutors, we get to choose the battlefield. We get the evidence first. We pick the charges. We have that advantage. The general who chooses the battlefield should almost always win."

"I never looked at it that way."

"Sure you have."

Lila gave Andi a blank stare.

"This morning, you told me to refer the Woggum case to the feds. How did you come to that conclusion?"

"Well...I thought I saw a weakness in the case. I wanted to shore it up."

"You were surveying a battlefield. You went through contingencies in your head, looking at moves, and countermoves. You played the case out from beginning to end and saw a flaw—so you suggested taking the fight to a more advantageous battlefield. You did well."

Lila smiled at the compliment, although she tried not to. "Thanks, Ms. Fitch."

"Andi."

Again, Lila felt like a puppy—this time one getting tossed a rare treat. "So, where's this case going...Andi?"

"When Ed gets back from meeting with Mr. Gray, he's going to be in a lather—all insulted that we would dare to charge his client with a crime that requires a predatory offender registration. Even if I offered Gray the disorderly, he'd have to register now. Ed will argue that the tape doesn't show enough to get a conviction for false imprisonment. He'll thump his chest and set the case for trial."

"You think he'll take it to trial?"

"Not in a million years. He'll challenge probable cause, and as we're waiting for that hearing, he'll tell me what a great guy his client is, and how this will ruin him. He'll put the wife out there and accuse me of re-victimizing her. But his only real leverage is to hope that I'm afraid to go to trial—and by now he knows better."

Andi looked at her watch, causing Lila to look at hers. They had ten minutes before court would convene, which made Lila nervous, not wanting her first hearing to begin with the judge lecturing her for tardiness. But Andi didn't seem fazed.

"Then, just before the probable cause hearing," Andi continued, "he'll propose a plea to misdemeanor assault and ask me to agree to a finding of no probable cause on the false imprisonment. With that, he'll at least have an argument against predatory registration. I'll agree to no probable cause on the false imprisonment, but only if Gray pleads to the felony assault. Give him a stay of imposition of sentence and call it a day. Ed will piss and moan, but in the end, that's the deal his client will take."

The door to the conference room swung open and Ed Chappelle stepped in, red-faced, a crumpled-up copy of the complaint in his hand. "False imprisonment!" The words came out half yelled and half snarled.

A gorilla, Lila thought.

"You charged him with false imprisonment? Are you out of your mind? There's no way in hell that'll fly. I'll have an acquittal before the jury can order lunch. This is bullshit and you know it."

Andi stood. "Lila will be doing the first appearance. We're asking that your client have no contact with the victim pending trial."

Ed choked on whatever words were in his throat, and Lila worried he might have a full-blown conniption fit. "They're husband and wife. They live in the same damn house."

Andi gave Lila a go-ahead nod, and Lila spoke. "It's the third time your client has assaulted his wife, Mr. Chappelle."

Chappelle looked at Lila and let loose his anger. "Those other cases were dismissed. She's preparing for a divorce. Weren't you listening?" Then he looked at Andi. "Tell your girl how this works."

Andi's face went cold, and she took a step toward Chappelle. "The way it works, *Ed,* is that Ms. Nash is handling your client's case today and she has my full support. And if you ever treat her with that kind of disrespect again, I'll burn you. I'll file an ethics complaint and let all these female judges know what a misogynistic asshole you are. You owe Ms. Nash an apology, and I'll expect it in writing by the end of the week."

Andi made for the door, and a stunned Lila followed.

Once outside, Andi remained expressionless as they walked back toward the courtroom, but she whispered to Lila, "What'd I tell you? A gorilla."

CHAPTER 15

Sadie had given Niki Vang two guiding stars to follow, in separate constellations but at least the same sky: the salon and the wedding. They agreed that Matty would go to the salon, a crime scene technician in tow, and Niki would track down the recent bride and groom.

She found the newly christened Mrs. Halloway at home in a small house in a tightly packed neighborhood, the kind of neighborhood where, she imagined, dreams had to fight to stay alive. The new husband wasn't home when Niki arrived, having gone to work his shift as a mechanic at a plastics plant. No honeymoon for the happy couple.

Janelle Halloway appeared at the door looking unkempt in her sweatpants and T-shirt, her hair pulled back in a ponytail. The color in her cheeks drained away when Niki introduced herself as a detective and asked to come in.

All around the house lay remnants of their wedding: stacks of gifts, flowers brought home from the church, a wedding dress draped over an ironing board. "Excuse the mess," Janelle said, moving a box of new dishes off the couch so that they could sit down. "We just got married on Sunday. Still puttin' stuff away."

"I understand," Niki said. "Actually, the wedding is what I came here to talk about."

"Did we do something wrong?"

"Not at all. But Sadie Vauk... she was one of your bridesmaids, correct?"

Janelle's "Yes" held threads of fear and hope and curiosity all balled up together.

"She was attacked last night."

"Oh my God." Janelle brought her hand to her mouth. "Is she okay?"

"She's in the hospital."

"Oh my God."

"It's bad, but she's going to be okay."

"What happened?"

"I can't go into it, but that's why I'm here. I want to ask about your wedding photographer. What was his name?"

"The photographer? I don't understand."

"What was your photographer's name?"

"Um... Gavin... Spencer, I think." Janelle stood and walked to the dining room table, where she picked through a stack of papers before pulling one from the pile. "Yeah, Gavin Spencer." She returned to the couch and handed Niki a price quote from GVS Photography—Gavin Vincent Spencer, proprietor.

"Do you know Mr. Spencer well?"

"No. I mean, we met when I hired him, and then at the wedding. A friend referred him to me. She said he was cheap but good. Did he do something to Sadie?"

"We're just gathering information right now. Did he have anyone working with him? Maybe someone named Kevin?"

"No. He worked alone."

"Was anyone else named Kevin taking pictures at your wedding, a family member or friend, maybe?"

Janelle thought for a long moment before answering. "I have an uncle named Kevin, but I don't think that he took any pictures."

The price quote listed the website of GVS Photography, so Niki punched it into her phone and found an extensive gallery of photos, broken down by category: wedding photography, corporate events, senior photos, fraternity and sorority parties, and children. Nowhere on the site could Niki find a picture of Gavin Spencer himself.

"Do you know if Mr. Spencer paid any special attention to Sadie?"

Janelle thought about it. "Honestly, I didn't notice. I was just—you know—enjoying my wedding day."

Niki's phone buzzed. It was Matty. "Excuse me. I'll be right back."

Niki left the house, answering the phone as she walked to her car. "Got something?"

"Not much. Bebe Kavenaugh, the owner of the salon, said when she opened this morning the window blinds were down—which they never are—and the back door to the alley was unlocked. Also, Sadie's phone was here. Bebe says Sadie would never leave her phone behind like that."

"Did you find Sadie's water bottle?"

"He must have taken it with him."

"What about hair clippings?"

"The floor's spotless," Matty said. "There were no prints on the chair, so I'm betting he wiped it down."

"Pull the traps off the sink, in case he washed anything down the drain."

"Already on my list."

Niki liked Matty. He was older than her by four years and had been a detective longer, but he had been in Homicide for less than a year, coming from Narcotics, where thinking on your feet was more important than attention to detail. Niki still found herself giving Matty *suggestions,* double-checking details to make sure that nothing got overlooked, and sometimes she could hear an itch in Matty's voice as he acknowledged her nudges. She was trying to do better.

"Cameras?"

"Not here, but I just got off the phone with Ainsley Holt in Sex Crimes. They requested surveillance footage from the restaurants along Nicollet Island. One of the bar owners sent in some digital. I haven't seen it yet, but Ainsley said the footage shows an SUV driving down Southeast Main, passing by about the time we think Sadie went into the river. It's driving in the direction of the power plant."

"Can she identify the vehicle?"

"She said it's an older SUV, like an old Blazer or Bronco, 1980s vintage, dark."

"I got a name," Niki said as she typed *Gavin Spencer* into her squad's mobile data computer. "But it's Gavin, not Kevin. Gavin Spencer was the photographer at the Halloway wedding."

"Maybe Sadie misunderstood him."

"Or he gave her a wrong name." A picture popped onto Niki's screen of a man with a round face, baby cheeks made rough with acne scars, and neatly trimmed hair. "I'm sending his DL photo. Ask around the plaza. See if anybody saw him."

"You got it."

Niki switched screens on her computer and brought up vehicle registration information for Gavin Spencer. "Well, son of a bitch."

"What?"

"Gavin Spencer owns a black Ford Bronco, 1986."

"Of course he does," Matty said, and Niki could almost hear him smiling through the phone.

"He lives on Franklin, near the top of Lake of the Isles."

"I'll check for cameras between there and the salon," Matty said. "There's got to be a stoplight camera or two along the way."

Pleased with the turn of events, Niki let Matty get back to work, and she returned to the Halloway home. She found Janelle sitting on the couch crying into a pillow, a picture of Sadie on her knees.

"What did he do to her?" Janelle asked.

Sadie's ordeal was an open investigation, confidential, so Niki dodged the question. "She's at the Hennepin County Medical Center."

"Did he . . . ?"

"Mrs. Halloway, I can't comment on a person's medical condition, but I can tell you that Sadie could use a friend today."

"I'll go as soon as we're done."

"I just have a couple more questions. Did you ever see Mr. Spencer driving a vehicle?"

"He came here to meet with us when we hired him. He drove a nice car, beige, I think, but I don't know what kind. I didn't get a good look at it."

"You never saw him driving any kind of SUV or truck?"

"No. Why?"

"One last question." Niki mentally crossed her fingers as she asked. "Did Mr. Spencer have any kind of speech impediment?"

Janelle's eyes lit up. "Yes. He couldn't say the letter S. It came out like..." Janelle tried a few different iterations of a lisp, shaking her head after each one. "I can't do it, but it was really bad."

It was all Niki could do not to pump her fist. "Thank you, Mrs. Halloway. You've been very helpful."

Niki was about to stand when Janelle reached out and put a hand on her arm. People never touched her like that. They usually went out of their way to keep her at a distance, as though shunning the messenger might stop the evil from happening.

"Is it my fault?" Janelle asked. "Did I bring someone bad to my wedding?"

"You didn't do anything wrong," Niki said.

"I'll never forgive myself."

"We'll find out who did this. You should go be with your friend. Focus on helping Sadie."

Janelle nodded. "Okay. But if Gavin Spencer hurt Sadie... promise me, you'll make him pay. Don't let him get away with it."

Niki didn't like making those kinds of promises. If she was right, Spencer had raped and murdered at least three times before. Low priorities, Lieutenant Briggs had called them. Bodies washed up along the river. But now Niki had a lead. No proof, but her gut told her this was her man, and if she had any say in the matter, Gavin Spencer would never again add another woman to his tally.

She looked at Janelle and said, "He won't get away with it. I promise."

CHAPTER 16

Sitting in his garage, alone with his Lexus, his Bronco, and his thoughts, Gavin ran through his cleanup tasks one more time. Something was bothering him. He had changed the tires on the Bronco, so if he had left any tread prints along the river, they wouldn't match. And there was no way they would find the dealership that sold him the used tires, and even if they did, the cash transaction severed the connection. He had cleaned the Bronco thoroughly—twice. He had used plastic sheathing so there would have been no transfer of fibers or hair. Nothing in the Bronco could link him to Sadie Vauk, but still, the Bronco bothered him.

Gavin knew that one of the biggest mistakes people made in committing illegal acts was to be cheap. A guy builds a bomb and keeps the wire cutter that links him to the device. A woman poisons her husband but refuses to throw away the computer she used for her research. As Gavin stared at his Bronco, he realized that he was being cheap. He loved the Bronco. It had been there for him from the beginning, and the hunk of metal felt almost like a friend. But a true craftsman would not tempt fate.

He thought about driving it into the river, but in broad daylight, that would be a high-risk move. What if he just parked it along a random, lonely street? Undoubtedly, some nosy neighbor would wonder about it and call it in. It was well past noon, the earliest time he'd given the detectives to track him down, and the possibility of them showing up at his door grew with every passing minute.

Then an idea came to him.

He drove the Bronco to the University of Minnesota, an area famous for its quick vehicle impoundment, found a quiet street with a No Parking zone, and parked. He watched the sidewalks and nearby porches and windows until he was satisfied that no one was around. Then he got out of the Bronco, screwdriver in hand, and slipped under the front of the truck. It only took him a few seconds to loosen the plug from the oil pan, letting oil stream to the pavement.

He rolled back out from under the truck, stood, and casually looked around again. He was still alone. He slid into the driver's seat one last time, wiped his fingerprints off the key and steering wheel, and started the Bronco's engine.

Then he shut the door and walked a block away to watch as his beloved Bronco coughed and shuddered. When the engine seized up, it sent a wisp of smoke into the air, as though its soul were leaving. His friend was dead—ruined. By the end of the day, it would be in the custody of an impound lot. An old truck like that with a blown engine would quickly be sold for scrap and crushed into a cube of rusted metal, forever hidden from his pursuers.

Gavin walked until he found a bus stop with a bus to take him downtown. From there, a taxi ride and he was home, pleased at the extraordinary measures he had taken to cover his tracks. He'd been surgical. A single strand of hair or a few skin cells was all a lab needed to put Sadie Vauk in his house, but if the police ever crossed his threshold, they would find nothing—not a hair, not a cell, not a speck to corroborate their theory.

There was a part of Gavin that yearned for them to show up at his house with a search warrant. He would encourage them to look. Hell, tear the place down board by board. The mere thought of an army of detectives and crime scene techs rooting around his house in vain, impotent at every turn, aroused Gavin in a way he hadn't expected, and he understood why other killers might send taunting letters to the newspapers. But Gavin would send no letter.

And if it ever came to the point where he found himself in court over Sadie Vauk, it would be her testimony against his—and Gavin had a plan for that contingency as well.

CHAPTER 17

Lila Nash was pretty certain that Donald Gray's bail hearing had been unremarkable for most observers, but for her it held the rush of a tsunami exploding against a rocky coastline. Gray had twice gotten away with attacking his wife, but not this time. And the best part was that Gray's wife wouldn't be the target of his anger; she hadn't asked for him to be held to account. Lila had done that. It had been Lila's work that had put him in his box, and as Andi had explained, there was only one way out. Men who harmed women should never get to walk away free—as her attackers had.

Judge Anderson, a kind woman with more years as a judge than Lila had as a human being, ordered Gray to have no contact with the victim—his wife—and specified that any such contact would constitute an additional criminal offense. He would have to move out of his house until the case resolved. This time there would be no retaliation, no arm twisting.

A very pissed-off Donald Gray glared at Lila as he left the courtroom, his expression stripped clean of the false humility he had so carefully presented to the judge. There was a part of Lila that thought she should be intimidated, but somehow it exhilarated her. The thrill of that moment, standing up to an abuser at her first real hearing, was something she would never forget. It fed a yearning that begged to be satiated.

As she often did, Lila met with Ryan and Patrick for lunch in the cafeteria of the Government Center, and as they waited for Patrick, Ryan asked Lila how she was getting along with Andi Fitch. The truth was that Lila found Andi to be the most amazing woman she'd ever met. Strong and brilliant, Andi was everything Lila wished she could be. However, telling all that to Ryan might rub him the wrong way, so Lila simply said, "Well, she hasn't thrown any books at me yet." Ryan seemed satisfied with that answer.

Patrick arrived, smacking down his tray of food and taking over the conversation as was his habit.

"Sorry, I'm late," he said, "but I have this new crim sex case. A woman attacked by three mimes. They did unspeakable things." He followed his punch line with a comedic rim shot, tapping his index fingers on the table and hitting an imaginary cymbal in the air. "Ba-dat, tsh."

Ryan cracked a smile and looked to Lila as if seeking permission to laugh.

Lila didn't laugh. "You're an asshole, Patrick."

"Get off your high horse, Nash. It was just a joke."

She looked at him coldly. "Fuck you." Then she stood, picked up her sandwich and milk, and walked off. As she left, she heard Patrick say, "What the hell's her problem?"

And just like that, Lila was a victim again.

She took her lunch back to her office, her anger on high boil. Patrick and Ryan would be talking about her now; she hated that. And she hated how she could so easily be thrown into a bad memory. And she hated Patrick for being such a jerk. Who the hell tells rape jokes in a professional setting?

Lila thought about Joe's words as she sat down at her desk to eat alone. He had called her a legal ninja Jedi, but there was nothing ninja about how she had handled Patrick that day. She had worked so hard to come across as confident and calm, only to have the façade crumble with one stupid joke. How could Ryan and Patrick not see her for the fraud she was?

She wanted a do-over. She wanted to go back and handle it the way she imagined Andi would have—a sharp word, scolding Patrick for his disrespect, followed by a cold stare, one that she would hold until Patrick wilted in apology. Instead, her panicked reaction would, undoubtedly, feed Patrick's misogynistic view of her.

Ryan, on the other hand, would likely ask her what happened, and if he did, what would she tell him? He could probably guess most of it. If word got around about Lila's past, she worried people in the office might treat her differently. They might even take her off of sex crimes cases altogether, to protect her tender sensibilities. Lila feared that far more than anything.

She knew now that she wanted to prosecute men like Donald Gray. She needed to prosecute them.

Lila had long ago resigned herself to the fact that her attackers would never be caught, but her hunger for justice—for vengeance—still burned hot. She could feed that hunger by convicting other men who hurt other women. It wouldn't be perfect, but it would be close. She'd experienced it when Donald Gray stared at her in court as if he wanted to punch her, and she wanted more.

If Ryan ever asked about her reaction, she would dodge his question. If he persisted, she would simply tell him that it was none of his business. She could not risk having her secret exposed.

CHAPTER 18

Summer days in Minnesota had a way of drifting, the sun lingering in the sky as though the earth has slowed in its steady rotation. The long days could play tricks on a homicide detective, dupe them into working far past a normal eight-hour shift, a circumstance that bothered Mateo Lopez—a father of two—but somehow invigorated Niki Vang.

She and Matty had been working different angles of the Sadie Vauk case all day and met up in Kenwood, at a café only a few blocks from Gavin Spencer's home. There they compared notes over a dinner of turkey sandwiches.

"Let's assume the tox report will find GHB in Sadie's blood," Niki said. "How did he give it to her?"

Matty looked at his notes. "Bebe Kavenaugh confirmed that Sadie had been drinking from a water bottle yesterday, but we found nothing at the salon."

"He was smart enough to take it with him."

"No one saw anyone matching Spencer's description, either."

"What about the truck?"

"I had one lady say she might have seen an older SUV like that but couldn't be sure. One of the stoplight cameras on Lake Street captured a truck that might be our guy, but it's coming out of an alley and the plates aren't readable."

"So, this is what we have: Spencer is a photographer at a wedding where our vic is a bridesmaid. The next day, the vic gets a call at her salon—some guy named Kevin wants a haircut—after hours."

"Waits until Bebe leaves. No witnesses."

Niki nods. "He comes in, sits, and right away wants to look at haircut samples."

"Because those books are in the reception area, she has to turn her back on him, leaving her water bottle unattended."

"He stalls—waiting for her to take a drink and for the GHB to kick in. But did he assault her in the salon?"

"That'd be taking a hell of a risk, leaving his truck in the lot all that time. What if Bebe came back? The windows had blinds, but not the front door. Anyone walking by could have peeked in."

"So he took her somewhere."

"His home?" Matty said.

"That'd be my guess. We need to get a search warrant—home, computer, phone—and we need it fast, before he has a chance to clean things up."

"All we have is speculation. A guy named Gavin taking pictures at a wedding isn't a guy named Kevin coming in for a haircut. We don't have anything hard."

"We have the speech impediment. Janelle Halloway confirmed it."

Matty leaned in. "A lot of people have a lisp. Hell, my own brother has one. That's not enough for a warrant."

"No, it's not. We need to do a lineup. If Sadie can identify Gavin, that'll get us our warrant."

"In-person lineup or photo?"

"I think we should try to get him to come in. If that doesn't work..."

"Think he'll agree?"

Niki shoved in the last bite of her turkey on toast and said, "Won't know unless we ask."

* * *

Gavin Spencer lived in a large house, far too large for a low-end wedding photographer. Two stories with a three-stall garage, a house big enough that Niki's entire family could have lived there, at least the ones who'd managed to get out of Vietnam after the war.

Boat people, they were called, even though Niki's family never set foot in a boat. They made their escape by walking over the mountains into Thailand. There, the family languished in the Ban Vinai refugee camp until 1986, the year Niki was born. It was Niki's birth that compelled the Lutheran church in St. Paul to sponsor their evacuation. Her mother still called Niki their good luck charm.

Niki parked on the street in front of Spencer's house and looked around for any doorbell cameras that might face Gavin's garage. The angle of the street and the vegetation along the sidewalk made the prospect of footage unlikely. Matty parked behind her and they paused for one last look around before heading up the walkway.

A curtain on a picture window moved as they neared the front door, and both Niki and Matty popped the thumb snap on their holsters. Niki could hear the sound of footsteps approaching the door, and before she even rang the bell, it opened. The man standing there looked nothing like the picture on his driver's license. He was bald. She looked hard at him, focusing on his eyes, and Gavin Spencer materialized.

"Gavin Spencer?" she asked.

"I am." His words came out slow and formal, as though he deliberated over each syllable.

"My name is Detective Niki Vang, and this is Detective Mateo Lopez. Can we have a word with you?"

Spencer gave the request a moment of thought and nodded. "Okay."

Niki assumed that they would go into the house, but Spencer came out, shutting the door behind him.

"What can I help you with?" he said, his delivery again slow and controlled.

"Mind if we talk inside?" Niki asked.

"I do," he said. Then he looked at the sky and added, "Beautiful evening."

Niki gave Matty a quick glance, which he returned. "Okay. Were you the photographer at the wedding of Darrel and Janelle Halloway on Sunday?"

"Uh-huh," he replied.

"Is that a yes?" Matty asked.

Spencer looked at Matty as though bored and said, "Yeah."

Niki asked, "Did you happen to meet a woman named Sadie Vauk at that wedding?"

Spencer chewed on his cheek and looked up in a thoughtful squint. "I met quite a few people."

"She was a bridesmaid."

"I may recall her, never got her name, though." Spencer looked back and forth between Niki and Matty then said, "Why do you want to know?"

"Where were you last night?"

"Here. I live alone."

Niki looked at Spencer's bald head. "How long have you been"—she pointed at his head— "without hair?"

"Am I . . . ?" Spencer paused as though to collect himself. "Do I need a lawyer? Why are you here?"

He hadn't asked for a lawyer, but he had come close to the line. If he crossed it, all communication would cease and they would have to walk away. They didn't have enough to arrest him or search his house, not without Sadie's identification. They could still do the photo lineup, but it would give Spencer time alone in the house, where he'd be able to clean things up.

Seeing no point to dragging things out, Niki asked the question she had come to ask. "There was an incident involving one of the bridesmaids. A witness thought you might have some information. We were hoping you'd be willing to talk to us about it, maybe come down and do a lineup so we can rule you out. It's routine. Won't take long."

"A lineup? I didn't do anything that would warrant a lineup, but...if it might help, I'll do it."

Niki exchanged another glance with Matty. Spencer hadn't bothered asking what had happened to Sadie. His demeanor and the slow cadence of his speech were odd, almost unnerving. Where was the nervous twitching? The shifting eyes? Gavin Spencer seemed as calm as a man feeding his fish.

Matty said, "You want to follow us down—"

"I'll take an Uber," he said.

They'd hoped to get a look into his garage, to see if he had the black Bronco parked there. Had Spencer seen through that?

"We can give you a lift," Matty said. "That is, if you don't mind riding in back."

"I don't mind."

"I'll need to pat you down, though. Rules."

"Fine." Spencer lifted his arms and turned his back to Matty, who patted him down thoroughly.

The three of them walked to Matty's squad car and put Spencer in the back. After securing his door, Niki and Matty convened at the rear of the car, where they spoke in whispers.

"This is weird, right?" Matty said. "What's with the bald head?"

"A bald man wouldn't go to Queen Bebe's for a haircut. And did you notice, he hasn't yet said a single word with the letter S in it?"

"Yeah, I noticed."

"He knows why we're here."

"So why is he willing to do the lineup?" Matty said. "You barely got the words out and he was on board."

"Because he doesn't look like he did when he went to the salon."

"He's playing us?"

Niki considered it and could find no better explanation. "If Sadie can't pick him out of a lineup..."

"We got no search warrant," Matty said. "Maybe we should cut him loose. Go with a photo lineup."

Niki looked at Gavin's head in the back of the unmarked car, giving thought to various scenarios. "We can get members of the wedding party to verify that he changed his appearance between Sunday and today. We can argue it shows his consciousness of guilt."

"What about the lineup, though?"

"We do it in person. If Sadie picks him out after all he did to change his appearance, it'll be catnip for the jury."

"But what if she doesn't pick him out?"

Niki tapped a finger to her lips as she played out that possibility. "Then we do the photo lineup later and hope the jury understands. But don't forget." A small smile crept across Niki's lips. "We have an ace in the hole."

CHAPTER 19

From his seat in the back of the unmarked police car, Gavin watched the two bootlicking public servants through the rearview mirror. He wanted to think of his interaction with the detectives like a chess match, but that would be a mischaracterization. In chess, you watch your opponent move each piece—their tactics exposing a strategy. But this was like playing chess blindfolded. For each move he could discern there had to be dozens kept from him. The challenge was to figure out the moves that took place in the dark.

And so far, from what little he could deduce, they didn't know as much as he'd thought they might.

Sadie must have been able to draw a line from the salon to the wedding, but she didn't remember being at his house, or in his Bronco; otherwise they would have shown up with a search warrant. That told him that the drug had done its job.

Gavin understood GHB. He had researched the subject at a level reserved for PhD candidates. On the street, they called it liquid ecstasy. Colorless, odorless, and tasteless, a capful in your drink and the world became a wonderful, euphoric place. A few capfuls in someone else's drink and you had complete control over them. Afterward, amnesia set in and covered your tracks.

A part of him wished that the detectives could see the true depth of his work. They would surely admire his attention to detail. But he knew it was for the best if they didn't. Now all he had to do was get through the lineup without Sadie recognizing him. If he could manage that, their case would come crashing down.

The male detective, Lopez, drove Gavin to the lineup, but at the house it had been the female who seemed in charge. At first Gavin hadn't been sure how he felt about sparring with a woman; he wanted to fight a giant. But the more he thought about it, the more he wished that they had put him in her squad car. It might have been fun to play a little cat-and-mouse with her on the drive.

At the jail, Detective Lopez gave Gavin a form to read, advising him that he had the right to have an attorney present. Gavin gave some thought to that option but decided against it. The lineup was part of the plan regardless of how it turned out. Gavin signed the waiver.

After that, they waited in a small room with plastic chairs and a metal table anchored to the floor. The female detective, Vang, would be rounding up decoys to stand in the lineup with Gavin. But would she get men with shaved heads or men that looked more like Gavin's driver's license photo—the Gavin Sadie knew?

After more than an hour, Lopez received a phone call and ushered Gavin down a hallway of cinder block and thick glass. A heavy door slammed somewhere in the distance, and the sound rattled Gavin's nerves a bit. His heart thumped in his chest, and for a split second, Gavin felt that most poisonous of all emotions—doubt.

A memory flashed in his mind, a video he had seen of some idiot in the Everglades sticking his head inside the mouth of an alligator, part of a roadside attraction. The man had done it a thousand times and never once did the alligator bite him—until it did. In a way, Gavin was about to put his head into that proverbial alligator's mouth. He could not let his guard down. *Stay focused. Don't mess this up. Everything depends on getting it right.*

He returned to the only thought that mattered. He had to be someone other than Kevin the Picture Boy. Sadie had to see no hint of the man who'd sat in her salon chair. He had to be perfect in his performance or the alligator's jaws might just snap shut.

He and Detective Lopez turned a corner and came upon five men dressed in civilian clothing, all about his age, height, and build—the decoys. Three of them looked reasonably similar to what Gavin had looked like before he shaved his head. The other two were bald. The detective placed Gavin second from the front of the line and gave them their instructions.

"Walk to the numbers on the floor and face the mirror. You're number six." Lopez pointed at the man in front of Gavin and counted them down, making Gavin number five. "Then just do what they ask."

A jailer opened the door for the men, and they filed in.

The room was smaller than what he had expected, gray walls with a panel of one-way glass. Gavin walked to where a number five was painted on the floor and turned to face the glass, keeping his expression blank.

Through the speakers, a man's voice asked for number one to step forward. The man did. There was a pause of about ten seconds and the man was told to return to his spot.

Then number two was told the same thing. This man looked like Gavin did before the shave, the same lumpy build and light-brown hair, not a doppelgänger, but satisfyingly close. He remained forward for a good thirty seconds before being asked to step back.

Number three looked nothing like Gavin and spent barely five seconds out of line before being asked to return.

She's not sure, Gavin thought. She must be the one determining how long each man stayed out front. She needed time to look at number two, which Gavin took to be a good sign. When his turn came, he could gage her level of recognition by how long they kept him forward.

Number four stepped forward. He stayed out front for even longer than number two had.

Now it was Gavin's turn. It all came down to this—his life, his freedom . . . everything rested on her inability to remember him. Would she see past his ruse? A lesser man would have been praying that she not recognize him, but Gavin wasn't a lesser man. Besides, what god would a murderer pray to? What god protects men such as him?

"Number five, step forward."

Gavin took a step and counted. *One Mississippi, two Mississippi, three Mississippi, four Mississippi, five Mississippi, six Mississippi, seven...*

"Number five, you can return."

Seven! She didn't recognize him. Gavin's heart hammered, and his chest rose and fell harder than it should have. He concentrated on slowing his breathing. *Look bored. This has nothing to do with you.*

They went down the line again, this time asking each man to turn to the left and right before stepping back. Again, number two and number four spent additional seconds being scrutinized by the woman behind the glass. When his turn came, Gavin barely got his feet planted before being asked to return. It took all of his self-control to keep his elation from spilling out. He had won. Gavin wanted to crow, but he remained rock-still. No smiling, no twitching—nothing.

Without a positive identification, they had nothing: no DNA, no hair, no Bronco—no evidence. If he walked out that door, unrecognized, it would be impossible to resurrect a case against him. The detectives would see his cunning but remain powerless to touch him. Gavin exhaled his relief in slow, calm breaths as he waited for the voice from the speaker to excuse them from the room—but it didn't.

"Number one, please step forward and repeat the following words: 'All you had to do was be nice.'"

And just like that, it felt as though someone had reached into Gavin's chest and ripped his lungs out. Those words—he remembered them now. He'd said them to Sadie on the bank of the river. Gavin wanted to scream and punch the wall. He had forgotten all about that brief moment of hubris. He'd felt such a deep need to teach Sadie her lesson, explain the sin she had committed, the one that condemned her. He'd thought he was being benevolent—but he'd really just been shortsighted. *No good deed goes unpunished.*

Of course, Gavin had already planned for the possibility that she might recognize him. He had worked out every detail of that contingency. But while he had absolute confidence in his backup plan, the thought of actually spending time in jail during its execution shook him. He needed to walk out of that room a free man.

Number one stepped forward and repeated the line in a fake lisp. Of course he would use a lisp—the decoys would have to. If Gavin were the only one in line to talk with a lisp, it would taint the lineup and get it thrown out of court. This was what Detective Vang had been up to while he sat in the waiting room with brain-dead Lopez. Gavin felt strangely thrilled. She was smart—she was worthy.

The lisp number one used was all wrong. He did a frontal lisp, sticking his tongue out between his teeth to replace the *s* with a *th*. It didn't sound anything like Gavin's lateral lisp, which resembled a wet slurp against his cheeks. Sadie would pick him out of the lineup on that alone. And if he refused to say anything, she would take a closer look at him and see past the shaved head.

"Number two."

Gavin still had a chance to beat this thing. The speech therapist Gavin's mother hired when he was in third grade had shown Gavin a technique. What did he call it? The butterfly technique.

"Number three."

Gavin hated that doctor, and he hated his mother for forcing therapy on him. She wore her embarrassment of Gavin like a plaster cast. Gavin resisted her attempts to change him and gave the doctor a piss-poor effort at best. Eventually, Gavin's mother quit trying and left him to his lisp.

"Number four."

How did the butterfly technique work again? The air had to flow over the tongue, not around it.

Number four stepped forward and said the line using the same incorrect technique as the first three.

"Number five, step forward and say, 'All you had to do was be nice.'"

Touch tongue to teeth. Push the air over the top. Gavin stepped forward, swallowed—and spoke.

CHAPTER 20

Sadie Vauk had been discharged from the hospital hours earlier, so Niki had picked her up at her father's house to bring her to the lineup. She'd looked healthier than she had in her hospital bed, with styled hair and makeup to give her face some color, but behind it, Niki could still see the battered woman from that morning.

Niki activated her squad camera for the drive in with Sadie, recording their conversation so that she would have proof that nothing was said to sway Sadie's opinion. The case against Gavin Spencer would live or die with the lineup, and Gavin's attorney would fight hard to keep it out, so it had to be done by the book.

"You'll be behind a one-way mirror," Niki said. "The men in the lineup won't be able to see you."

"Will he be one of them?"

"All we're asking is that you look at these men, and if you recognize one as the man who came to your salon, let us know. If you don't, that's okay too. There is no right or wrong answer."

Sadie nodded her understanding while folding her finger into knots on her lap.

"It'll be okay," Niki said. "Just do your best."

The room where Sadie would stand had a single sixty-watt bulb to keep things somewhat dim behind the one-way mirror. Niki positioned Sadie, then stepped behind her so that there could be no claim that a nonverbal cue had exposed Niki's preference for Gavin. Then Niki called Detective Tony Voss, who had collected the men to stand with Gavin in the lineup. When they were all in place, she called Matty to bring Gavin to the party.

As they waited, Niki thought about something that had been bothering her. She had worked in the Sex Crimes unit for years before moving to Homicide, and in that time, she had handled scores of lineups, but the weight of this one seemed out of proportion. Rapes tended to be impulsive and sloppy, a crime of opportunity driven by urges and anger. This case had none of those hallmarks.

If Niki's theory held true, Gavin Spencer had never laid eyes on Sadie Vauk until the wedding, and in the span of a day, he had stalked her, kidnapped her, assaulted her, and tossed her into the river. Gavin's speed and proficiency made him a whole new order of evil. And he was smart. She and Matty had yet to find a single piece of corroborating evidence: no DNA, no witnesses, no footprint or fingerprint.

All they had was a tire track from Nicollet Island and some grainy camera footage of a Bronco near both the island and the salon. And if he had been this careful with Sadie, how were they going to prove murder in the other cases, going back six years? If Sadie failed to pick Spencer out of the lineup, the case would fall apart. It would become just one more unsolved file. Niki couldn't let this be shelved next to the other "low priority" women pulled from the river.

As the jailer escorted the men into the lineup room, Niki went out of her way not to focus on Gavin, just in case Sadie could see Niki's reflection in the glass. Each man stood facing Sadie, who again twisted her fingers together in a knot, pressing her hand tightly to her stomach. She studied the faces of the men, going from left to right. Niki watched as Sadie glanced at Gavin and moved on.

The jailer spoke. "If you want, I can have them step forward."

"Maybe number two . . . and four."

Two and four, but not five? Niki thought. "We'll ask them to each step forward, one at a time," she said. "What we asked of one, we have to ask of them all."

The jailer pushed a button on an intercom beside the window. "Number one, take a step forward."

The man did as he was instructed and Sadie gave him a look, her head moving, almost imperceptibly, from side to side in a *no,* before she whispered, "Okay."

"Number one, step back. Number two, step forward."

Sadie narrowed her gaze on number two, looking hard at the man as though struggling to connect his face to a memory. The jailer reached for the button on the intercom and Sadie said, "Wait." The man remained ahead of the line for several seconds, an eternity that caused Niki's pulse to quicken.

Then Sadie nodded to the jailer. "Okay."

The jailer returned number two to his place in line. Number three's turn came and went quickly and Sadie paused again when number four stepped out of line. Sadie scrutinized his face the way she had with number two.

When Gavin stepped forward, Niki watched Sadie's face in the glass, looking for any sign of recognition and seeing none. Sadie closed her eyes as though trying to conjure up the memory of the man in the salon chair. When she opened them again, she shook her head no and said, "Okay."

Number six took his turn and obviously struck no chord with Sadie.

"I'm not sure," she said when he stepped back. "I didn't look at the man straight on. He was sitting in the chair. I saw him in the mirror and from the side. Can I have them... maybe turn to the side?"

"Absolutely," Niki said, relieved.

The jailer had each one step forward and turn to the left and then to the right. Again, Sadie paused on number two and number four. When they were finished, her gaze bounced back and forth between those two men.

Niki handed a piece of paper to the jailer. "Ask them each to say these words."

The jailer read the sentence on the paper, and then cued the intercom. "Number one, please step forward and repeat the following phrase: 'All you had to do was be nice.'"

Niki watched Gavin's eyes and saw fear flash in them. He'd replaced his practiced expression of boredom with what looked to be concentration.

The men, one by one, followed the jailer's instructions, repeating the phrase that the man who had called himself Kevin had said to Sadie. When number two and number four said the words, Niki saw, in Sadie's reflection in the glass, a hint of disappointment.

"Number five?"

Gavin Spencer stared at the wall ahead of him, intensely focused. Niki could almost read his mind. *He's trying to cure his lisp.*

Gavin hesitated just enough to expose his struggle. Then he spoke. "All you had to do... wasch be nische." His words fell thick and wet to the floor.

Sadie inhaled sharply, her eyes wide with fear. She put her hands on the glass, her face only an inch away as she studied Gavin Spencer. Then she stepped back, almost stumbling, to put distance between herself and the man on the other side of the glass.

"That's him! That's the man," she said in sharp, breathless shots. "I'm sure of it. But... his hair—he had hair."

"You're telling me that number five is the man who came to your salon yesterday evening?"

"Yes." Sadie trembled as she spoke.

"The man who told you his name was Kevin?"

"Yes, that's him." Sadie began to hyperventilate, and Niki eased her into a chair in the corner. "Just breathe, Sadie. You're okay."

"I'm sorry, I can't..."

"I'll get you some water. I'll be right back."

Niki stepped out of the viewing room, into the hall where Matty waited. She looked at him, smiled, and said, "He's our guy."

CHAPTER 21

Two days later, on Thursday morning, Lila began her day in Andi Fitch's office, sitting with her back straight and knees together, a stack of files on her lap. She took notes on a legal pad, trying her best to write as fast as Andi spoke. Lila looked the part of a professional, but inside she felt like a child running to keep up with the long strides of a parent.

"They have a guy named Gavin Spencer in custody. His first appearance is set for eleven. Put a rush on this." Andi handed the file to Lila. "There's not much to work with. I'm meeting with the detectives in an hour, and I want you there."

Gavin Spencer's file was the last case that they discussed that morning, but with the clock ticking toward his first appearance in court, it would be the one that Lila would start on. She went to her office and gave the file a quick read-through and saw that Andi was right—there wasn't much there. A woman named Sadie Vauk had been pulled from the Mississippi River unable to stand or talk. Although she had no memory of the attack itself, she identified Spencer as the man she had been with prior to blacking out.

Then Lila read that investigators were testing Ms. Vauk's blood because they believed she had been given a date-rape drug. A shiver ran through Lila's body. She knew in that second that this would not be just another file. She took in every word of the police report, letting her mind paint the picture of what happened to Sadie Vauk. She read between the lines, searching for the smallest detail, anything that might pull her into the mind of Gavin Spencer and offer up a clue about the monster beyond the page.

Surveillance footage showed an older black SUV near the scene where Vauk had been abducted and also near where they believe she was put into the river. Spencer owned a black Ford Bronco, but detectives had not yet been able to locate it. One neighbor thought she saw Spencer drive by in his Bronco around seven o'clock the night of the abduction, but she wasn't sure.

They had searched his home but found nothing to link him to the crime. Lila read the reports again, hoping that she may have missed something: some tiny drop of semen on the girl, or maybe a strand of her hair at Spencer's house, but other than Vauk picking Spencer out of a lineup, the investigators had come up empty. And after his arrest, Spencer invoked his right to remain silent.

Lila typed up a skeletal outline of the complaint and headed to the meeting—hoping the detectives might bring something to bolster the case.

The conference room in the County Attorney's Office had two walls lined with old law books, decorations from an era when you needed more than fingers on a mouse to find a statute, but it gave the room character. A long oval table took up the majority of the room, and in the corner, a single plant—a dusty silk ficus—stood as a sad witness to the many serious conversations that room had held.

In the months that she had worked under Oscar Hernandez, Lila had never once been asked to sit in on a meeting in the conference room. Her eagerness caused her to be the first to arrive, so she took a seat and waited.

A few minutes later, she heard two voices approaching, a man and a woman, chatting about where to buy the better coffee. When they walked in, Lila recognized the woman and held out a hand. "Lila Nash, I'm working with Andi on this case."

"Niki Vang." The detective shook hands with Lila. "And this is Detective Mateo Lopez."

"Matty." The detective gave Lila a kind smile as they shook.

Lila turned her attention back to Niki. "I believe we've met before—kind of. The Ben Pruitt case?"

Lila watched as recognition slowly took hold, although Lila didn't know whether this was a good thing or bad. Niki Vang and her then-partner, Max Rupert, had been the investigators on the Pruitt case, and Lila had been at counsel table with Boady Sanden as he picked their case apart.

To Lila's great relief, Niki's face lit up. "Lila Nash. Of course. I thought the name sounded familiar." They took seats, leaving an empty chair for Andi. "I haven't seen you around here before," Niki said. "You just start?"

"They had me in White Collar since March. I just started with Andi this week."

Niki looked at Gavin Spencer's file in front of Lila. "What do you think of this one?"

Lila almost answered honestly but thought better of it and said, "The lineup is strong?"

"I think so," Niki said. "The victim had a visceral reaction once she recognized him."

Lila thought about asking Niki to clarify what she meant by "once she recognized him," but Andi entered before she could, nodding to Niki and Matty as she joined them at the table.

"What have you got for me?" Andi said.

The detectives shared a glance before Niki spoke. "I wish we could say we have a lot more than what we had yesterday, but..." Niki slid a piece of paper to Andi. "We had them rush the tox report and they confirmed the presence of GHB—enough to incapacitate a person."

"Any GHB in the house?" Andi asked.

Matty said, "Crime scene techs covered every inch. Didn't find a thing."

Andi laced her fingers into a church and steeple and touched them to her chin, her gaze fixed on the middle of the table as she concentrated. "Maybe the house isn't the crime scene."

"We're pretty sure it is," Niki said. "Gavin went to the salon at six o'clock on Monday. Add up how long it might take to slip the victim the drug and get her home and we're looking at about an hour. We have a neighbor saying that she thought she saw the black Bronco drive by around seven. It fits."

"Did he take his phone to the salon? Can we trace his whereabouts?"

Niki shook her head. "As far as we can tell, the phone never left the house."

Andi leaned in, keeping her focus on that same spot. "What about computer forensics?"

"Odd thing there," Matty said. "Preliminary forensics show that the guy used his home computer that day—looking up email and stuff, nothing that helps us—but we couldn't find a router. He used the internet but had no connection. We think he threw the router away as part of the cleanup. If nothing else, it suggests he had something to hide—that he knew we were coming."

Andi looked up from the table. "So, what we have so far is a missing router, a woman with GHB in her system who claims to have been with Spencer just before she lost her memory, and a black truck that we can't find."

Niki leaned in as if to match Andi's posture. "Sadie Vauk didn't knowingly take GHB—we are sure of that. It causes amnesia going forward in time, not back, so we can get an expert to testify that the gap in her memory would have started shortly after she ingested the drug. Gavin Spencer was the only person around."

Andi looked at Niki. "It's circumstantial."

"We have evidence of sexual trauma," Niki said. "And she sure as hell didn't jump in the river of her own volition."

Andi shook her head slowly. "You have enough to get past probable cause, but proving it beyond a reasonable doubt is going to be tough."

"There's something else," Niki said. "We think he's done this before."

As Lila listened to the conversation about GHB, her throat had grown tight, and she gave her head an almost imperceptible shake as if to push the feeling away.

Niki opened a folder and slid a picture of a young woman across the table to Andi. "This is Eleanora Abrams. Her body was found in the Mississippi River six years ago in St. Paul. They found signs of sexual assault, although her body was pretty beat up—postmortem. She likely went into the river above the falls, just like Sadie Vauk."

Matty picked it up from there. "She had GHB in her system, but the ME couldn't say definitively if it was produced by her body or if it came from an outside source."

Niki pulled a second photo out and gave it to Andi. "This is Virginia Mercotti. She was pulled out of the river at Gorge Park four years ago. Same MO: sexual trauma, fully clothed, and elevated levels of GHB, source undetermined."

Andi put the two pictures beside one another on the table, "before" pictures of the two young women smiling at the camera, oblivious to the horrific turn their lives were about to take.

Niki slid a third picture across the table. "Two years ago. Her name is Chloe Ludlow. Found her floating in Ford Parkway. We believe all three were put into the river upstream of the falls. None of them had defensive wounds or ligature marks. All three had elevated levels of GHB, and we can prove that Ms. Ludlow's GHB came from an external source."

Andi laid the picture of the third victim next to the others. "Do we have a connection between these women and Spencer?"

"Not yet," Niki said. "We focused on getting him off the streets. The guy has money—well, his mother has money. Either way, he's a flight risk. We didn't want to give him a chance to run."

Andi tapped a finger lightly on the picture of Virginia Mercotti as she considered what to do. "Will you be able to shore up the case for Vauk? I can get a judge to sign the complaint, but in front of a jury..."

Matty said, "We're waiting for the forensics on some hair and fingerprints from the salon, but to be honest, we don't hold out much hope for a match. This guy was pretty thorough."

"We're looking for his Bronco," Niki said. "They found a tire print on Nicollet Island, so we may get something there."

Andi looked at Lila. "Arrange a meeting with Ms. Vauk. I want to see what kind of a witness she'll be. I'll charge this out, but I'm telling you now, if this is all we have to give a jury, he may walk."

CHAPTER 22

The jail smelled of old sweat and dust, and it clattered with the voices of unbathed men socializing in the common area as if it were just another Thursday morning. Gavin awoke from sleeping on a concrete bed for a second night, although to call it sleep would be overstating it. The grind of his thoughts kept him awake through most of the night, as did the tormented howls of one of his neighbors down the row.

It angered Gavin to be in jail, not so much for the loss of his freedoms but because Detective Vang had slipped one past him. Summoning his lisp to clench the lineup had been a smart move, and in doing so, Niki had proved herself a worthy opponent. Finding a way to put Vang in the river would become a special project for Gavin once he got out.

He was also angry to be there because of someone as common as Sadie Vauk. He should have kept his mouth shut that night. Exposing his lisp to her, even if what he said had been a truth she needed to hear, had been a lapse in judgment, and he could not afford such mistakes.

When he'd first arrived in jail, Gavin introduced himself to the inmate residing in the cell next to his, a guy in his forties named Gideon Doss, who had a tattoo of a dragon that snaked up his pale left arm. Doss seemed peaceful enough, even though he had once done a four-year stint in Stillwater for—as he put it—beating the tar out of a spic. His current charge was stabbing his cousin over a girl. He wasn't one of the chatty ones, which Gavin appreciated, and he came across as a bit of a dullard, which Gavin suspected might come in handy for him.

Gideon took pride in having been through the system before, and he warned Gavin about going to his bail hearing without an attorney. "It's not fair," he said. "They have lawyers talking about why you need to stay in jail, and you ain't got nobody to talk for you. And once your bail's set, it's near impossible to get it changed."

But for Gavin, choosing an attorney was the cornerstone of his plan. It had to be a certain type of attorney. Gavin had the resources to hire the best in the Twin Cities, but he didn't need the best. He didn't even need competent. What he needed was an attorney who would take orders, one willing to bend a rule here or there. It would take some time to find the right man—and it would be a man. Gavin's mother had long ago shown him to never trust a woman.

Around ten-thirty that morning, a jailer came to his cell and handed Gavin some papers. "Be ready for court in ten minutes."

The first document was a complaint, charging him with various levels of attempted murder, criminal sexual assault, and kidnapping—eight counts in all. If they thought this might ruin his day, they were wrong. He needed the charges to be heavy for the next phase of the plan. The second document was a bail study recommending that Gavin be held without bail. That too was part of the plan.

He rolled the papers into a scroll and made his way to the pod entrance, waiting there while the jailer gathered five others. After being cuffed at the wrist and shackled around the ankles, the six men, wearing orange jumpsuits, orange socks, and orange sandals, marched through the underground tunnel that led to the Government Center. On the third floor, they were ushered into a courtroom through a special side entrance and told to sit in the jury box, where they would await their respective hearings.

Gavin had never been in a courtroom before, although he had imagined it—planned for it—a thousand times. He looked around at the laminate tables, the gray carpeting, and the cheap ceiling tile, and he felt disappointed. Where was the majesty? Remove the judge's bench and the gallery pews and the room could just as well be cold storage. It was hardly a venue befitting the intrigue he had planned in the coming days.

People who he assumed were attorneys walked in and out with the casual gait of shoppers at a farmers' market. Where was the drama? Shouldn't these attorneys be under some modicum of stress? They were dealing with people's lives—their freedoms—and not a one of them seemed to have a worry in the world. But then it occurred to Gavin that for them this is just another day at the office. Convictions and prison sentences were just words when you weren't the one sitting in the box. And at the end of the day, the lawyers all went home.

Gavin settled into his chair and watched the goings-on, soon figuring out which table belonged to the prosecutors and which was reserved for defense attorneys. Prosecutors occupied the farther table, sitting like lords of the manor as they received a host of groveling defense attorneys whispering their requests with bowed backs.

One of the prosecutors, a younger woman who seemed less involved than the others, sat in the gallery just behind the others and held a single file on her lap. She read a document from that file over and over. Something about her held Gavin's attention—the way her nose curved, or the line of her chin. He couldn't put his finger on where or when, but he had seen her before.

The bailiff called for everyone in the room to rise.

A grim-faced woman with gray hair and a black robe entered and took a seat behind the bench. An administrator to her left handed her a stack of files, and she lifted the top one and called, "State of Minnesota versus Gavin Spencer."

The sound of his name announced like that, official and damning, jarred him a bit. He stood, and the jailer pointed for Gavin to walk up to a podium in front of the judge's bench.

"Sir, please state your name for the record," the judge said.

"My name is Gavin Spencer." The words slogged through the muck of his slur, causing the judge to pause as though she needed a second to understand—even though the file with his name on it lay right in front of her.

The judge then said, "And for the State?"

No answer came.

Gavin looked over his shoulder at the young woman he'd been trying to place. She now stood at the counsel table, her face pale, her fingers wrapped tightly around the edges of that file, her eyes locked on Gavin.

"For the State?" the judge repeated.

The young woman began to breathe heavily. And still no words came out of her mouth.

"Ms. Nash, are you okay?" the judge said.

Nash? Gavin looked closer at her face and chin and eyes, but it was the name that triggered the memory. In a flash, it all came flooding back with the chill of an April lake. *It couldn't be.*

Another prosecutor, a polished Black woman with a cold confidence, stood and took over the hearing. "Andrea Fitch for the State, Your Honor."

Gavin turned to look at the judge, but all he could see was the face of a ghost, a woman he'd met only once, eight years ago in the backseat of a car.

CHAPTER 23

Lila had read and reread Gavin Spencer's bail study, looking for arguments that Spencer might make to keep bail low. He might point out that he had no criminal history and had lived in Minnesota all of his life, with the exception of three years when he attended a private high school in Indiana. Lila would counter with the fact that Spencer was facing serious time in prison and had enough money to take flight. She went one step further, though, and prepared rebuttals for arguments that didn't jump out as obvious, such as medical concerns, turning in his passport, or a request for home confinement.

Lila had come away from her meeting with the detectives seeing that Gavin was both smart and careful. The lack of physical evidence meant that Sadie Vauk's abduction had been meticulously planned. And if she hadn't been a champion swimmer, she would have been just as dead as the other three women pulled from the river. More than any other defendant in her stack of files, Gavin Spencer seemed to be playing a game. And although he chose to appear without an attorney that morning, Lila had vowed not to underestimate him.

As she had waited for court to start, the creak of the courtroom door pulled Lila's attention to the back of the room, where Frank Dovey was walking in. He carried no files, no briefcase. He looked at Lila, locking his gaze on her for an uncomfortable few seconds before taking a seat in the back row of pews.

Lila turned back around and looked at the file on her lap, although her focus floated away from the pages. Why was Dovey there? Had he come to watch her? It sounded paranoid, but why else come when he had no cases to handle?

She did her best to shake Dovey from her thoughts, shuffling through the Spencer file to calm her anxiety. Then a side door opened and a jailer ushered six men in orange jumpsuits into the room, Gavin Spencer walking at the head of the line. She recognized him from his booking photo. He took a seat in the jury box and Lila returned to her prep work. He looked unimpressive—insignificant—his skin soft and squishy on his bones.

The hum of conversations stopped when a bailiff entered through a hidden door behind the judge's bench. He tucked his thumbs into his belt and called out, "All rise." Everyone did. "The District Court of Hennepin County is in session, the Honorable June Anderson presiding."

Judge Anderson walked to the chair behind her bench and sat down. "You may be seated."

This would mark the fourth time that Lila would appear before Judge Anderson, the first being the Gray case—Lila's very first court appearance. She liked Judge Anderson.

Lila had barely taken her seat when the judge called the Spencer case, so Lila took her place at the prosecutor's table, standing beside Andi, who remained seated. Gavin Spencer sidestepped the other inmates to get out of the jury box and followed the bailiff, who directed him to a podium just ahead of the judge's bench.

Judge Anderson asked Spencer to confirm his name for the record. He answered by saying, "My name isch Gavin Schpenscher."

Something in those words sent a bullet through Lila's chest, opening a hole that stole her breath away. Her world tilted, her face flushed hot, and her tongue turned to dust. White noise filled her ears, and her peripheral vision began to fade as though she were about to pass out. She didn't understand what was happening.

Through the hum of her panic, she heard Judge Anderson say, "And for the State?" Lila tried to speak but nothing came out—no air, no sound, nothing. She looked at the judge, and then at Gavin Spencer, confused.

"For the State?" the judge repeated.

Lila put her hands on the table for balance.

"Ms. Nash, are you okay?" the judge asked.

Lila felt hands touch her shoulders as Andi stood up beside her, disappointment on her face. Lila sat down as Andi took over. Not much of what happened after that registered, other than Gavin telling the judge that he was okay with being held without bail.

Andi walked out of the courtroom after the hearing, leaving Lila alone at the table. She felt naked, everyone's eyes fixed on her as she stood to leave. The weight of her embarrassment was made a thousand times worse when she saw Frank Dovey watching, a slight smile angled into his cheeks.

The sight of Dovey weakened Lila's knees, but she took a step.

Ten.

Then another.

Nine.

She kept her focus straight ahead, counting down each step until she pushed the door open on the count of three.

Two.

The door closed behind her.

One.

Lila stopped and took a full breath, her first since that moment she heard Gavin Spencer speak.

CHAPTER 24

Gavin wanted to punch something. He would have torn the metal sink from the wall and flung it across his cell had it not been bolted and welded and immovable. His mouth went dry as he tried to swallow the anger that burned his throat. He needed to think.

It's panic. Just keep your head—figure this out.

The yapping of inmates in the common area kicked at his concentration, breaking his thoughts apart before they could form. On top of everything else, a voice in his head barked like an angry dog, the words *You're fucked* ricocheting off the cinder blocks that surrounded him.

He took a seat on the edge of his bunk, squeezed the thin mattress in his fists, and clenched his jaw to hold back a wail. Gavin Spencer had walked into the Hennepin County Adult Detention Center with a perfect blueprint for his escape, a lifeline to freedom that he had formulated as he waited for the detectives to show up.

Jails were designed to stop men from breaking out through barriers of stone and steel. Gavin's strategy looked beyond the walls. In the end, his captors would be the ones to escort him out. His plan had been playing out exactly as he had anticipated, until he came face-to-face with Lila Nash, a contingency that had never crossed his mind.

What the hell was she doing in court—an attorney, no less? She had been a wasted party girl, someone he had always imagined would drink her way to a stripper pole. He had dismissed her as fodder, a first draft that he could wad up and throw away, but there she was—a prosecutor.

Had she recognized him? The thought of growing old in prison—surrounded by troglodytes and sodomites—suddenly filled Gavin with a dread so strong that he nearly lost his ability to breathe.

Slow it down. Settle. Gavin moved to the floor of his cell, closed his eyes, and tipped his head down to concentrate. He needed to control the panic, calm the flurry of thoughts banging around his head.

She'd frozen at the sound of his voice. That had to mean something, but what? If Lila remembered him, could they put a case together after all this time? What do they have? No DNA. No trace evidence. They have a victim with no memory. When he laid the chips on the table, they added up to nothing—not yet, at least. They would need time to put it together, and Gavin could use that time to bring this new threat to an end. He was Gavin Spencer, for God's sake, a scalpel in a drawer full of meat cleavers. He would find a way.

And just like that, Gavin's heart rate began to slow, his lucidity returning. He stepped out of his panic, a butterfly freed of its chrysalis. He had time—not much, but enough. The plan remained the plan; he would just have to speed things up. He would fix the mistake he'd made eight years ago, but he had to get out to do it. How long did he have before they put him in the backseat of Lila Nash's car, too?

The race was on.

CHAPTER 25

It had happened once before, the panic attack, three summers ago when Lila drove to Iowa to visit her grandmother. She'd passed an old rusted car parked out in the middle of a fallow field, and the sight had nearly squeezed the breath from her chest. Her skin had turned hot and cold at the same time, and her stomach knotted up so tight that she had to pull over to the shoulder.

To anyone else it was just a car in a field, but not to Lila. That was how her attackers had left her, unconscious in the backseat of her own car in the middle of a bean field, her memory stolen by a date-rape drug. It had taken several minutes on that long-ago morning for her eyes to find their focus, the backseat materializing out of nothing, and a few minutes more to understand why her clothing lay at her feet.

After that first panic attack, Lila had made a trip to the university library, where she'd spent hours researching post-traumatic stress triggers: images, sounds, and scents that could transport a person back to the moment of the trauma. She'd understood why the car in Iowa had been such a powerful trigger. But why had Gavin Spencer now sent her spinning? Before she could face Andi, she had to understand.

In her office, she spread his file on her desk, laying his picture on top. His face meant nothing to her. She studied his eyes, the roundness of his chin, his thin lips. He could have been cut from cardboard and construction paper for all that his image affected her. Gavin was a small man accused of a crime that made him even smaller in Lila's eyes. But her reaction in court had the same debilitating effect on her as what she'd experienced in Iowa. Something in her gut opened the door to the unthinkable: What if they had crossed paths before?

According to the bail study, she and Gavin were the same age. For their freshman years of high school they'd gone to schools geographically close yet miles apart economically—she went to South while he went to Southwest. But halfway through his freshman year, Gavin got shipped to a private school in Indiana. They had never been classmates, and after combing through every word of his file, she found no connection.

She went online and searched for the private school in Indiana and found a link with pictures of his graduation ceremony. She read and then reread the date, the exact night that she had been attacked. Lila scrutinized each picture, looking for Gavin's face in the crowd. He wasn't there. Eight pictures in all and Gavin didn't appear in any of them.

His absence sent her mind racing with possibilities, a strange yet grim anticipation taking ahold of her. Her last memory before waking up in the bean field had been of a house party, one like so many others before it. Could Gavin have been at that party too? She always assumed that her attackers had been boys from her school, boys at the party that night, and Gavin was far removed from that crowd. Still, something had happened up in court. There had to be a reason.

She hadn't realized that she was holding her breath until she noticed the attribution beneath the pictures on the website: *Photos courtesy of Gavin Spencer.* Lila closed her eyes, breathed, and cursed to herself. Of course he wouldn't be in any of the pictures. He was the photographer. She moved from optimism to despair in the span of a single heartbeat.

She pulled up another link where some of those same graduation pictures had been published in the local newspaper, and each carried the same attribution. Yet another link took her to the school's yearbook, where she found Gavin in a group photo of the yearbook staff, a camera strapped around his neck.

Lila wanted to cry for letting hope bloom so easily.

But if Gavin hadn't triggered her panic attack, then what had? He'd used GHB on Sadie, the same drug that had been used on her. Had that been what sent Lila reeling? She dismissed that notion out of hand. GHB was a popular drug among the date-rape ilk. If that was all it took to throw Lila for a loop, then she might as well hang up her prosecutorial spurs now.

Then she remembered that the panic attack didn't start until she heard Gavin speak. Could she have been triggered by something as simple as a lisp?

She started a new query on her computer, one focused on PTSD triggers rooted where the victim had no memory. In time, she found an article that talked about triggers causing a reaction even when the person had no recollection of the original instance. If one of her attackers had had a lisp, could she have buried the memory that deeply? But as she read on, she started tripping over terms like *autonoetic awareness* and *intrusive traumatic memories*. She was out of her depth—but she knew someone who could walk her through that labyrinth.

She paused to consider whether she could go down that path.

Dr. Roberts was the best person to make sense of what was happening to her, but seeing him again would take Lila back to that year, the one that nearly killed her. Those channels in her soul that once roared with fury and pain had dried up in the eight years of his absence—or so Lila believed. Just the thought of seeing him again brought back the heaviness that she had carried to every one of those early sessions.

Her time with Dr. Roberts had been like crossing a bridge built of rotted wood, each step exposing new vulnerabilities. He'd explained that her suicide attempt had been about much more than a single attack. It had been about her father abandoning her. It had been about the uncle who touched her when she was too young to understand. And it had been about Sylvie Dubois, Lila's best friend, and the betrayal that Lila still held close to her heart.

She had expected Dr. Roberts to chastise her when she told him about her downward spiral of alcohol and boys. She was smart enough to understand that the self-worth she craved could never be found in the backseats of their cars, but that didn't stop her from looking for it there. She thought her confession might dishearten the good doctor, but he simply nodded as if Lila were telling him what she ate for breakfast.

Then he explained that her reaction to boys was not unexpected of someone who had been abused. And the drinking was simply a form of self-medication. He had a way of explaining things so that none of it seemed to be Lila's fault, as though she were a casualty of some war being waged deep in her subconscious mind.

But it was her fault, no matter what Dr. Roberts said. She chose to drink because it hid the ugliness. Lila embraced it—a hand to hold when she acted out. She could laugh when she was drunk, if only for a moment. Vodka had been the friendly nudge at her back when she flirted with the boys. It blunted the sharp edges of her regret and softened the memory of how they touched her. It whispered promises in her ear as she followed them to their cars. With enough alcohol, the broken parts no longer seemed vital.

But those moments always came to an end, and when they did, she had to pretend that it didn't hurt, pretend that she didn't notice how the boys, who gave her so much attention at the parties, turned away when she passed them in school. She understood why. She heard the nickname, the one whispered by boys and girls alike—Nasty Nash. Even Sylvie, the one friend Lila thought she had left, called Lila by that name the day she spat in Lila's face—the day Lila destroyed the last remnant of their friendship.

And just when Lila thought she had found rock bottom, a place so low that her world could not hold any greater pain, there came a morning when she woke up naked in the backseat of her car. No one believed her—not even, it seemed, the detective assigned to investigate her abduction. Lila wanted to cry as she told him what happened, but she couldn't.

When she reached for emotion—any emotion—she found nothing. So she stared at the floor and told him what little she remembered.

In the days and weeks that followed, a vile rage began to spread through Lila's veins, thickening her blood and filling her chest to the point that she could barely breathe. Her world became a muddle of emotion and chaos, all of it straining for release. Crying did nothing, and screaming only made it worse.

Lila's mother kept a utility knife in the kitchen, a packet of clean blades tucked inside its handle. Lila took one of the blades to her bedroom one night and examined it through her tear-filled eyes, the light dancing off the razor's fine edge. She put the blade against her tongue and tasted the steel. Then, with her bedroom door locked, she pulled the blade across her left biceps, pausing halfway into the cut to let a wave of nausea pass. The bite of the razor chased a pathway of nerves straight to her heart, jolting her with a mixture of pain and pleasure—and release.

Days later, when she cut herself the second time, there had been no hesitation, no nausea, and the relief she felt didn't quite give her the same kick. Five more times, she pulled that razor blade across her arm, the respite from her anguish shrinking with each new incision until it seemed little more than an exercise for drawing blood.

But the rage persisted—and Lila found her mother's pills.

How many Ambien would it take? Were there enough in the bottle? Could a person even overdose on Ambien? Lila would soon find answers to those questions. She had downed the pills with vodka and lain on her bed, no note to explain why. When she awoke in the Hennepin County Medical Center, Dr. Stephen Roberts had been at her side.

Lila typed Dr. Roberts's number into her phone and held her thumb over the send button, contemplating the hell out of which she had climbed. Phantoms of those dark days once again whispered in her ear, their soft voices tightening ropes around her chest. But something about Gavin Spencer had opened a door, and she had to find out why.

She closed her eyes and pressed the send button.

CHAPTER 26

Six years ago, joggers in St. Paul's Crosby Farm Park found the body of Eleanora Abrams floating at the edge of the Mississippi River, snagged in a fallen cottonwood tree. She had been missing for three days, having disappeared from a bar on Halloween night. Still wearing the sexy nurse costume, she was assumed to have gone into the river on the same night that she disappeared. The lead detective from the case had retired, so Niki sat alone in the St. Paul Homicide Unit as she culled through the reports.

Abrams had been a sophomore at the University of Minnesota, living in an apartment with Paula Schmidt, her best friend from high school. The two women had gone out dancing the night that Eleanora disappeared, getting into a club using doctored IDs because they were only twenty years old at the time.

Just before midnight, a camera at the entrance showed a man dressed in a pirate costume escorting a tipsy Eleanora out of the club, his broad-brimmed hat covering his face as he passed. Footage from earlier in the evening caught a glimpse of the man's face, but it had been at such a distance that all they could ascertain was that the man was Caucasian and had a beard—whether that beard was real or part of the costume, they couldn't tell.

Paula swore that Eleanora wasn't the type of girl to wander off like that. She would never just up and leave a club without telling someone.

And she wouldn't go off with a man she had just met. Yet Paula didn't report Eleanora missing until the next day, just in case she had done one of the very things that Paula swore she wouldn't do.

The medical examiner didn't rule the case a homicide at the time because she found no clear evidence of foul play. There had been sexual activity with borderline trauma, but there was no way to know whether the sex had been consensual or not. The lead detective had the foresight to request a screen for date-rape drugs, and they found GHB in her system, levels on the cusp of what could occur naturally in a dead body. The roommate swore that Eleanora—Ellie, as Paula called her—never took liquid ecstasy. Still, the medical examiner concluded that the GHB levels proved nothing definitive.

They found no defensive wounds, no ligature marks, and she was fully dressed. The cause of death was drowning, and the water in her lungs came from the river. Her body had been badly damaged postmortem, which led to the belief that she had gone into the river upstream of St. Anthony Falls. Interviews with friends, classmates, and family found no enemies or suspicious stalking activity. And none of them could identify the man in the pirate costume.

After spending the better part of a day digging through Eleanora's file, Niki tracked down Paula Schmidt and headed out to the suburbs to re-interview her. On the drive, she got a call from Matty.

"We got the forensics back on Spencer's computer," he said. "No search history on Sadie Vauk, the salon—nothing to link him to our victim in any way."

"Pictures?"

"He took pictures of her at the wedding, but nothing unusual. It wasn't like he was fixated on her or anything."

"What about the Bronco? Any idea where it might be?"

"No online payments for a storage unit. Nothing on his phone, either. He didn't disable the location tracker, and according to the phone data, he's never stopped at a storage unit."

"All we know is where his phone's been, not him. If he's smart enough to get rid of his router, he's smart to leave his phone at home."

"I think we should apply for a second search warrant—specific to the Bronco," Matty said. "Go back to the house and look for a paper trail. He's good at keeping things off his computer, but maybe he slipped up and kept a receipt."

"Can't hurt."

"Any luck in St. Paul?"

"Nothing yet, but I'm on my way to meet with a witness. Now that we have a suspect, maybe I can shake something loose by coming at it from a new direction."

"I'll get to work on that search warrant."

"Thanks, Matty. I'll call if I get anything on my end."

* * *

Paula Schmidt lived in a blue town house in Eagan, along with one husband, two small children, and three cats. She kept a pleasant home that seemed to hold the exact amount of clutter one would expect with toddlers and pets running around, and she struck Niki as being overly eager to talk.

"Are you reopening the case?" Paula asked as they took their seats at a dining room table.

"I'm looking into some things, but I can't say that I'm reopening anything just yet. I need to ask you a few questions about the night Eleanora went missing. You knew her pretty well, right?"

"We'd been best friends since seventh grade. I lost a sister that night."

"In the report it says that you were roommates?"

"At the U of M. We lived in Dinky Town."

"You went to the club about nine?"

"Right."

"And you don't recall seeing the man in the pirate costume that night?"

"I mean, I might have seen him, but the place was packed with people in costumes. I was dancing... and we'd been drinking a little."

"They showed you the picture from the security camera?"

"It was so blurry, I couldn't even see his face."

"Did Eleanora do anything in the week or two prior to her disappearance where... there would have been a photographer involved?"

"A photographer?" Paula looked confused at first, thin lines wrinkling across her forehead. Then she closed her eyes as if to focus on her recollection. "It was a long time ago."

"Take your time. It's important."

"It was Halloween... and before that...." She opened her eyes. "The party."

"Party?"

"We were members of Alpha Chi Omega— Give me a second." Paula jumped from her seat and ran upstairs, coming down a few seconds later holding a picture in a frame. "Our sorority had a costume party that week with Sigma Nu. There was a photographer there."

Paula handed Niki the picture. It showed two women with their arms across each other's shoulders. On the left, a younger version of Paula toasted the photographer with a cup of beer. On the right, Eleanora gave a peace sign with her raised hand. She wore the nurse costume that she would wear on the night she died.

"It's the last picture I had with Ellie. You think the photographer had something to do with..."

"Can I take it out of the frame?"

"Sure."

Niki pressed the clips aside and pulled off the back of the frame, her breath catching slightly when she saw the stamp. *GVS Photography.*

"Can I keep this?"

"Anything you want. Does it help?"

Niki carefully lifted the photograph by its edges and slipped it between the pages of her notebook, where she could carry it without contaminating it any further. "Was the photographer who took this picture a man or a woman?"

Paula again closed her eyes as if to transport herself back to the night of the party. "A man, I think—yes, a man."

"Was he wearing a costume?"

"I don't... Wait... yeah. I think he wore... a Phantom of the Opera mask."

"Beard or clean-shaven?"

"I'm not sure."

"Would you recognize him if you saw him again?"

"I barely remember him being a man, so... Who was he?"

Niki had come to that meeting with Gavin's face, his name, and his lisp in her quiver. Paula had already made it clear that the face was a nonstarter, but maybe the name might ring a bell. "I believe the person who took this picture is named Gavin Spencer. Does that name—"

"Gavin Spencer?" Paula lit up. "Gavin Spencer took that? He went to school with us—with me and Ellie. He... Oh my God... that was Gavin?"

"What?"

"That fucking bastard! That..."

"What?"

"He took Ellie to homecoming. It was horrible. He talks with a bad lisp, right?"

Niki almost broke her composure. "Go on."

"Ellie felt sorry for the little prick. She was just being nice to him, and he..."

"What happened?"

"Gavin's mom threw hot coffee on Ellie after the dance. We called the cops and everything. Did he... did he kill Ellie?"

"We don't know," Niki said. But that wasn't true—Niki did know. Unfortunately, the gap between knowing a thing and proving a thing could be as wide as a canyon.

Putting Gavin Spencer at a party with Eleanora Abrams the week she was murdered didn't put him in the club. The Phantom of the Opera wasn't a pirate, and nothing they'd found in their search of Gavin's house hinted at a connection. Even with the homecoming story and the photo, Niki was a hundred miles away from probable cause, and even further away from proof beyond a reasonable doubt. But in her heart, she had no doubt—she knew.

"Tell me everything you know about Gavin Spencer."

CHAPTER 27

Dr. Roberts worked at the Hennepin County Medical Center, but also had an office in a nearby high-rise built of steel and blue glass, a building Lila used to call the Aquarium. Her mother had driven Lila there for her visits with Dr. Roberts back in that summer when Lila's gloom had sent her to the hospital.

Gloom—that's the word her mother, Charlotte, used when talking about Lila's downfall. "You seem so gloomy," Charlotte had said. "You need to get some fresh air. Call Sylvie. Maybe catch a movie. That'll cheer you up." But Lila could not call Sylvie. They were no longer friends, and explaining why they weren't friends would have taken more energy than Lila cared to muster. Instead, Lila chose to resolve her gloom with a handful of her mother's Ambien.

Even after the suicide attempt, Charlotte used words like *gloom* and *doldrums* to talk about Lila's circumstances, avoiding any true conversation. As for the suicide attempt itself, her mother called that *the incident,* as though not calling it what it was raised doubt as to whether it happened at all. It was *the incident* that happened back when Lila was *in the doldrums*.

Lila paused outside of Dr. Roberts's office, the harsh florescent light in the corridor behind her casting her shadow against the door, a phantom inviting her back into the room where she had shed so many tears. In those months with Dr. Roberts, she had loved him and hated him. He'd guided her through a dark place, opening wounds that she refused to acknowledge. And when she lashed out, he had let her. All of those old feelings—emotions she thought she'd tamped down long ago—found new life and now itched beneath her skin.

And as he had done all those years ago, Dr. Roberts greeted Lila with the smile of an old friend. He hadn't changed much since she had last seen him. A smallish man with a balding head and thin wire glasses, he liked to walk around his office in his socks, a practice that Lila thought was meant to ease her anxiety—and it had.

"It's so nice to see you again," he said. "Please, have a seat."

His office had a desk in the corner, but Lila had never seen him behind it. Instead, they sat across from each other in leather chairs separated by a mahogany coffee table. A shelf behind the desk held some books, but beyond that, the office had been decorated like a fine parlor. Wood trim, Persian rugs, and oil paintings—abstract pastels hanging on the taupe walls—gave the room a soothing ambience.

Lila and Dr. Roberts took seats in the very chairs they'd sat in eight years ago, as if nothing had changed, but to Lila everything had. She wasn't the same girl who shook with anger as they cut through the tangle of her past. But then she thought about how she'd seized up at Gavin Spencer's hearing and felt as if those eight years had never happened.

"I've often wondered how things worked out for you," he said.

"Honestly, life's pretty good," she said. "I went to college, like I said I would. And then law school. I'm working at the Hennepin County Attorney's Office. And I've been sober now for..." She paused to think back to the date of her suicide attempt—the last time alcohol had passed her lips. "Eight years and forty-three days."

Roberts received this news with a satisfied smile, which stayed for only a moment before he turned serious and said, "And yet here you are."

Lila squirmed in her chair, the way she had back then. "It's just that...something happened, and I think it goes back to the night I was raped."

Raped. It felt strange to say that word. Her mother would leave the room if ever Lila used it. Even around Joe, Lila had taken to saying things like "the night I was assaulted," or "the night of the attack."

Dr. Roberts settled back into his chair, a cue to Lila that she had his full attention.

"I was in court, doing a first appearance—that's when they bring people in to have their bail set—and this guy came in. I've never seen him before—at least, I don't think so—but when he spoke, I...I don't know how to describe it."

"Take your time," Dr. Roberts said. "Just tell me one detail at a time."

Lila took a breath and willed her heart to slow down. When she was ready, she said, "I felt a chill flush through me, but it was warm, too, like the way you feel just before you throw up. And I couldn't talk. I tried, but it was like all the air drained out of my lungs and I couldn't fill them up again. Then I started shaking. It scared the hell out of me."

"Had anything like that ever happened before?"

"A few years back, I was driving to my grandmother's house and saw this car. It was sitting out in the middle of a field and...I don't know...it tripped something, and I almost passed out. I had the same reaction in court this morning. I thought it might also be a trigger or something."

"It's hard to say. With all the work being done in the field of PTSD, we still don't have a full understanding of how triggers work. The men who assaulted you had left you in a car in a field, so I can see why that car would have triggered you. But the guy in court—is there any chance you'd met him before?"

"There's nothing in his file to suggest that we ever crossed paths. He wasn't even in Minnesota at the time of my attack."

"Was there anything unusual about him—anything that stands out?"

"He had a lisp, a heavy one, but I don't remember anyone from my past like that."

Roberts put his hands together, fist in palm, as he considered Lila's suggestion. "Triggers aren't necessarily tied to concrete things we remember. Sometimes a trigger could be associated with something deeper in the subconscious."

"That's why I wanted to see you. We did that one session with Dr. Eggert when she hypnotized me. I was wondering if I said anything about a guy with a lisp when I was under. I know it's a long shot."

Roberts stood, walked to his desk, and retrieved Lila's file. After returning to his chair, he paged through the papers to find a particular set of notes, pausing to read to himself.

"You talked about a guy named John." Roberts let the file tip away as he raised his eyes to look at Lila. "That would be your friend's boyfriend?"

Lila nodded without making eye contact with Dr. Roberts.

"Did you ever resolve things between you and..."

"Sylvie."

"Right, Sylvie."

"I tried, but..." Lila trailed off, unable to continue the lie. But was it a lie? On the one-year anniversary of her suicide attempt, Lila drove to Sylvie's house and sat in the car for almost an hour, trying to build up the courage to knock on her door. In the end, she couldn't do it. Did that count?

Roberts returned to his notes, cocking his head slightly as something snagged his attention. "There is something here. You mentioned a man...you couldn't understand him, like he was drunk. You said he slurred."

Lila leaned in. "He slurred? Did I describe what he looked like?"

"No. You had no memory of his face. Did the police interview anyone with a lisp?"

"I don't know."

"That's all I have," Roberts said, folding the file closed. "There's nothing more about anyone with a lisp—just that one mention of a slur."

"If he had a lisp and not a slur, might that explain why I fell apart in court? It could have reminded me?"

"It could, but like I said, there's a lot we don't understand about PTSD."

"The only alternative is that I folded under pressure. I don't want to believe that's true."

"I doubt that's the case. You're stronger than you think. I've always felt that about you."

"Thanks," Lila said, acknowledging his compliment even as she silently disagreed with him. "I miss our talks."

"Me too. I thought we were making some important breakthroughs when you ended our sessions."

Lila thought that she might have misunderstood him. She looked at Dr. Roberts in confusion. "When *I* ended the sessions?"

"Yes. You had a number of issues that warranted deeper discussion. But it was your right to end the relationship."

"I didn't stop our sessions, Dr. Roberts. You told my mom that you didn't need to see me anymore."

Dr. Roberts raised an eyebrow. "I'm sorry, Lila, but that's not true." He opened the file again and began to dig. "You wrote me a letter."

When he found what he was looking for, Dr. Roberts handed Lila a piece of paper with a single typed paragraph. It informed Dr. Roberts that Lila was terminating her therapy. The signature at the bottom came close to being Lila's—but it wasn't.

"I..." Lila could find no words. How could this letter even exist?

"I called your house, spoke to your mother. She said that you decided to work with a different therapist. Was that not true?"

So many memories had been lost back then, disappearing into the murky dark of Lila's denial—her self-loathing—but there had never been another therapist. Lila shook her head slowly as she remembered her mother's many objections: the cost, the constant driving to appointments, and, of course, the embarrassment. People were talking about it: the rape, the investigation, the suicide—the ugliness that was Lila Nash. Which one had been the final straw that pushed her mother to forge that letter?

On the inside, Lila felt like she was back on that rotted bridge, the boards beneath her feet crumbling and falling into the abyss. On the outside, though, she tucked her mother's betrayal into a tiny corner of her heart, and asked Dr. Roberts to make a copy of the letter for her.

CHAPTER 28

The names of criminal attorneys got tossed around the jail like baseball trading cards. This one'll get you out. That one sucks. The woman with the big tits is nice to look at but doesn't know her way around the courtroom. The pod buzzed with scouting reports given by men who knew this stuff firsthand, which was helpful, because the right attorney was crucial to the next step in Gavin's plan.

There were only a few names that piqued Gavin's interest, and they were the least coveted of the trading cards. The first guy he called wanted Gavin to wait nearly a week to meet, on account of him being in trial. That wouldn't do. The clock was ticking on Gavin's plan, and now that Lila Nash had been thrown into the mix, he had to trim his timeline by weeks. How dare that asshole ask him to wait!

The first attorney to visit Gavin in jail spent his time bragging that he'd handled dozens of cases like Gavin's. He didn't actually say that he'd won those cases, but that didn't matter to Gavin. When he finished his pitch, Gavin asked the man a single question.

That lawyer failed his test.

The second lawyer did no better, trying to come across as though Gavin would be lucky to have him. "I have an opening at the moment, but I'll be meeting a guy tomorrow—a possible white-collar case—so if you want that slot, now's the time to pull the trigger." Did that timeshare-sales pitch actually work? Again, Gavin asked him the critical question, and that man, too, failed.

The third, a man named Leo Reecey, seemed particularly well suited for Gavin's purposes. His license had once been suspended because he'd stolen money from a client's trust account. He'd been sued by another client for failing to disclose a conflict of interest. The two men in Gavin's pod who had Reecey as an attorney wore an aura of dread as they paced the common area. Leo Reecey seemed a perfect pawn.

Reecey showed up wearing a slept-in corduroy jacket mismatched against his khaki pants. He had bags under his eyes, etched in permanent half-moons, and the bulbous nose of a man who needed a few nips to get through the day. He may as well have worn a sandwich board reading WILL SELL SOUL FOR CASH.

They met in a small conference room, a ten-by-ten space with a stainless-steel table mounted to the floor and four seats sprouting up out of the concrete like toadstools. No cell phones allowed. No guards listening in. No cameras rolling in the corner. The room was built to ensure attorney-client privilege. It had a red panic button near the door, but if an inmate decided to kill his attorney, the lawyer would have little chance of getting to that button in time.

Reecey greeted Gavin with a handshake and a tired smile.

"It's nice to meet you, Mr. Reecey," Gavin said, putting his speech impediment on full display. "May I call you Leo?"

"That'd be my preference." The two men took seats at the table. "I read up on your case," Reecey said.

"Don't believe everything you read."

"That's one of the Ten Commandments in my line of work. I'm here to get you through this as best I can. What other people say about you doesn't matter to me."

He didn't say that he would get Gavin acquitted, but simply promised to help him through the process. Gavin appreciated that Reecey wasn't a man prone to overpromising. It also suggested Reecey understood that he was a glorified seat warmer. It was a terrible sales pitch, but an honest one.

"Attempted murder, kidnapping, and first-degree criminal sexual conduct. Those are some serious charges." Reecey spoke as though he was the first person to deliver this bad news to Gavin. "It's going to take a lot of work to put together a good defense." He was prepping Gavin for the price tag, an amount almost sure to be well below what Gavin was prepared to pay. Gavin let Reecey prattle on.

"I don't think that lineup they did was kosher. Looks to me like they were trying to get her to pick you out—with that whole lisp thing. We may need to bring in an expert to talk about different kinds of speech impediments. By the way, the cost of an expert is separate from my fee. But the lineup is the key to your defense, and that's where we'll put up our biggest fight. Even if we win, though, we have to deal with her pointing you out at trial."

"She'll have to testify, right?" Gavin knew the answer to his question but wanted to hear Reecey say it.

"You have the right to face your accuser. It's in the Constitution. If they don't meet that threshold, they don't have a case."

"And what if I have an alibi? How do we present that?"

"Well, that's about as good as it gets—as long as the alibi has legs. I'd want to shore it up—you know, make it airtight, maybe get an investigator to take the stand and explain it to a jury. Do you have an alibi?"

"Maybe."

"Maybe?"

"Like you said, it has to be shored up." Gavin liked Reecey's choice of words, and the ethical gray area they implied. Shoring up an alibi sounded an awful lot like creating one.

"The thing is," Reecey said, "that kind of thing takes resources, especially in a case like this."

Resources—lawyer code for money. Reecey was bringing it in for a landing.

"I have resources," Gavin said.

"We're talking significant amounts here." Reecey had probably done enough homework to know that Gavin had the means to pay "significant amounts." Gavin could almost see Reecey juggling the numbers in his head—set the amount high enough to sound upscale but not so high that it might scare Gavin off. "Probably... I'd say, I'd need... fifty grand?"

Gavin almost laughed at the lowball request. Gavin's mom gave him four times that amount as a yearly allowance. *Allowance.* He liked that term. It was a word he and his mother agreed upon in their negotiations. It sounded much more refined than terms like *extortion* or *hush money*.

"I assume you brought a retainer agreement?" Gavin said.

Reecey put his briefcase on the table and popped it open.

As Reecey dug to find the retainer agreement, Gavin rang a Pavlovian bell that he knew would make Reecey salivate. "I'll give you two hundred thousand dollars up front to be held in trust. I assume that would constitute sufficient resources to get the ball rolling?"

Reecey could just as well have done a spit take, the way he reacted. When he pulled himself together, he said, "That'll do fine." He began writing Gavin's name in the blank spaces on the retainer agreement.

"I want you to add a couple lines to the contract. Once we get past the contested omnibus hearing, you'll get a flat fee bonus of fifty thousand dollars on top of your hourly rate."

Reecey stopped writing and looked at Gavin. "Why would you do that?"

"By then, I'll know whether or not I have an alibi, and you'll have earned the bonus one way or the other."

Reecey put his pen down. "What will I have done to earn a fifty-thousand-dollar bonus?"

Now came the test—the question that had sent the other two lawyers scurrying away. "What I say here is confidential, correct?"

"Attorney-client privilege. I can't utter a word of it."

"Not to anyone? Not ever?"

"Not ever."

"What if I told you that my alibi is a woman—a married woman?"

"Wouldn't be the first time that's happened."

"But here's the thing. I've been in here a while now, and she hasn't come to see me. I have to assume that she's not willing to give up her marriage to save my neck. But if I could get ahold of her..."

"Have you tried giving her a call?"

"I can't do that. We only communicated through text messages. Her husband's crazy jealous, so she bought a special phone, one she could use to text with me. If I could communicate with her—text her—I could convince her to give a statement."

"I could send an investigator—"

"No. It has to come from me. She won't talk to anyone else."

"Well, how do you propose we do that?"

Gavin leaned in to the table and lowered his voice. "That's how you earn your bonus. You'll need to buy a burner phone and let me use it."

"They won't let me bring a phone here."

Gavin smiled on the inside. Reecey's objection was how to get a phone past a jailer, not the ethics of providing a phone to an inmate. He liked where this lawyer's head was at.

"Not here," Gavin said. "You'll bring it to court. I have a Rule Eight hearing coming up. When we meet in the holding cell at court, you let me send her a text message or two—whatever it takes to get her to come in and give a statement. I need to convince her how important this is. That's all you have to do, and the fifty grand is yours."

Reecey stared at Gavin as he considered the proposal, and Gavin could almost see the man contemplating the boat he would buy with the money.

Gavin had gamed his moves with precision; the only gamble in the plan was getting his hands on a cell phone. His freedom, his life, everything hinged on finding an attorney willing to turn a blind eye.

Gavin held his breath as the lawyer weighed right versus wrong. When Reecey finally made the decision, it came not with a smile or handshake but with the slumped shoulders of a man who had just calculated the price of his integrity.

CHAPTER 29

Andi had taken that Friday off, which gave Lila three days to ponder her panic attack and come up with a way to explain it to Andi—to Joe. It also gave her three sleepless nights to contemplate one inescapable truth: Gavin Spencer had triggered something in her. Whether it was Gavin himself or some characteristic of his, she had no way of knowing, but something about him had shaken her.

Lila ran through a thousand iterations of what she would say, but every version collapsed beneath a tiny voice that whispered: *What if?* What if Gavin had something to do with her attack? It was absurd on its face, she knew that. Other than the GHB, nothing of what happened to her matched up with what Gavin did to Sadie. Besides that, he had been in Indiana that night.

Still, *what if?*

Those two small words created an enormous problem for Lila. No matter how inconceivable that *what if* remained, its mere existence could get her kicked off Gavin's case. Andi would apply an over-abundance of caution and lock Lila out for nothing more than a wisp in the wind. That seemed an injustice that bordered on cruelty. Andi needed her on that case. Lila understood the fog of Sadie's amnesia, the mix of memory and imagination that might cause her to stumble in her testimony. No one was better suited to prep Sadie for trial than Lila.

But more than that, Lila wanted to be there when they put Gavin in prison. It didn't matter that he was in Indiana the night she was raped; his crime echoed what had happened to her, and she'd be damned if she was going to step aside because of something as implausible as a *what if*. She wouldn't lie to Andi, but there was a large gray sea between the truth and a lie—a sea she would have to find a way to navigate.

What to tell Joe was another matter. He would ask questions and pry, dig into the meat of that far-fetched suspicion. Just the fact that she and Joe would have a conversation about it gave weight to Lila's need to tell Andi. And if Joe asked how she planned to tell Andi... Well, that's where it all fell apart.

The more Lila played out that conversation with Joe, the easier it was to persuade herself that she need not have it. She had to figure out what had tripped her up in court, fit all the pieces together, first. Then, like an artist revealing her work only after it's finished, she could lay it out for him. He would forgive her keeping a secret from him, because that's the kind of guy he was.

By the time she went to bed Sunday night, Lila was convinced that keeping her circumstances to herself was more an act of discretion than deception. It posed no harm to anyone. But as she lay awake, listening to Joe sleep next to her, she found little comfort in the twists of her logic, knowing that she cast a far bigger shadow in Joe's eyes than she deserved.

* * *

At eight o'clock Monday morning, with her stomach tied into a Gordian knot, Lila took her seat in the chair across from Andi, her back straight, her knees together, and her heart thumping as she awaited judgment.

Andi, who had been writing on a legal pad when Lila entered her office, continued to write as she asked, "You want to tell me what happened in court on Thursday?"

What little Lila had prepared for that moment drifted out the window, and she answered, "I'm not sure."

Andi stopped writing and looked at Lila, her countenance falling somewhere between the stern disapproval of a teacher and the soft disappointment of a mother. "You're not sure what happened? Or you're not sure you want to tell me?"

Both, Lila thought. "I had some kind of... attack, I guess."

"You guess? I had to take over your hearing. I've never had to take over a hearing before, and I plan to never have to do it again. What would have happened if I hadn't been there? If you become an attorney here, you'll be on your own. I need to know you can handle yourself."

Andi's use of the word *if* didn't escape Lila's notice. "I've taken steps to make sure it never happens again. I promise—"

"Taken steps?"

Lila had hoped those words might slip past Andi's keen ear, because behind them lay a sordid entanglement of things like PTSD, and therapy, and hospitalizations. To suggest that her panic attack was nothing—that they happened all the time—would not only be a lie, but would surely get her pushed to a division of the County Attorney's Office where the consequences of a mistake like that would cause little harm.

But to say that it was a rare occurrence—which it was—planted the proverbial time bomb under her table in court. Andi could never be confident that it wouldn't happen again, maybe at the height of an important cross examination or during a closing argument.

Lila tried a third option—deflection. "Being here is everything to me." Lila heard the begging in her voice, and it sickened her. She could only imagine how those words sounded to a woman like Andi Fitch. Lila gathered her nerve and tried again. "I promise you, it will never happen again."

"Lila, this is not an easy job. You were handling a first appearance. You should be able to do those in your sleep. What happens when there's real pressure and you have the family of a murder victim in court watching you? You make a mistake at this level—you freeze up when it counts—and a murderer or a rapist walks free."

Lila felt like she was clawing at the icy side of a glacier, desperately trying to keep from sliding down. "You've seen my résumé. I've handled pressure before."

"This isn't law school. It's not pretend, and it's not like TV. You won't sleep the week of a jury trial. Your appetite messes with you. First you can't eat, and then you're famished but puke it up in the end. It's pressure like nothing you've known before. If you can't handle a first appearance, maybe there's another part of the office where you might feel more comfortable."

Be strong, Lila thought to herself. *Show Andi what this means to you.* "I didn't go to law school to haul deadbeat dads into child support hearings. I want to be a prosecutor. I want to protect women from abusers like Donald Gray. I want to help you lock Gavin Spencer away so he'll never rape anyone ever again. This job was why I went to law school in the first place. It's here or it's nothing. Give me another chance; I'll show you. Please." *Begging. Stop it!*

Andi considered her answer for a moment before saying, "Give what I said some thought." Andi's words took on a gentler tone as she continued. "I've seen people fall apart doing this job. Busted marriages, alcoholism—a good friend of mine got marched out of court for showing up drunk. If you have any doubts—"

"I don't." Lila's words finally landed sharp and hard.

Andi appraised Lila and gave her a nod. "So, you want to tell me why Frank Dovey has taken an interest in you?"

"Frank?"

"He stopped by my office on Thursday. He saw you...freeze in court. He wants a report on your work. And he said that he'll be doing your next quarterly evaluation. I have to go through him to put anything into your personnel file. That's outside of the norm, so do you have any idea why he gave me that order?"

The answer that came to Lila first—that Dovey was out to get her—sounded over-the-top paranoid, even to her. Instead, she said, "The only time we ever met was when I worked with Boady Sanden on the Pruitt case."

Lila saw what looked like a twinkle of understanding in Andi's eyes. Then she nodded. "He wants me to draft a letter for your file regarding Thursday's incident. I told him I'd give it some thought. Well, I've given it some thought, and I don't think I'll be writing any such letter. I'm taking you at your word that it was an aberration and won't happen again. But, Lila, if this thing—this attack—isn't an aberration, I'll have no choice. Are we clear on that?"

"We're clear."

* * *

Lila ate lunch at her desk, finishing up on the more pressing of Andi's assignments. She passed the afternoon working on a research memo that she could have done in her sleep, her attention continually wandering away from her task and to her meeting with Dr. Roberts. Something he said—a minor point that Lila hadn't given much thought to at the time—had become a pebble in her shoe, growing in size until she could no longer ignore it.

Had the investigators, eight years ago, interviewed a man with a lisp? She remembered giving Detective Yates her account of the party and waking up in the bean field, but after that, she never heard from him. Now she couldn't help but wonder how far he had gone to find her attackers.

Somewhere in the back of a police precinct lay a box—or maybe only a thin file—holding the investigation of the rape of a girl named Lila Nash. If Yates had interviewed a man with a lisp back then, he wouldn't have known that it mattered. Was it possible that somewhere in those reports lay the seed of what happened to her in court? Might she find her attackers in those pages?

As a victim, she didn't have an absolute right to see her case, but she wasn't just another victim—she was also a prosecutor with connections on the inside. Lila paged through Gavin's file until she found the business card of Niki Vang stapled to a report. Lila paused for only a couple of seconds before tapping out a message to Niki's number and hitting send.

* * *

They met in the courtyard of the Government Center, a green space in the middle of downtown where people could sit and enjoy the warm August sun. Lila had no sooner claimed a bench in the shade of a tree when Niki appeared at the other end of the courtyard. Lila stood and waved her over.

"I appreciate you meeting with me, Detective Vang," Lila said, as they took seats on the same bench.

"Please, it's Niki."

"Okay... Niki. The reason I asked to see you is that I need a favor. It's kind of a gray area, so if you have any qualms about it, I want you to refuse."

Niki considered Lila for a moment and said, "Okay."

"An active investigation is confidential, correct?"

"That's right."

"As a peace officer, you have access to any active file, and you can share that information with a prosecutor."

"Yes."

"And technically I'm a prosecutor."

"Is there a file you want to see?"

Lila leaned forward on the bench, lacing her fingers together, her forearms resting on her knees. "Eight years ago, I was at a party near Uptown and something happened. I was drugged and... raped."

Her words lingered in the air for a few seconds before Niki said, "I'm sorry."

"I reported it, but there wasn't much I could tell the detective. I remember getting dizzy and really tired all of a sudden, but I don't remember leaving the party. The detective handling the case, a guy named Yates, told me that people said that I was bouncing off walls, trying to walk. They thought I was being my usual drunk self." Lila looked up at Niki. "I used to drink a lot back then."

Niki gave Lila a smile that said *No judgment* and Lila continued.

"I woke up the next morning in the backseat of my car, parked out in a field. I didn't know what happened. I didn't understand how I got there. I was naked and confused. They did a rape kit and screened for drugs. I had GHB in my system."

Niki leaned forward, elbows on her knees to match Lila's posture. "I take it they never caught the guy?"

"Guys. There were two of them. They took a picture that made the rounds among my... my friends. It showed..." Lila paused to let a lump in her throat melt. "It showed me from the waist up, no clothes. My eyes were half open. I looked drunk. One guy took the picture while the other posed me. You can see his blue jeans—his knee—stuck under my ribs to prop me up."

"That must have been... I can't imagine."

"It was. But that brings me to my favor. Last week, I was supposed to handle Gavin Spencer's first appearance, but when he spoke, I froze. I couldn't talk or breathe—almost passed out right there in court. I talked to my therapist, and he thinks that Gavin's lisp might have triggered my reaction. It's possible one of my attackers had a speech impediment."

"Is it possible... that Gavin Spencer might have been your attacker?"

"I thought about that, but it doesn't fit. Spencer kills his victims; I was left alive. He takes them to his house; my attack happened in my car. He puts their clothing back on; that didn't happen with me. Spencer's a lone wolf; my attackers worked as a pair. And they took a picture. Don't serial rapists stick to their habits?"

"They do, but they also learn from mistakes."

"There's one more thing. I looked up Gavin's high school graduation on the internet. It was the same night that I was attacked, and he was there taking pictures—in Indiana. Honestly, other than the use of GHB, I don't see a connection."

"I could follow up with his high school just in case," Niki said. "I agree it's unlikely, but leave no stone unturned, right? So, how do I fit into all this?"

"I want to see my case file—see if there's anything in it that might jog my memory. I reacted to Gavin's speech impediment. My therapist said that years ago, when I was under hypnosis, I mentioned a guy with a slur, someone I couldn't understand because he sounded drunk. Maybe there's something in my file that might mean something to me even if they didn't make the connection back then."

Niki mulled it over for a moment and said, "If the party was in Uptown, that'll be the Fifth Precinct. I can't imagine anyone would have a problem with you taking a peek. When do you want to go?"

Lila hadn't expected it to be that easy. "Um, whenever you're available."

"How about right now?"

CHAPTER 30

The common room of Gavin's jail pod held tables and chairs—all anchored to the floor—where the inmates could play games, or talk, or work on the pecking order. Gavin did his best to avoid it, having learned early in life that a speech impediment and a doughy appearance made him a target for anyone wanting to pick a fight. Knuckle-draggers hated to have their ignorance put on display, thus even the most innocuous conversation could turn deadly. So, when it came time for Gavin to write his letters, he pulled his mattress to the floor and used his bunk as a table.

Outbound mail was subject to inspection by jail staff, and Gavin knew that copies of his letters would find their way to Detective Niki Vang. It brought him joy to picture her reading each, incapable of grasping the significance of what she held in her hands.

After an hour of contemplation, Gavin put pen to paper and wrote the first of his two letters.

> Dear Jack,
>
> Keep your chin up old friend, and ignore what you've read about me. I did not commit the crime for which I am accused. Life has taken a sad turn for me, but I find strength in the detailed memory of our friendship. Little things like

time and distance can't erase those pictures from my mind. So many times I have thought of you and of our days together, all those years ago. All I can do now is hope that you hold those memories as close to your heart as do I. Did you ever think that our paths would cross again after so much time apart? I must admit, I never expected to be where I am. Every day I find myself stunned that I could be accused of so heinous a crime. Vicious lies are being told about me, and they cut me to my core. As I write this, they are marshalling their forces to bring a case against me based on nothing but a lie. Unafraid, I will meet their challenge, knowing that justice will prevail. Karma shall be my salvation.

Yours in confidence,
G.

Pleased with his effort, he went to work on sneaking his message past the jailers. This second step of the plan involved his next-door neighbor, Gideon Doss, whom he found sitting alone in the common area, a game of solitaire spread in front of him. Gavin took the seat across the table.

"You winning?"

Gideon didn't look up. "Not yet."

"Any luck calling your girl?"

Gideon had discovered that his girlfriend had gone to the hospital to visit his cousin—the man Gideon had stabbed. Too broke to buy a prepaid phone card, Gideon called her collect every day, but she refused to accept. Suspicion tormented him to the point that he cried in his cell at night.

Gideon looked up, a scowl on his face. "All I can do is yell that I love her when the operator's askin' if she'll take the call. I ain't got the money to talk to her the way I wanna."

"Man, that sucks."

"Got that right."

"I can't stand the way they rip a guy off in here—charging an arm and a leg just to call his girl."

"No shit. I called my mom collect and they charged her ten bucks just to say hi."

"That's bullshit," Gavin said, dumbing his vocabulary down to put Gideon at ease. "And your cousin's out there free and clear, doggin' on your girl all he wants, and ain't nothing you can do. You can't even tell her how you feel."

"Why you doin' me that way, man? Why you fuckin' with me—making me feel like shit? It's bad enough I'm locked up and all."

"I have an idea that might help you out." Gavin nodded in the direction of his cell, then stood and walked.

Gideon hesitated, but followed Gavin. Once inside, Gavin stayed near the door to make sure that they weren't overheard. "I feel bad about your situation, Gideon. I mean, you didn't do nothin' but defend your honor. Hell, folks used to expect a man to defend his honor. Now they throw you in jail for it."

"Ain't that the truth?"

"There ain't much I can do to get you out of here, but I can make your stay a little better—if you let me."

Gideon looked at Gavin with a suspicious eye. "What the hell you talkin' 'bout?"

"I want to buy you a phone card, and put a little scratch in your commissary fund."

"Why would you do something like that?"

"You're a good guy, Gideon. I saw that right away. You didn't make fun of my speech impediment or go all predator on me. I appreciate that."

"You do talk funny, but I figure that ain't somethin' you got control over."

"That's an honorable way to look at it, Gideon."

"Ain't no big deal," he said. "And I thank you for the callin' card and stuff."

"No problem. We have to help each other out, because no one else is going to do it. Am I right?"

"Amen to that." Gideon held his fist up and Gavin gave him a bump.

"I do have one small problem, though," Gavin said. "It's not much, but I could use your help."

"What's that?"

"I have this friend who might be important to my case. I need to reach him, but I don't really want the powers that be to know about it. I mean, he might help me, but then again, he might hurt my case quite a bit—if you know what I mean. I wrote him a letter."

Gavin went to his bunk and pulled the letter from beneath the mattress. "I was hoping you might mail it for me. There's nothin' that'll get you in trouble. Go ahead, read it."

Gavin gave the letter to Gideon and waited as the man slowly read the content, a process that took far longer than it should have.

"See? It's harmless. I just don't want the guards to flag it as coming from me. If my prosecutor gets ahold of that guy's name I could be in a ton of shit. All you have to do is mail it."

"I mail this and you give me a calling card?"

"That's the deal."

"Hell, I'll do it right now."

Gavin put the letter inside an envelope and gave it to Gideon, slapping him on the back as he left the cell.

With that letter on its way, Gavin moved his mattress to the floor again and began writing the second letter—also addressed to Jack. The second letter was far more difficult to construct, and it ran two pages long. No matter how hard he tried, Gavin could not get the words and sentences to make sense, so he embraced the incoherency of it all, filling the pages with symbolized cursing and disjointed babble. When he finished, Gavin delivered the second letter to Gideon Doss, who once again acted as courier.

The day's tasks completed, Gavin retreated to his cell to lie on his bunk and contemplate his next step. Should he write a third letter, one to set Jack on the trail of Lila Nash? No. That would be a bridge too far. He would have to handle Lila himself once they freed him.

For all of his life, Gavin had cherished his time alone, his mental journeys soothing him as though he were walking through a garden. But Lila Nash brought strife to his paradise. She had seen his face and heard his voice. She had his file, so she knew about his use of GHB. What else did she know? What had she remembered? What could she re-create from that night eight years ago?

It had been Jack who had slipped the GHB into Lila's drink and driven her out to that bean field. Gavin had taken the picture, but it had been Jack who sent the email. Gavin had been little more than a shadow that night. If Lila were ever able to trace a path back to Gavin, it would have to go through Jack.

How could Gavin have been so stupid as to leave both a victim and an accomplice alive? He calmed himself by working through his plan to rectify those mistakes.

In a couple days, Jack would receive the letters and read them in confusion, Gavin's words coming off as the ramblings of a lunatic. But soon, all would be made clear and Jack would know what to do.

CHAPTER 31

The Fifth Police Precinct reminded Lila of an elementary school, flat and long, the building blending in to the community with a quiet confidence, as might a sleeping pit bull. Niki and Lila entered together, Niki showing her badge to a woman behind a thick window. A duty officer escorted them to a conference room and then left, returning a few minutes later carrying a brown box with Lila's name written in black marker on the front. Niki opened a binder that lay on top of the box and signed her name at the bottom of a list of people who had pulled the file over the years.

"Is there some movement in this case?" the sergeant asked.

"Nothing special, why?"

"It's the second time in a week that I dug it out."

Niki looked at the logbook again. "I'll be damned." She turned it so that Lila could read, tapping her pen on the line just above where Niki had signed.

Lila read the name. *Frank Dovey.* "What the . . . ?"

Niki slid the binder back to the sergeant, and after he left, Niki said, "Why would Frank Dovey be looking into your old assault case?"

"I'm not sure. I think he holds a grudge because of the Pruitt case. But I was only a law student. Is he really that petty?"

"Yes, he is," Niki said. "I know we're supposed to be on the same team and all, but I can't stand the guy. He's a political prick, and if he's gathering intel on you, you'd be smart to watch your back."

"You're preaching to the choir."

Inside the box, Lila saw evidence bags sealed with tape. She would find her clothing from the night of the rape in those bags. She steadied her breathing and let Niki decide what to do next. Niki opened the folder that held the investigative reports. The first page was a photo of Lila, bare-breasted and groggy, the picture that had made the rounds at South High.

Nausea passed through Lila, and the further realization that Frank Dovey had seen that picture brought bile up to the back of her throat. Niki casually turned the photo facedown on the table.

"Let's divide this up," Niki said. "I'll take the police reports and you go through the medicals."

Lila opened a folder and began reading. The words the doctor used were cold and emotionless: *petechiae,* and *laceration,* and *acute trauma.* Other clipped phrases made Lila sound like a classroom cadaver. *No observable blood or skin cells under the fingernails. Gamma-hydroxybutyric acid present. Negative presence of sperm and saliva. Swabs preserved.*

Lila felt as though she were floating outside of herself, reading about some other poor girl brought to an emergency room with no memory of an attack. The doctor asked a lot of questions, but none of Lila's answers seemed helpful. And none of them mentioned a man with a speech impediment.

"Tell me about John Aldrich," Niki said, without looking up from a report.

Lila flushed hot with embarrassment. If Lila were being honest, she would have told Niki that John Aldrich was her best friend's boyfriend. But Lila knew what questions would follow, so she merely said, "We went to high school together."

"They found his semen on the backseat of your car."

The investigator from eight years ago had also gone down that path, asking Lila if she and John had ever engaged in consensual sex. Lila's mother had been in the room when Lila admitted having sex with John.

She went on to explain that they had been intoxicated, but that tidbit didn't stop her from feeling small and ashamed.

"We were never together," Lila told Niki. "Not like boyfriend and girlfriend."

"And... the semen? Were you ever together that way?"

Lila looked down at the papers in front of her, the memory of what she had done stinging as sharply now as it had all those years ago. In a meek voice she answered, "We hooked up one time. I put a stop to it after that."

"How did he feel about that?"

"I didn't care how he felt about it." That wasn't an answer to Niki's question, so Lila tried again. "He didn't agree with the decision, but it was final."

Niki moved on as though she hadn't noticed Lila's reaction. "Do you remember him being at the party that night?"

"Yeah, he made a scene. His girlfriend, Sylvie—I guess his ex-girlfriend at that point—she saw him try to kiss me. I pushed him away. Like I said, he didn't agree with my decision."

"One of the witnesses from the party said John grabbed you by the... buttocks. Said it looked aggressive."

Lila pondered that for a minute. She remembered him trying to kiss her, but the grab? Now it came back to her. It had been rough and sudden, a show of ownership. How could she have forgotten that?

"I think he did," Lila said. "Who was the witness?"

"A guy named Sean Daniels. He gave Detective Yates a picture—not of the grab, but it's from that party."

Niki handed Lila an eight-by-ten photo of John Aldrich holding her by the wrist, a squint of anger wrinkling his eyes. It was probably the last picture taken of her before her world changed forever. Lila was pulling away from him. She remembered that John wanted to kiss her, and she remembered that Sylvie was there.

"What about Sean Daniels," Niki asked. "What's his story?"

"He was in my class—kind of quirky."

"Quirky?"

"He asked me out a couple times, but he wasn't my type. He was one of those socially awkward guys who came across a little creepy, even when he wasn't trying to."

"Do you remember anyone else from that night?"

Lila looked at the picture, at the people in the background. She studied their faces but recognized no one. "There were a lot of people there, so I'm sure there were others from South, but I can't remember. Is there any mention of a guy with a lisp?"

"Nothing."

Lila returned to her medical reports and came upon an addendum that cataloged her suicide attempt. It had been authored by Dr. Roberts and included notes from her stay in the psych ward as well as the failed hypnotherapy session. The report didn't mention the guy with the slur, a point possibly too minor to be included.

Niki leaned back in her chair as though pondering some new thought. Then she said, "How did you hear about the party in Uptown?"

"John—" Lila stopped to pull a memory from the darkness. Detective Yates had never asked her that question. "John told me about it. He called to say he was getting a carload of kids from South together to go to this party. He wanted to know if he should save a seat. By that point, I didn't want anything to do with him, so I drove myself."

"A carload of kids?" Niki picked up one of the reports and read. "He told Detective Yates that he left the party alone. If he went there with a car full of kids... wouldn't he have given those same kids a ride home?"

Lila thought about that for a moment. Had he said those words—about taking other kids from South? Yes, she was sure of it.

"Maybe he was trying to get you alone," Niki said, "for old times' sake. Maybe it was part of a bigger plan."

"A bigger plan?"

"I'm just thinking here, but... the one fact we know for sure in your case was that there were two of them. We have the picture."

"Okay."

"And then there's your reaction to Gavin Spencer in court. It could have been nothing more than you hearing a lisp, but what if it wasn't? What if Gavin was there?"

"The modus operandi doesn't fit."

"I know, but there were two of them. We don't know what the MO of the other guy is—or was. The pattern could be different because of the second guy being there."

"But Gavin was in Indiana."

"Well, there's that, but Gavin Spencer isn't your run-of-the-mill criminal. It's possible he faked an alibi. It's a stretch, I know."

"How could we find out?"

"I can look into that graduation ceremony, see if anyone remembers seeing him there."

"It's been eight years."

"Yes, it has—eight years of this case gathering dust. Eight years of this thing hanging over your head. That has to be... pure torment."

It was as if Niki understood something about Lila that no one else—not even Joe—understood. "Sometimes I think it's made me insane... paranoid. I walk down the street and I'm sure someone's following me. I memorize the cars around me when I drive, just in case I see them again. I've woken up in a cold sweat, sure that I saw one of their faces in a dream. I don't think a day's gone by when I don't think about them being out there."

"Well, it's time we take another look at it." Niki pulled out a pen and wrote down John Aldrich's name and date of birth on a pad of paper.

"You think John...?"

"He was the prime suspect. With you breaking it off, he had motive, and that picture of him holding your arm shows he had opportunity. Plus, whether it was about taking other kids to the party or about leaving the party alone, I think it's clear that John Aldrich lied."

CHAPTER 32

Gavin knew his mother would come for a visit. Amy had to sign Leo Reecey's two-hundred-thousand-dollar check. He'd given his lawyer her phone number. "And if she has any questions," he'd said, "tell her to come talk to me."

The jail used a video-conferencing system so Gavin sat in the guts of the jail staring at a screen while his mother did the same from the visiting area. Even remotely, Gavin could see that Amy had dressed inappropriately for the occasion, wearing a blouse that hung low off the shoulders and had a drawstring in the middle—a look far too provocative to wear to a jail. But then, Amy rarely had the good sense to hide the cleavage that Richard Balentine had bought for her.

Amy held the phone receiver with the tips of her manicured nails to keep the plastic from touching the skin of her fingers. "I got a call from some lawyer named Leo Reecey. He said I was supposed to give him a check for two hundred grand."

"He's my lawyer. I can't access my money, so you'll have to pay him."

"Did you do any research on the man? I mean, he's just barely a lawyer at all. Last year he was suspended for stealing from his clients. What do you even know about him?"

"I'm on top of it."

Amy furrowed her brow. "Honey, he ain't worth that kind of money. Let me take care of this for you. You're in jail, for God's sake. They wanna lock you up and throw away the key. I can find a lawyer who—"

"Mother, all I need from you is a check."

"At least let me get you a good lawyer. If I'm footing the bill, I should get some say in it."

Gavin knotted his hand into a fist to redirect his anger. He then stated his position in a calm voice. "You will pay the man his two hundred thousand dollars. You owe it to me, so stop interfering and do what I tell you to. Okay?"

Gavin watched as the words, and the unspoken understanding behind them, slapped his mother in the face.

"You don't have to get that way, honey. I just want the best for you. We can afford any lawyer you want. But if he's the one...I'll cut him a check. I just want to make sure you walk out of here when this is all done. You're my baby."

"Everything's going to be fine, Mother. They can't convict me if I didn't do anything."

"But why do they think it was you? How could they think—?"

"It's a case of mistaken identity. Some girl picked me out of a lineup, but it's not true. You'll see. They don't have anything—no DNA, no witnesses, nothing—because I didn't do it."

"They have that girl. Ain't she a witness?"

"It's her word against mine, and she's lying."

"The paper said you met her at a wedding." The detectives had no evidence that Gavin had actually met Sadie, but Amy threw it out there anyway. She was a dullard that way.

"I was the photographer. She must have confused me with someone else."

"They came and talked to me—a Mexican and a little Asian woman."

Gavin expected this. In those stagnant hours, as he'd waited for the detectives to show up, he had contemplated calling his mother to warn her. He didn't, because she would undoubtedly let it slip that he had warned her. And if she had done that, they would argue to a jury that the phone call showed a consciousness of guilt. How would Gavin Spencer know that detectives were on their way if he hadn't done anything wrong?

"What did you tell them?" he asked. "And remember, they're recording what you say here." Gavin hated that he had to remind her not to be stupid.

"They asked me where you were Monday night. I told them I didn't know."

"Because you *don't* know."

"Maybe you called me from home, and I can tell them that—"

"But I didn't call you, did I?"

"No."

"And if you told them that I did, all they would have to do is check your phone records and see that you were lying. Don't add. Don't improvise."

"They asked if I knew when you shaved your head. I said I didn't know. Why'd you cut your hair? You had such beautiful hair."

"For God's sake, Mother."

"I'm sorry."

"What else did they ask?"

"They wanted to know where you kept your Bronco—if you had a storage unit or something. I told them I didn't think you owned it anymore."

"Why would you tell them—" Gavin closed his eyes and took a breath. His next words came with a sharp point. "They have access to my vehicle registrations. They know I own a Bronco. Don't try to help!"

"I'm sorry." Amy seemed to choke on a cry that was trying to get out. "I'm your mother. I'm supposed to help. That's my job."

"It's okay, Mom. I didn't mean to yell." Gavin paused to let his aggravation settle. "Was there anything else?"

"They wanted to know if you ever wore a beard."

Something cold ran through Gavin's chest. A beard? Why would they ask about that? He grew one after high school to try to give shape to his rounded chin. He'd hated the way it itched, and he'd hated the way it filled his shirts with dandruff. Still, he kept it for a while because he'd liked the way it put bones into his gelatinous face.

Then came the night he ran into Eleanora Abrams again.

He hadn't seen her since he left for Indiana. After high school, he started his photography business and got hired to take pictures at some fraternity's Halloween party. He went, dressed as the Phantom of the Opera.

He had been working for about an hour before he saw her, dressed as a nurse, her uniform short and tight. At first, he wanted to throw up. His second reaction was to hide. But as he circled the room, his camera flashing away, a dark confidence took root. With the mask and the beard hiding his features, he walked up to Eleanora and snapped her picture. She thanked him and gave him a smile that assured him that she had no idea who he was.

That's when a plan began to form, one that involved the GHB left over from his night with Lila Nash. It had been tucked in a boot in the back of a closet, where it had continued to call to him.

After the party, Gavin quietly followed Eleanora back to her apartment. She would, no doubt, head to the bars that weekend—it's what college girls did, especially girls who filled out their costumes as well as Eleanora did. When she left her apartment to hit the clubs that Saturday, Gavin was waiting and followed her.

He'd dressed as a pirate that night, his face barely recognizable in his own mirror. The club they went to had a camera at the entrance, so Gavin kept his head lowered, even though there would be little chance that he could be identified dressed up as he was. He watched Eleanora from a safe distance, gauging the pace of her drinking, watching for an opportunity. When it came, she had no idea what was happening.

It didn't take long before Eleanora's movements turned sluggish. As he expected, the drug made her queasy, and she made her way to the restroom, her friend—dancing with a man in a zombie costume—oblivious to Eleanora's plight. Gavin positioned himself near the restroom, and when she came by, he offered to help, carefully hiding his lisp. In her befuddled state, he easily coaxed her out of the bar, getting almost to his Bronco before her legs gave out and he had to carry her.

Gavin shaved his beard off the next day.

Now, as Gavin stared at the screen and his mother's confused face, he ran through all the possible reasons why a detective might ask about his beard, and the only answer that came back to him was *Eleanora*.

He leaned in to the screen to get his mother's undivided attention. "What did you tell them about my beard?"

His mother's confusion turned to concern. "I said...I said you used to have one, but not for a long time."

"Did they ask you anything else about it?"

"They wanted to know what year you had it."

"What did you say?"

"Gavin, what's wrong? Why do they want to know about your beard?"

"Mother! What did you tell them?"

"I said you shaved it off about six years ago."

CHAPTER 33

Lila was packing up to leave work when she saw the text from Niki Vang. *Do you have a minute?* It had been two days since they went to the Fifth Precinct together, and the message caught Lila by surprise. They decided to meet in the courtyard of the Government Center again.

"I just wanted to give you an update," Niki said as she took a seat on the bench. "I called some of Gavin Spencer's teachers and classmates in Indiana. Seems he doesn't stand out in a crowd. Some didn't remember him at all, and the few that did needed me to mention his lisp before they remembered. As for graduation, I don't have anything more than what you found. It appears that he was the photographer at the ceremony, although the only proof of that is that the photos are attributed to him."

"So his alibi stands?"

"It's possible he had someone take pictures for him, and he then sent them in. I asked if he walked across the stage to get his diploma, but no one remembers. I'm trying to track down his roommate from that year, but the guy's out of the country. His alibi might be a load of crap, but right now we have nothing to put him anywhere near Uptown that night."

"I appreciate you looking into it."

"I also did a search of John Aldrich's family tree, at least what I could find online. There's nothing to suggest that he's related to Gavin Spencer, and neither is he friends with him on social media—but then again, other than the website for his photography business, Gavin's pretty quiet online."

"I didn't expect...I mean, all these years of wondering, and then this guy with his lisp comes along." Lila looked around the courtyard, the way she sometimes did when the memory of that night breathed with life. Would there ever be a day when that feeling of being watched died away? "It's not easy...knowing they're still out there."

"I'm not giving up," Niki said. "The statute of limitation hasn't run, so I'll see what I can do. In the meantime, is there anyone I can talk to about John Aldrich? Maybe someone who knew him back then?"

Lila almost said Sylvie's name but stopped herself. Of course Sylvie knew John back then. He had been her boyfriend, even though he treated her like shit. He had tried to kiss Lila at that party in Uptown, even though he knew Sylvie was there. But John had been Sylvie's only love, which was probably why she forgave him everything—and married him.

According to the police reports, Yates had talked to Sylvie eight years ago and gotten a strong shot of venom for his effort. Niki Vang would have no better luck. There was only one path to get to Sylvie, a path beset by rot and risk, a path that filled Lila with dread. She pushed the notion away as soon as it formed. Instead, Lila told Niki that she would try to come up with a name or two. The lie of omission made her chest tighten.

* * *

That evening, as Lila and Joe ate delivery pizza, he asked her why she was being so quiet. She shrugged him off, saying, "Hard day at the office." Later, he caught her staring into space as they watched TV, and again asked what was on her mind. She lied once more and said, "Nothing."

In bed, after Joe fell asleep, Lila stared at the ceiling as the memory of those last months with Sylvie looped in her mind. Over the years, Lila had been judicious in what she told Joe about her.

She'd told him about meeting a Sylvie Dubois in kindergarten, and the way they bonded over dolls and crayons. She'd told Joe about the Christmases—she would run to Sylvie's house after opening her presents to show her best friend what Santa had brought. And Lila had even shown Joe the secret handshake they'd devised, which was little more than a fancy game of patty-cake.

But she'd never told Joe how their friendship had ended. She had come close so many times, walking up to the edge of that precipice only to wither at the sight of the drop.

Sylvie had been Lila's anchor in those years when cootie shots gave way to stumbling compliments and awkward flirtations. They'd sat on the swings at the park and talked about the boys they would date once they got to high school. They'd planned their homecoming and prom dances—double dates, of course—but when the time came, the boys only wanted to go with Lila.

As they'd rounded the turn into their junior years, Lila could see her friend slipping away. That was about the time that Sylvie met John Aldrich. Lila was happy for Sylvie but sad that John gave Sylvie a reason to pull even further away from Lila. The true split in their friendship, however, began when Lila saw a side of John that he'd kept hidden.

It had started with glances, short flashes of eye contact that pulled the corners of his mouth up into a grin. Then came the jokes and the comments, thinly veiled flirtations that popped up when Sylvie wasn't around. Lila tried to tell Sylvie about John's flirting, but it went horribly wrong, and by the end of senior year, they rarely spoke to each other.

Then came the night that drove a stake into the heart of their friendship.

Lila was at a party, drunk enough that driving was a risky proposition.

John was there without Sylvie, who'd had to work her waitressing job. John had focused his attention on Lila, and at the end of the night, offered to drive her home—in her car—just to be a nice guy. And Lila let him.

In the aftermath, Lila convinced herself that John had planned the whole thing from the beginning. He'd coaxed her to play drinking games at the party. He had been the one to park at the end of the block instead of in front of Lila's house. He had been the one to kiss her first.

She remembered thinking at the time that if she gave in to John, she could prove to Sylvie once and for all what kind of jerk he was—a rationalization that would not survive in the light of the sun. It didn't occur to Lila until she sobered up that her act did more to show who she was. Faithless. Cold. Monstrous. Lila had betrayed her best friend, and eight years later, the thought of that act still made her sick.

Lila had told herself that she would confess her sin as soon as she saw Sylvie at school, but the opportunity came and went. It wasn't until after lunch that things came to a head. A classmate had seen Lila and John leave the party together and told Sylvie. When Sylvie confronted John, he confessed, putting the blame entirely on Lila, painting her as the villain, saying that Lila all but attacked him in her car that night. With the reputation Lila had built up for herself, his lie was one that Sylvie easily believed.

When Sylvie confronted Lila in the hallway, her eyes were red from crying but alive with rage. She walked up to Lila, spat in her face, and said, "When they called you Nasty Nash, I stood up for you." Then Sylvie walked away and never spoke another word to Lila.

A great many bad things had happened to Lila in her lifetime, but what she did to Sylvie—she had been the one to commit that sin.

As Lila lay beside Joe, remembering what she had done to Sylvie, tears began to etch their way down her face. She eased out of bed and went to the living room to sit on the couch, wiping her tears and her nose on the sleeve of her T-shirt, the words of Niki Vang echoing in her ears. *We need to talk to someone who knew John back then.* If anybody would know about John's friends—one with a lisp—it would be Sylvie.

But to ask her those questions, Lila may as well just come out and accuse John of rape. It wasn't hard for Lila to see that side of him, but Sylvie's walls would be thick, especially now that they were married. She would be protective and vicious.

Lila dreaded facing her old friend, but she could no longer turn away from where this path led. How could she? As a prosecutor, she would ask others to make this kind of sacrifice. Sadie Vauk fought her way out of a river and was willing to face Gavin Spencer, laying herself bare before twelve strangers and a judge. How could Lila ask that of Sadie if she wasn't willing to face her own ghosts?

Lila yearned for the comfort of her bed and Joe's arms. She longed to have her mother's talent for ignoring the ugly parts of life. She wanted to look into her broken mirror and see only those fragments that pleased her—ignoring the shards with blood on them—but she knew that she didn't have that right anymore.

CHAPTER 34

It had been four years since they found Virginia Mercotti floating in the Mississippi River, but unlike Eleanora Abrams, Virginia hadn't been seen with any suspicious men in the hours before she went missing. She had been nineteen years old, and the investigators could only say that she had left her night class at Minneapolis Community College around nine p.m. and never made it back to her home in northeast Minneapolis.

She lived with her brother, Arnold Mercotti, and his wife, Lisa, in a house that used to belong to her parents. Arnold had been eighteen when their parents died in a car accident. He dropped out of school to raise his twelve-year-old sister.

Virginia's file was thinner than Eleanora's but mirrored it in that Virginia's body was also found in the river, fully clothed, with no ligature marks or defensive wounds, and with extensive postmortem injuries. She showed signs of sexual trauma and had inconclusive levels of GHB in her system.

Niki had called ahead before driving to the Mercotti home, and was greeted at the door by a plain woman in her midtwenties who wore a melancholy smile—Arnold Mercotti's wife.

"Arnold's upstairs, washing," the woman said as a way of inviting Niki in.

The house was clean—a childless clean—no toys shoved in the corners, no sippy cups by the sink—and the only ambient sound came from the pipes. The woman led Niki to a kitchen table and offered her a seat.

"Can I get you something to drink? Water? Juice?"

"I'm fine," Niki said, sitting down and laying her notepad on the table. The sound of running water stopped and heavy footsteps moved across the floor above them before coming down the stairs.

Arnold was a big man, not muscular or fat, but large. He wore a Vikings jersey, blue jeans, and work boots, the entire ensemble splashed with patches of black asphalt. Niki knew from the file that he worked on a road crew, having passed up a junior college football scholarship so he could raise Virginia.

When he saw Niki, Arnold paused at the door to the kitchen and said, "Are you here to tell me that Gavin Spencer killed my sister?" He walked to the table, turned a chair around backward, and plopped down, his eyes on Niki the whole time.

Niki choked back her surprise and said, "I'm here to look into your sister's case." She slid her business card across the table to Arnold. "Tell me about Gavin Spencer."

"A couple weeks ago I read about some asshole who threw a woman in the river. I was only half paying attention and didn't think much of it at the time, but then I get your call today. I think to myself, *It's been four years since Ginny's death—why would a detective be coming out here?* That's when I remembered the story about the asshole. I looked it up and read it again—and it clicked. I've met Gavin Spencer."

Arnold nodded to his wife. "Lisa, you wanna grab those pictures?" Lisa left the kitchen and Arnold turned his attention back to Niki. "You read Ginny's file, right?"

"I did."

"So you know that I raised my sister after our folks got blindsided by a truck."

Lisa walked back into the kitchen and set down a small stack of four-by-six photographs, one in a frame.

"I think I did a pretty fair job, for the most part," he said. "Ginny was an easy kid—smart and funny as hell. And we were close. We were like a team, Ginny and me. And then Lisa came along."

Arnold put his hand on his wife's and gave a small squeeze. "We started dating, and I worried that Ginny might feel left out, like a third wheel or something. But no, she loved Lisa almost as much as I did—like they were sisters. The three of us...we were a family, as close as any, I 'spect. I always planned on asking Lisa to marry me, but I thought I'd wait till Ginny finished college."

Arnold paused to smile at the memory before he continued. "Then one day, Ginny and me were watching TV—Lisa was out somewhere—and Ginny just up and asks me why I hadn't proposed. I said I didn't have a good reason for it, so I told Ginny I'd do it just as soon as Lisa got home. Well, Ginny called me a lunk-head and took over the operation. She planned my proposal so that I'd do it right. It was her idea to take Lisa to the park down at Minnehaha Falls. That's where Lisa and me had our first kiss. Ginny said I should propose in that same spot, so that's what I did."

Arnold picked up the photos and held them tightly in his thick hands, as something dark and cold filled the air around him. He looked at the pictures and swallowed hard.

"It was her idea to hire Gavin Spencer. He was supposed to walk behind Lisa and me, like he was just another tourist. There's this rise in the path, just before you get to the falls. I was gonna stop there and get down on one knee, and Spencer would take the picture."

Arnold handed Niki the picture on the top of the stack. Crooked and slightly out of focus, it showed Arnold kneeling down, a tiny box in his hand. Both he and Lisa faced the camera—Arnold looking angry and Lisa confused.

Niki turned the picture over. *GVS Photography.*

"He screwed it up. Right as I got down on my knee, the dumbass tripped and fell. Not only that, but when he fell, he yelled, 'Fuck!' You believe that? Ginny hired him to capture a magical moment, and he hollers 'Fuck.' He was on his side when he took that. I hadn't even asked Lisa to marry me yet. I had the ring out, and here we are looking at that asshole lying on the ground behind us."

Arnold handed Niki the picture that was in the frame. It was a shot from a vantage point above the falls looking down on Arnold and Lisa. This one was taken the very second that she saw the ring. Lisa's hands were moving up to her face as if in surprise. Even from that distance the photographer had caught Arnold's nervous smile.

"Ginny was waiting on the bridge above the falls with a picnic basket and champagne—that was part of her plan. She took that picture with her phone, snapped it a split second before that dumbass fell on the ground."

"How long after the day in the park did Virginia go missing?"

"About a week and a half. When the cops asked if I knew anyone who might want to hurt her, it never occurred to me. I mean, sure, Ginny was mad. She showed him the picture she took with her phone and told him she wasn't gonna pay him."

"If it's all right with you, I'm going to take these with me."

Arnold pointed at the shot Ginny took from the bridge. "Can I get that one back when it's all done? That picture means a lot to me."

"I'll get a copy made for you," Niki said as she slipped the picture out of its frame.

Arnold looked at Niki's card, then at her. "Detective Vang, this man—Spencer—he took something important from us. At my folks' funeral, I knelt down beside their caskets and made a promise." Arnold folded his hands together to stop them from trembling. "I told my mom and dad that I'd take care of Ginny. I swore I'd protect her. She was a good kid. She was beautiful and kind and..."

A tear left his eye and traced a ragged path down the big man's cheek. "She didn't deserve what he'd done to her."

He wiped the tear away and looked hard at Niki, his anger turning his face red. "You put that evil son of a bitch away, Ms. Vang. Lock his ass in prison till he rots, because if you don't, I'll put him in the ground. I know you're a cop and I shouldn't be saying it, but if he walks, I'll kill him."

CHAPTER 35

Sylvie lived in a carbon copy of the stick house she had grown up in. Two stories, rust on the corners of the gutters, the exterior in need of both paint and elbow room—a far cry from the mansion she dreamed about as a child.

Lila remembered a sleepover back when they were still young enough to enjoy the glow-in-the-dark stars glued to Sylvie's bedroom ceiling. They lay in Sylvie's bed, their pajamaed bodies angled slightly so that their heads touched, and they talked about babies, and weddings, and the houses they would live in when they grew up. Lila's house was a simple thing, but it had a big yard, and a driveway long enough that you wouldn't be able to hear cars as they drove past. Sylvie, however, dreamed of marble floors and walk-in closets and backyard pools, a fantasy heaved upon the poor girl from birth.

It had been Sylvie's mother who encouraged those impractical dreams. It was Sylvie's mom who taught her to say her name with that silly French accent—Sylvie Jacqueline Dubois—when everything else Sylvie said came from the hollowed-out throat of a Scandinavian. It had been her mother who entered Sylvie into Little Miss beauty pageants only to complain when she placed no higher than a participation ribbon. And it had been her mother who sent Sylvie out every Halloween dressed as a Disney princess, Sylvie's head filled with dreams of a glass slipper—but that slipper would never fit her foot.

Lila thought about those dreams now as she parked her car in front of Sylvie's house, which leaned half a bubble off-plumb and had pieces of plastic taped over the upstairs windows to keep out the winter chill.

Lila hadn't called before going there. She didn't know what she would have said and doubted Sylvie would have taken the call anyway. Lila stayed in her car for several minutes, watching the house, waiting for some sign of life to push her to that next step. When she spotted a little boy playing in the fenced-in backyard, Lila got out of her car, walked to the door, and knocked.

Footsteps approached, the soft padding of bare feet, and Sylvie opened the door. Was it anger Lila saw on her face? Confusion? Disgust? The woman looked as though she had just bitten into a bitter seed. "What are you doing here?"

"Hi, Sylvie."

Sylvie said nothing.

"Been a while, huh?"

Still no answer. Sylvie wore sweatpants and a T-shirt, the attire of a woman not expecting company. She'd cut her hair short since high school, had put on a little weight, and her face seemed older than the eight years it had been since they had last seen each other.

"I was hoping we could talk," Lila said.

"You don't own a phone?"

"I didn't think you'd answer."

"I wouldn't have."

"Can we talk?"

"We're talking now, aren't we?"

"Come on, Sylvie."

Sylvie looked over her shoulder as if to inspect the cleanliness of her house, then pointed at two camping chairs on the front porch and walked past Lila.

They sat down and Sylvie remained silent, waiting for Lila to say something. When she finally spoke, Lila looked at her feet. "I never got the chance to say I'm sorry. You have no idea how much it's bothered me—what happened..."

"What happened? You make it sound like some kind of accident. What happened was you screwed my boyfriend—the man who is now my husband."

Sylvie's words burned a hole inside of Lila, who could do little more than nod in agreement.

"You hurt me," Sylvie said. "You hurt me more than I thought anyone ever could."

"I know, and I'm so sorry."

"I never understood." Anger flashed in Sylvie's eyes as she spoke. "You had everything. You were pretty...and smart. It all came so easy for you. John was the only thing I had that was mine. He loved me, not you, but you couldn't let that be. You had to take him, too."

"What I did...I don't expect that you'll ever forgive me. But I wish you would. You were my best friend—my only friend. I was a different person back then. I was messed up in so many ways. I don't deserve it, I know, but I'm asking for your forgiveness."

Sylvie stared out at the street, looking at nothing in particular, as though thinking through the steps of a dance she had all but forgotten. The seconds ticked away slowly and quietly as Lila waited for her friend to find a sliver of who they had once been, before the fall. When Sylvie finally spoke, she did so in a low, somber voice that seemed to have clawed its way up from a great depth. "We were all different people back then."

The little boy that Lila had seen playing came running around the corner of the house, stopping when he saw Lila on his porch. He had Sylvie's blond hair but John's sharp features. "You have a son?" Lila acted surprised, not wanting Sylvie to know that she had been staking out the house.

"Dylan, come here," Sylvie said. The boy, maybe five years old, stepped onto the porch, sliding a hand under his runny nose.

"Hello, Dylan," Lila said, holding out a hand for the boy to shake. He turned into his mother's side and buried his face in her shirt.

"He's shy," Sylvie said, putting a protective hand on her son's head.

"He must get that from John," Lila said the name before she could stop herself, and it felt wrong coming from her lips, as though she hadn't earned the right to speak it just yet. But once it was out there, Lila decided to push on. "How is he?"

Sylvie sat up a little straighter. "Dylan, go inside and wash up."

The little boy eyed Lila as he shuffled into the house.

"He works at the airport," Sylvie said. "Should be home pretty soon, so you should probably go."

That struck Lila as unfair. John had been a willing participant in every step of Lila's treachery. He had been just as unfaithful to Sylvie as Lila had been. In fact, despite what Sylvie believed, he had been the pursuer. He had been the one to lean across the console and kiss her first.

Lila let the injustice of that memory pass as she tiptoed back to the question she needed to ask. She would have preferred a little more time to ease into it, but that didn't seem to be in the cards. "There's something I've been wondering. Do you remember anybody from high school with a speech impediment?"

The question came as an awkward shift, and Sylvie looked at Lila with the same agitated expression she wore when she'd first seen her at her door. "What are you talking about?"

"Nothing, it's just...I have this vague memory of this guy with a lisp, kind of a flashback, really."

"Flashback?"

"It's like I remember him but I don't. I thought maybe you might."

"I don't know anyone like that."

"I might have met him at that party in Uptown. Maybe he was a friend of John's."

"A friend of—" Sylvie's eyes bloomed with understanding. "I don't fucking believe this!" She stood up and backed a step away from Lila. "Haven't you done enough?"

"What?" Lila's half-hearted plea fell to the ground with the heavy thud of a lie.

"You bitch! You come to my home, talking about being sorry, when all you really want is to drag my husband back through that sewer. I have a family now."

"That sewer—as you call it—is my life."

"John had nothing to do with it."

"I never said—" Lila stood, but kept her distance. "I just want to know what happened to me."

"What happened is—John didn't touch you that night. He left that party with me."

"He told the police that he left alone. Why are you lying for him?"

"It doesn't matter. He didn't touch you. He didn't rape you. Quit accusing him. Just leave us alone!"

"You were my friend. Why don't you care?"

"I *was* your friend!" Her words came out like the snarl of an angry dog. "That was before you fucked my boyfriend—before you sent the cops after him for something he didn't do."

"How do you know he didn't do it? Did you ever ask him? Did he ever talk about it?" Lila could feel her anger getting the best of her.

"You need to leave. Now!" Sylvie looked at Lila but pointed to the street.

Just then a silver SUV turned in to the driveway, John Aldrich behind the wheel. He parked and stepped out. "What the fuck's she doing here?"

"Leaving," Sylvie said, her eyes fixed hard on Lila.

Lila stepped past Sylvie, absorbing the heat of the woman's stare, and walked down the porch steps.

John hadn't aged well, having put on a good twenty pounds of girth while losing an inch of hairline. Lila paused at the bottom of the steps for only a second, but that was all it took for John's face to turn red and hot. "You get the hell off my property, you bitch," he yelled at Lila.

He said more after that, stammering as he struggled to find ever-greater insults to hurl at her, but Lila had stopped listening, filling her head with numbers as she counted her steps back to her car. *Ten. Nine. Eight. Seven. Six. Five. Four. Three...*

Once inside, she started the engine and pulled out from the curb, nearly hitting a truck passing by. John and Sylvie stood in their yard, shoulder to shoulder, John's face red as he continued his tirade, Sylvie simply glared at Lila, letting her husband speak for both of them.

Lila could barely breathe as she fought to keep it together. She had failed in spectacular fashion, and it took all of her strength to keep her eyes from filling up with tears. Sylvie had pledged her loyalty to a man who might be Lila's rapist. She was willing to lie for him. For better or worse, she had chosen his side—truth be damned—and now Lila understood that Sylvie, a woman who had once been like a sister to her, would defend John to the end.

CHAPTER 36

Leo Reecey tried to convince Gavin that they should waive his Rule Eight hearing, telling him that the proceeding was superfluous. Then the pompous ass felt the need to explain that *superfluous* meant "meaningless," as if Gavin were just another cave-dweller in an orange jumpsuit.

"The Constitution grants you the right to an attorney," Reecey said. "The Rule Eight is there to make sure that step gets accomplished. You have an attorney, so going in for a Rule Eight is a waste of time."

But Gavin Spencer did not waive his hearing. He had prepared for this moment over the course of years, sitting alone in his big house, watching true crime reruns, his mind racing with half-formed ideas about how he'd do things better—perfecting his craft. How many nights had he awakened with plans and ideas wriggling like larvae inside his temples, twisting and grinding at his brain until he was forced out of bed to do more research—the only task that could calm the squirming.

Like an obsessive in search of order, he'd scoured the internet for information. What charges could they bring? How did the jail system work? He studied the rules of evidence and criminal procedure with more vigor than some law students. *Know your enemy* became his mantra.

What Gavin understood about the Rule Eight hearing was that he would be brought to court and given an opportunity to meet with his attorney away from the strict procedures of the jail. This was his chance to be in reach of a cell phone.

At the courthouse, a guard walked Gavin and another inmate, Bart, to a cinder block holding cell where Gavin expected to find Leo Reecey waiting. The attorney wasn't there. Bart gave a stab at conversation, but Gavin ignored him, focusing instead on the image of choking his lawyer until the man's eyes filled with blood. Two hundred thousand dollars and the son of a bitch couldn't bother to get to court on time. *God damn that lazy bastard.*

Three minutes before the start of the hearing, the door clanked with the sound of a heavy metal key. "Spencer, you're up." The jailer walked Gavin through a side door and into the courtroom, where Leo Reecey sat at counsel table.

"Where the hell you been?" Gavin hissed the words into Reecey's ear as he took a seat.

"Traffic," Reecey answered.

"Bullshit," Gavin whispered. "Did you bring the phone?"

Reecey put a finger to his lips as the bailiff announced Gavin's case.

"Did you bring it?" he asked again with more insistence.

Reecey hesitated for a second and then gently tapped his breast pocket.

Gavin relaxed, and let his gaze track across the floor to the prosecutor's table, where Lila Nash sat askew in her chair, looking at him, her expression perplexed, as though she were trying to shove a square memory into a round hole. Gavin averted his gaze and leaned back in his seat.

Judge Anderson asked Reecey if his client wanted the complaint read. Reecey declined.

"Would you care to address the issue of bail?" the judge asked.

Reecey looked at Gavin, who shook his head.

"No, Your Honor."

"Are there any omnibus issues to be addressed?"

Reecey stood. "I filed a motion requesting a contested hearing on the issues of probable cause and the admissibility of the lineup. We do not waive our right to have the matter heard in an expedited fashion, as my client is in custody."

"Would the State care to be heard?"

Lila Nash rose to her feet, swallowed as if nervous, then said, "Defendant's motion is boilerplate, Your Honor." Her words came across weak—a scared mouse. "We understand that the only issues going forward are those set forth on the record today. We further assume that all other issues will be waived. If counsel for the defense has any additional issues, we ask that he serve us with specific notice in a timely fashion."

The judge looked at Reecey, who had retaken his seat. "We're litigating just those two issues, correct, Mr. Reecey?"

"Correct."

"If you decide to raise any additional issues, you'll need to give proper notice to the State."

Reecey partially stood to give his answer. "Absolutely, Your Honor."

When the hearing adjourned, Gavin glanced sideways to watch Lila Nash as she put her papers into a briefcase. When she left counsel table, she passed within a few feet of Gavin and their eyes met, the contact lasting less than a second. It was enough for Gavin to see the flicker of turmoil. She was struggling.

Would she piece it together? Even if she did, they would still need to reopen the case, find the string that connected Gavin to Lila. He had taken great care to create an alibi, bribing his roommate to take pictures at graduation, pictures that would mark Gavin present at the ceremony. The move seemed over the top, but even back then he was a craftsman. They had nothing that could put him anywhere near Lila Nash that night. Plus, they would need to find Jack—Jack, who was on the outside, free to carry out what needed to be done to keep them both out of prison.

Reecey stood, as if to leave the courtroom, but Gavin grabbed him by the sleeve. "We need to talk."

Leo's nod seemed reluctant, but he said to the guard, "I need a minute with my client."

The jailer walked them through the side door to the holding cell, where Bart awaited his turn in court. The jailer swapped Gavin for Bart, telling Reecey, "When we're done with his hearing, I'm taking 'em back. You got till then."

In the room, Gavin took a seat at the lone table, his back to the door, and beckoned the phone from Reecey with a flick of his fingers. Leo hesitated but handed it over.

"I'll need a paper clip," Gavin said.

"What? No."

Gavin opened a texting app on the phone.

"Give me a goddamned paper clip. I'll give it back."

As Reecey dug through his briefcase, Gavin typed in a phone number from his memory, and then—typing in proper sentences, as he despised the crude language of textspeak—he wrote:

Hi, Jack. It's Gavin. Surprise! By now you've read about me in the papers. I'm famous. You will be too unless you do as I say. You will receive two letters signed G—one long, one short. It is VERY IMPORTANT that you do exactly what I tell you to do. Write down the first letter of each sentence. The short one will give you your instruction. You will want to refuse, but that would be a grave mistake. The long letter will lead you to a private URL. There you will find a file. Open it. Do what I say or I promise I will send you to prison. I am not fucking around!

Send.

The jailer rapped at the door, causing Reecey to jump. He gave a thumbs-up to the jailer at the window and held his other hand out to Gavin, wanting the phone back.

"Paper clip," Gavin whispered as he deleted the text from the phone.

Reecey slid the paper clip to Gavin. "You're gonna get me in trouble."

Gavin ignored him, punching the tip of the paper clip into the side of the phone, popping open the SIM card tray. He tapped the memory chip out of the tray and closed it again.

The door clanked as the jailer pushed the key in.

"Give me the goddamned phone," Reecey said.

Gavin slid the phone and paper clip to Reecey and slipped the SIM card under his tongue.

The door opened. "Let's go, Spencer."

Reecey—with tiny droplets of sweat clinging to his temples—stood with Gavin and walked out of the cell. Before they parted company, Gavin leaned in to Reecey and whispered, "Next time, don't be late."

There was a lightness to Gavin's step as he walked back to his cell. Eight years ago, he'd been the sidekick, following Jack's instructions, but he had learned a lot. He'd learned that leaving a witness alive leads to regret and sleepless nights. He'd learned that he had a darker appetite than even Jack could have suspected. But the true lesson that Gavin carried out of that bean field was that he could do it better if he did it on his own.

Now the tables had turned. Jack would be the one taking orders. Gavin pictured Jack sitting down to decipher the secret messages, a child's code, really, the letters and symbols in the longer correspondence taking Jack to a file stored on the server hidden in his mother's garage attic.

It disappointed Gavin that he wouldn't be there to watch Jack open that file. Gavin had been the photographer who took that picture of Lila, the one that made its rounds among her classmates, but there were other pictures from that night, pictures that Gavin had sworn he had destroyed. One of those captured Jack's smiling face. That little taste of blackmail should leave no doubt as to just how serious Gavin was. Jack would obey, or the picture would be turned over to the police.

Jack would then decipher the shorter of the two correspondences—thirteen letters that, when laid in order, read KILL SADIE VAUK.

CHAPTER 37

Lila had prepared for Gavin Spencer's Rule Eight hearing by staring at his mugshot. She propped it over a framed photo of Joe on her desk, and looked at it to try to dull the flutter in her chest. Something about him had seeped through the cracks of some very thick walls, finding a place where lost memories clung to life, and the more she stared at the picture, the more convinced she became that it was the man, not his lisp, that shook her.

But at the same time, she knew the research on false memories and eyewitness fallibility. The Innocence Project had secured the release of over three hundred inmates, some on death row, who were put there by eyewitness testimony. Those victims probably felt certain as they accused their attackers, yet DNA would later prove those men to be innocent. She'd studied the infamous preschool abuse cases where subtle cues from an investigator steered children to describe things that never happened. How could Lila not have glimpses of Gavin in her memory? She'd been obsessed with him ever since that first day in court.

She put the mugshot back in the file, closed it, and set off for the courtroom.

On the way, she recited legal responses she could make to Gavin's attorney, simple, throwaway phrases she'd memorized in case the panic returned. Andi had, no doubt, assigned the hearing to Lila to scrutinize her performance. Dovey would probably be there too, waiting for Lila to stumble. But the person Lila didn't expect to see that morning was Sadie Vauk.

She sat on a bench in the corridor, her fingers twisted together on her lap. Lila recognized her from the pictures in the file and took a seat beside her.

"Sadie?"

Sadie looked at Lila with guarded eyes, and didn't answer.

"My name is Lila Nash. I'm one of the prosecutors working on your case. I'm handling the hearing this morning."

"Oh, hi." Sadie tried to smile, but it looked forced. "I thought you might be one of his lawyers."

"You don't have to be here, you know."

"I know. That lady from your office, the . . . um . . ."

"Witness coordinator?"

"Yeah. She said I didn't have to come—that nothing much was going to happen, but . . ." She shrugged instead of finishing her thought.

Lila saw a slight tremor in Sadie's hands, and she wanted desperately to hold those hands until the tremor passed. But despite seeing Sadie as a kindred soul, she and Sadie were strangers.

"You want to see him in handcuffs," Lila said. "You want to know that he's not out there anymore—that he can't get to you."

Sadie cocked her head, her eyes widening slightly as though Lila had just read her thoughts. Then she looked away and lightly nodded. "I see him in my dreams, his hands . . ." Sadie shuddered. "And when I wake up, I . . . I can't seem to convince myself that I'm safe—that he's not coming to kill me. So I thought . . . if I could see him, just for a second or two . . . if I could be sure."

"You don't need to be afraid, Sadie." The words felt like something she needed to say, even as they tasted like a lie on her lips.

"But now I don't think I can go in there. I'm terrified."

Lila thought for a moment and an idea came to her. "Follow me."

She led Sadie to the bailiff's station, the office that organized security for the whole building. A bank of monitors lined the wall, one for each courtroom. And each monitor could switch views between cameras. Lila explained the situation to the chief bailiff, and he agreed to let Sadie watch the hearing on the monitor.

"You can go to the hearing if you want to," Lila said. "But if you would be more comfortable, you can watch it from here. There's no sound, but you'll see Gavin in his jail scrubs and handcuffs. It's up to you."

"I'd rather watch from here," Sadie said, and in her words, Lila thought she could hear a small measure of calm. "I'm just not ready to see him face-to-face. Not yet."

Lila reached out, wrapped her fingers around Sadie's hand, and gave a light squeeze, holding the connection long enough to let Sadie know that she meant it when she replied, "I understand."

Lila left Sadie in the bailiff station and walked to court, where Dovey once again sat in the back pew. She counted her steps to counsel table, the silent tick of numbers easing the anxious swell that bloomed in her chest. This case had her walking on the edge of a blade.

Lila didn't look at Spencer when they brought him in, but after he was seated next to his attorney, she couldn't stop her head from turning. The man was wholly unremarkable, a guy who could blend into any backdrop, disappear in a crowd with the ease of a copperhead in a bed of dead leaves. He was the kind of guy that Lila would never have noticed or remembered. But isn't it the copperhead you don't see that bites you?

Then Spencer glanced at her, and Lila could remember his voice, how his name fell heavy and wet from his lips. A chill touched her lungs and began to spread through her chest like frost. The panic had returned.

Judge Anderson opened the hearing by addressing Spencer's attorney, which gave Lila a moment to thaw. She ran through her script in her head, paying enough attention to what Mr. Reecey was saying to know which of her practiced responses would fit. When the time came, she stood, humming softly to herself to prime her vocal cords. She swallowed, and then spoke in a voice much softer than she had intended. "Defendant's motion is boilerplate, Your Honor."

She cleared her throat and continued, yet the tremble behind her words made her sound like a child caught misbehaving. She was glad that Sadie couldn't hear the shake in her voice. Had Dovey noticed? Had Andi? If she had, she didn't show it. Lila finished her points and returned to her seat, relieved to have kept the panic at bay behind its paper-thin veil.

At the end of the hearing, when she vacated the table to make room for the next prosecutor, she knew she would pass within a few feet of Gavin Spencer. He turned his face up to watch her leave, and she willed herself to look at him, hold the focus of his stare. She studied him with the eye of a poker player. He turned her stomach, but she wanted to take in all that she could in that brief moment. She wanted to shake something loose, some new crumb. What was it about this man that turned the air around her so thin?

Next, Lila passed Dovey, who looked at her with an expression of mock indifference, but Lila could see calculations moving behind his eyes. He had come there to confirm that she was weak, and she may have given him what he wanted.

As she rode the elevator back up to her office, she continued to think about Gavin, and an idea occurred to her. If his lisp could trigger a bad memory, whisking her back to those stolen hours, might not a different trigger unlock a more helpful memory?

Sean Daniels had been at the party in Uptown, but Lila hadn't remembered that until she went to the Fifth Precinct with Niki. After hearing his name she could now see him sitting on the back porch, alone, arms folded as he watched her. The image was fleeting, but it was real, and it had been resurrected from dust. Could there be a way to let more of that light in?

Lila had yet to face so much about that terrible year. Like a woman standing blindfolded on a cliff, she once believed that if she never took a step, there could be no fall. Others had looked for her attackers and failed, so Lila told herself that there was nothing more to be done.

But that wasn't true, and now she knew it. The scars those men inflicted reached deep into her soul, and if an answer were to be found, it would have to come from her. She would have no peace as long as those men walked free. She needed to shake loose some new memories, helpful memories, and the place to start would be the home she lived in on the night she tried to kill herself.

⋆ ⋆ ⋆

Charlotte Nash lived a mere twenty minutes away from Lila, but Lila hadn't been to see her mother since Christmas. She would phone on her birthday and Mother's Day, but those conversations held no more depth than a shadow, both mother and daughter making a point not to veer off happy topics.

Charlotte Nash had been tireless in her fortifications against the winds of change. She lived in the same house where Lila grew up, went to the same church she had when Lila was a child, and played canasta on Saturday evenings with the same group of friends. The house had the feel of a time capsule, with Lila's high school speech medals still hanging next to a family picture taken just before her father left for the Philippines—where he took up with a woman whose name remains unspoken in Charlotte's house.

"You should have called," Charlotte said when she answered the door. "I'd have made cookies or something."

It was by design that Lila hadn't called. It was the best way to keep the visit short.

Charlotte backed into the house with Lila in tow. "You should've brought Joe. I haven't seen him since Christmas. I wish you'd bring him around more often. I have some lemon bars left over from canasta. You want a lemon bar?"

"No, Mom."

"It's so good to see you." Charlotte sat on a couch and pointed to the love seat with her eyes as if to direct Lila to sit, but Lila stayed on her feet, causing Charlotte's cheek to twitch ever so slightly.

"I happened to be in the neighborhood," Lila said, knowing that her mother would appreciate the lie. "Thought I'd stop by and say hi."

"You look healthy."

That was Charlotte's preferred compliment for Lila. It came from the heart but had its roots in a time when Lila didn't look healthy—a time when the overdose and the cutting had turned Charlotte's daughter into a tattered scarecrow of a girl.

"I can't stay long, though." Something Lila said to her mother on most of her visits. "I was hoping—"

"Are you sure you don't want a lemon bar?" she said. "I have more than I can eat."

"I'm sure, but I was hoping to take a look—"

"You can take some home for Joe. He loves my lemon bars. I think he ate a whole plate full at Christmas?"

"Remember that metal box I used to keep in my sock drawer, the one with my high school stuff in it?"

A tinge of worry materialized in the lines around Charlotte's eyes. "What do you want with that?"

"I need to look at something. I know you took it out of my room."

"I haven't seen you in months."

"It's important, Mom."

"What could be important about a bunch of old pictures?"

"I'm trying to figure some stuff out."

"Stuff?"

"I want to look at those pictures."

"Oh, honey, are you sure that's wise? I mean..." Charlotte didn't finish her thought; she didn't need to. Lila knew what followed. *I mean, won't that make you gloomy again? Won't that take you back to those days when you tried to kill yourself?*

"Can you please tell me where it is?"

Charlotte knotted her hands together. "I put it in my bedroom...for safekeeping."

Lila headed toward the steps. "Where?"

"The closet, but...shouldn't you let sleeping dogs lie?"

Lila paused to look at Charlotte. She pictured her mother writing the letter to Dr. Roberts, and forging Lila's signature. The image summoned an army of harsh words and made her cheeks get hot, but Lila held her tongue. She shook her head, and walked upstairs in silence.

Lila found her box in the closet, shoved beneath a winter quilt. She pulled it free and took it to her old bedroom. The key to the box was where she'd left it, taped behind the back side of her sock drawer.

Among the relics, Lila had kept four decks of wallet-size photos bound together by rubber bands, one stack for each year of high school. She pulled the band off her senior photos and started flipping through the faces, searching for a memory that might not even exist. She turned each picture over to read the inscriptions on the back, their sentiments starting with phrases like *Hey wild thing,* or *To my favorite party girl,* or *Remember that crazy night we...*

About halfway through the deck, Lila had to pause. She had never noticed it before, but not one of her classmates offered a sentiment that ran deeper than the swill in the bottom of a shot glass.

She returned to her task, her mood much heavier than before, and when she came to Sean Daniels's picture, she read his inscription: *Every dog has its day*. Quirky was how she'd described Sean to Detective Vang, but this seemed to blow past quirky and land in the area of full-blown creepy. Lila put his photo into her pocket to show Niki.

Then she came to Sylvie's senior picture, a remarkable shot that caught her friend in a beautiful light. Sylvie stood waist-deep in a calm lake, the water so still that it captured her reflection on its surface. Sylvie's hair danced off her shoulders, and her eyes burned like flames behind her smoky eye shadow.

Lila turned the picture over and read: *To my friend.*

Sylvie's freshman picture looked up at Lila from the top of another stack, and Lila pulled it free to read the inscription on the back.

You are my sister
My deepest soul
My best friend
You make me whole.
I love you forever.

Lila put the two pictures side by side. How had Lila gone from being Sylvie's *deepest soul* to barely being her *friend* in four short years? It occurred to her that maybe her mother had been right about letting sleeping dogs lie.

In the bottom of the box Lila found a stack of pictures of her and Sylvie that she'd collected over the years, spanning from when they were children splashing in a plastic pool in Sylvie's backyard to the time right before the fall of their friendship. Lila began slowly going through them, the memories bringing tears to her eyes.

Deep in the stack, Lila came upon a picture taken the fall of their senior year. Lila had forgotten about it, but now recalled the day when Sylvie invited her to play Frisbee golf with John and some of his friends. In the picture, Lila and Sylvie sat on a picnic table, talking. In the background, John chatted with a guy whose face Lila recognized, but whose name escaped her. He didn't go to their school, but he and John had some connection—relatives, maybe.

Something about the man's smile caught Lila's attention. She studied his face and then closed her eyes to try to remember. She could see him standing in a doorway, pointing at her. He had a beer in his hand and a sharp grin that gave his face an elfish quality. She remembered body odor and a sense that she disliked the man. Had he been at the party in Uptown?

Lila turned the picture over and read Sylvie's handwritten notes: *Me, Lila, John, and Silas.* Silas. Lila closed her eyes and repeated the name, trying to conjure something, but the only thing that came to her was the word *jackass.* Silas Jackass. She could hear John calling him by that name. She looked at the picture again and it came to her. Silas Jackson—John's cousin. She'd only met him a couple times and had always been less than impressed. Did he have a lisp? She tried to remember if she had ever heard him speak, but got nothing.

She put that picture in her pocket and locked the box shut before returning it to its rightful place in her sock drawer, the key tucked once again into its hiding place.

Downstairs, Charlotte was waiting for Lila, holding a plate of lemon bars on her lap. She looked at her daughter with a smile that begged to start the visit over. But all Lila could think about was that her mother had lied to Dr. Roberts and ended Lila's sessions. And now she wanted to eat lemon bars and pretend that none of that had happened—as if it didn't matter.

A powerful anger churned in Lila's gut, kicking to get out. Lila stopped at the bottom of the steps, her eyes fixed on her mother, who tapped the edge of the plate with a nervous finger.

"I used to make these for your father," Charlotte said. "To be honest, I've never been a fan of lemon bars. I don't know why I still make them. So... if you want one."

The sadness in her mother's eyes hobbled Lila's anger. Lila wanted to have it out with Charlotte, but the woman seemed so small and weak, a wounded deer barely able to look into the eyes of the wolf. Lila couldn't do it. So she left, saying nothing.

CHAPTER 38

Niki and Matty met with Detective Tony Voss in an interview room of the Homicide unit to go over the Chloe Ludlow case. He had been the lead investigator when it went cold.

Voss placed his box of evidence on the table. "You think your boy might be good for Ludlow?"

"There's a pattern," Matty said. "White female, fully clothed, no defensive wounds, no ligature marks, but evidence of a sexual assault. COD is drowning, river water in the lungs and GHB in their systems—how are we doing so far?"

"Batting a thousand," Voss said.

"Our boy's a photographer," Niki said. "Ring any bells?"

"A big one. Ludlow was an aspiring model, last seen getting into an older black SUV outside of her apartment. She told her roommate the guy was a photographer who offered to do some headshots on the cheap."

"Did the roommate have a name for the photographer?" Niki asked.

"No. And we checked Chloe's phone records, but the number she'd called was a burner. Cell towers had it moving all around the metro, so we figured he kept the phone off and only returned her calls while driving, so we couldn't trace it to a house."

"What about the SUV? Anything more specific than black?"

"Not according to my notes. I got the feeling the roommate didn't like Chloe all that much. We didn't rule her out as a suspect, but the photographer made more sense."

"What's her name—the roommate?"

Tony dug through the file and pulled out a report. "Alice Kempker. A kindergarten teacher at the time. They became roommates when Ludlow answered an ad, and by the time she went missing, the two were at each other's throats. Kempker stayed at her boyfriend's house that night, so it's possible Chloe came home after the photo shoot. Her body wasn't found right away."

"Did you get any surveillance footage of the SUV?"

"No cameras at the apartment. We looked around the neighborhood, but didn't find anything. Does your guy drive a black SUV?"

"An 'eighty-six Bronco—black," Niki said. "But we haven't been able to locate it."

"Are we talkin' serial killer?" Tony asked.

"We have four possible victims," Niki said. She thought about saying five, adding Lila's name to the list, but the connection remained far too remote. "Same MO and all with a nexus to a photographer named Gavin Spencer."

"He's an awkward guy," Matty said, "a loner with a bad speech impediment. Probably uses his camera as a way to interact with people—women in particular."

Niki added, "He's independently wealthy, so we think he uses the photography business to scout victims. Once he chooses a girl, he figures out her habits. Then, when the opportunity presents itself, he drugs her, assaults her, and drowns her in the river."

Matty said, "He covers his tracks like nothing I've ever seen. We think he puts them in the river off Nicollet Island—lets them float over the falls. He uses the falls like...Excuse the analogy, but he uses the falls like the agitator of a washing machine—lets it hammer away the evidence."

Tony tapped the lid of the box. "We weren't even sure she was murdered," he said. "She drowned, so we couldn't rule out an accident or suicide."

"But we have Gavin Spencer now," Matty said. "Virginia Mercotti hired him for her brother's marriage proposal, and Spencer took a picture of Eleanora Abrams at a party two days before she turned up dead."

"And get this," Niki said. "Spencer went to homecoming with Eleanora Abrams when they were freshmen in high school. Things got ugly." Niki slid a police report across the table to Voss. "Abrams ignored Spencer all night. They went home separately, but not before Gavin's mother threw a cup of hot coffee on the girl."

Voss leaned back in his seat and read the report, whistling when he came to the part about the hot coffee. "This guy's a piece of work—so is his mother."

"Did the name Gavin Spencer come up anywhere in your investigation?"

"No, and we grilled the roommate pretty hard. She just happened to look out the window when Chloe got into the vehicle—that's the only reason we know it was a black SUV."

"What about a speech impediment?" Niki asked. "Spencer has a bad lisp."

Voss churned through the pages of his report. "No mention of it, but Kempker never met the photographer or heard him speak."

Niki shook her head. "It's him. I know it is."

The three detectives sat in silence for a few seconds before Voss spoke. "Did you know that Ted Bundy was the top suspect for multiple murders in Utah and Washington while he was killing women in Colorado? They knew he'd done it. Had a ton of circumstantial evidence, but nothing that got them to court."

"Like we got here," Matty said.

"Exactly."

Niki said, "We can put him with Eleanora and Virginia within days of their abductions, but not on the actual day. We can tie a black SUV to both Chloe and Sadie Vauk, but can't prove that it's Spencer's vehicle. Sadie puts him in her salon chair right before her memory goes blank, but to get a guilty verdict, the jury has to believe a woman with no memory."

"Lots of smoke," Voss said, "but no fire."

"We're so damned close," Niki said. "I feel like we're trying to open one of those Chinese puzzle boxes. If we could look at it the right way, we'd see the answer."

"I wish I had more to give you," Voss said. "But the file was thin from the get-go."

Niki stared at the picture of Chloe Ludlow, young, beautiful, but with intelligent eyes that added depth to her features. Niki put the three faces side by side in her mind.

Matty and Tony continued talking, but Niki shut their conversation out. Something was wrong—missing. She couldn't put a finger on it, so she lined up their fact patterns in her head, carefully running down the list, checking off where they matched up—and where they didn't.

"Chloe's MO doesn't fit," she said.

The men stopped talking and looked at Niki.

"Her modus operandi is missing a step." She paused to give Matty an opportunity to see the flaw.

When he didn't say anything, she continued as though the pause had been for her to organize her own thoughts. "Mercotti and Abrams both met Gavin Spencer several days before they were abducted. For Sadie Vauk it had been twenty-four hours. In each case, though, he used that time to stalk them. Chloe Ludlow went missing after climbing into that black SUV, but where was the first meeting? When did Spencer make her a target? If he plans his abductions, then he and Chloe would have met before he kidnapped her."

Niki jabbed a finger at Chloe's picture. "We know his MO. Maybe we can work backwards and put them together before her death. We might get lucky."

Then Niki turned to Tony. "Any problems if I go have a chat with Ms. Kempker?"

"I think you should," Tony said.

CHAPTER 39

Lila spent the drive home searching her memory for Silas Jackson and finding the cupboard all but bare. She dug deep and kept coming back only to an image of him standing in a doorway, pointing at her. She couldn't shake the belief that that image came from the party in Uptown. But surely if he had a lisp, she would have remembered it by now.

Lila walked into her apartment to find Joe in the kitchen, a pot full of water on the stove in front of him.

"About time," he said. "I've been holding up dinner." On the counter nearby lay a brown paper wrapper, unfolded, with four king crab legs inside. "Thought I'd make something special."

"Okay," Lila mused. "It's not my birthday . . . so, what's up?"

"Can't a guy make an incredibly expensive meal for his girl without there being some hidden agenda?"

"Yeah, but you're Joe Talbert, so out with it."

Joe shrugged and smiled. "Fine, but someday I'm gonna make crab legs just to confuse you."

"I'm listening."

Joe took a beat, and then said, "They want me to go to North Dakota to cover that pipeline story."

Lila hadn't expected that to be Joe's answer. He'd mentioned the possibility, but she'd let it fall off her radar. "So this meal is a peace offering?"

"I was thinking distraction, but peace offering works too."

"When do they want you to go?"

"In the morning. The protest is heating up. There've been some skirmishes already, so—"

"So, that's your cue to go?"

"They don't harm reporters. They need us to get their message out to the world. That's the point of a protest."

"Still..."

"I made biscuits."

"Well, in that case..." The words came with a pout.

"It's a big story, Lila, and no one else is covering it—not nationally, at least. I could really make a name for myself."

"How long will you be gone?"

"Few days—maybe a week—I don't know."

Lila then noticed the suitcase pulled from the hall closet. "You've already made up your mind?"

"I thought the crab legs made that clear?"

Lila didn't smile. The timing seemed all wrong, but Joe had no way of knowing that. She had kept him in the dark about so many things.

He must have sensed her reticence because he stopped joking. "I'm only getting this assignment because Liz is out on maternity leave. I'm the new guy, remember? This is a great opportunity. I'll stay home if—"

"No. I want you to go. It's not like you're going to the Antarctic—it's North Dakota. Just...be careful."

"Absolutely." Joe pulled her into his arms and gave her a kiss. "I'll do my story and get back here as soon as I can."

"Do me a favor, though?" Lila said.

"Anything."

She looked deep into his eyes and said, "Make sure you set the timer on those crab legs. You overcooked them last time." She pulled back, gave him a wink, and walked out of the kitchen, picking a pile of mail off the countertop.

She flipped through the mail on her way to the bedroom and came across a letter from the Minnesota Board of Law Examiners. The results of the bar exam weren't due for another month at least. Confused, she unsealed the envelope with her fingernail and read.

Dear Ms. Nash,

The Minnesota Board of Law Examiners has been notified of a concern regarding your application for admission to the Minnesota Bar, having to do with your character and fitness to practice law. Specifically, the Board had been informed that your answer to question 4.37 (b) may be inaccurate or incomplete. That question asked:

Do you have, or have you had within the last two years, any condition, including but not limited to, the following:

b) A mental, emotional, or behavioral illness or condition that impairs, or has within the last two years impaired, your ability to meet the Essential Eligibility Requirements for the practice of law set forth in Rule 5A of the Rules for Admission to the Bar?

It has been brought to the Board's attention that a supervising attorney in your office has concerns about your fitness pursuant to Rule 5A. The informing party has written an affidavit and has provided documentation of a prior involuntary hospitalization and suicide attempt. While the hospitalization falls outside of the two-year look back, a more recent in-court event has raised concern.

To address this concern, the Board asks that you submit a letter from a treating therapist regarding your mental and emotional fitness as well as a letter from your supervising attorney as to your fitness to handle the stresses of the practice of law. We will then set up an interview with you.

Please understand that this letter is not intended to make

your path to admission to the bar more difficult, but rather to ensure that any and all concerns are properly addressed. We look forward to working with you to address this issue.

Respectfully,
Lucius Wolterman
Director of Character and Fitness Evaluations
Minnesota Board of Law Examiners

"What the fuck?"

"What's wrong?" Joe asked from the kitchen.

Lila read the letter again. "That son of a bitch!"

Joe walked in and Lila handed him the letter. "He's going after my license."

"Who is?" Joe started reading.

"Frank Dovey."

"How?"

"You have to pass a character and fitness requirement before you can be admitted to the bar. Dovey must have sent something to the board."

"I don't understand. What do they mean by 'in-court event'?"

Of course Joe didn't understand. She'd never told him about freezing in court, or about Gavin Spencer's lisp. She hadn't told him about her trip to see Dr. Roberts or the afternoon she spent with Niki at the Fifth Precinct. She wasn't ready to tell him yet, and she couldn't tell him now that he was about to leave for North Dakota.

"I had a little stumble in court, that's all. It was nothing, but Dovey was there. He has me under a microscope."

"How would he know about you being in the hospital?"

"As a prosecutor, he has access to my case from...that night. All he'd have to do is type my name into the system, and there I am." Lila remembered the list at the Fifth Precinct. He had done much more than just type in her name.

"And Dovey is using that to..."

"Stop me from becoming a lawyer."

"That stuff is so old. Can he do that?"

"I don't know. Maybe." Lila's knees softened, and she sat down on the bed.

"That's bullshit," Joe said.

"He's head of the division. If he doesn't stop me from getting sworn in, he could transfer me—or fire me. The only reason he hasn't done something like that already is he knows he'll catch heat when Beth comes back."

"I'm not going to North Dakota," Joe said.

"What?"

"It's not right."

"You're going to North Dakota, Joe Talbert." Lila spoke in that same tone her mother had always used when she put her foot down.

"It's no big deal—"

"I'm not letting that asshole ruin your career too." She turned to Joe and cupped his face in her hands. "I appreciate the thought—I really do—but I want you to go to North Dakota. Write a great story, and when you come back, I'll have this all figured out—I'm not sure how, but it's my dragon to slay." She kissed him to keep him from saying anything more, and when she drew back she added, "I'm a legal ninja Jedi, remember?"

That brought a smile to Joe's face. Lila smiled too, even though, in her heart, she felt the weight of her lies. How was she going to be okay? She pulled Joe in, wrapping her arms around him before he could notice the deception in her eyes.

CHAPTER 40

Alice Kempker wanted to meet with Niki Vang at a coffee shop rather than her house. Niki was more than happy to oblige, choosing a café on Southeast Main Street, a quaint and quiet place with outdoor seating where they could enjoy the morning sun and watch people stroll by on the cobblestone sidewalk. The place had a true old-town feel and just happened to look out over the Mississippi River at the spot where Chloe Ludlow would have floated by after Gavin Spencer killed her. The roar of St. Anthony Falls was unmistakable in the distance.

Niki arrived before Kempker and used the time to walk to the river, slipping into Spencer's world. Niki imagined Spencer's panic as he'd watched Sadie Vauk start to swim, heading toward the power plant instead of the falls. In trying to reach her he would have driven right past where she now stood. Niki looked at the line of shops and bars along Southeast Main and saw no cameras. The Sex Crimes unit had already canvassed the area for witnesses and footage, coming up with only a single shot of the Bronco, taken from a distance.

She could see the cameras of the power plant a block away, white bobbles stretching out at the corners of the building. With the abundance of outdoor lighting at the power plant, Spencer would have seen the cameras as well and ended his pursuit. He might have even parked within a few yards of where Niki now stood to watch the security guard pull Sadie from the river. Niki had scoured the footage from the plant and found nothing more than the shine of headlights in the periphery.

As she listened to the water churning in the distance, a woman in her late twenties hesitantly approached. Niki recognized her from her driver's license photo as Alice Kempker.

"Ms. Kempker, I'm Detective Vang."

Kempker held out a hand to shake, but extended no pleasantry beyond that, not even the slightest hint of a smile. The woman had pretty eyes, green like olives, but the rest of her carried a plainness that murmured, *Leave me alone*.

A waiter showed the two women to an outdoor table and took their orders for coffee.

"I appreciate you meeting with me like this," Niki said. "I only have a few questions."

"I don't know what more I could say that I didn't tell your people two years ago."

"I understand, but we're taking a fresh look at the case. Just making sure that nothing was overlooked."

"Fine, what do you want to know?"

Niki opened her pad of paper. "Chloe had been your roommate for how long?"

"About six months."

"How would you describe your relationship?"

"We got along all right." The answer came across as snide.

Niki paused, tapping her pen against the pad as she contemplated the path the interview was about to take. "Alice, it's really important that you be straight with me. We have reason to believe that Chloe's attacker had killed before, and might kill again. I need honest answers from you today."

"Are you calling me a liar?"

"Tell me about your relationship with Chloe Ludlow."

"She was a..." Alice pursed her lips as though to hold back some venomous words. Then she proceeded in a calm tone. "I should've never taken her in. We were a bad fit from the start. She was pretty and tall—not that I have anything against that, but the way she flaunted it in my face. I had a boyfriend, and she'd walk around the apartment wearing next to nothing—prancing in front of him like she was trying to seduce him or something. I told her to stop, but she'd just say, 'I can't help it if boys like to look at me.' She had no respect for other people—none at all."

"Was Chloe seeing anyone—a significant other?"

"She saw lots of men, but significant? She used to bring guys to the apartment, guys she met at the bars. Sometimes she didn't even remember their names. What do you expect when you act like that? I told her she was gonna get herself in trouble, acting that way. I told her—I said, 'One of these days, you're gonna run into the wrong kind of guy and end up dead.' I said that to her. You can't live that way and not expect consequences."

"You make it sound...like you think she deserved what happened to her."

"I'm not saying she deserved it, but what'd she expect?"

Niki said nothing for a moment, letting the rumble of St. Anthony Falls fill the silence. "Hear that?" Niki asked. "The falls?"

Alice looked toward the river but didn't answer.

"He drugged Chloe—then he raped her. When he was finished, he drove her over there to Nicollet Island. She was probably groggy because he wanted as little of the drug in her system as possible when he dragged her down to the river and held her under the water. When he was sure she was dead, he pushed her out to let her wash over the falls. The pull of the undertow probably held her body at the bottom of the spillway for a while—minutes, hours, who knows—before letting go. Chloe might not have lived up to your expectations, but nobody—*nobody*—deserves what happened to her."

Alice looked at her hands on the table and didn't say anything.

"Now, I want you to tell me everything you can remember about Chloe's last days in that apartment. Don't leave a single detail out, no matter how small. Did you meet the man who came to pick her up?"

"No, I was in my bedroom. He never came in."

"Prior to him coming to pick her up, did she say anything about him?"

"We weren't exactly speaking at that point."

"In the days or weeks before her death, did Chloe have any event she attended where there might have been a photographer—a wedding or a modeling job?"

Alice paused to think. "Yes. She did some modeling. She was behind on rent and got this gig at...I think it was the auto show. Is that in March? She paid her March and April rent with the money."

Niki pulled out her phone and sent a text to Matty. *Check auto show for connection to Chloe.* "Did she say anything about meeting a photographer at the auto show?"

"Like I said, we weren't talking much, but maybe. I think it was later that week when she said something about getting some headshots done."

"And you told Detective Voss that the guy drove a black SUV?"

"He pulled up in front and honked, and that irritated me. I went to the window and saw Chloe get into this older, black— It was big, but I wouldn't call it a truck either."

Niki pulled up a stock photo of a 1986 Chevy Blazer she had on her phone. "Did it look like this?"

"Yeah. It could have been one of those."

Then Niki pulled up the same year model of a Ford Bronco. "What about this?"

"They look alike to me, but yeah—except it had that mark on the door."

Niki perked up. "What mark?"

"A faded spot. It looked like a big teardrop. I told the other detective about it—at least I think..." She looked at Niki as though struggling to find a memory. "I'm sure I did."

"There's nothing in the file about any tear-shaped mark. Can you describe it more?"

Alice held up her hands to indicate a circle the size of a turkey platter. "It was about this big around, with... you know, a point at the top like it was a tear or a drop of water. The truck was black and the mark was kind of gray, like it had faded where there used to be a sign or something."

"And you're sure about this?"

"I'm sure I told that detective about it."

"Did you see the driver?"

"No. The windows were tinted."

"Anything else you remember about the truck or the guy?"

Alice took a minute to think on it then shook her head no. "I'm sorry, I can't remember anything more."

Niki's phone dinged. "Excuse me a second." She opened the text and found a set of pictures from Matty. High-end cars—Bentleys, Ferraris, Porsches—all parked inside the Minneapolis Convention Center. Niki had seen those pictures on Spencer's website, filed under corporate events, but hadn't given them much thought. Matty's message read:

Spencer shot publicity for
T.C. Auto Show. March 15-17.
1 week before death.

There would be surveillance footage and photos from that event, tons of them. If they could find one with Chloe and Gavin together, it would fill in Gavin's MO. It wasn't a lock, but this was a step in the right direction.

She put her phone away. "Chloe's gig, was it the Twin Cities Auto Show?"

"That sounds right."

"Did Chloe say anything about meeting a photographer at the auto show? Think hard."

Alice stared out at the river, the unrelenting thunder of the falls permeating the air around them. "I can't remember. I'm trying—I really am."

"I know." Niki slid her business card across the table. "Keep thinking on it, and if you come up with anything more, promise me you'll call."

"I will."

As Niki stood to leave, Alice said, "You were right, you know... about Chloe not deserving what happened. I feel bad for saying what I did."

Niki wanted to say that it was okay, but it wasn't. It wasn't okay that Alice Kempker let her dislike for Chloe interfere with the statement she gave Tony Voss. She left out the identifying stain on the side of the Bronco. It might not have changed things, but who knows? If she'd mentioned it, maybe Sadie Vauk wouldn't have gone through her ordeal. So Niki only gave Alice a slight nod.

"Did I give you anything that helps?"

"I hope so," Niki said.

CHAPTER 41

Lila carried the letter from the Board of Law Examiners into the Government Center that Friday morning, rolled up in her hand as she made her way past the metal detectors. She'd brought it to show Andi, hoping that there might be a way to get around Frank Dovey, although in the back of her mind she knew there wouldn't be. That letter had been the reason Dovey ordered Andi to go through him with Lila's personnel matters. It was simply one more maneuver in a much longer strategy.

When she arrived at the bank of elevators, she spotted Frank standing amid a handful of people waiting to go up. Lila stayed back away from Dovey's view. Two elevators dinged their arrival at the same time, one in front of Dovey, the other closer to her. The small crowd divided toward the two open doors, and once inside, Lila pushed the button for the twentieth floor. The doors juked as if wanting to shut, but popped back open—and Frank Dovey stepped in.

He stood close enough to Lila that she could smell the cutting scent of his cheap cologne. The doors closed and didn't open again until they got to the fifth floor, where Lila stepped off to let a woman behind her out. As she waited, it occurred to her that if she stayed there—let the doors shut—she could take a different car up to the twentieth floor.

After the woman stepped out, Lila didn't move to get back in the elevator, and neither did she walk away. She watched the bottom of the elevator door, paralyzed, waiting for it to close, to make the decision for her. And when it didn't, she looked up to see Frank Dovey holding it open. He gave a subtle wave of his free hand as if to gesture her back into the car, and she obeyed.

Floor by floor, people stepped off, the crowd thinning until after the fifteenth floor only she and Dovey remained. And when the doors closed, Dovey turned toward her and stared, no words, no sound, just like he had done before. Lila wanted to say something, but her words died at the back of her throat. Her breath quickened, and her palms began to sweat.

She started counting, the numbers ticking down as the elevator crept upward. *Ten, nine, eight, seven*... The elevator crawled so slowly that Lila had to slow her counting. *Six... five... four... three... two...*

A ding announced their arrival on the twentieth floor. *One.*

Lila's heart thumped inside of her chest hard enough that Dovey should have been able to sense it. Her fingers still clutched the letter from the Board of Law Examiners, now damp from the sweat of her fists. She should confront him. This was her chance, but she wasn't ready. She hadn't prepared for this.

After the doors opened, he continued to stare at her, making no move to exit the elevator, and when she glanced up at him, he wore the smile of a man on the verge of saying, *Checkmate*. Lila stepped past him to exit the elevator, and as she did, he murmured, "You don't belong here."

Lila pretended that she hadn't heard him, both furious and sickened by her cowardice—and counting her steps in measures of ten.

By the time she got to her office, Lila was so mad that she could barely think. She wanted to punch something, but she also wanted to curl up on her chair and cry. She would allow neither. The heat in her chest reminded her of that rage she felt when she'd first drawn a razor blade across her arm. *Stop it!* Lila grabbed her desk and squeezed her anger out through her fingers. *You're not that girl anymore.*

As her anger slowly eased, Lila saw Sadie Vauk's file lying on the desk in front of her. She and Andi were scheduled to meet with Sadie that morning. She picked it up and opened it to the pictures: Sadie after they'd pulled her from the river, weak and confused, Sadie showing the cuts and bruises she got as she clung to the rocks, Gavin Spencer at the lineup, the beauty salon where he'd kidnapped her, his house where they were sure he'd taken her. With each new image, the thought of Frank Dovey faded further into the distance until it was little more than a dust mote floating on the breeze.

Her job—her calling—was to put monsters like Gavin Spencer in prison. If she let Frank Dovey sidetrack her from that mission, she would become someone small, like him, focused on her career and not on her job.

It would take time for Dovey to drive her out, and she vowed to use that time to make a difference. When the time came for her to leave, she would walk out with her head held high.

* * *

Just before nine a.m. Lila walked into the conference room, carrying three bottles of water and a legal pad, as it was her job to write down everything Sadie would say, to give to Leo Reecey. Prosecutors can keep no secrets from the defense.

Sadie entered a few minutes later and the two women shared a smile that went deeper than a simple hello. The black business suit Sadie wore aged her at least five years, and with her hair pulled back she could have passed for a colleague instead of a victim. She seemed far more calm and self-assured than she had at the Rule Eight hearing, but when Lila shook her hand, Sadie's fingers still held a tremor.

"How are you feeling?" Lila asked.

"Good, I think—a little nervous."

"There's no reason to be nervous," Lila said. "This is simply an opportunity for you and Ms. Fitch to meet—get to know each other. That's all."

"She wants to see if I'm gonna flake out."

"Not at all," Lila lied. "She doesn't want your first conversation to be when you're on the witness stand."

"It's okay. I'd want to meet me too, if I was her. To be honest, I'm scared to death. I don't know how I'll react...when I see him face-to-face. I'm scared I won't be able to talk."

"You'll do fine." The words Lila spoke made her feel like a hypocrite.

Andi entered the conference room in that get-down-to-business way she had, barely managing to fake a smile as she introduced herself to Sadie. She took a seat directly across from her witness, and in a cold, toneless voice asked Sadie to detail what she remembered from the wedding. Sadie answered with nothing more and nothing less than what she had told Detectives Vang and Lopez. Andi asked Sadie about the evening at the salon, and Sadie again followed the script she'd given the investigators.

Then Andi asked about after the salon.

"I wish I could tell you that I remember Gavin Spencer raping me, but I don't."

"Just tell me what you do remember, if anything."

"It's not so much a memory as...Well, it's more like a dream. I was tired. I couldn't keep my eyes open. And I felt sick to my stomach. I remember sleeping, and I think I remember the hum of a car, but I'm not sure."

"Were you in the car?"

"I must have been. It was like when I was a little girl and my dad would take me on a drive. The hum of the tires just kind of made me want to sleep."

"Anything after that?"

"I have a vague memory of walking to the river, but that doesn't seem right. Why would I walk to the river?"

"Was he with you then? Do you remember anyone with you?"

"He had to be. I think that's where we were at when he said that thing about 'All you had to do was be nice.' I think that's where we were, but..." Sadie closed her eyes. "It's all so murky."

"That's okay, Sadie. You can only remember what you remember. Is there anything else I haven't asked you about, anything that might be important?"

"No." Sadie stared at the top of the table as if embarrassed by her answers.

"Do you have any questions of me?"

After a long pause, Sadie looked up and said, "Why me? Why'd he do that to me? I didn't do anything to him. I didn't even know him. Why did he think it was okay to hurt me like that?"

"I don't know, Sadie," Andi said.

"I can't sleep. I feel sick when I eat. My dad had to take off work to stay home with me." Sadie's lip began to quiver slightly. "I know he's locked up, but I still feel like someone's following me. I can't stop looking over my shoulder. I'm trying to get back to normal, but..."

Lila wanted to reach out to Sadie, hold her hand the way she had for that brief moment in the bailiff's station, but she didn't, and Andi offered the woman no comfort. Was this why Andi lived behind that cast-iron shell? Was it better to keep distance from this kind of pain? Lila hoped not. The job might one day eat her up for it, but Lila yearned to carry as much weight as Sadie would allow.

Sadie pulled a tissue from a box on the table, dabbed her eyes, and wadded it in her fingers. "Last night, I was swimming laps and...I started shaking. I kept seeing his face. I couldn't breathe." She knotted her hands into fists and spoke through gritted teeth. "I'm a good person. Why'd he rape me? Why did he think he had the right? And for what—sex? He tried to kill me because he wanted sex? How can people like that exist in the world?"

Sadie swiped the tears from her cheeks with the wadded tissue.

"I'll never be the same. I can't be. I look in the mirror and I don't see myself. I see..." She paused as the anger behind her eyes turned sad. "I see something broken."

Sadie's words found their way to Lila, passing through some door she'd forgotten to close. And in that moment, Lila hated Gavin Spencer as much as she had ever hated anyone in her life. Sadie probably believed that no one in the world could understand what she was going through—but Lila did.

Lila had lost track of the conversation but was brought back when she heard her name being repeated. Lila looked at Andi, whose face held an expression somewhere between puzzlement and irritation.

"Are you with us, Lila?"

"Um... yeah, sorry."

"So... do you have any questions for Ms. Vauk?"

Sadie looked expectantly toward Lila, the wadded-up tissue in her hand, as though waiting for something.

"No," Lila said. "I don't have any questions... except to say... things will get better. You may not believe that right now, but they do."

Sadie smiled at Lila, a silent thank-you. Andi stood, and they all followed suit.

"I'll walk you out," Lila said.

To Lila, Andi said, "I'd like you to stay for a minute." There was something cold and empty in her tone that filled Lila with dread.

"I can find my way out," Sadie said, giving Lila another small smile, this one to say goodbye.

After Sadie left the room, Andi turned to Lila and said, "What's going on? That's twice now that you've disappeared on me. Do I need to be concerned?"

Lila *had* disappeared. But Lila couldn't tell that to Andi. So instead, she pulled the letter from the Board of Law Examiners out of her pocket.

"I'm fine... but..."

"But what?"

She handed the letter to Andi. "Frank Dovey's coming after me."

Andi read the letter, glancing up at Lila about where suicide was mentioned. She finished reading and handed the paper back to Lila.

"I was hoping," Lila said, "that you might write that reference for me."

"I can't," Andi said. "Frank ordered me to run everything through him." She pointed at the piece of paper in Lila's hand. "That, I assume, is why. I may not like it, but he's the head of the division. My hands are tied."

Lila sank into a chair, the sense of powerlessness rising around her. "If I can just hold out until Beth comes back."

Andi walked to the conference room door and closed it. When she returned to Lila, Andi chewed on the inside of her cheek as if contemplating something, her eyes serious. "Lila, I'm going to tell you something, but it's confidential. You understand?"

"Sure," Lila said.

"I visited Beth in the hospital on Wednesday." Andi paused as if rethinking her decision, then said, "She's retiring. I don't know if she told Mr. Nelson yet, but if she hasn't, she will soon."

The words blindsided Lila. Within the chaos of her thoughts, one unavoidable truth rang out—she would be out of a job soon. "What should I do?"

"Don't quit." Andi sat down next to Lila. "If you let him win, you'll carry that regret with you forever. If that's where Dovey's going, make him own his decision."

"That's easy for you to say."

"Not as easy as you may think." Andi slid a hand toward Lila in a gesture that had all the makings of an offer of comfort, but she stopped short of touching Lila's arm.

"My first job out of law school was at one of the big firms. A dream job. About a year in, I caught the eye of one of the partners, but not for my talents as a lawyer. He was a married man, and, like Frank Dovey, a conniving prick. He was careful in how he tested me, and when I refused his advances, I started getting poor performance evaluations. He never left his fingerprint on anything, but after a while, it was clear my days were numbered. Just like you, I was faced with saving my dignity or saving my résumé. I left. That was twenty years ago and I regret quitting to this day."

Andi cleared a catch from her throat and sat up straight in her seat, the moment of connection slipping away. "I can't tell you what to do, but know that if you quit, it will come with a price."

"I can't even think straight right now. I feel like I'm at the end of my rope."

"You have a lot more rope than you think, Lila. If only you—" Andi stopped mid-thought, paused for a long moment as if struck by something profound, and then said, "What size shoe do you wear?"

Lila looked up, confused.

"About a six, maybe?"

"Yeah, six. Why?"

"Have you ever been to Interstate State Park up by Taylor's Falls?"

"No, but—"

"What are you doing tomorrow?"

"It's Saturday."

"My question stands."

"Nothing."

"Then meet me at the information center there, and wear something athletic. We're going rock climbing."

CHAPTER 42

Matty Lopez had earned undergraduate degrees in both accounting and computer science before turning his eye toward law enforcement. He had a gift for numbers and research, which made him a perfect fit for Niki Vang, who thrived in the open air of the crime scene. She sometimes felt guilty letting him do so much of the background work, but he kept reminding her that he enjoyed that part of the chase, so she left him to it. As they drove out to visit Gavin's mother for a second interview, Matty brought Niki up to speed on Amy Spencer.

The daughter of a mechanic from Mountain Iron, a small mining town in the heart of the iron range, Amy had managed to stay out of trouble for most of her life, with only a single arrest for underage consumption at the age of eighteen—no conviction.

But then, at twenty-two, she'd shown up in the Twin Cities when she was questioned in a case of aggravated robbery. According to the victim, Amy came on to him in a bar. After several drinks with this very attractive young woman, he'd followed her out to her car. When they got there, a man with a knife stepped out of the shadows, stole the victim's wallet, and ran off. The victim, an out-of-town businessman, told officers that Amy didn't appear to be spooked by the attack, and he'd thought it suspicious that the thief didn't take her purse. No charges were filed.

Three years later, Amy married David Spencer, a man who owned a small catering business in South Saint Paul. Gavin was born four months after the wedding.

Over the course of their two-year marriage, police visited the home of David and Amy Spencer on three occasions, disorderly conduct calls that came in from neighbors tired of the yelling and screaming. No charges were ever filed. David filed for divorce, but before the process played out, he died in a motorcycle accident. A year later, Amy shuttered the failing catering business and went to work as a hostess at the Minneapolis Club.

"That's where she met Richard Balentine," Matty said. "He was a member there."

"And Balentine is...?"

"Amy's second husband. Drowned in his own swimming pool when Gavin was twelve. Man was rich as hell, and Amy inherited the works."

"Sounds like she hit a jackpot. Was the drowning investigated?"

"They ruled it accidental. Amy said she and Richard were having drinks by the pool one night, two lovebirds celebrating the sale of one of Richard's companies. She got a little tipsy and went to bed, while Richard stayed up to finish his cigar. In the morning she found him floating in the pool. His blood alcohol was a point two six. Apparently, Balentine liked his Scotch."

"Signs of a fight?"

"An injury to the back of his head. They found blood at the edge of the pool along with a wicker footstool that had been knocked over. The theory was that he stumbled, tripped over the footstool and fell, hitting his head on the concrete. Then, groggy and drunk, he tried to stand up and fell in the pool. It's plausible, but..." Matty shrugged.

"But it's bullshit."

"Gavin called it in. I listened to the 911 tape; if it was bullshit, he put on one hell of a show."

"Why do I get the feeling that Gavin offed his stepdad?"

"Who knows?" Matty said. "He was only twelve, but the old man was drunk, so it wouldn't have taken all that much effort. Honestly, I wouldn't put anything past that evil son of a bitch."

Niki pulled the car into the driveway of a redbrick colonial with a black wrought-iron fence. The house rose two stories, with white pillars, black shutters, and enough ivy climbing its face to tell a story of old money. Now it was the home of Amy Spencer.

She had been visibly nervous when they'd talked to her the first time, exhibiting the kind of tics that liars often show: fidgeting, delayed gesturing with her hands, looking away at key points as if trying to find an answer, and filibustering—rambling on and on when just a word or two would do. They had gone there to ask a few simple questions about Gavin and his Ford Bronco, but after that first meeting, the detectives agreed that something about the woman was off.

"Why, hello, detectives. I wasn't... expecting... Um, come in."

Amy wore an outfit that probably looked great on the mannequin at Forever 21: a loose V-neck sweater over skinny jeans, and a pair of Chelsea boots, an ensemble that seemed as mismatched on her as rhinestones on a work glove. Her desperately youthful clothing seemed designed to draw attention to the obvious augmentation she'd done to her fifty-one-year-old frame.

"Sorry to bother you again," Niki said, "but we just had a couple follow-ups."

"If you'd called, though, I could have had coffee ready."

"That's okay," Niki said. "This won't take long."

Amy showed the detectives to the same room where they had convened on their last visit, a room that held a leather chaise across from two matching Queen Anne chairs. Niki and Matty sat in the Queen Annes while Amy struck a pose of nonchalance on the chaise.

Niki spoke first. "I wanted to ask you if you had any updates on Gavin's Ford Bronco. We're having some difficulty locating it."

"I haven't seen it since... Well, it's been probably a month or two, but I don't know where he keeps it."

"Where was it when you last saw it?" Matty asked.

"I suppose it was in his garage."

Niki and Matty had watched the video of Amy's jail conversation with Gavin, so they knew she was putting on a show.

"The thing is..." Matty flipped through a small notebook. "Last time we were here, you told us that he didn't own it anymore. You said..." Matty stopped flipping and read. "Here it is. You said, 'He used to own one some time ago, but he sold it.' Now you're saying you saw it a month ago in his garage?"

Amy looked at the floor near her left foot, her brow furrowing as she searched for a response. Her tells were easy to spot. "I don't remember saying that. I mean, I don't keep tabs on Gavin, so I can't tell you anything about his vehicles. He and I, we see each other sometimes—not a lot, not enough that I know what's going on with his cars. I know he's working and stuff, but, like... what he buys or sells, I don't keep tabs on that kind of thing. But I do seem to recall seeing his Bronco lately, now that I've had time to think about it—although I couldn't say for sure."

Again with the filibuster.

Niki said, "What can you tell us about his photography business?"

"Oh, he loves photography. Started taking pictures when he was just a boy."

"Does he get hired a lot?" Matty asked. He already knew the answer because he had seen Gavin's bank accounts. Gavin didn't bring in more than thirty grand a year as a photographer. The nice house he lived in was one that Richard Balentine's money bought for him.

"I suppose so. I can't really say. Like I said, I don't keep tabs on him."

Matty said, "But you still support him—financially—isn't that right?"

"Support him? I don't know..."

"You put money in his bank account every year?"

Amy put her hands together on her lap, one cupping the other. "I give him an allowance of sorts. I have means, you know."

"An allowance?" Matty said. "According to his bank records, you gave him over two hundred thousand dollars last year. I wish my parents gave me that kind of allowance." Matty chuckled to keep the mood light, but Amy didn't seem to find it funny.

"Like I said, Detective, I have means."

Niki said, "I understand you have a swimming pool. Do a lot of houses around here have pools?"

"I don't think so. We're just lucky, I guess."

"Could we see it?" Matty asked. "I love pools. Always wanted one, but... you know." He shrugged and grinned. "A cop's salary."

"I... suppose so." Amy stood. "It's this way."

They walked through a kitchen big enough to quarter an army. Beyond that, Amy led them through a set of French doors and onto a concrete patio.

Niki went to the edge of the pool. It had been sixteen years since Richard Balentine died there, so she knew she would find nothing of evidentiary value—but she looked anyway. "Has Gavin ever had any girlfriends that you know of?" Niki asked.

"I'm sure he has," Amy said. "But that's another thing I don't keep tabs on. A boy needs his privacy."

"Excuse me for saying this," Niki said, "but it sounds like you and Gavin weren't all that close."

"We're very close," Amy said, her nervousness momentarily replaced by indignation. "He's my only child. I just don't pry into his life, that's all. His affairs are his affairs."

"Do you and Gavin talk much?" Niki asked, turning from the pool to face the woman.

"I guess, maybe once a month or so."

"And he never told you about dating any girls?"

"Oh, I'm sure he told me, but I'm no good at remembering stuff like that."

Niki took a couple steps toward the wilting Amy Spencer, closing the gap to about four feet, holding Amy's attention so that she could read the woman's eyes. "Did he ever mention a woman named Chloe Ludlow?"

"Chloe Ludlow? I don't... That name doesn't ring a bell."

"It would have been about two years ago."

"No, I don't think so."

"What about Virginia Mercotti?"

"I can't say I remember that name either."

"She also went by Ginny. Would have been about four years ago."

"I don't think I can help you with that."

"Did he ever date a girl named Eleanora Abrams?"

Amy looked at Matty, then at the ground. "What's this all about, anyway?"

"Eleanora Abrams? Does that name mean anything to you?"

Amy tried to hold her gaze on Niki but failed. "Of course not." She smiled as her eyes fell away, laying bare the knots that twisted inside of her. "I told you, I don't keep tabs."

"That's strange," Matty said. He reached into his pocket and pulled out a piece of paper, then handed it to Amy. "Because I have a police report here that says you threw a hot cup of coffee on Eleanora Abrams at a homecoming dance."

Amy didn't bother reading the report. "That was a long time ago." Her cheeks turned red as she crumpled the paper into a wad and threw it to the concrete. "What does any of that have to do with Gavin now? It didn't mean nothing."

"You assaulted a fourteen-year-old girl. That's not nothing."

Anger flared in Amy's eyes. "She treated him like shit. A mother's supposed to protect her child, ain't she? And the cops didn't charge me because they saw the truth. That girl was a mean little bitch and deserved more than what I gave her."

"Is that why you lied to the police?" Niki said. "To protect Gavin?"

"You're twisting my words."

Niki turned back to the pool, walking to the edge again. "Is this where Richard died?" She looked over her shoulder and saw Amy on the verge of apoplexy. Her lip had curled up into a snarl and her cheeks blazed with color.

"You need to leave now," Amy hissed.

Niki gave Amy a soft smile, one that said, *Yeah, we know what you did.* Then she nodded to Matty and they headed toward the front door.

On the way, Niki had a thought. Gavin had an alibi for the night Lila Nash was raped, but Gavin was also a cunning little shit. Niki had no evidence that he faked his alibi, but at the same time, she was becoming more convinced he was not in Indiana that night. If Gavin was clever enough at the age of twelve to kill his own stepfather, he could surely manufacture an alibi.

Niki stopped in the doorway. "Ms. Spencer, I have one last name for you—Lila Nash. Did your son know anyone in high school named Lila Nash?"

"I told you to get out," Amy said.

Niki nodded a polite goodbye and left.

As Niki walked with Matty back to her car, she wondered how long it would take for Amy to make her next trip to visit Gavin. And more important, how Gavin would react when she gave him the list of names—especially the last one, Lila Nash.

CHAPTER 43

Lila woke up that Saturday morning, rolled over to touch Joe, and found him gone, his side of the bed cold. He had texted her when he got to North Dakota, and they'd spoken on the phone last night, but that didn't stop her muscle memory from seeking him out.

She hadn't told him about Beth Malone's plan to retire. If she had, he would have driven home, chucked the story so he could swoop in with some misguided impulse to rescue her. That was the last thing she wanted—or so she told herself. In truth, she wanted Joe there more than anything. She craved his strength. She would need him more than ever once her world fell apart.

She thought about staying in bed and dreaming about Joe, holding him in that hazy penumbra between wakefulness and sleep, and she would have had she not had an invitation to go rock climbing.

Lila still didn't understand why Andi had asked her to go. It wasn't as though they were friends. Hell, the woman had yet to crack a smile in Lila's direction. If Andi hadn't been her boss, there was no way she would have spent a Saturday climbing up the side of a bluff with her. But Andi *was* her boss, so Lila had decided to make the best of it.

* * *

Interstate State Park was a small slice of land along the St. Croix River. When Lila arrived, she found Andi waiting at the trailhead, wearing light pants, tight around the ankles, similar to the yoga pants that Lila wore but made of sturdier material. She wore a simple sports bra top that exposed a hard table of abdominal muscles, and she carried a backpack over her shoulder and a helmet in her hand.

"You're late," Andi said as Lila approached.

"You said nine, right?" Lila had glanced at her watch, which read 9:02. So it was going to be one of those days.

Andi pulled a pair of shoes from her backpack, light and colorful with hard, pointed toes. They looked expensive. "Size six, right?"

"Yeah."

Andi handed the shoes to Lila and started down the trail without any further greeting.

"We're doing what's called a top-rope climb. I'll be taking a trail up here to go to the top of the wall and set the anchor. You follow the main path until you can't go any farther. That's the wall we'll be climbing today. I'll meet you there."

With that, Andi cut to the right, taking a small path into the woods. Lila stopped, hoping to ask a few questions, but Andi was gone.

The path to the wall sloped down to the river, passing a landing where a riverboat was taking on tourists for a trip down the St. Croix. After that, the path turned rocky and followed along the bottom of a hundred-foot-tall bluff, the trail disappearing beneath fallen chunks of basalt that littered the base of the wall.

The coppery river churned a dozen feet away, giving the warm summer air an earthy aroma. Lila followed the trail until she could go no farther, stopping at the bottom of a bluff, dark and scarred with fissures cutting both horizontally and vertically like a Stone Age Tetris.

Soon Andi appeared at the top of the wall, bent over as she connected the rope to the anchor. Lila had watched a video the night before and knew that top-roping meant the rope ran through a pulley so that one person could climb while the other—the belayer—held the opposite end from the ground below.

When she stood up, Andi yelled, "Rope!" Two ends of a blue rope unfurled as they sailed down the face of the cliff. Andi then hooked the rope to a harness around her hips and slid over the side, easing herself down with the grace of a bird.

At the bottom, Andi took off her backpack and pulled out a second harness, which she handed to Lila. "This end goes in front."

Lila slipped her legs through the straps and pulled the harness on like a pair of pants. Andi gave it a jerk and then tightened the strap around Lila's stomach, shoving a hand between the padding and Lila's belly, to check the snugness of the fit. Then she inspected the leg straps, tightening each slightly to account for Lila's thinner legs.

"How's that feel?" Andi said.

"Tight."

"Tight is good. We don't want you falling out of your harness."

"Is that a thing?" Lila asked.

Andi didn't answer.

"Am I climbing today? I thought I was just gonna . . . you know, belay for you."

"Oh, you're climbing, all right. This is a figure-eight knot." Andi stretched an arm's length of rope, made a loop, and wrapped the end around and through. "Do that first, then—" Andi slid the rope through two loops on the front of Lila's harness. "Always make sure you connect through both hard points."

"Shouldn't I take a class first? I've never climbed before. I mean, I did a wall at the Y, but not—"

"Pay attention," Andi snapped. "Your life depends on doing this right. Now take this end and follow the path of the figure eight." Andi moved the rope, snake-like, through the figure-eight knot. Lila was lost.

"Is there going to be a test, because I have no idea what you just did."

"You'll just have to trust me, I guess." Andi gave the knot a yank and then took the opposite end of the rope and passed it through what Lila recognized from her brief research as a belay device, connected to Andi's harness.

"You don't have your shoes on," Andi said.

Lila hadn't thought to put on the climbing shoes Andi had given her, and sat down to swap out of her cross trainers.

"Now, before you start climbing, you'll need to plan your path. I've always found that rock climbing is a little like handling a case in court. You don't just charge in; you plan it out—have a strategy that covers every contingency. If you make a wrong turn on the wall, you'll end up under an overhang or stuck in water or mud."

Lila stood in her new shoes and pressed her toe against a rock, getting the feel for the hardness in the soul. Andi handed Lila the helmet, and as she strapped it on, Andi attached a bag of chalk to the back of Lila's harness.

"The object of top-roping is to climb to the anchor. Touch it and I'll let you down."

"And if I don't touch it?"

Andi didn't answer, but instead gave Lila a look as if she had just been insulted. Then she pointed at the bluff. "Start wherever you want."

Lila walked to the face of the wall and put a hand against it. The east-facing rock was warm to the touch, but cool in the fissures where sun didn't reach. She was about to start climbing when she remembered Andi's instruction: Have a strategy. Lila stepped back.

The place where she stood seemed the obvious starting point, the cracks in the wall rising like a ladder. She followed the ladder with her eyes to the point where it ended, about forty feet up. From there, the wall turned smooth. That route was a trap.

A second starting point angled into a corner about halfway up and looked doable after that, but then Lila noticed the trickle of water painting the rock green. There would be no way to get to the top without climbing through mud and water for several feet. It might become impossible to climb with wet shoes. Another dead end.

On her left, the wall rose with very few places to grip, but seemed to offer relief about halfway up. She followed that path with her eyes and saw every step she would take until the last ten feet, where shadows obscured her view. She decided that that would be her path. If she was going to struggle on her first climb, she preferred that it be at the lower elevation.

When she looked for her first handhold, she spotted a patch of white—chalk from previous climbers. She had chosen correctly.

Lila had no cadence to her climb. She pressed her chest into the stone and made slow yet deliberate moves. She had never gone out for sports in high school, but she could keep up with the best of them in her PE classes. Still, this climb was putting her to the test, and she hadn't gone more than thirty feet.

Andi called out encouragement, things like "Rely on your feet!" and "Your legs are stronger than your arms!" Lila looked for the chalk remains of those who had climbed before her, and even when the hold seemed too small, she put her faith in the chalk—her yellow brick road to the top.

A little over halfway, she came to a ledge where she could rest. It was the first time she'd had a chance to look down, and when she did, her stomach turned to jelly. Lila had never been afraid of heights, but she had never clung to the side of a cliff sixty feet off the ground before. Her lungs began to heave, pumping more breath through than she needed, making her dizzy.

"Oh my God," she whispered. "What am I doing? This is stupid."

"What'd you say?" Andi called up.

"I'm dizzy. I don't think…"

"Breathe like you're standing on the ground. It's the same air up there as down here."

"You sure about that? It seems thin."

"Take a moment. Look around. Find your next hold. Focus on the climb."

Next to her, Lila could see chalk on both sides of a crevice. She tried to figure out how those two smudges could possibly work together.

"You're going to have to do a lay-back," Andi hollered.

"A what?"

"That edge of rock nearest to you is called a flake. Grip it like you want to pull it toward you. Then put a foot on the wall on the other side of the gap. Pull yourself toward the wall with your hands while pushing away with your legs. The tension will let you walk up the wall to that next hold."

"I can't... I—"

"Grip the flake!"

Lila put her hands where the chalk dictated. Then she put one foot on the chalk smear beyond.

"Once you start the maneuver, don't hesitate," Andi yelled. "If you stall, you'll drain out. Just three steps and you can rest on that ledge above you."

Lila would have stopped there, demanded to be lowered back to the ground, had Andi not seemed so certain that Lila would make it to that next ledge.

Lila patted her hands with chalk, and then dusted the soles of her shoes in case they had gotten damp along the way. She gripped the edge of the flake with both hands, took a calming breath, and pressed her foot into the wall.

Just like Andi promised, the tension lifted her off the tiny ledge. She slipped one hand higher along the flake and took another step. A third step took her to where the next hold was within reach. Her fingers shook with exhaustion as she swung her left leg up to the next ledge and pulled herself onto the eight-inch shelf.

She sat on the ledge as her body trembled and burned. Adrenaline release? Exhaustion? Both? She didn't know. She could hear a quiver in the panting of her breath. The ground was so very far down. She was close to the end of her strength, but she was also close to the top.

She carefully stood up.

Behind her, the wall was as smooth as a playground slide. To her left, a crack ran upward, and on her right the wall flattened and dropped a good forty feet to a ledge below.

"You're almost there."

Lila looked up and saw that the top of the wall was a mere two feet beyond her reach. She looked for chalk marks and saw none. Had she boxed herself in? This is where her yellow brick road had led her, so what was she missing?

"There's no handhold."

"There is," Andi yelled. "You just don't see it."

Lila looked again and saw nothing.

"Go to that crack."

Lila shuffled along the ledge to the crack on her left, about five inches wide.

"You know how to play rock paper scissors?"

"Yeah."

"With your left hand, do paper."

Lila made paper.

"Now slide your hand into the crack just above head height."

Lila moved her paper into the crack.

"Go deep enough so that the rock presses against the knuckles on both sides of your hand."

Lila did as Andi instructed.

"Now make a rock."

When Lila made a fist, her hand expanded, filling the gap, pressing against the walls of the crack.

"That's your handhold—that fist. You need to jump, using your fist as a handhold and—"

"I need to what?"

"Jump. Pull yourself up with your left hand and grab the top of the wall with your right."

Lila's arms were heavy and weak. Her legs shook so badly, she thought she might collapse and fall off the ledge at any second—and Andi wanted her to jump? "I can't," she said, more to herself than to Andi.

"Don't think about it—just do it."

"No, I'm serious. I don't have anything left. I can't jump. I—"

"It's all in your head. Your mind will give up long before your body will."

"I'm shaking. My legs feel like—"

"Don't do that, Lila. Don't give up. You're stronger than that. Trust me—trust yourself!"

"I'm coming down."

"That's fear talking. Don't let your head get in the way! You know what to do, so do it."

"It's too high."

"God dammit, Lila." Andi's voice turned hard with exasperation, or maybe anger. "You get your ass to the top of that wall or don't expect to see the inside of a courtroom again—not under my watch!"

"That's not fair." Lila stared at the top of the wall, which seemed to move farther away.

"If you let your mind fuck with you like that—"

"You can't do that. I worked hard—"

"It's your fear that's stopping you. Nothing more."

Lila started counting down in her head. *Ten, nine, eight*...

"Dig in," Andi yelled. "Trust yourself."

Seven, six, five.

"Do it!"

Four, three... *Fuck it!*

She clenched her fist as tight as she could in the gap and jumped with all her strength, her hand slapping the top of the wall. She brought her other hand up and fought to pull herself chin high. The anchor lay right in front of her face, but her arms were failing her.

She threw one arm out, her wrist slapping hard against the stone. Her feet scuffed against the wall until her toe found the crack. She jammed a foot in as far as it would go. It gave her the boost she needed to hoist herself onto her elbows. She reached out, grabbed the anchor, and pulled herself over the top of the wall.

Exhausted, she lay on her back, gasping, her ears ringing, her forearms burning. Her stomach felt so tight that she wasn't sure she could move, but she managed to roll onto her side to peek over the edge. Andi was jumping up and down in celebration, a huge grin on her face.

Lila rose up on shaky legs and screamed her excitement, the sound filling the valley and bouncing back from the Wisconsin side of the river. She had done it. She had conquered the wall, and the wave of chemicals that rushed through her made her feel invincible. But there was something else, something she couldn't quite put a finger on, something that hadn't been there when she started her climb—and it filled every cell of her body.

From below, a chorus of whoops and cheers caught Lila by surprise. The riverboat, the one that Lila had passed on her way to the wall, now floated down the river, its passengers lining the rails, waving to Lila and cheering. Lila nearly exploded with exhilaration. She raised her arms above her head, punched her fists into the sky, and howled her triumph.

CHAPTER 44

Bright and early on Monday morning, Niki and Matty executed a second search warrant on Gavin's house, this time hoping to find something that might lead them to the Ford Bronco. After her meeting with Alice Kempker, Niki spent some time examining the Bronco's history through the vehicle's registration and found that it had once been owned by a well-drilling company from Glencoe. They told her that they had owned three black Broncos, all purchased new in 1986, and all sold at an auction in the mid-nineties, one eventually finding its way through a maze of used-car lots to Gavin Spencer.

According to the company, all three vehicles had sported magnetic door signs featuring the company's logo. The owner wasn't sure if the signs had oxidized the paint, telling Niki that his mechanic took care of the vehicles before auctions, but he said if there had been a stain it would have been in the shape of a drop of water.

A stoplight camera a few blocks from Bebe's Salon had caught what looked to be a black Bronco driving nearby on the evening Sadie disappeared. The grainy footage showed the vehicle at a poor angle, but Niki convinced herself that she could see a tear-shaped stain on the passenger door. Niki knew that wasn't enough—the photo was like one of those trick images that could be either a frog or a horse, depending on the viewer.

But if they could find the Bronco itself—and it had the water-drop stain on the side—the jury might buy the argument that the surveillance camera had caught a picture of Gavin Spencer on his way to abduct Sadie Vauk.

Unfortunately, the second search wasn't going any better than the first.

Niki and Matty spent the morning digging through the stacks of old bills and papers that Spencer kept under his staircase. They were hoping to find evidence of a storage unit or any place where Gavin might be able to hide a vehicle, but after three hours they'd found nothing: no receipts, no notes, not even a picture of the Bronco in the possession of a man who took pictures for a living.

A crime scene technician examined the floor of the garage and driveway for tread prints or dirt that might tie the vehicle to the soil of Nicollet Island, but found nothing.

They assigned two patrol officers to traipse up and down the surrounding streets, double-checking for surveillance footage from doorbell cameras. They all came back empty-handed. By noon, Niki had sent the tech and the patrol officers away.

Matty went for sandwiches while Niki paced through the house, trying to figure out what they had missed. How could there be no hair or DNA anywhere? The complete lack of forensic evidence would give Gavin a powerful defense argument.

When Matty pulled up, Niki joined him in his car to eat.

"When's the omnibus hearing?" Matty asked.

"In three days, and we got nothing more than Sadie's faulty memory and a couple grainy shots of what could be a Bronco."

Hearing the defeat in her voice, Matty worked through it again. "Sadie puts Gavin in the salon—so we have that. That's where she was when the amnesia kicked in. She didn't knowingly consume the GHB, which means that someone had to slip it to her. We have a man with a lisp telling Sadie that all she had to do was 'be nice'—and that was right before she ended up in the river. We have Sadie's testimony, and it's like you always say, a woman's word should be enough."

"Should be, but you know how this works. The defense attorney's going to spend an entire day asking me about all the things we *didn't* find. 'Did you find any of Ms. Vauk's hair in my client's house? Did you find any of Ms. Vauk's DNA in my client's house? Did you find any computer forensics, any GPS, any texts, any skin cells?' And I'll have to say no to all of it. All we'll have is Sadie."

Niki finished her egg salad sandwich and was taking the first bite of a cookie when a postal worker rounded the corner pulling a cart. She walked up to the mailbox on the porch, inserted some mail, and walked away.

Niki and Matty looked at each other. "Did you look in the mailbox?" Niki asked.

"Not today. Did you?"

"No."

They exited Matty's car and walked to the porch, Niki pulling letters out of the overstuffed box and flipping through them. Near the end of the stack, Niki came upon a notice that a certified letter was being held at the post office for Gavin.

"What do you think it is?" she asked.

"A mirage," Matty said. "Something to get our hopes up before it disappears."

"That'd be our luck," Niki said. "Your car or mine?"

* * *

With badges and a search warrant, they passed the tellers at the post office and went straight to the branch manager, an affable man with a Santa Claus beard who—once he saw the warrant—delivered the certified letter. Niki looked at it, grinned, and showed Matty.

Hideker's Towing and Impound.

Niki opened the envelope and read.

Mr. Gavin Spencer,

This letter is to inform you that your vehicle:

1986 Ford Bronco (blk) Minnesota plate number DSM-345 has been impounded for: **illegal parking**.

You have thirty (30) days from the date of this notice to retrieve your vehicle and pay all associated costs and fees. If you do not retrieve your vehicle within that time, your vehicle may be sold at auction or scrapped, and any proceeds from such sale will be held to cover those costs.

* * *

Hideker's Towing was a small, private operation that cleared cars away from a number of public facilities throughout the city. Because they weren't on the city's impound database, Matty hadn't gotten a hit when he ran the Bronco's plates. The company had a small lot just outside of city limits, and within ten minutes, Niki and Matty were in the office talking to Oliver Hideker.

"We towed it from a No Parking zone on campus," he said, looking at the vehicle records. "Ain't gonna be able to recover our costs, though. Strangest thing. The keys were in the ignition, turned on, and the plug for the oil pan was gone. It's like they drained the oil and left it running—like they were trying to ruin the motor or something."

"Can we take a look at it?" Niki asked.

"Absolutely."

Oliver led the detectives out to the lot. Turning down a row near the end, Niki spotted the Bronco parked nose-out about forty yards away. From that distance, the car beside it blocked her view of the door, so she quickened her pace. When the passenger door came into view, she took it in as if beholding a stunning desert sunrise.

There on the side of Gavin Spencer's black Ford Bronco was a gray patch, a stain in the shape of a tear.

CHAPTER 45

Lila spent her Monday morning drafting in-custody complaints, the charges fed by simple facts and well-written police reports. After delivering those documents to Andi, she turned her attention to a name that had been poking at her ever since she left her mother's house—Silas Jackson.

Through her office's databases, Lila found the highlights of Silas's criminal history. She could see when he was arrested, and for what, and in those cases where he had been charged, she had access to all the documents filed with the court. She found that he had been arrested at the age of eighteen for peeping into a neighbor's window where a fifteen-year-old girl slept. Two years later, he was charged with stalking an ex-girlfriend—although she later dropped the charges. The cherry on top of Silas Jackson's hot fudge sundae came a year after that, when he slipped into a bedroom at a party and touched the breasts of a woman who was passed out. A roommate walked in before Jackson could do more than partially undress the poor girl. He spent a year in prison for his act.

Reading through Silas Jackson's transgressions was like viewing a constellation one star at a time; each incident burning a new pin-point into the dark sky. But Lila could not see the whole. Where was the GHB? Where was the boldness? Nothing in his record rose to the audacity of what happened to Lila. He'd come close with the girl on the bed, sure, but guys like him were supposed to get more daring as they went along, not less.

Had he lost his nerve? Had the two men fed off each other out in that bean field, crossing a line only because they were together? And still, no mention of a lisp. There had to be more to the story, but Lila's head hurt from trying to see it.

Then, just before the clock struck noon, Ryan Kent stuck his head into her office, breaking her focus.

"Got a second?"

"For you, always. What's up?"

He came in and closed the door behind him. "Beth Malone gave Nelson her notice this morning. She's taking an early retirement."

Even though Lila had been expecting the news, it still sent a spike through her. She closed her eyes and sighed.

"I know, right?" Ryan said. "Looks like Dovey's going to be the permanent head of Adult Prosecution. I'm meeting Patrick for lunch. Wanna come?"

Lila nodded her answer, still unable to muster up words.

After Ryan left, she looked around her office. With Beth gone, Lila's departure would be in a matter of days, and her bare walls whispered, *I told you so.*

On her desk, Sadie Vauk's file lay open, a picture of Gavin Spencer staring up at her. It wasn't fair. She wanted to be there for Sadie, to sit with her before she took the stand to testify. Lila wanted to see Gavin's face when a jury convicted him, and when a judge sentenced him to prison. None of that would happen now.

Lila had no appetite, but she stood and began the long walk to the cafeteria to have lunch with her fellow newbies—knowing it could be the last time. She arrived at the bank of elevators just as Frank Dovey stepped into one of the cars. He was with Colin Nelson, and the two men seemed lost in conversation. It grated on Lila to see them so friendly together, and she waited to take the next car.

On the ground floor, Lila spotted Dovey and Nelson heading for the north exit of the Government Center. In the opposite direction was the escalator that would take her down to the cafeteria. She stood still for a moment and remembered Andi's words about making Dovey own his decision to fire her. She thought about the weight of her own regret if she were to hand Dovey her letter of resignation. And she thought of Gavin Spencer and felt a cold sting of defeat in her chest.

Then she thought of Sadie, her words whispering in Lila's ears. *Why'd he do that to me? Why did he think he had the right?* Lila wanted to join her friends in the cafeteria, but a powerful gravity pulled her toward Dovey and Nelson, who were leaving the building. She couldn't abandon Sadie—not without a fight. With no idea what she planned to do, she turned and followed the men.

Dovey and Nelson chatted seriously as they walked across the brick courtyard. At the street, they paused, as if deciding where to go for lunch. It was a beautiful summer day, a day that would normally have made Lila feel light and agreeable. But something about the sun on her face now turned her blood hot.

The men made their decision, crossing Third Avenue and entering the building on the corner. Lila followed at a careful distance. The atrium was full of glass, and sun, and people. Straight ahead of her, an escalator carried Dovey and Nelson to the second level.

At the top, they made their way into a restaurant with tablecloths and waiters in white shirts, a far cry from the cafeteria where the rest of the employees ate. But this was Colin Nelson—the big boss—having lunch with his division head. Their meal was important and weighty and would be paid for by taxpayers' money. Why not eat at a restaurant with a wine list?

The hostess seated the two men while Lila stayed outside, peeking in and pretending to look at a menu on the wall. She had no guiding force beyond the absolute unfairness of it all. Dovey had attacked her with every arrow in his quiver and all because she had rightfully beaten him in court. He had sunk so low as to use her suicide attempt against her, exposing the darkest part of her life to the Board of Law Examiners. Again, Sadie's words echoed in Lila's ears. *Why did he think he had the right?*

Why indeed, Lila thought to herself, and with those words, something took hold deep within her, a thought so powerful, it nearly caused her to stumble backward. He didn't have the right—why hadn't she realized it before? And just like that, the pieces on the chess board shifted around until Dovey's king stood vulnerable in the corner.

She started to walk into the restaurant but paused briefly to consider Joe. What would he say if he were there? She smiled. He would tell her that she was a legal ninja Jedi. This was the woman he saw when he looked into her eyes. Then she heard the echo of Andi's voice, yelling up to her as she stood frozen on that stone wall. *You know what to do, so do it.* If she was going down, it would be on her terms, not Dovey's.

She walked into the restaurant with a purposeful stride, grabbing a chair along the way, and dragging it to the two-person table where Frank Dovey sat with Colin Nelson. When the two men looked up at her, she felt the same dizziness she'd experienced on that cliff ledge, but she continued forward, clapping the chair down to join them at their table. The look of stunned confusion on Dovey's face was enough to make getting fired worth it.

"Hi, Frank," she said, taking a seat.

"Um...Ms. Nash, this is a private meeting," Dovey said, a far more polite reaction than what Lila had expected. She'd caught him off-guard.

"This won't take long." Then to Colin Nelson, she said, "My name is Lila Nash. I work for you." She held out a hand, and a bewildered Nelson shook it. "I'm one of your new hires. Frank here's my boss."

"Ms. Nash," Dovey said, "what are you doing?"

Lila ignored him. "Here's the thing, Mr. Nelson. There's a rumor going around the office that Beth Malone is retiring, and that you may be thinking about giving Frank her job. I'm here to tell you that that's a terrible idea." Lila's pulse raced, but she spoke with the ease of a storyteller, her words flowing like fine cursive writing. She had been waiting for this moment for a long time and didn't even know it.

"Have you lost your mind?" Dovey's eyes popped with indignation, his words starting to jam up in his throat. "If you don't leave this table..."

"You need to hear this, Mr. Nelson."

"Of all the..."

"I just need three minutes of your time, and then I'll leave."

Dovey drew in a breath to continue, but Nelson held up a hand to stop him. Then he looked at Lila and said, "You work for me?"

"In Adult Prosecutions. I'll be sworn in this fall, and whether or not I'll still be working for you then... Well, that's what this is all about."

Nelson said, "Go ahead, Ms...."

"Nash. Thank you, sir. You see, when I was in law school, I worked on a case with one of my professors, Boady Sanden, and we—"

"I know Professor Sanden quite well," Nelson said. "We came up through the ranks together. A damned fine attorney."

"I agree," Lila said. "We had this case against Frank and... well, to put it bluntly, we kicked his ass. Rumor has it, he lost a judgeship as a result, and I think that's why he's been trying to push me out of my job."

Again Dovey tried to interject. "Push you out—?"

Nelson lifted a finger to silence Dovey.

Lila continued. "Just the other day he cornered me alone on the elevator and told me that I didn't belong here. But here's the thing, Mr. Nelson, I do belong here. I'm damned good at this job."

"You froze in court," Dovey said. Then to Nelson, "She has emotional issues—significant ones."

Lila shot Dovey a cold glare. "And how would you know about that, Frank?"

Dovey looked back and forth between Lila and Nelson, but didn't answer.

She turned her attention back to Nelson and softened her tone. "When I was eighteen, I was raped by two men. It was..." She paused, not to wrestle with her emotions but to find the right word. Her hands remained calm and folded in front of her. Her voice held no quaver.

"Mr. Nelson, I honestly don't think there's a word in the English language that could tell you all that I went through. Those men took something from me that will never be replaced. The shame from something like that can be devastating. People look at you like it's your fault. Hell, my own mother refused to acknowledge what happened to me, and when it became too much, I swallowed some of her pills."

Nelson seemed to balance discomfort and empathy better than most people. It fed Lila's resolve.

"That was eight years ago," she said. "And I clawed my way out of that hell. I went to college and law school, and now I have the job I've always wanted—except Frank doesn't think I'm cut out for it. He sent a letter to the Board of Law Examiners telling them about my suicide attempt."

Nelson looked at Dovey. "Frank?"

"Ms. Nash had to be relieved in court because she had some kind of episode. I was being prudent."

Lila said, "But you didn't just tell the board about the *episode,* did you? You told them that I'd been involuntarily committed in a psych ward because of a suicide attempt."

"I didn't tell the board a single word that wasn't true."

Lila leaned back in her chair, turning her focus toward Dovey. "Fair enough; it was true. But, Frank, you found out about my hospitalization and my suicide attempt by reading the investigation file for my rape."

"I have a legal right to access to those files."

"Yes, you do, but you don't have the right to share that information with anyone else, do you? The Data Practices Act is clear on that point. Active investigations are confidential—especially with regards to medical reports. Sharing that information with anyone is a crime. My case may be old, but it's still active. You broke the law, Frank. You wanted me gone so badly that you committed a crime to get me out."

Bright red patches began to mottle Frank Dovey's neck and cheeks. He opened his mouth to speak, then, apparently finding no words, closed it again.

Lila turned back to Colin Nelson. "I just needed to tell you what he's been doing. I expect I won't have my job much longer, and I regret that, but you needed to know who this man is at his core. I care too much about the mission of your office to let this go unsaid."

Lila stood up. "I apologize for interrupting your lunch, Mr. Nelson."

With that, she turned and left the restaurant, her back erect and her mind clear. She didn't even feel the need to count her steps.

CHAPTER 46

Every day, Gavin waited for the news that Sadie Vauk no longer walked the earth—and every night he went to bed disappointed. Committing murder, at least for most people, didn't come easily, and Gavin understood that Jack would need time to see the inevitability of what had to be done. But time—like Gavin's patience—was quickly running out.

He had two days until his status hearing and an opportunity to send another text to Jack. It would be more urgent than the first text, more demanding, a message delivered with the nuance of a sledgehammer. After that, Gavin would have a mere twenty-four hours between the status hearing and the omnibus hearing on Thursday. Sadie Vauk had to be gone by then. Gavin needed to make it clear to Jack that if Vauk wasn't out of the picture by Thursday, there would be consequences.

Jack's failure to act weighed heavily on Gavin as he busied himself with a small side project that day. He had purchased a simple green folder from the commissary to carry his legal papers. It would have a more important purpose soon—a hiding place for the burner phone's SIM card. Gavin used a piece of plastic from a pen to jab along a seam until he created a slot big enough for the card.

He had barely completed his task when a voice on the intercom called him to the guard station. He had a visitor.

As he neared the visiting room, he could see his mother's face on the screen, and it angered him. "What are you doing here?" he asked.

"I have something to tell you."

"Can it wait until I get out?"

"Those detectives came to see me again."

Gavin hadn't expected that, and he held his expression in check as he considered the news. It should mean nothing to him. An innocent man would welcome a more thorough investigation. "Good," Gavin said. "I hope they're getting closer to catching the guy."

"They asked some strange questions."

"Like what—and remember, Mom, Big Brother is listening."

Amy nodded. "They wanted to know about the money I give you."

"And what did you tell them?"

"What do you think I said? I told them it was an allowance. I'm taking care of my son. That's what mothers do; they look out for their children."

"You are a good mother," Gavin said, doing his best to sound sincere. Amy smiled as if she believed him. Was she really that stupid? Yes, she was. If it weren't for Gavin, she would have been locked up a long time ago.

His mother and Richard hadn't been celebrating that night, they'd been arguing. It had been one of those long, simmering fights that grew in heat as the Scotch in Richard's bottle dwindled, their insults whispered and hissed to hide their acrimony from the neighbors. But their harsh words climbed the ivy up to Gavin's window, words like *cheat,* and *gold digger,* and *divorce*. He heard Richard say that he was *sick of that retarded kid,* and Gavin knew what kid he was talking about.

He'd dug his camera out of its bag and trained its lens on the patio below, zooming in to watch his mother and Richard.

Richard had downed the last of his Johnnie Walker Black Label and thrown the bottle to the concrete, smashing it into a thousand shards. Then he'd pointed his finger at Amy and said, "You think I don't know what you're doing?" He struggled to form consonants as the alcohol thickened his tongue. "You think I'm an idiot? I'm done with you . . . and that defective kid of yours. I'm done with the whole thing. You wanna be a whore, go be a whore."

Richard turned to stumble his way toward the house and nearly lost his balance as he tried to navigate around the wicker footstool. That gave Amy the opportunity to grab a paver stone from the edge of the flower garden.

Gavin snapped a picture—no flash—the aperture set for the low light of the patio.

Amy brought the brick down on the back of Richard's head.

Gavin's chest filled with a breath that refused to leave. What had she done? He snapped another picture.

Richard crumpled to the ground, falling onto his back at the edge of the pool. Amy dropped the brick and took a step back, her hands pressed against her mouth as if to hold in a scream.

Gavin dropped his camera and ran downstairs. When he got to the patio, he saw his mother with a phone in her hand—she was dialing.

"What are you doing?"

"He's hurt. I need to call for help."

Gavin took the phone away from his mother. The look of shock on her face made no sense to Gavin. "You can't call for help. You'll go to jail."

Amy began to shake. "But he's . . ."

"He's a jerk. We don't need him."

"But . . ."

"If he wakes up, he'll tell the cops what you did. You'll be arrested. You'll go to prison."

"I don't know what to do."

Gavin put his mother's phone down and knelt beside Richard, who looked like he was simply asleep. He grabbed the man's shirt and lifted to try to roll him over. He never asked his mother to help. He had planned to do it all himself, but when he failed at his first attempt, Amy joined him at Richard's side. Together they rolled him into the pool.

Richard never moved. He didn't struggle or kick. As Gavin watched him drift, facedown, his only thought was that Richard Balentine had been killed by Amy's "retarded" son.

His mother tossed the brick into a shrub and suggested that they now call the cops—the woman was hopeless. Gavin told her to clean up the shards of glass from the Scotch bottle. There could be no signs of a fight. Gavin pulled the brick out of the shrub and cleaned it in the pool before replacing it in the flower bed. Then, using a paper towel to prevent leaving a fingerprint, he drained a full bottle of Scotch into the kitchen sink and placed the empty bottle on the patio next to Richard's chair.

When he finished the cleanup, Amy again suggested calling 911.

"We can't call until morning," Gavin said. "We need that brick to be dry."

Gavin stepped back to survey the scene, re-creating it in his head. Then he pointed at the stub of a cigar in a nearby ashtray. "You went to bed, and he stayed up to finish his cigar. You have no idea what happened—got that? I'll find him in the pool in the morning and call the police. If they ask, you were celebrating and drinking, but you don't know what happened after you went to bed."

He made his mother repeat the story three times before they left the patio. Even then he didn't trust that she wouldn't screw it up.

Yet, she now sat on the visitor side of the video screen while he was in jail. He shook the thought away and reminded himself that being locked up was all part of the plan.

"I'm scared for you, Gavin," she said. "I just want to help."

"I don't want your help." And then, for the benefit of the detectives who would be viewing this later, he said, "I didn't do anything, so they can't convict me of anything. Have faith. I'm innocent."

The smile Gavin shared with his mother carried the weight of their history, a wink between conspirators, saying more than words ever could. "Is that all they asked about—my allowance?"

"No, they asked me about a bunch of names."

This caused Gavin to twitch ever so slightly. He took a second to compose himself and asked, "What names?"

"They asked me about that girl you went to high school with, um, Eleanora what's-her-face. And then there was a Chloe and a Virginia and…" Amy paused as she counted the names off on her fingers, stumbling to find the fourth one.

Gavin stopped breathing as each name jammed a new scrap of rusted metal into his chest. How had they made those connections? They were random bodies, floating in the river. Were they guessing? Taking a shot in the dark?

No, Vang wasn't guessing. She must have puzzled together the thin nexus between his photography business and their disappearances. Surprisingly, the thought of those names passing through her lips brought Gavin a strange sense of accomplishment. His hard work, his art would finally be appreciated. But he had also been careful, and if that was all she had, then Gavin had nothing to worry about. Those women were all dead. There would never be a lineup. They could never sit in a courtroom and point a finger at him.

Gavin almost smiled at the thought of Vang watching him walk out of court a free man. She would know the truth of his deeds, the depth of his skill, but she would be able to prove nothing.

"Now I remember," Amy said. "The fourth girl's name was Lila Nash. That was the one."

Lila Nash? Had she finally remembered him? He had seen a look in her eye on that last trip to court, but he didn't believe it. He pictured her sitting on the witness stand, pointing a finger at him and saying his name. The image filled his chest with something cold and thick and heavy. It suffocated him. Was this what it felt like to drown?

"Are you okay?" Amy asked.

Damn it! Gavin forced a smile onto his face, took in a slow breath. They wanted him to react. That's why they fed Amy the names. If Nash had truly remembered him, they wouldn't have given that information to his mother. They were grasping at straws and he had fallen for their trick.

He pushed the panic from his mind and let his intellect cool the heat of those embers. He still had time to fix his mistake, put an end to the threat that was Lila Nash. He had a plan—a good one—and if he stuck to his strategy, everything would work out in the end.

Gavin painted his face with a look of boredom, shrugged, and said, "Never heard of her."

CHAPTER 47

Lila didn't go back to work after leaving Dovey at the restaurant—stunned and muted and covered in red blotches. She refused to treat the remainder of her day as just another afternoon, a page plucked from the calendar and thrown onto a pile with the rest. She wanted to bask in her audacity. She wanted to let the tremble of adrenaline work its way out of her fingers. And she wanted to call Joe, but this—along with everything she needed to tell him—seemed like a conversation best had in person.

A termination letter would likely be on her desk by morning. Or would they email it to her? She hoped that Dovey would at least have the balls to do it himself and not drag Andi into it. She sent Andi an email from her phone to let her know that Spencer's status hearing was prepped and ready for the morning, adding a cryptic note about having a family emergency and needing to leave for the day. Then she climbed into her car and drove.

Lila followed the flow of the traffic through downtown Minneapolis, replaying those few minutes in the restaurant, the memory both thrilling and horrifying. She tried to convince herself that her rash act had been a huge mistake, but every time she relived the memory, it played like music in her ears.

Yet, there had been one moment at the table that didn't feel right, a single sentence that had nothing to do with Dovey, or Nelson, or the letter from the bar examiners. In truth, that one sentence had no place in the discussion at all, but having said it, Lila could not rid it from her mind. *My own mother refused to acknowledge what happened to me, and when it became too much, I swallowed some of her pills.*

It wasn't the statement itself that bothered Lila. She'd understood long ago that her mother closed her eyes to the ugly parts of life. That's how Charlotte coped with her husband flying off to the Philippines or her daughter carving lines in her skin. But at the restaurant, Lila had presented her mother's oblivion not as a reaction to the suicide attempt, but as a cause of it.

My own mother refused to acknowledge what happened to me, and when it became too much…

As she slowed for a red light, another voice entered the conversation. *Healing requires forgiveness,* Dr. Roberts had said. *Forgiveness isn't for them. It's for you.* She had always seen those words aimed at the men who attacked her. Weren't they the ones who Dr. Roberts wanted her to forgive?

And when it became too much…

Lila aimed her car south, toward her mother's house.

* * *

Charlotte answered the door wearing a smile that had no memory, as if Lila's last visit hadn't ended the way it did. "Well, look at this—twice in one week?"

"Can we talk?" Lila's tone made clear that bad news lurked behind the request.

"Of course, honey." Charlotte stepped aside to let Lila in. "Is everything okay?"

Lila took a seat on the couch. Charlotte sat on a chair across from her, apparently sensing that some distance between them was warranted.

Despite having practiced her lines on the drive there, Lila struggled to start the conversation.

"Mom, I'm going to ask you an important question, and I want you to give me an honest answer."

Charlotte nodded. "Okay."

"Do you know what happened to me... that night in Uptown?"

"Oh, honey, why are you stirring that up again?"

Lila kept her tone flat as she repeated her question. "Do you know what they did to me?"

"Do you always have to bring that up? Can't we—"

"I've never brought it up. When have we ever talked about this?"

"It was a long time ago."

"That doesn't mean it didn't happen. It's still there. You understand that, don't you?"

"It's there because you never tried to move on. How can you get past something if you hold on to it like that?"

"I'm not holding on to it, Mom." Lila couldn't stop her voice from growing louder. "For Christ's sake, it holds on to me. Don't you understand that?" Lila closed her eyes and took a breath to calm down. "I can't move on unless I face what happened to me."

"Wasn't that the point of all that therapy? Where did that get you? It's like all he did was make it worse."

"Is that why you stopped my sessions with Dr. Roberts?"

"I never stopped—" Charlotte saw the look in Lila's eyes and didn't finish her sentence.

"I saw the letter. You forged my signature. Why would you do that?"

"For goodness' sakes, Lila—what good can it do to bring all this up again?"

"I deserve an answer. Why did you stop my therapy sessions?"

"All he was doing was rehashing it over and over. A wound can't heal if you keep jabbing it like that. And look at you now. Look how you turned out. You went to law school, and you have Joe."

"Dr. Roberts was helping me."

"No, he wasn't. He had you all mixed up. And they always blame the mother. One way or another, it's always the mother. I have no doubt that that's why he wanted me to come in. I was a good mom. I loved you. I tried—"

"Wait. Dr. Roberts wanted you...to come in?"

Charlotte looked down at her fingers and didn't answer.

"Why didn't you tell me?"

"I know how these things work. I wasn't about to sit there and let him blame me for what happened to you. I did my best."

"You stopped my sessions because you didn't want to talk about it?"

"You were better. I could see it. You didn't need—"

"I wasn't better!" Lila yelled, causing her mother to flinch.

Lila had never before wanted to hit her mother, and the urge scared her. She clenched her hands into fists and squeezed, her teeth gritted, her eyes pinched shut. Then she took in a slow breath. "You didn't answer my question, Mom."

"What question?"

"Do you know what happened to me at that party in Uptown?"

"Oh, Lila...please."

"I drank a lot back then—but you knew that."

"Can't we—"

"The night of that party, someone put something in my drink—a drug called GHB."

Charlotte closed her eyes like a child hiding from a monster. "I don't want to hear that ugliness."

"That ugliness is a part of my life."

"Not anymore. It's in the past."

"No it's not—that's the point." Lila couldn't stop the emotion from lifting inside of her. "You can't know who I am if you keep pretending it never happened."

"I was watching you kill yourself and there was nothing I could do.

First came the drinking. Every time you walked out that door I prayed that you'd come back safe. I'd stay awake, just to hear you walk in. Then the incident—"

"It wasn't an incident, Mom. Can't you even say it?"

"You were my little girl, and you were killing yourself right in front of me. I didn't understand."

"You didn't want to understand."

"Why didn't you come to me?"

"I'm here now. I'm coming to you now."

"What do you want from me, Lila?"

"I want..." A lump in Lila's throat nearly blocked her words from coming out. "I want to know that it wasn't my fault."

"Your fault? Oh my God! No!" Charlotte knelt on the floor in front of Lila. "No. No. Of course it wasn't your fault. Why would you ever think—?"

"What did I do wrong?" Tears trickled down Lila's cheeks. "You wouldn't look at me... you couldn't. You were ashamed of me."

Charlotte took hold of Lila's hands, her words falling between sobs. "I was never—"

"I felt dirty." Lila let her tears flow as she spoke. "You couldn't stand me."

Charlotte moved from the floor to the couch, wrapping her arms around Lila and kissing the top of her head. "I just wanted my little girl back. I didn't know."

Lila could hear the beat of her mother's heart and the quavering of her breath as Charlotte gently rocked and cried.

Then Charlotte said, "When you were born, I held you in my arms, and I promised I'd never let anyone hurt you. It never dawned on me that I would be the one... I'm so sorry. I was never ashamed of you. And what I did, I did because I wanted to protect you. I thought that if we could just get past it..."

A shaky inhale followed, and Charlotte paused for a long time as if to gather her strength. "I know what those men did to you. They...they raped you. They raped my little girl. I know that. It wasn't your fault. None of it was your fault. I just didn't know how to handle it. I'm sorry I got it so wrong."

Something softened inside of Lila when she heard her mother finally speak those words, and Lila settled into an embrace that she had once thought she would never again feel.

CHAPTER 48

On the morning of Gavin Spencer's status hearing, Niki Vang carried four files to her meeting with Andi Fitch, three cold case homicides and the Vauk file. The Vauk file now held a stack of pictures of the Bronco, taken by the crime scene tech. Every inch of the vehicle had been examined, photographed, and pressed with tape in an attempt to draw the tiniest speck of evidence out of hiding. And yet she and Matty had nothing more to give Andi beyond those pictures.

"He probably took it through a car wash before ditching it," Matty said as he handed the pictures to Fitch. "I've seen brand-new cars dirtier than this."

"Vacuumed, wiped down, the floor mats and cargo mat gone," Niki said. "I'm surprised he didn't rip the leather off the seats."

"What about the tread?" Andi asked. "Does it match the cast from Nicollet Island?"

"No," Niki said. "Either that wasn't his tread print, or...he was smart enough to swap out his tires before he ditched the truck. We've been calling some tire shops, but it's a needle in a haystack."

"Do you have any good news for me?" Andi asked.

"A couple things," Niki said, pointing at two of the pictures in front of Andi. The first was of the side of the Bronco taken at the impound lot. "Look at the door. The Bronco used to belong to a well drilling company. There used to be a magnetic sign on the door and you can see where it faded the paint."

Then Niki pointed at a grainy shot from a stoplight camera taken a few blocks from Bebe's Salon. "See the spot on the door?"

Andi picked the picture up and examined it carefully. "I think so."

"It's the same vehicle. We can put Gavin's Bronco within a few blocks of Sadie Vauk within an hour of her abduction."

Andi squinted as she looked again at the picture. "I'm not sure a jury will buy it. I mean, I see the spot because I want to—but a jury?"

"We sent the footage to the FBI to see if they can clean it up, but this might be as good as it gets," Niki said.

"It helps, but the case is still weak. You got anything else?"

Niki laid the three cold case files on the table. "I've been looking into the other women pulled from the river, and..." She opened the Ludlow file first. "We think we have something that might bolster the Vauk case. Chloe Ludlow was a model. She worked the Twin Cities Auto Show a week before she died. Gavin Spencer was there as a photographer."

Niki slid a photo across the table to Andi. "Matty found this picture of Gavin at that same event, taking pictures of cars."

Matty said, "They hired him to do publicity for the high-end room. Notice that green shirt he's wearing."

Niki slid a second photo to Andi. "This one's from a distance, but—you see that man in a green shirt standing in front of that booth with the orange logo?" Niki pointed with the tip of a pen. "That's Gavin Spencer standing at the booth where Chloe was working."

Andi looked hard at the second photo. "So, you have Gavin standing at her booth. Do you have them talking? Are there any pictures that put them together?"

"No," Niki said. "But a week later, Chloe climbs into a black SUV with a stain on the door in the shape of a teardrop—her roommate saw it. Chloe also told her roommate she was leaving with a photographer to get some headshots done. That was the last time anyone saw her alive."

Andi didn't respond, as though waiting for more.

"We have a pattern," Niki said. "He meets them before the abduction, puts together a plan, gets them alone, and slips them GHB. The Bronco connects the two cases."

Andi thought for a moment before saying, "The problem is the proof—or lack of it. Gavin's prior bad act with Chloe is only admissible in the Vauk case if we first prove by clear and convincing evidence that Gavin killed Chloe. We don't have that. No judge will let that in."

Niki wanted to spit. She was so close she could taste it, but again, the damned rules got in the way. "Chloe's killer had a tear-shaped stain on his door. That's why I knew we'd find that stain on Gavin's Bronco. I can draw a line from Spencer's homecoming date with Ellie Abrams to her death on Halloween. Ginny Mercotti disappeared days after she refused to pay Gavin for a photo shoot. He's as guilty as hell. Those women didn't commit suicide. They didn't jump or fall into the river. They were pushed there, drowned and discarded by Gavin Spencer. If a judge would just let the jury see the damned evidence, they would know he was guilty too."

"I'm on your side," Andi said, "but I need more than your beliefs. We have to have proof that Spencer killed Ludlow. We can't get his other bad acts in unless we can cross that threshold."

"Chloe Ludlow got in that Bronco the night she disappeared," Niki pleaded. "We can prove that it's Spencer's truck. That's got to count for something."

"I'm sorry," Andi said. "But Sadie's jury will never hear about Chloe Ludlow. No judge will let that in." Her words sounded like an apology.

Lila, who had been sitting quietly next to Andi, sat up straight and held out her hand as if to stop the conversation, her eyes darting back and forth in thought. After several seconds of silence, she said, "We have it backwards."

"We have what backwards?" Niki asked.

"We don't use Chloe's case to convict him for Sadie—we use Sadie to convict him for Chloe."

The room fell silent, and Andi looked at Lila to explain.

"Rule 404 allows us to bring in evidence of other wrong acts, but not to prove action in conformity therewith—"

"Action in what?" Matty said.

"Sorry," Lila said. "Say John Doe gets arrested for shoplifting ninety-nine times. You can't use those prior thefts to prove he shoplifted that hundredth time. But you can bring those acts in to show that he commits his crime in a specific way—his modus operandi. And for modus operandi, it doesn't matter which crime happened first, as long as it shows the pattern."

"But don't we still have the issue of proving he killed Chloe?" Matty asked.

"We convict him for Chloe's death by proving Sadie's case."

"I don't understand," Niki said.

Something came alive in Lila. She leaned in to the table as if feeding off the attention. "In order to get a conviction in Sadie Vauk's case, the jury will have to agree—beyond a reasonable doubt—that Gavin drugged her, raped her, and then dressed her back up and drowned her in the river. That's his MO. The jury can't convict him for Sadie's case unless they agree that we've proven the modus operandi beyond a reasonable doubt."

Andi picked it up from there. "If we convict him for Sadie's case . . . we could use that MO as evidence in the Ludlow case—show how the facts in Sadie's case line up with Ludlow's."

"Exactly," Lila said. "The jury would hear about what he did to Sadie."

Andi continued. "Sadie's case is only attempted murder, but Chloe's case—and the others—are all first-degree murder. Life without parole."

"First we win Sadie's case," Lila said. "Give him fifteen years or so, but then we go after the others and put him away forever."

"So, all we have to do is win Sadie's case," Niki said.

"Yeah," Andi said, with an obvious dip in her mood. "That's all we have to do."

CHAPTER 49

On the day of Gavin's status hearing, Lila had come to work certain that it would be her last at Hennepin County. Before going to see Andi, she fired up her computer to look for an interoffice message from Frank Dovey. It wasn't there. She remained at her desk for a moment, looking around the small room, realizing with a touch of sadness that she would take nothing with her when she left other than the picture of Joe on her desk.

In Andi's office, Lila took her seat as she did every day, and waited for the swing of the scythe. Andi had her head down in thought, a set of police reports spread out on her desk. When she finally looked up, she launched into a to-do list for Lila. Lila hadn't bothered to bring a legal pad, thinking "You're fired" didn't require recording.

When her meeting with Andi adjourned—with no bad news—Lila eagerly joined Andi in her meeting with Vang and Lopez. If nothing else, she would have one last chance to contribute to Gavin Spencer's conviction before she left. Even if she only got to read about it in the newspaper, it would brighten her day to know that she had a hand in bringing him down.

She put Dovey out of her mind and let her thoughts drift through the tangles of the problem at hand, listening as Niki and Matty laid out the wall they were up against.

The modus operandi seemed to be the key to it all. They had evidence that Gavin had met Sadie, as well as the other three victims, in the days and weeks before they were abducted. But they had no proof that Gavin had killed the three women. Without that proof, the connection was speculative at best, so Sadie's jury would never hear how Gavin had drowned the others and floated them down the Mississippi—just as he had tried to do to Sadie. He might be convicted for Sadie's case, but he would walk free on the others.

That's when it hit her. They needed to reverse the order. The voices in the room faded into a low hum as Lila moved pieces around in her head. It would work. Suddenly excited, she explained her idea to the detectives, and they gave her their complete attention. In their eyes, she wasn't a girl with broken parts. She was a prosecutor. And she felt the way she had when she stood atop that rock wall.

As they left the conference room, Niki said to Matty, "You go on ahead. I'll meet you in the atrium." To Lila, she said, "I have something I want you to see."

In Lila's office, Niki pulled a flash drive from her pocket and handed it to Lila.

"What's this?" Lila took a seat at her desk.

"Spencer's mother paid him a visit last night."

Lila plugged in the drive and pulled up the footage.

"Fast-forward to minute seven," Niki said.

"What am I looking for?"

"Watch his reaction. I'm curious if you see what I see."

Lila moved the indicator to the seventh minute and hit play. The screen was split. On the left was a woman who Lila assumed to be Spencer's mother, and on the right sat Gavin. The footage started with Gavin talking, making no attempt to hide his lisp.

"Is that all they asked about," he said, "my allowance?"

"No," the woman said. "They asked me about a bunch of names."

Lila saw Gavin cock his head as if curious. "What names?"

"They asked me about that girl you went to high school with, um, Eleanora what's-her-face."

Gavin's eyes widened slightly before returning to a heavy-lidded stare, held without a blink. Recognition?

"And then there was a Chloe and a Virginia and..." Amy was counting the women off on her fingers, pausing at number four to come up with a name. Gavin's breathing had shallowed. A line formed between his eyebrows, flashing a note of worry before it disappeared again.

"Now I remember," Amy said. "The fourth girl's name was Lila Nash. That was the one."

The change was, at once, subtle and stark. Gavin's eyes deepened, and the line on his forehead returned—and stayed. His lips went tight until he pressed out his tongue to wet them. His breath stopped in his chest long enough for his mother to notice and say, "Are you okay?"

Gavin's features turned blasé once again as he answered, "Never heard of her."

"He knows me," Lila whispered. "His face when she said my name...He knows me."

"That's how I see it too. It's nothing we can take to a jury, but...there's something there."

"What about his alibi?"

"I don't know. I'm still looking for his roommate. I'm also trying to track down footage of the graduation ceremony. There has to be a video out there showing that he didn't walk across the stage to get his diploma."

A cold wave washed over Lila, a fear so pure that it blinded her for a second. She spread her fingers open on her desktop just to feel something stable. One of her ghosts now had a face and a voice. She had no memory of him, but at the same time, she had no doubt. A man who had murdered at least three women—and almost a fourth—had left her alive. He had made a mistake and would surely seek to rectify that.

"He knows that we know," Lila said. "If he gets out..."

"He's going down for Sadie," Niki said, "and the others." She put her hand on Lila's arm. "I promise, he'll never get near you."

"There were two of them that night. What if he doesn't need to get out?"

"We'll protect you. I promise."

Lila looked at the hard steel in Niki's eyes and knew that if grit could carry the day, the detective would stand by her word. But Gavin Spencer was smart and careful. He would never come at Lila from the front; he would find a way to snake the blade in from the shadows. Niki couldn't protect her—Lila knew that—but she gave Niki an appreciative nod all the same.

Lila handed the flash drive back to Niki and walked her out of the office, her thoughts lost in a maze of *What ifs*. Gavin stopped at nothing to wash away his crimes—she had seen the bodies. And now he knew they were on to him.

When Lila returned to her desk, she pulled Gavin's mug shot up on her computer screen and stared into his eyes, her fear melding into anger. Gavin had raped her, and now that the secret was out, she was certain he would try to kill her.

Lila knew how far Gavin would go to silence her, but as her anger grew, she began to wonder how far she would go to stop him.

The game had changed. The entire world of right and wrong now played out like a coin tossed into the air. For her, it all came down to a simple choice. *Him or me.*

CHAPTER 50

Gavin's attorney came early to the status hearing that Wednesday, walking into the court's holding cell with pictures of Gavin's Bronco in his hand.

"They just gave me these," he said, handing Gavin the pictures.

"I need the phone." Gavin had his back to the door. The green folder with his paperwork lay on the table in front of him.

"They have pictures of your Bronco only three blocks away from where Sadie Vauk was kidnapped."

"It's not my Bronco. Give me the phone."

"Look at that patch on the door. You don't think they can match that? A jury's gonna—"

"Give me the fucking phone!"

Leo Reecey looked at the window on the door, clear of any guard, and handed Gavin the phone. "I think I have a right to know who you're texting."

Gavin slipped the SIM card from its hiding place in the folder and slid it into its tray. "Tomorrow's my omnibus hearing. You have a right to collect that fifty grand. That's the only right you have. Cough if you see a guard."

He typed Jack's number and began his text message.

What the Fuck Jack? You think I'm joking? You know what I'm capable of. You know what you have to do. Look at the time stamp on this message. You have twenty-four hours and not one minute more. If she's not silenced in twenty-four hours, I will send your picture to the police. We will both go to prison. I don't fucking care. I have nothing more to lose—you have everything to lose. The clock starts now!

Gavin had a backup plan should Jack fail him—Gavin always had a backup plan—but that plan came with a high level of risk. Jack would do what was needed, Gavin was sure of it, but time was running out. He needed to get out before they could build up any of the other cases—especially Lila Nash's. She had seen his face and heard his voice all those years ago. Was the fog of her amnesia somehow lifting?

He needed the plan to move faster. He needed to get out so he could take care of things himself—do it right.

He deleted the text from the phone after he sent it. Then he removed the SIM card and slid it into its hiding place in the green folder. Reecey sat sideways at the table, his eyes studying the cinder block wall, as though his act of looking the other way—literally—somehow absolved him of his involvement in Gavin's offense.

"Did they give you anything else?" Gavin asked. "Reports about other women?"

"Other women?" Reecey turned a shade whiter. "What other women?"

"None—never mind."

"Are there others? No, wait. Don't answer that. I don't want to know."

"Of course there's not, Leo. I didn't kidnap Vauk, but they're accusing me of that, aren't they? So who's to say they won't try to tag more on for good measure?"

Reecey accepted Gavin's answer with the blind eye of a politician taking a bribe. "We have a fighting chance tomorrow," he said. "But don't be disappointed if the judge keeps the lineup in. Even if the judge kicks it, they'll bring Ms. Vauk in at trial to point at you. We'll use the faulty lineup to show how they planted your lisp in her head. We'll turn their best evidence against them."

Gavin was barely listening. He didn't want to hear the man's glass-half-full assurances. This had to end the way Gavin had planned it. If the case made it to trial, he would lose. Jack had to put an end to it.

The guard opened the door and ushered them into court, Gavin doing his best not to acknowledge that Lila Nash sat at the prosecutor's table. How far down that path had the detectives traveled? They hadn't charged him, so there had to be a hole in the case. Were they re-interviewing witnesses from the party? Had they talked to Jack yet? All he needed was another twenty-four hours. If things could go his way for one more day, he'd be golden.

Gavin stared at the wood trim on the judge's bench for the entirety of the proceeding, hearing very little of what was said. It was a sideshow as far as he was concerned. Leo Reecey was a joke. The man had few skills and could do no more to set Gavin free than the Tooth Fairy.

The lead prosecutor, Andrea Fitch, handled the hearing that day, and the confidence in her voice raked across Gavin's nerves. He calmed himself by fantasizing about that moment when her case would fall apart. The thought of her smug face crushed in defeat as he walked out of court pleased him. He would smile at her but not say a word, letting his silence echo off the walls as a final *fuck you.*

As he listened to the two attorneys drone on, something pulled his attention to the left, to the table where Fitch stood in argument and Lila Nash sat in obedience. He wanted to look at her, but he kept his focus on the courtroom's outdated woodwork. What was she thinking? Was she looking at him? How much did she remember—if she remembered anything at all? If he looked, he might know.

Don't do it, he thought to himself. *She has to believe that she means nothing to you.*

"All right," the judge said, after the thrum of attorney prattle died away. "It looks like discovery is completed and we're set for a contested hearing tomorrow at three o'clock. Is there anything further, Mr. Reecey?"

One glance, Gavin thought. *Just a peek.*

"Nothing further," Reecey said.

Look at Fitch and then a quick glance. She won't even notice.

"Anything further, Ms. Fitch?"

Gavin snaked his eyes to Fitch, standing at counsel table with the poise of a show horse. Next to Fitch, Lila Nash sat sideways, facing Gavin. They locked eyes for only a second, and where he had hoped to see confusion—or maybe even fear—he saw something else, something deep and powerful.

He saw resolve.

CHAPTER 51

At the status hearing, Lila had put all of her concerns about getting fired aside and studied Gavin Spencer, paying particular attention to the way he stared straight ahead like a man not wanting to be noticed. She watched his head veer in her direction a couple times, his eyes leading the way, only to return front and center. It wasn't until the proceeding waned to its final seconds that he looked at her.

The connection lasted barely a second, but in his eyes she saw that same strange flash of recognition she'd seen in the jail video. And behind that spark, Lila thought she saw something that looked an awful lot like fear.

He turned his head back sharply, but Lila didn't look away. She kept her eyes locked on the man who she now believed had raped her.

But how was that possible? How had Gavin found her that night? Had he been at that party in Uptown? What about his alibi? And if Gavin had not been the one to choose her, then it had to have been his accomplice. Gavin's partner was still out there, and if she could find him, she could destroy Gavin's alibi, attack his flank where he had no defense.

The sight of him being led away drew her rage to a fine point. It made her want to drive a pen through his neck, and at the same time it made her so sick, she could barely stand up. She wanted Gavin to look at her. She wanted him to see that she knew.

As she walked back to her office she pondered her strategy. Once there, she again stared at Gavin's picture, trying to place him at the party, or anywhere in her past, but it was like trying to grab smoke.

She stood and paced. Maybe she was coming at this from the wrong direction? *Don't think about Gavin. Think about the party.*

Up until a few days ago, she could only remember two people there that night: John and Sylvie. But now she believed that Silas Jackson had been there, and she knew that Sean Daniels was there. If she tracked down more people from that night, she might be able to color in enough of the scene to make a picture. It would take time—weeks, maybe months—but what were a few more months after living a nightmare for eight years? Besides, she would have plenty of time on her hands once Frank pulled the trigger on her termination.

Lila wrote Sean Daniels's name on her legal pad. Maybe he could remember a few names from that night, fresh bread crumbs for Lila to follow. It may lead nowhere, but at least she wouldn't be sitting on the sidelines. She would start with Sean.

* * *

Lila made it to quitting time with no message from Dovey, leaving work a little early to avoid running into him at the elevators. She drove to Sean Daniels's house in Lake Elmo, a quiet little burb on the outer ring of the Twin Cities, having found the address online. On the drive, Lila tried to remember everything she could about Sean. He had been a smallish boy who hung around the fringe of the conversations, piping up at the oddest moments with jokes that weren't funny. Wasn't he on the yearbook staff? She seemed to remember him taking pictures at high school events. He was a photographer?

And then there was his senior picture. She had kept it in her car after leaving her mother's house and now glanced at the inscription as she moved it to her pocket. *Every dog has its day.* What the hell was that supposed to mean? She wasn't sure why, but it seemed important that she surprise him—capture his honest reaction to her showing up out of the blue.

She parked in his driveway and paused before getting out of her car. His house was one of the largest on a street full of large houses: two stories, a stone façade, a three-car garage, and at least an acre of land. Clay pots filled with flowers framed the front door, suggesting a woman's touch, and on the driveway, a toy horse lay on its side. Children?

She walked up, rang the doorbell, and waited as footsteps approached. An amiable woman in her midtwenties opened the door and smiled at Lila.

"Hello," Lila said. "Is Sean here?"

"He is, and who can I say...?"

"Could you tell him that it's Lila Nash... from high school?"

Curiosity passed across the woman's face, but she smiled and invited Lila inside.

The home was lovely, full of windows and light. An open staircase in the entryway rose in a graceful curve to the second floor. Lila remained at the door, admiring the grandeur of the home as the woman left to get Sean. The sound of at least two children, young ones, came from somewhere beyond the foyer. A minute later, Sean emerged from a long hall.

"Lila?" Sean looked legitimately confused. He hadn't changed all that much since she'd last seen him, although he had put on some muscle weight and his acne had cleared up.

"Hello, Sean."

"This is... Well, 'a surprise' doesn't quite seem to cut it."

"I'm sorry for dropping in unexpected like this." It was a sentiment that Lila had planned to express even if she didn't mean it—which she now did. "This is going to sound strange, but I was wondering if I could talk to you."

"Sure. I have an office back here."

As he led her through the house, she took in not only the size but the simple pleasantness of the home. She had been in nice houses before, but not one owned by someone her own age.

The office was bigger than her bedroom back at the apartment, and held a drafting table and a desk made of what she thought might be mahogany. Sean pointed at one of the two leather chairs in the room, and they sat down.

"I gotta tell ya, Lila. If you gave me a million guesses, I never would have thought that was you at the door."

"And again, I'm sorry for not calling. My coming here was kind of a spur-of-the-moment thing. Is that your wife?"

"Mallory. Going on four years now."

"And did I hear kids?"

"Bill and Kelly. Four and three. But I suspect you didn't come all this way just to catch up."

"No, I didn't."

Lila had planned a dozen ways to ease in to her questions, each determined by her read of Sean, but now she struggled to remember any of them. It all came down to one thing: What did he remember?

"The weekend before graduation I was at a party in Uptown. That's the night that..." She watched Sean's face fall, and she knew he understood which night she was talking about. "I've been trying to re-create what happened. I know it was a long time ago, but—"

"I'm sorry about what happened to you."

"Thank you. What exactly do you know about...what happened to me?"

"Just what people said—and what the cops asked about."

"You took a picture of John Aldrich holding my arm."

"I remember. I gave it to the police after I heard what happened."

"Why? I mean, what was it that made you feel like that picture was important?"

"I don't know. I remember him treating you like that, and I..." Sean shifted uncomfortably in his seat.

"It's important, Sean. My memory of that night is pretty much missing, so if there's anything you can tell me about the party, I'd really appreciate it."

Sean stood, closed the door to the office, and returned to his chair, his face tinged in melancholy. "I don't know if you know... how I felt about you back then."

Lila swallowed but didn't answer.

"I had a bit of a crush on you."

Lila felt her face go flush, and nodded. "I had my suspicions."

"It tore me up to see you with assholes like John Aldrich. To hear people talk about you—the things they called you behind your back."

And just like that, the memory of those taunts came rushing back. "Yeah, I know about that."

"I used to ask myself, 'Why not a guy like me?' But I guess I always knew the answer."

"I had a lot of issues back then."

"I didn't like the way Aldrich treated you. I think that's why I took the picture. You were so..."

"Drunk?"

Sean nodded. "I thought that if I had a picture, I could show you later—show you what a dick he was, and with Sylvie right there."

"Did you see who I left with?"

"I think I left before that."

"Have you ever heard the name Gavin Spencer?"

"Um... I don't think so." Sean's eyes showed no hint of a lie.

"Did you know anybody back then who had a bad lisp?"

"A lisp? Not that I can remember. Why?"

"Just a shadow I'm chasing. How about the name Silas Jackson? Does that name ring a bell?"

"No."

"Was anyone at the party acting weird toward me, besides John, that is?"

"It was a long time ago. I honestly don't remember, but...that picture I gave the cop wasn't the only one I took."

"You have more?"

"I think I still have 'em." He went to a cupboard and started pulling boxes out.

"Didn't the detective ask to see them?"

Sean paused and turned to Lila. "The guy I talked to asked me about you and Aldrich—asked me if you were dating. When I said no, he said..." Sean dropped his eyes as though embarrassed.

"He said what?"

"He said that *dating* was the wrong word—hooking up was what he meant. When I said I didn't know, he said..." Sean looked at Lila and she could see pity in his eyes. "He said he was trying to get a handle on all the guys you'd been with. I got the impression he was just going through the motions. When I gave him that picture of you and Aldrich, he acted like I was bothering him."

Sean lifted one of his boxes onto his desk and began digging through it. The box held external storage drives, each drive with a date written on it in Sharpie. Sean smiled. "I'm a pack rat when it comes to pictures."

"You took pictures for the yearbook, right?"

"Yeah."

"Are you a professional photographer now?"

Sean held up one of the drives and squinted to read the date on it. "Oh, God, no. I'm a computer coder. I wrote an algorithm that tracks buying habits." He looked up from his box and smiled at Lila. "Bought this house with the money Amazon paid me for it."

"It's beautiful," Lila said.

Lila slipped his senior picture out of her pocket and held it out.

"Holy crap!" His face lit up with a smile. "You still have that?" She turned it over so he could read the inscription, and his smile fell away. "Yeah, I was a bit of an asshole back then."

"What did you mean by 'Every dog has its day?'"

"I wrote that on all my pictures." He gave a self-conscious shrug. "I know what people thought of me—the annoying twerp with bad social skills. But I never saw myself that way, and I wanted to prove you all wrong, stroll into my ten-year reunion like a boss. That's all."

Lila dropped her head a touch. "I'm sorry for my part in all that. I wasn't a very good friend back then."

"Don't worry about it." His smile returned, and he handed the picture back to Lila. "I found a woman who... Well, she's everything to me. I got two great kids, and at the end of the day, I don't really care anymore what you guys think— No offense."

"None taken."

He returned to his search and soon held up an external drive about the size of a cell phone. "I think this is it." He attached the drive to a cable on his desk and opened a file to show a picture from the party, although not the picture of John and Lila.

"May I?" Lila asked, and Sean slid the mouse to her.

She clicked through the pictures slowly, looking at each one carefully. Three pictures in, she came to the one of John holding her wrist. She moved on, slowly, until she came to a picture of a boy shotgunning a beer. He had his head tipped back, and his face was mostly covered by the beer can, but Lila could see enough to know that it was Silas Jackson.

Lila inhaled sharply. "Do you know that guy?" she asked.

Sean looked closer and shook his head. "Don't think I've ever seen him before."

"Can you email me a copy of this one?"

"No problem."

Lila clicked on the next picture, and her heart nearly stopped. It showed two girls in a red-faced argument. Lila saw herself at the edge of the crowd, a beer in her hand. But it wasn't the two girls fighting that caught her attention—nor was it seeing herself standing half drunk at the edge of the fray. What made Lila's blood freeze was the image of a boy in the background. He sat on a cushioned chair alone, invisible to the rest of the partiers, and he wasn't watching the fight like everybody else. The boy stared at Lila.

It was Gavin Spencer.

CHAPTER 52

When the jailers called Gavin's pod to dinner that evening, he stepped into line with the other men. The guy ahead of Gavin looked like he belonged there, tall and broad-shouldered, his greasy hair dangling down between his shoulder blades. He glanced over his shoulder at Gavin and gave a sneer—then a smile. Gavin should have trusted his instinct and moved to the back of the line, but he hadn't.

They marched, single-file, into a concrete hallway, one jailer at the head of the group, one at the tail, the odor of forty unwashed men filling the small space. Gavin hated chow time. He needed to eat, so he made that walk three times a day, but he loathed being lumped in as just another dreg in an orange jumpsuit, no different from the toothless meth heads and the idiots who blew their snot to the floor when there was a tissue within reach.

But he took comfort in knowing that unlike the rest of them, he would be out soon; he was only there for the alibi.

The line turned a corner, placing Gavin out of view of the guard in back, and the man ahead of him suddenly turned and punched Gavin in the stomach—once, twice, three times. It happened so fast that Gavin didn't have time to react. He dropped to the floor, his body curling in upon itself, his lungs empty, and his stomach heaving bile up into his throat.

The man did not continue the attack, but simply turned and walked on as though nothing had happened. The men behind Gavin stepped around him as if he were a pile of dog feces.

By the time the rear guard got to him, Gavin had worked himself up onto his knees. The man radioed to the control center, telling them to look at the security footage to see if anything was caught on tape. He lifted Gavin to his feet and asked what had happened. Gavin wasn't sure he could explain it even if he wanted to, so he simply shook his head.

In the mess hall, Gavin took a seat far away from the long-haired man. The attack had beaten the appetite out of him, but he cut a piece of Salisbury steak and put it in his mouth anyway.

As he was cutting a second piece, Gideon Doss took the seat across the table from him. "That was quite the tumble you took back there," he said.

Gavin didn't answer. At first his silence was because he wanted to be left alone with his thoughts, but then it occurred to him that Gideon had been one of the men to step around him as he lay on the hallway floor, trying to breathe.

"Jail can be a dangerous place," Gideon said. "Lots of accidents. Prison's even worse if you piss off the wrong people."

"What's going on, Gideon?"

"Word is, you have some enemies in the big house."

"Big house? What are you talking about?"

"Stillwater, Oak Park Heights, Lino, St. Cloud...It don't matter which prison you go to—there's some folks who are pretty pissed off at you."

"I don't even know anyone..."

"But they know you." Gideon reached across the table, picked up Gavin's Salisbury steak in his fingers, and took a bite. "That's the thing about prison," he said. "It's like its own little world with rules and... What's that word? Hi-er... hierarchs...?"

"Hierarchies?"

"That's it. You're a smart fella." He took another bite of steak and tossed the remains onto Gavin's tray, licking the gravy from the tips of his fingers.

"What's any of that got to do with me?"

Gideon opened his jumpsuit and pulled the collar of his T-shirt down enough to show Gavin a tattoo on his chest, a lightning bolt with an A on one side and a B on the other. "I'm bettin' a smart man like you can figure out what this is."

Gavin's stomach knotted up. "Aryan Brotherhood?"

Gideon smiled—a teacher pleased with a slow-learning student. "Remember how they sent me up for beatin' that spic some years back? Well, it put me in good with some mighty particular folks. They asked me to pass on a message to you."

"Wait—you knew what they were going to do to me?"

Gideon pursed his lips in disappointment. "You don't get it. What happened today ain't nothin'. You're a marked man."

"Why?"

"What you did—raping that white girl and throwin' her in the river? I mean, that by itself's gonna get you hard time. But you fucked up. That girl—she's connected. They say her uncle's inside, and he's put the word out on you."

"What..." Fear swallowed Gavin's words.

"I'm sorry, buddy, but you're fucked."

"What'll they do?"

"Not much till you get sent up. They'll mess with you a bit here in County, but the real stuff won't start until later. That little tussle in the hallway was just to show you how far they can reach. The guy that hit you, he'll do some time in seg for it, but he did what he was told to. We're just—you know—like soldiers following orders."

"I thought we were friends."

"We are, but that don't make no difference."

Gavin's brain clamored—fear bouncing off the walls of his skull. "Are they...going to kill me?"

Gideon leaned back in his seat, his desolate features bringing to Gavin's mind an executioner. "They're gonna have a high time with you. It pains me to say this, Gavin, but there'll come a day when you're gonna wish you was dead." Gideon shook his head. "You done fucked up."

With that, Gideon stood and left.

⋆ ⋆ ⋆

After dinner, Gavin headed straight for his bunk. On his way, he passed a cell that had its door open, and a large hand reached out and pulled him in. A man—different from the man who attacked him in the corridor—punched Gavin in the stomach three times, fast. Then he drove a fourth blow into Gavin's ear and shoved him back out the door. Gavin stumbled to his cell, the pain so intense that he could barely walk.

He didn't leave his cell for the rest of that day, remaining on his bunk, his back to the corner, his legs and feet ready to fend off any new attackers.

That night, he fought to keep thoughts of failure from poisoning his mind. He had a plan—and a backup plan. They would work. But if they didn't, these men would kill him, a slow, torturous death that would take years. Gavin would do the hardest time a man could do.

CHAPTER 53

Lila's memory sometimes seemed like a quilt that she could never quite stitch together, the patches lying around her, visible to the eye, tactile against her fingertips, but forever disconnected. As she lay in bed that night, she stared at that picture of Gavin Spencer sitting in a chair at the party in Uptown. He was looking at her the way a lion watches a fallen wildebeest.

She held in her hand proof that he had not been in Indiana on the night of her rape—the final puzzle piece tying his lisp to her panic attack. She had found the man who raped her, yet she could summon no memory of him, or of his partner.

There were moments, in those dark hours, when she retreated into self-pity, mourning the events that befell her that long-ago night, the attack that would happen within a couple hours of that photo being snapped. There were other moments when she could not hold back the guilt she felt for letting Gavin walk free for so long. If Lila had remembered what had happened to her, Eleanora, Virginia, and Chloe would be alive, and Sadie—the only other survivor—would never have suffered at the hands of a monster.

Joe would have told her that none of that had been her fault. He would have kissed the top of her head as he explained that she had done everything right. She almost called him but stopped herself. He would race home and lift this burden from her shoulders, but this time that wasn't what Lila wanted. She loved him to hell and back, but she knew she needed to stand against this wind on her own.

She had managed only a thin dappling of sleep before her alarm clock woke her.

The first item on her agenda—assuming Dovey didn't fire her first—would be a discussion with Andi, another cause for her sleepless night. Lila had become a witness in *Minnesota versus Gavin Spencer.* It didn't matter that she had no recollection of Gavin raping her; Lila had uncovered evidence that she had been Gavin's first victim. She could no longer be involved in prosecuting his case.

But how could she walk away? She had been the one to devise the plan to send him to prison for what he'd done to Chloe, Virginia, and Eleanora. It killed her to do it, but those were the rules.

And what was worse, those rules might get Andi kicked off the case as well. Lila's conflict of interest might spread like an infection to the person best suited to take Gavin's case to trial. What if Gavin walked free because Lila found the thread that connected them?

When she arrived at Andi's office, Lila was surprised to see Niki Vang and Matty Lopez sitting across the desk from Andi. They looked over their shoulders at her, their expressions hollow. Andi's eyes were red and heavy, her hands folded in front of her as if in prayer. Lila had never seen her so shaken.

Lila stopped in the open doorway. "What's wrong?" she asked.

It was Niki who spoke. "Sadie Vauk is dead."

CHAPTER 54

Gavin left his cell that next morning to claim a spot in the common area as close to the guard station as possible. Feeling like a picked-on child, he walked to breakfast at the head of the line, a jailer only a few feet away. Back in the pod, he dealt himself a game of solitaire and looked out from under heavy-lidded eyes at the faces of the other inmates, trying to decide which of them meant to do him harm.

So when the jailer told Gavin that he had a visitor, he simply had to lean across the control panel and say, "Spencer, your attorney's here."

Gavin found Leo Reecey sitting comfortably in the small room reserved for attorney visits, one leg crossed over the other, a briefcase on the floor next to him. He didn't stand to greet Gavin, but motioned for him to take a seat, as if Gavin hadn't planned to do that anyway.

"You here to talk about the omnibus hearing?" Gavin asked.

"In a way, yes," Reecey said. "I got a call this morning from the prosecutor. There's been a development."

Reecey seemed determined to drag this out, but the mere possibility of what that development might be sent a rush of relief through Gavin. He swallowed his excitement and played along. "What development?"

"Sadie Vauk died last night."

Gavin feigned confusion, with a touch of surprise tacked on for good measure. Inside he jumped and screamed and turned imaginary cartwheels, but outside he cocked his head slightly and blinked. "What do you mean?"

"I mean she'd dead. She was murdered outside of a fitness center where she'd been swimming."

Gavin paused as he pretended to take in this information. Then he perked up and said, "You think the guy who threw her in the river finished the job? I mean, it kind of proves that I'm innocent, doesn't it?"

"Doesn't matter. They can't prosecute you, not with the evidence they have now."

Gavin furrowed his brow to deepen his pretense of disorientation. "I don't understand," he said, even though he did.

"An accused has the right to confront his accuser—force them to testify in open court and be subject to cross-examination. They have to testify, especially in a case like this, where they have nothing more than her word. They have no forensics, no corroboration, just her picking you out of a lineup. They have no case without her testimony."

"So... the stuff she told the cops... and the lineup...?"

"They can't use it unless they can prove that you had a hand in killing Sadie Vauk."

"I was in here. How could I...?"

"That's their only path forward, and Fitch would have said something if they had any evidence that you were involved last night. We'll know for sure by the time we have the hearing today."

"What's gonna happen at the hearing... now that...?"

"I have my probable cause motion on the table already, but I drafted a habeas corpus petition to go along with it."

"Habeas corpus?"

"It means produce the body—your body. It's a mechanism to get someone out of custody if there's no basis to keep them there. I want to make sure that if they have an argument to keep this case going, they lay it out today. If not—"

"I'm free?"

"Yeah," Reecey said, with a hint of regret. "As free as the wind."

CHAPTER 55

Clouds to the west painted the sky in shades of gray and black, promising a heavy rain. For now, though, people moved through the city unencumbered by the impending storm—or the death of a hairstylist named Sadie Vauk. Lila didn't have that luxury.

After learning that Sadie had been murdered, Lila left the office and walked north, pulled by some need to be near the place where Gavin had thrown the women into the river. She was now his lone survivor. She walked until she found herself in the middle of the Stone Arch Bridge, a structure that looked like it belonged in the Middle Ages, its graceful limestone arches leapfrogging across the river. Originally built for trains, it now supported bicyclists, joggers, and pedestrians.

Lila leaned against the steel rail and gazed up the river at St. Anthony Falls. Beneath her, the river's coppery foam carried a tree branch past the spot where it had once carried the bodies of Eleanora Abrams, Virginia Mercotti, and Chloe Ludlow. Sadie Vauk would have made that same journey had she not been such a good swimmer.

Sadie's father had told Niki that swimming laps helped Sadie deal with what Gavin Spencer had done to her. That's why she had gone to the fitness center, to clear her head of those poisonous memories. They'd found her in the parking lot, one bullet in her head and one in her chest. The night-shift detective identified Sadie by her driver's license but hadn't made the connection to Niki's case until morning.

Niki had brought surveillance footage to show Andi. It showed Sadie leaving the gym and walking to the parking lot. A light-colored SUV pulled up. The view was grainy and the car was near the end of the lot, but they could see Sadie stop as if someone in the SUV was talking to her. Then she walked up to the car and pointed north.

"Probably asking directions?" Niki had said.

Two muzzle flashes sent bullets ripping into Sadie. Then Lila watched Sadie fall to the ground as the car drove away.

"We're ninety percent sure it's an SUV, smaller, white or silver," Niki had said. "It's just too grainy to get a lock on the make or see the driver. But we all know who's responsible."

"But can we prove it?" Andi had asked.

Niki dropped her head in defeat. "No."

As Lila stood on the Stone Arch Bridge, she ran through their few remaining moves. Andi would go to the hearing and argue that Sadie's statements be allowed to go before a jury under a good-faith catchall of inherent reliability, but that argument would fail. With no proof that Gavin helped to plan Sadie's death, they couldn't use the lineup or anything she had said without violating Gavin's constitutional right to confrontation. Andi's final line of defense remained a dismissal without prejudice. They could refile the charges in the future if they found new evidence, but to go to trial now meant an acquittal and double jeopardy.

Lila looked out over the river, searching for a strategy that might bend fate, but no matter how she moved the pieces, it always ended with the white king tipped on its side. Lila had gone to law school to stop men like Gavin Spencer and to protect women like Sadie Vauk. She had failed, and now Gavin was about to walk free.

He would hunt her. They didn't have enough evidence to put him away for what he did to her eight years ago, because proving that he was in the state that night was a far cry from proving that he'd raped her. But she was onto him, and he knew it. He would have no choice but to put an end to her as a threat.

If Gavin had orchestrated Sadie's death, he would have needed an accomplice—like the one he had with him eight years ago. And if Sadie's killer was that second man in the car that night, was he already looking for Lila?

Lila glanced in both directions across the bridge and spotted a man forty yards away, elbows resting on the rail, his gaze cast toward the churning of the falls. He paid no attention to Lila, but his presence shook her. Was he Silas Jackson? He was about the right age and had a similar build.

Lila looked at the lampposts that lined the bridge, hoping there might be a surveillance camera, but saw none. There were a few walkers passing by, which eased her fear. He wouldn't try anything with witnesses around, would he? Lila wanted to run, but where would she go? If Gavin wanted to get to her, he would get to her—if not on the bridge then somewhere else.

The flurry of possibilities muddled Lila's thoughts as she watched the man. Then he turned toward her and started walking, a smile on his face. He raised a hand and waved. Lila shook her head slightly, confused, but then looked behind her to see a woman approaching, her hand in the air, waving back. Lila looked at the man's face again and saw that he couldn't be Silas.

Feeling foolish, she turned toward the rail and waited as the couple embraced and walked away. She hated Gavin for making her see threats in the faces of strangers. She hated him for the evil he brought to the world. And she hated him because he was about to get away with his fourth murder.

Lila, and Andi, and Niki were bound by rules, and yet he could cheat. If only she didn't have those constraints.

Somewhere in that thought a seed took root, its tendrils reaching to the sky in search of inspiration while its roots burrowed down to find strength. She could feel it grow inside her, consuming all her air until she understood—the time had come to start playing by a new set of rules.

And just like that, she saw what had to be done. She tapped her fingers on the rail as pieces of a plan moved through her head, cogs and wheels locking into place one by one. Gavin had chosen the playing field. He had chosen the game. He had been controlling the moves from the beginning, and the time had come to turn that around.

She started walking, and by the time she stepped off the Stone Arch Bridge, Lila knew how she would finally get Gavin Spencer.

CHAPTER 56

Sitting at his table near the guard station, Gavin wanted to crow. Even with the added curveball of Lila's involvement, his plan had worked just as he had conceived it. In a matter of hours, he would be free to take the next steps, the ones that would ensure that he would never again lose sleep over his mistakes. He would put a stop to Lila before she could put a stop to him.

Like a child waiting for Christmas, he felt as though time had slowed to a near dead stop, the clock's second hand cruelly lingering before sliding to the next dot. Yet at the same time, Gavin's mind spun at a fever pitch, jumping from one idea to the next.

He finally calmed himself by thinking about war, specifically the idea that in every war there has to be a last soldier to die—that guy who did everything right, surviving battle after battle, dodging bullets and bombs, only to get shot by some asshole who refused to believe that the end had come. That last soldier let down his guard, believing that some finish line had already been crossed when in truth it remained miles away. Gavin resolved that he would not be that last dead soldier.

The dismissal of his case would not mark the end of a war but merely the start of a new battle. There was still much that Gavin needed to do, beginning with the task of eliminating Jack and any other path that might lead back to him. Once again Gavin's mind turned to war, but this time he thought of the great generals who in the midst of loss and disarray, ignored calls for retreat and instead ordered counterattacks. They understood that opportunity is found in chaos, and that victory belongs to the bold and to those who kept their wits.

Gavin would not fall back. He would not watch as detectives drew a line from Sadie to Jack to him. Gavin would be bold.

At two-thirty, Gavin walked with a guard through the tunnel that led to court. He carried his green folder and secret SIM card with him because he expected them to toss his cell while he was gone. How could they not? Sadie Vauk had been murdered, and no one in the world wanted her dead more than he did. They would know he orchestrated her death. But it's not what they knew that mattered, but what they could prove. Those were the rules.

The jailer paused outside of the courtroom and asked Gavin to hand over his folder. Pulling the papers out, the jailer shook them as though expecting something nefarious to fall out. Then he checked inside the pockets, a quick glance into each, before returning the papers and the folder to Gavin.

Could they have been any more predictable?

The guard walked him into the courtroom and to the table where Leo Reecey sat waiting.

"Any surprises coming?" he asked Reecey.

"Nothing I know of."

The door at the rear of the courtroom opened and a somber Andrea Fitch strolled up to her table, looking at neither Reecey nor Gavin. Gavin took that as a good sign. Then Lila came in, but she did not go to counsel table; instead, she took a seat in the back. Gavin contemplated the significance of this subtle change in protocol but decided that it meant nothing.

The hearing began, and the discussion unfolded just as Leo Reecey had thought it would—one after another the State's arguments fell to the floor. When Andi had exhausted all of her options, the judge called the attorneys back to her chambers. Reecey had predicted this move, telling Gavin that judges often explained a decision in chambers—especially one that might be hard for one of the parties to accept—before stating her ruling from the bench. Reecey also said that Fitch would dismiss the case rather than wait for an adverse ruling. The hearing was playing out exactly as Reecey had said it would, which raised Gavin's opinion of his lawyer—if only slightly.

Andi and Leo stood and followed the judge through a door behind her bench, leaving the jailer, the bailiff, Gavin, and Lila alone in the courtroom. Gavin wanted to say something pithy, gloat over his victory, but he held it in. He wasn't going to be that last soldier.

Then from the corner of his eye, he saw movement. Lila had risen to her feet and was walking his way. Gavin kept his eyes forward. The swinging gate that divided the well of the courtroom from the gallery squeaked as she walked through. She stopped in front of him, facing him, barely an arm's length away.

"It took me a while," she said, "but I remember you."

"I don't think you should be talking to me," Gavin said, his lisp slipping out.

"I knew your voice but I didn't understand why. Now I do."

"You need to leave." Gavin looked in the direction of the bailiff, who watched Lila with curious fascination.

Lila reached into her jacket pocket, and for a split second Gavin expected her to pull out a gun. But it wasn't a gun; it was a picture. She slapped it to the table in front of him. Gavin glanced at the picture and recognized himself, sitting on a chair at a party, his eyes fixed on Lila. Gavin's blood went cold and thin in his veins.

"You think you've won," Lila whispered, her eyes pinned on his. "But I won't let that happen."

Then she turned and walked out of the courtroom.

CHAPTER 57

It took nearly an hour for the jailers to book Gavin out, an excruciating march of time that caused Gavin's heart to pound. He was close—so damned close.

As he waited, he relived Lila's actions. There was no way that her memory had miraculously returned after eight years of amnesia. It didn't work that way. If she accused him, it would be a lie. But did that matter? Even if she concocted an absolute fairy tale out of bits and pieces, she had a photo to back it up. Where the hell did she get a photo?

But they were still processing him out, which meant they didn't have a prosecutable case yet. They would need to re-interview witnesses from the party, focus their attention on Gavin's movements that night. They would dig through the evidence bags in search of anything that might put Gavin in the backseat of that car. He had been careful, even if Jack had not. He knew they would find no DNA or trace evidence—but they might find Jack.

With Vauk dead, they would be frantic in their efforts to get him back behind bars. His window of opportunity would be small, a matter of days or maybe even hours.

And still the clock on the wall refused to tick.

If the State's best evidence rested on the word of a single woman, he merely had to silence that woman—Sadie Vauk had proven that. With

Lila gone, the photo would become meaningless. And with Jack gone, the last remaining witness would be eliminated.

At 4:27 p.m., Gavin Spencer became a free man, stepping out of the jail into a heavy downpour of rain, his green folder held over his head as an umbrella. He needed to move quickly to put his plan into motion. Step one—find out where Lila lived. With any luck, he might catch her leaving work.

He didn't go directly to the Government Center, though, just in case anyone was watching him. Instead, he slipped into a parking ramp, which he knew connected to the Government Center via the skyway. He crossed the skyway, dropped his folder with the hidden SIM card into a trash receptacle, and grabbed a newspaper to hide behind.

The atrium of the Government Center buzzed with people heading home for the day. Gavin found a bench facing a calm reflecting pool, beyond which lay the bank of elevators. He opened his newspaper to a random page and began watching—and thinking.

How could he follow her if she had driven to work? Getting a cab would be impossible in the rain; besides, a cab would keep a record of the route. He seemed to recall seeing one of those bike sharing racks out in the courtyard. He had a credit card in his wallet. It would record his rental, there at the Government Center, but he'd just gotten out of jail, so that could be easily explained. With the rain and the congestion of rush-hour traffic, he might be able to keep up with her. If all else failed, he would buy a new laptop—a throwaway—and hunt her down that way, but he would have to move quickly.

Gavin breathed in the sweet air of freedom, reveling at how it carried no hint of desperation, or fear, or sweaty men who wanted to beat him to death. Gavin was a free man, and he would stay that way. There was nothing he wouldn't do—no labor too difficult, no risk too great, no price too high—to stay out of prison now. Lila would die. They would suspect him, of course, but if he left no evidence, he would face no greater jeopardy than what he had with Sadie or the others. Do it soon. Do it cleanly. But do it, and put the nightmare to rest.

Gavin manned his post, his eyes lifted above the top edge of the paper, his thoughts pumping faster than the beat of his heart, contingencies gushing like blood from a ruptured artery.

Then he saw her step off the elevator. She wore a red raincoat and carried one of those classic umbrellas, long and thin with a silver point on the top. She didn't look around the atrium for Gavin, which told him all he needed to know about her naïveté. She headed for the north exit and not the parking ramp, which lifted Gavin's spirits. She walked to work? Gavin waited until she had left the building, her blue umbrella opened against the rain, before he stood to follow.

CHAPTER 58

Lila walked through the north exit of the Government Center, popping open her new umbrella as she stepped into the rain, the handle sturdy and thick in her hand. The heavy droplets fell hard and loud against the nylon, the cacophony making it difficult to hear anything beyond the edge of the umbrella—traffic, voices, footsteps. Above the skyline to the west, the clouds appeared to be thinning.

She crossed the courtyard, walking north toward the Stone Arch Bridge, the sidewalks mostly empty in the rain. A couple of men ran by, racing against the downpour. One came up behind her so quickly that it startled her, his large shoes splashing water onto her pant legs as he rushed by.

As she walked seven blocks to the bridge, the rain, carried easterly by the wind, grew lighter, but it had emptied the bridge of pedestrians. She followed the curve of the bridge as it ran past the ruins of an old mill, and slowed her pace as she reached the middle of the river.

Had she planned for every contingency? She thought so, but she knew the price of even one small mistake. What she was doing—this gambit—she owed to Sadie and the others. No one could walk this path except her.

She arrived at the center of the bridge and turned to look downstream, thinking about Joe for just a moment. There was so much she hadn't told him, and if he knew why she was standing on that bridge, he would have lost his mind. She hadn't called him, but it would have been nice to hear his voice—tell him that she loved him—just in case.

He's coming.

From the corner of her eye, Lila saw the dark figure getting closer. He was about a hundred feet behind her and moving slowly. The rain had lightened enough that she could hear the water rushing over the falls. Soon she would be able to hear his footsteps. She went through her final preparations—a few more seconds and she would be ready.

Forty feet away.

Lila closed her umbrella, strapping the canopy to the handle, turning it into a weapon.

Thirty feet.

She reached into the pocket of her raincoat and armed the canister of pepper spray.

Twenty feet.

Lila pulled the pepper spray from her pocket and turned.

CHAPTER 59

He had planned to keep his distance as he followed her home, but when she neared the middle of the bridge, she stopped. The rain had settled enough that he dropped the newspaper he'd been holding up to keep the rain at bay. He slowed his pace as he closed the gap between them.

She stopped at the rail and looked out over the river, her body at an angle that kept her back to him. She was all but begging to be thrown off that bridge. He had big plans for Lila, true, but he also had a gift for improvising. There were no cameras on the bridge. No people. The view from shore would be frustrated by the misty rain. He could steal her umbrella to cover his face as he escaped. One simple shove and his troubles would be over.

Be smart. Be bold. Strike when they expect you to retreat.

He slowed down even more, to let the plan gel. It would work.

She closed her umbrella.

He was almost there.

She reached into her pocket, and before he could charge, she spun around to him.

Gavin saw a flash of black in her right hand, and the way she thrust it out made him think it was a gun. He stopped in his tracks, even stumbled back a step before he realized that it was only pepper spray.

"Get back!" she yelled.

She held the umbrella in her left hand the way a child might hold a toy sword. The absurdity of it nearly made Gavin laugh. He took a step closer.

"I said get back!"

"What the hell's wrong with you?" Gavin glanced from side to side to make sure they were alone. He thought about charging her and being done with it, but his curiosity got the better of him. How much did she remember? Did she know about Jack? What had she told the cops? *Find that out before you kill her.*

He said, "What was that about—up there in court?"

"You raped me."

"I what?"

"I remember everything."

"I don't even know you."

"I know the truth."

Gavin looked hard at Lila, unable to mask his contempt. "You wouldn't know the truth if it walked up and spat in your face."

"You and your buddy."

"What buddy?"

"Silas Jackson. He was with you."

"Silas—?" Gavin could no longer suppress his laughter.

"He confessed."

"Who the hell is Silas Jackson?"

"He was with you that night. I remember."

Gavin subtly checked both ends of the bridge again—still no travelers. He took a small step forward and dropped his voice to a deeper register, drawing his words up from a cold, dark place. "You can't bluff after you've shown me your cards, Lila." She stood with her back to the rail. Foolish. No escape. "Silas Jackson? You overplayed your hand. We both know you're lying."

Lila's eyes narrowed on him. "But you wouldn't know that unless you were there, would you?"

A spike of heat ran up Gavin's neck and into his cheeks. *The last soldier to die,* Gavin thought to himself. He had let down his guard and said too much—only Lila's rapist would know that Silas Jackson hadn't been there—but it didn't matter now. Lila Nash wasn't leaving that bridge.

CHAPTER 60

Lila had her confession—at least it sounded like a confession to her ears. And it didn't escape her notice that Gavin had been carefully stepping closer to her with each word—preparing for his attack. The time had come to end it.

"You're a rat," Lila hollered. The odd choice of words seemed to confuse Gavin, who paused in his tracks. And then, like an explosion, both ends of the bridge lit up with strobing lights. They had heard her signal; the squad cars were on their way.

Gavin looked north and south, and smiled—not the reaction Lila had expected. He tipped his head back to look at the sky, the rain soaking his face. He opened his mouth to catch some of the droplets on his tongue. When he returned his gaze to Lila he said, "No good deed goes unpunished."

"When did you ever do a good deed?"

"I let you live, didn't I?"

The lightness drained from his eyes, and he lunged at her. She hit the trigger on the pepper spray, catching him in the eyes but not slowing his attack. She jammed the umbrella tip into his chest with all the force she could muster. He shrieked in pain. Then she aimed the pepper spray onto his opened mouth. But none of it stopped him.

He crashed into her, slamming her against the rail, the steel hitting her back and nearly knocking the wind out of her. His arms shot around her chest, gripping her in a bear hug, and his momentum pulled her off her feet and over the rail. There was nothing she could do.

They toppled over and fell—six feet.

The climbing rope snapped tight, and the full-body harness clamped hard around Lila's thighs, jerking her back. She smacked against the stone of the bridge, her head cracking so hard that it jarred her teeth. And somehow, Gavin held on, his arms locked so tightly around her waist that she couldn't breathe.

She had planned for Gavin's attack. It had been the final contingency, the break-the-glass emergency. The harness had a dorsal ring in the back between her shoulder blades, making it easy to feed the rope up through her raincoat. She had clipped the rope to the bridge with a brand-new carabiner in those seconds as she'd waited for Gavin to catch up.

Niki Vang hadn't agreed to the plan at first, but Lila explained about the harness, and that, with Gavin just getting out of jail, he wouldn't have a weapon. "Put an unmarked car on both ends of the bridge, and wire me so we can hear each other. I'll come across as weak, vulnerable—even stupid. It'll feed his ego, make him cocky. He'll see me as a loose end, not bait."

Niki still didn't agree, so Lila put it as bluntly as she could. "If we don't do this, he'll walk, and then he'll kill me, and there'll be nothing you can do to stop him."

It never occurred to Lila that Gavin might hang on. His eyes remained pinched closed, blinded by the pepper spray, but it was the shot he took to the mouth that was putting the hurt to him. He gaped, trying to pull in a breath.

"Who was with you?" Lila yelled.

"Fuck you." His throat had closed up so that she could barely make out the words. He wrapped his legs around hers, let go of her waist with one of his hands, and grabbed her lapel. He was heavy, and his weight caused the leg straps of the harness to dig into her thighs.

He let go with his other hand and grabbed the collar of her coat. He could barely breathe, yet he was climbing up her body. She kicked and flailed, boxing the sides of his head with her palms, and still the snake continued to climb. She grabbed his ear and twisted it. She stabbed at his eyes with her thumb. *It's him or me.*

He thrust a hand up to her throat, digging his fingers into the sides of her neck, cutting off her air.

Above her Niki yelled something, but the words got lost as pain clotted Lila's ears. Gavin kept squeezing, his face red and wet with spit, his tears streaking down his cheeks.

Lila punched him in the face as hard as she could, the crack of her knuckles against his nose sending a jolt up her arm. He reacted by jerking his head back, exposing his throat. She punched a second time, landing her fist on his Adam's apple. She heard a crunch.

Gavin let go of Lila's throat and grabbed her coat again, his reddened eyes searching Lila's face for something. His mouth opened and closed, but his lungs didn't fill. His eyes grew large, and she heard a gurgle as his body began to jerk.

He announced no surrender as he let go of Lila and fell into the dark, cold embrace of the Mississippi River.

CHAPTER 61

Matty Lopez and a uniformed officer hoisted Lila onto the bridge, her eyes still fixed on the body of Gavin Spencer bobbing and twisting in the frothy river below, facedown—dead.

On the bridge, Niki helped Lila out of her harness, and another officer brought a blanket from her squad car to wrap around Lila's shoulders. They were treating her like a victim, like someone they had pulled out of a burning house, but she didn't feel like a victim. She could still see his face as he fought to breathe. The elation of watching him fall to the river still pulsed in her veins. She felt nothing like a victim.

A third detective joined them on the bridge, a man named Voss whom Lila had met when they were working out the details of the plan. He handed a green folder to Niki.

"He dumped this in a trash can on the skyway," Voss said.

Lila didn't get to watch them fish Gavin's body from the river. Instead, they took her to the Homicide office in City Hall, where she listened to the recording of her confrontation, filling in those words that had been lost behind the rustle of her clothing. As she worked with Niki on the transcript, Matty dug through the green folder, inspecting the pages one at a time. As Lila was finishing her account, Matty lifted the hidden SIM card into the air.

In the moment of silence that followed, Matty and Niki must have formed the same thought, because they both reached for their phones and opened their SIM card trays to try and slide it in. It didn't fit. Lila laid her phone on the table and Niki popped it open, fitting the card into place. A few taps on the screen and she said, "Two text messages sent to a single number. Nothing else."

Lila leaned in for a peek and saw the phone number—and recognized it.

* * *

At six o'clock on a dreary Thursday evening, Lila Nash knocked on Sylvie Dubois's door, a microphone once again tucked beneath her clothing. In those few seconds as she waited for Sylvie to answer, Lila contemplated the truth she now knew, the one that broke her heart. Lila watched through a small window in the door as Sylvie approached, padding her way as if this were just another day and the knock at the door just another visitor.

When Sylvie saw Lila, she paused, one hand on the knob, but then opened the door and said, "What are you doing here?"

Lila looked into Sylvie's angry eyes and struggled to find words, as though the axe she brought to destroy her friend's world had suddenly become too heavy to swing. Finally, she managed to say, "Is John here?"

"No, and you need to go."

Sylvie started to close the door, so Lila blurted out the one thing that she knew would stop her. "Gavin Spencer's dead."

Sylvie tried to hide her shock, but failed. "Who's Gavin—?"

"Your cousin." Lila watched the color drain from Sylvie's face. Matty had been the one to find the connection. Sylvie's mother and Gavin's birth father were stepsiblings, a tie that Matty found only because he now had an idea of what to look for. It had been the last piece Niki needed before sending Lila in.

"I don't know what... you're talking about." The shake in her voice said more than words ever could.

"I was with him when he died, Sylvie."

Sylvie looked behind her, to where her son Dylan stood in the hallway, a stuffed dachshund under his arm.

"We need to talk."

Sylvie turned to her son, her voice so weak that Lila could barely hear it. "Mommy's gonna talk to her friend. Go watch TV till I get back."

Dylan hesitated, but then headed into the living room. Sylvie walked onto the porch, and she and Lila sat in the same chairs they'd sat in the last time. When they got settled, Lila said, "I know it was you, Sylvie, in my car...that night in the bean field."

Sylvie shook her head and looked away, her breath faltering as it left her body. Lila watched as guilt wrapped its cold fingers around Sylvie's throat.

"Gavin told me it was you."

Sylvie's breath caught in her chest.

It was true that Gavin had confessed that information on the bridge, but not so bluntly. *You wouldn't know the truth if it walked up and spat in your face.* In the heat of the moment, Lila had dismissed the odd phrasing as the ravings of a psychopath, but his words hadn't been random. When she saw Sylvie's phone number on the screen of her phone, Lila understood.

"Why, Sylvie?" Lila whispered. "Why would you help him rape me?"

Sylvie's eyes shot up to Lila. "I didn't. I swear. It wasn't supposed to happen that way. We were only gonna take a picture. That's all. I didn't know he'd go back. I swear to God—"

"Take a picture? Why would you do that?"

Tears began to stream down Sylvie's cheeks. She pulled her thighs up to her chest and wiped her face on the knees of her jeans. "You could've had anyone. John was all I had, and you took him."

"Gavin raped me!" Lila almost snarled as her emotions got the better of her. "Do you have any idea how that...? I tried to kill myself, Sylvie. I almost died because of that night."

"I was a stupid kid—and I was hurt. I just wanted to embarrass you. I wanted to hurt you the way you hurt me. Gavin was just supposed to take a picture, that's all. He wasn't supposed to—"

"But he did. And you helped him."

"I didn't know. I swear. When I found out... I'm sorry. If I could take it all back, I would."

"And all these years, you let me suffer."

"But you got better." Sylvie looked at Lila with something hopeful in her eyes. "You went to college and law school. You got over it."

"You never get over something like that. You have no idea what you've done, do you?"

"I didn't know what to do. He was my cousin."

"He was evil—a monster—and you helped to create him."

"I hadn't spoken to him since that night. I swear. I wanted nothing to do with him."

Lila leaned back in her chair to watch Sylvie's reaction, and said, "Sylvie Jacqueline Dubois. Did he call you Jack because he couldn't say Sylvie—because of his lisp?"

Sylvie didn't answer, but looked at Lila as though Lila now aimed a gun at her heart.

Lila reached into her jacket pocket and handed Sylvie the printout of the text messages. When she saw them, Sylvie began hyperventilating. "I didn't." She looked at Lila, pleading. "He wanted me to, but I didn't. I couldn't. I swear."

"What happened to you, Sylvie?"

"No! Listen! I got those texts and the letters, but I didn't do anything. I would rather go to jail for what I did to you than to... Please, you gotta believe me. I didn't—I wouldn't."

"The police are going to arrest you, Sylvie."

Two unmarked police cars lit up at opposite ends of the block. Sylvie could barely breathe as she pleaded. "I have a son. Please—"

"They're going to charge you with my kidnapping."

When Niki and Matty got out of their cars, Sylvie slid off her chair and fell to her hands and knees, her sobs heaving in her chest. "I swear I didn't. I swear." Lila could only imagine the chaos spinning around inside Sylvie's head as the world folded in on her.

Then Sylvie looked up at Lila, her cheeks wet with tears and said, "Please...forgive me?"

Niki walked onto the porch, eased Sylvie's arms behind her back, and ratcheted handcuffs around her wrists. Lila stayed in her chair as Niki escorted Sylvie to the squad car. Only then did Lila feel strong enough to stand and walk to her car, tears blocking her vision.

In her car, Lila sat in silence as Sylvie's pleas echoed in her head. Could she forgive Sylvie for what she did? They were different people back then, weren't they? Dumb kids whipped around by torrents of emotion. Lila wanted to believe that Sylvie didn't know that Gavin would rape her that night, that what happened in the bean field went far beyond what Sylvie had planned.

Then she heard the gentle voice of Dr. Roberts say, *Forgiveness isn't for them. It's for you.*

CHAPTER 62

Niki read the Miranda warning to Sylvie in the squad car, while Matty stayed in the house with Dylan, waiting for the social worker to arrive. Sylvie jumped at the opportunity to tell her side, repeating, between sobs, that she had nothing to do with the death of Sadie Vauk, swearing that she was at home with her husband that evening.

Niki and Matty had already prepared a search warrant, but in the end, they didn't need it. Sylvie agreed to let them search her house, telling them where they could find the two letters that Gavin had sent. Because of the text messages, they knew that the letter held a code and easily read the first message: *Kill Sadie Vauk*. The second letter led them to a URL and photos of Sylvie Jacqueline Dubois posing Lila Nash the night she was raped.

From there, they went in search of Gavin Spencer's hidden server.

"Think of the IP address as a telephone number," the tech told Niki. "Every computer has one so they don't get all mixed up online." He continued to click away on his keyboard as he talked. "And with an IP address, we can get a longitude and latitude for the server. I should be able to narrow the location down to . . . Here you go."

The map on his screen had a pinpoint in Kenwood. When Niki leaned in to read the streets around it, she recognized the address.

An hour later, Niki, Matty, and a crime scene tech named Bug Thomas pulled up to Amy Spencer's house, a search warrant in hand.

Amy opened the door, dressed in black, mascara smudged at the corners of her reddened eyes. "You killed my son" was her only greeting.

Matty did the honors. "Ma'am, we have a warrant to search your house."

Her cheeks turned red with anger as he handed her the search warrant. "Haven't you done enough?" she hissed.

"I'd like you to step outside while we search, or if you prefer to remain inside, I can come in and sit with you—"

Rage lit fires in Amy Spencer's eyes. "I'm gonna sue you for killing my boy."

"Inside or out, ma'am?" Matty said.

Amy turned and walked into her sitting room, lying down on the chaise without saying a word. Matty took a seat in one of the Queen Anne chairs to watch her.

Niki and Bug began their search on the outside of the house, Bug carrying a flashlight, expecting to spend time in either a crawlspace or an attic. He located the junction box where the internet cable connected to the house, which led them to a utility room in the basement. Behind a hinged panel Bug found a splitter.

"See this?" he said. "You normally have a single cable going from here up to a router, but there's a second cable going somewhere."

The utility room had a dropped ceiling, so Bug climbed atop a washing machine, lifted the tile, and shined the flashlight along the joist. Niki could hear him mumbling to himself but couldn't make out the words. When he jumped down, he walked upstairs without saying a word. He found the router, paused to consider something, then, like a coonhound on a scent, he followed something invisible into the garage.

The space was large and clean—white walls, epoxied floors—and it held three cars: a Jaguar sedan, a vintage Corvette convertible, and a white Porsche SUV. Above the Porsche, a scuttle hole led to an attic.

Bug grabbed a ladder that hung on the wall and set it up below the scuttle hole. "Not a very sensible place to have a computer," he said as he climbed.

"Unless you wanted to keep it hidden," Niki said.

He shined his light around the attic. "Is there a pry bar down there?"

Niki found a crowbar and handed it up to Bug. He took it and crawled into the darkness.

As she waited, Niki leaned against the Porsche, a beautiful automobile, sleek and compact, more expensive than anything Niki would ever be able to afford. She glanced down at the driver's-side window, her curiosity pulled by the red leather interior, and something caught her eye.

Above her, Niki could hear the screech of floorboards being pried up, but her attention remained on the door of the Porsche. The rubber seal at the bottom of the window had a tiny smear of something dark, a patch about the size of Niki's thumbnail.

"There's a server up here," Bug yelled from the attic. "Fully functional. They hid it below the floorboards."

"Bag it," Niki yelled.

She bent down to look more closely at the spot, pulling a lock-blade knife from her pocket and scraping loose a tiny speck—dark red, almost black. Blood? She stepped back and looked at the car, a white SUV. Sadie Vauk's killer had driven a white SUV.

Then Niki remembered the videos of Amy and Gavin in jail, some of the comments coming into a new focus. *That's what mothers do; they look out for their children. I'm scared for you, Gavin*, she had said. *I just want to help.* And then there was that comment Amy made while standing beside the swimming pool, when she and Matty cornered Amy about Eleanora Abrams. What had she said? *A mother's supposed to protect her child, ain't she?*

She pulled out her phone and called Matty. "You okay in there?" she asked.

"I'm fine. Why?"

"Put cuffs on Ms. Spencer. I think we found Sadie Vauk's killer."

CHAPTER 63

The weight of all that had happened didn't fully hit Lila until she got to work the next day. Some of the attorneys actually applauded as she stepped off the elevator on the twentieth floor. She tried to act like it was just another day as she went about the to-do list that Andi had given her, but people kept popping into her office to ask her about her confrontation on the bridge.

Ryan stayed the longest and stared at the fingernail scrapes on her neck as he peppered her with questions. Even Patrick stopped by to offer congratulations. But it was the last visitor of the day that surprised her the most.

Lila was packing to leave, relieved to have survived one more day without getting fired, when the knock came. She looked up to see Andi standing there. Andi had never been to Lila's office.

"Um... come in."

Andi took a seat in the visitor's chair and glanced around at the bare walls. "I like what you've done with the place."

Lila shrugged. "Yeah, I haven't gotten around to hanging stuff up."

Andi said, "I came to tell you that I can't be your supervisor anymore."

Those words turned the air suddenly chilly, and it occurred to her that certain pigeons might now be coming home to roost.

"I wanted to tell you before they announced it officially, but Frank Dovey tendered his resignation this morning."

Lila had to fight to keep the smile off her face.

"I'll be taking over Adult Prosecution in two weeks."

Lila let her smile go free. "Congratulations."

"I'm hearing rumors that Frank's resignation wasn't his idea. Word has it, someone got tired of his bullshit and did something about it." Andi paused and gave Lila a knowing look. "If that's true, I'd love to hear the story someday. For now, I wanted you to know that I'll be the one writing that letter to the Board of Law Examiners. By the time I get done, they'll be falling over themselves to admit you."

"Thanks, Andi. You've been great to work for—"

"Work with. You're my colleague, and you need to get used to that idea."

"Gladly."

Then Andi's demeanor turned somber and she said, "I also wanted to tell you that they found a server in Gavin's mother's attic." Andi leaned in and lowered her voice. "There were four pictures—of you—and one of them showed Sylvie Dubois's face. They'll be stored in a password-protected file until we resolve Sylvie's case."

It sickened Lila to know that those pictures might someday be shown to a jury at Sylvie's trial. Lila would have to testify and point at Sylvie and accuse her in court. Thinking about it made Lila's stomach churn, but it had to be done.

"There were four other files, with pictures of Abrams, Mercotti, Ludlow, and Sadie Vauk. Those cases will all be closed now."

Lila felt a wave of satisfaction, knowing that those families would finally get closure.

"And there was another file," Andi said with a hint of a smile. "It had pictures of Gavin's mom, Amy, hitting her second husband with a brick."

"Assault?"

"Murder. When they showed her the pictures, Amy confessed to killing her husband, but claims it was self-defense."

"A family of sociopaths."

"She also killed Sadie Vauk."

"So Sylvie... She didn't...?"

"Apparently Sylvie told you the truth about that. The mother hasn't confessed to it yet, but they found a gun under her mattress. It's the right caliber. We're testing blood found on both the gun and the car. I'll give you ten-to-one odds that it's Sadie's. Amy's never going to see the outside of a prison."

Lila felt a sense of relief wash over her. Sylvie was willing to go to prison rather than help Gavin with his plan. "What about Sylvie?" Lila asked. "Who's handing that case?"

"I'm holding on to it."

"I believe her—that she didn't plan for Gavin to rape me that night. What she did was... reprehensible, but she didn't set out to have things go that far. I guess, what I'm trying to say is... I forgive her. I know she has to face the consequences, but... I've given this a lot of thought, and I don't want to see her go to prison."

"You're the victim, so of course your position will be taken into consideration," Andi said in a very lawyerly tone. Then she gave Lila a slight smile and added, "I'm sure we'll work something out."

Andi stood to leave, but stopped. "Oh, I almost forgot." She reached into her jacket pocket and produced a piece of paper, then handed it to Lila.

Lila unfolded the paper and saw the letterhead of Edward Chappelle, Attorney at Law. She read.

> Dear Ms. Nash,
>
> I wish to extend my sincere apology for acting rashly in our first meeting. I look forward to many years of cordial yet spirited contests with you.
>
> Respectfully,
> Ed Chappelle.

Lila laughed to herself, and said, "I think I'll frame it... and hang it on my wall."

CHAPTER 64

Joe called Lila that night to tell her that his assignment had run its course and he was coming home. It was a nine-hour trip and she ordered him to stay in North Dakota one more night. She didn't want him driving tired.

She didn't tell him about Gavin Spencer or the bridge. She would save that discussion for when he got home—she knew it would be a long one.

The next morning she stepped into the shower, excited for Joe's return home. Like oil on an old hinge, the hot water seemed to work things loose. Her throat still hurt where Gavin had clawed her. She had a lump on the back of her head where she'd hit the stone of the bridge. When she closed her eyes, she could see Gavin's face looking up at her as he fell to the river. She could hear Sylvie pleading as Detective Vang put the handcuffs on her. And she could feel Sadie's hand in hers as they stood in the bailiff's station.

The more she thought about all that had happened, the more she wanted to cry—so she did. She reveled in the emotion as it pushed her to the floor of the shower, the water washing over her.

Then she pictured the look on Joe's face as she told him what she had done—dangling above the Mississippi River with a psychopathic killer wrapped around her—and she started to laugh, hard and loud. He would be pissed that she took the risk, and he would be disappointed at the secrets she'd kept. But in the end, he would be proud of her—although he could never match the pride she felt in herself.

As she continued getting ready for the day, she rubbed a dab of scar-reduction cream on her arm and noticed that she didn't feel the ridges strum against her fingertips. She looked more closely and saw lines so thin and small that they were nearly invisible.

Lila went to her closet and found one of the few sleeveless shirts she owned and slipped it on. She could still see her scars—she would always see them, even if they became invisible to the rest of the world—and she was okay with that.

At first she planned to welcome Joe home with a dinner of king crab legs, but that was her favorite meal. His was spaghetti. She would need to run to the store for some meatballs, and she skipped like a little girl as she went to her car. Joe was on his way home.

When she parked at the supermarket, she caught sight of a jewelry store a few doors down. She remained in her car for several minutes, staring and contemplating something crazy. Lila was willing to concede that she wasn't in the proper frame of mind to make a wise decision. She was far too manic to be giving voice to the thoughts in her head, but she ran with her happiness anyway.

What was it Joe had said? *The woman has just as much right to say when the time is right as the man. And if that time ever came...*"

Lila stepped out of her car and walked toward the jewelry store, pondering whether Joe would prefer gold or silver.

ACKNOWLEDGMENTS

I couldn't do what I do without the love and support of my beloved wife, Joely. I would also like to thank the many people who have helped bring this work to the world, starting with my first readers, Nancy Rosin, my agent, Amy Cloughley, and my wife, Joely. I also want to extend my deep appreciation to Helen O'Hare, my editor, for helping me to shape Lila's story. I remain forever grateful to my team at Mulholland/Little, Brown, including: editorial director, Josh Kendall; marketing manager, Ira Boudah; publicist, Shannon Hennessey; cover designer, Lucy Kim; production editor, Mike Noon; and copyeditor, Allison Kerr Miller.

ABOUT THE AUTHOR

Allen Eskens is the *USA Today* bestselling author of *The Life We Bury,* which has been published in twenty-six languages and is in development for a feature film, and five other novels, including most recently *The Shadows We Hide* and *Nothing More Dangerous*. His books have won the Barry Award, the Rosebud Award, the Silver Falchion Award, and the Minnesota Book Award. He has also been a finalist for the Edgar Award, Thriller Award, and the Anthony Award. Eskens is a former criminal defense attorney and lives with his wife, Joely, in greater Minnesota.